Over The Wall

Trisha FitzGerald

A Wings ePress, Inc.
Contemporary Romance Novel

Wings ePress, Inc.

Edited by: Karen Babcock
Copy Edited by: Rosalie Franklin
Senior Editor: Anita York
Executive Editor: Lorraine Stephens

Wings ePress Books
www.wingsepress.com

Copyright © 2007 by Patricia FitzGerald-Petri
ISBN-13: 978-1-59705-835-3
ISBN-10: 1-59705-835-1

Published In the United States Of America

Wings ePress Inc.
3000 N. Rock Road
Newton, KS 67114

What They Are Saying About

Over The Wall

The heartbreak of mother loss anchors this tale of interwoven Irish lives in a tender, funny and tragic rendering of the fate of two lifelong friends. From a feisty adolescence in a small boarding school to big city adulthood, the two friends explore the limits of loyalty. In this spirited, atmospheric portrayal of a quintessential Irish coming-of-age, FitzGerald pulls together the lives of friends, family, and lovers around a haunting call for a lost mother, touching the reader's heart when the yearning is unexpectedly fulfilled.

—Dr. P. R. Preciado.

(Dr. P. R. Preciado, a member of The Frankfurt Writers' Group, has actively participated in writers' workshops in America and Great Britain. Furthermore, she leads creative writing courses for native and non-native speakers at the Volkshochschule in Frankfurt am Main.)

Over The Wall by Trisha FitzGerald is an intelligent and timely story in which two girls from opposite sides of society become life-long friends.

You will follow Fudge Ginnane and Lilly McDermott from girlhood into womanhood, from one drama to another, sometimes laughing hilariously, other times crying. Ms. FitzGerald writes a stunning story about the struggles of everyday people. She shows money isn't always the solution, but it can often be a problem. Over The Wall is a recommended read, but be sure to keep a tissue handy. I give this outstanding novel

FIVE STARS.
—Jacqueline McGuyer
Author, Blood Secrets
Wings Press

Over The Wall is written in the author's familiar descriptive style, displaying Irish countryside, Dublin slums, and characters themselves with equal panache, and a wry sense of humour. For example: "The last time she'd seen him his face consisted mainly of a nose, but now the other features had caught up."

The subject of class differences crops up in the story, and is handled with deft and poignant awareness. One of my favorite characters, Skids Curry, appears late in the book as a blustering, down-to-earth businessman who shamefacedly hides a tender heart. From college professor to Irish housewife, from socialite to a delivery van driver, FitzGerald treats all her characters with understanding affection.

—Jeanette Cottrell
http://www.simegen.com

While the central focus of this novel is the friendship of Fudge and Lilly, and the way in which each woman searches for love, the author also takes the time to explore a non-traditional romantic attraction between two middle-aged characters, one married and one widowed.

I thoroughly enjoyed this story and found it a compelling study of female friendship, romantic entanglements that creep in when you least expect them, and the ways in which people deal with the ups and downs of life.

http://www.longandshortreviews.com

Over The Wall is an enchanting story about life, love, and

friendship. The story begins with the account of two unlikely friends at a boarding school—one spoiled, rich, and motherless, the other a farm girl from a close-knit family. Years later, they are reunited and their friendship blossoms into adulthood and along with it work, responsibility, and love. The story is a wonderful concoction of various relationships and how some children grow up to be very different adults and others don't change much at all. The bonds between the characters take surprising turns throughout and Trisha does a fantastic job developing the characters and making them feel like our friends, too.

—Edee Wilcox
Author (Saved Times Three)
www.edee.org

What a fantastic page-turner! It's been ages since I read a book that so enthralled me, maybe because there's a bit of Lilly and Finnula, the two friends whose story Over The Wall focuses on, in me.

Lilly, the bragging adventurer eager to defy authority, the tough cookie with the stunning looks who, in reality, is but an injured bird, forever wounded by the loss of her mother. Fudge, the serious girl who despairs at finding love, true love, but short of finding it, becomes her friend's most loyal ally, her life savior.

Over The Wall takes the two lifelong friends from girlhood to womanhood, thrusting us into situations that are in turn funny, often tragic. It deals with the kinds of emotions and human experiences—friendship and love for instance—that most of us have all gone through in one way or another.

Fitzgerald's "coup de maitre" is to make these emotions so credible that they make us laugh and cry.

—Isabelle de Pommereau
free-lance journalist
(Christian Science Monitor
The Observer Alternatives Internationales)

Dedication

For my sisters, Gráinne and Kathy, who have supported me along the way with their honest opinions and daring critique!

"Life is a test and this world a place of trial. Always the problems—
or it may be the same problem—will be presented to every
generation in different forms."

Winston Churchill (1874—1965) Speech 1949

One

A milky ray of sunlight crept inch by inch along the wood-panelled gymnasium wall, illuminating a universe of dust particles which whirled and danced every time the matron expelled a huff of aggravation.

"Six pairs of sky blue knickers."

"...four, five, six... yes."

"Six pairs of navy blue knee socks."

"Yep."

"I beg your pardon?"

"Yes, Miss Brody."

"Four white, short-sleeved Airtex shirts."

"I've got five."

The matron heaved a great sigh, wiped her moist lower lip with a talon-like finger and fixed Fudge with a withering look.

"Oh, for Pete's sake, girl. If you have five, then you have enough. Now stop wasting my precious time!"

Fudge eyed Miss Brody as she ticked off the uniform checklist with a red pencil. Her mouth was pressed into a thin line, the high brow furrowed in concentration. Under the prominent nose a shadow of dark hair played across her upper lip, creating a butch appearance, an impression not enhanced by the slightly bulging, watery eyes peering over a pair of gold-rimmed bifocals, which, when not perched on the tip of her nose, rested safely upon her ample chest on the end of a large-linked chain.

"Three royal blue wool skirts."

"Hmm..."

"Miss Ginnane! If you don't mind—I really haven't got all day! They're waiting for me upstairs—now, three wool skirts!"

"Sorry, yes."

"Three navy blue, V-neck sweaters."

"Two—my mother's ordered a new one."

"Have you got a note?"

"A note?"

Miss Brody stamped her Hush-Puppied foot in exasperation. Checking the uniform list at the beginning of the school year was something the matron clearly detested, but then again, Fudge decided, she seemed to detest everything. The young boarder couldn't even be sure she'd ever seen the woman laugh. Miss Brody. Unfortunate name, that. Inevitably, the moustached matron with the froggy eyes became known as Toady Brody and although Fudge presumed she had a Christian name like everyone else, in the three years at boarding school she'd never actually found out what it was— and nobody dared to ask. Years later, she would ask herself if anyone had ever tried to look behind the whiskers and the bifocals. Surely there had also been sadness there, a sense of lost chances, of crushed expectations. How brutally clear things become in adulthood—how utterly blind in adolescence.

"From your mother... about the sweater! Don't you know the rules—you've been here long enough!"

"Sorry, I forgot all about it, Miss Brody."

"Well, please ask her to forward it to us when you write home on Friday afternoon."

"Yes, I will." While Brody scribbled a note on the corner of the clip chart, Fudge risked a glance at her watch. It was already well after five. If Lilly didn't arrive by the rapidly approaching six o'clock deadline, she'd be up shit creek, Fudge considered, hoping her friend wouldn't be condemned to eating supper alone. She was simply *aching* to exchange all the gossip and could hardly wait to discover if the other girl had actually *done it* during the summer holidays. Lilly had solemnly sworn to impart with all the succulent details so Fudge was optimistic, but even if she had chickened out of the *Big F.K.*, there would surely be lots of other exciting news from Salthill. A few years later, the *Big F.K.* would take on a whole new meaning, but in that summer of 1975, thirteen and still somewhat innocent, it meant for Fudge and Lilly the first French kiss.

At the end of the gymnasium the door opened. She and Miss Brody both looked up, Fudge almost jumping to her feet in anticipation. The last rays of sunlight shining through the bubble-glassed windows were now throwing long streaks of dusty light across the room. The millions of twirling specks danced in the draught from the open door. With a pang of disappointment, Fudge watched as Irene O'Neill waddled backwards through the door dragging an ancient trunk behind her.

"Ara, feck it!" she cursed as the cumbersome piece of luggage became wedged in the doorframe.

Fudge cringed and closed her eyes.

"Irene O'Niell! Shame on you!" Miss Brody bellowed down the length of the gymnasium, her nasal voice resounding along the rafters.

Irene whipped around as fast as one can when your arse is in the air and your bathroom scales read almost eleven stone. Snagging her foot on the rough boards mid-pirouette, she tottered and fell, sitting down heavily on the trunk, causing the locks to snap open. Her mouth formed a perfect "O".

"Miss Brody, I... sorry, I didn't see you!" Irene stuttered, her face the colour of a ripe tomato and just as shiny.

"I should sincerely hope not! Is that the kind of language you use at home? Does your... Oh get on with it, will you?" She stopped herself in time, the thin line of her lips working furiously.

Irene swallowed. "It... it just slipped out," she answered feebly, knowing there was no point in denying it.

The matron glared at Irene for a moment longer, nervously tapping the pencil on her pad.

"Prepare your clothes for the uniform check immediately, and afterwards you can report to Mrs. Oldfield. Tell her you'll be taking supper alone for using abusive language in my presence. Now hurry up—I don't want to hear another word!"

Full of indignation, Irene opened her mouth to speak, only to clamp it shut again when she saw Toady Brody's eyes narrow challengingly. Resigning herself to spending supper on her own at a table with her face to the wall, the podgy teenager turned to the job of getting the trunk dislodged. As soon as Brody's attention had returned to the checklist, Irene glanced back briefly—just long enough to mouth "feck you" and flash the older woman's back the two fingers.

Fudge stifled a snigger and started rearranging her socks in the suitcase.

Miss Brody, happy to have been able to vent her frustration so satisfactorily, calmly continued to list off the remaining articles, now hardly caring if Miss Ginnane had the correct number or not. Five minutes later, she chalked an "OK" on the top of the case and marched over to the disgruntled Irene O'Niell. Fudge stood up from where she'd been kneeling and wiped the dust off her knees, grimacing at the imprints of knots and ridges the rough wooden floor had left in the soft skin.

If Lilly doesn't come within the next few minutes, she realised dolefully, *I can forget squeezing all the facts out of her until bedtime, and even then there won't be much opportunity before "lights out" and Kelly starts her hourly patrol.* Playing for time, she bent down and started picking a Butlins sticker off the side of the large suitcase. She'd only just managed to ease her fingernail under the dog-eared plastic when the sound of her name reverberating down the gymnasium made her jump.

"Finnula Ginnane! What are you waiting for? The cases will be brought up to the dormitory while you're having your tea. Hurry along and get ready!"

Fudge slunk off towards the door, disappointed that Lilly hadn't turned up. Across the cobbled yard she could hear the school bell ringing out six o'clock. In fifteen minutes one of the kitchen girls would hammer the gong in front of the dining room where everyone would subsequently assemble in an orderly queue outside the door.

Out in the corridor the worn-out linoleum smelt freshly scrubbed as it always did at the beginning of term, before the odour of hundreds of sweaty gym shoes and socks filled the air. A long line of burnished metal coat hooks stood out in the gloom. The benches lining the walls were empty. A day later, the corridor would be humming with activity as scores of quibbling and shrieking schoolgirls fought to bag a place for their drawstring sports pouches, tunics and runners. And as always at the commencement of every school year, it was first there, first served—the survival of the fittest. If you arrived late or weren't devious enough, you might very well find yourself changing for gym squashed in behind the door, fighting to keep your balance as it banged against your backside every time anyone rushed in. There would be jostling, pushing and, presupposing no teachers were lurking in the vicinity, effing and blinding. Assuming an air of indifference, all and sundry from the second class on would try their utmost to sneak a fleeting glimpse at everyone else's breasts, terrified that their own pubescent development could in any way be anomalous. Depending on their observations, they would then proceed to the gymnasium, their expressions either the picture of triumphant complacency or sheer horror.

Fudge glanced down at her shirtfront, wondering would she pass the test. She'd thrown herself into the summer holidays sporting two peas on a baking tray and stepped off the train at Westland Row ten weeks later to discover the manifestation of two kiwi-sized convexities on her scrawny chest. The holidays had flown by and, to be honest, she hadn't paid a lot of attention to the physical changes taking place while sailing on Loughrua Lake, helping to make raspberry jam sandwiches for the silage makers and secretly learning how to drive her mother's Vauxhall up and down the front field.

It was only when the train pulled into Dublin did she realise they were there. The convexities. Her astonishment was great. Convinced they'd popped out somewhere between Athlone and Portarlington, she was glad no one had been sitting opposite her at the time. The minute the taxi dropped her off at the front door of Castleglen Park, she'd rushed to the privacy of the locker room loo and gawped down the front of her Airtex shirt. They were there all right. Slightly perturbing, however, was the fact that they appeared somewhat wide-set, the nipples pointing to ten and two o'clock respectively. Fudge chewed on her lower lip uncertainly as she strolled past the rows of shiny coat hooks; maybe she'd voluntarily take the changing place behind the door after all.

~ * ~

She was still contemplating her chest and the endless weeks which lay ahead before the next holiday, when the doorway leading out to the central court yard suddenly flew open, sending a splash of light across the dark wooden wall-panelling. Like a flaxen whirlwind, unruly blond curls swirling back from her face, Lilly emerged into the hallway and sprinted towards the gym door, eyes blinking rapidly in the relative darkness. When the two girls saw each other they squealed with delight, Fudge stepping back to let her best friend pass as she rushed to smather Miss Brody in justifications for her delayed return.

Fudge smiled. *She'll get away with it, too*, she thought to herself, and was confident that if Lilly called Brody a dried-up old fart to her face, the matron would merely titter and tell her not to be so cheeky. Lilly got away with everything.

Tiptoeing back down the corridor to the door of the gymnasium, she strained to hear Miss Brody's reaction, but could only decipher dull murmurings. Even though Lilly came from Ballsbridge, she was still always the last one to turn up, arriving long after the boarders from Letterkenny and Cahirciveen had unpacked their trunks and made up their beds, and while other late-comers were forced to succumb to such disciplinary measures as picking dried-up clods of earth out of the prefects' hockey boots or dragging a rug sweeper over the Persian carpet in the reception room for a week, Lilly's punishment never amounted to much more than staying in prep for an hour longer.

There was something special about her—and not only because she had three L's in her first name. She was, in effect, the kind of precocious schoolgirl most people would love to hate—if only they could. Lillian McDermott had every teacher in the place wrapped around her finger, flirting unashamedly with Bertie Barrett, the school gardener, and bamboozling day-girls into bringing her fairy cakes and cream éclairs from the corner shop at the bottom of Glenageary Road. Naturally bright, she wouldn't have a problem absorbing with ease the intricacies of trigonometry and calculus, appreciating knowledgeably the explosive qualities of trinitrotoluene and digesting with a hearty appetite, compositions on truncated spurs and mica schist. However, if ever caught on the hop, there wasn't a girl in her class who wouldn't let her copy the homework.

Tragically, her mother had died of cancer when Lilly was eight, and her father, a scatty art historian, highly acclaimed critic and rose-cultivating dilettante, was left to raise her and Julian, Lilly's older brother, all on his own. It was a task that got the better of him, and after two years of juggling household and profession, he finally capitulated, sending them both off to boarding school in the hope that there they might learn to understand the meaning of order and discipline—something he had difficulty understanding himself. That was why Lilly always arrived late—and another reason why staff were rarely angry as a result. Not that they felt sorry for her. Lilly had blossomed into the kind of witty, attractive teenager one would go out of their way to know, but when she first turned up on the doorstep of Castleglen Park at the age of ten—a motherless waif with a broken heart—she immediately awoke the protective instincts in everyone who crossed her path—a feeling which many, over the years, had difficulty shaking off.

Fudge shifted nervously from one foot to the other and tried to get a peek through the keyhole. She could only just make out the back of Lilly's head bobbing up and down in emphatic affirmation. A moment later she moved to the side offering Fudge a view of Miss Brody, whose thick eyebrows knitted together despite an amused grin dancing around the corner of her mouth.

"Come on, Lilly, will you?" Fudge whispered to herself. "You've buttered the old cow up enough."

It was almost time for the supper gong to go off. She couldn't wait around much longer without getting into trouble. Finally Fudge heard Lilly trotting down the gym. A moment later she appeared, all smiles.

"And?" Fudge hooked her arm through Lilly's.

"I have to clear away the staff table after supper."

"That's all?"

"That's all!" Lilly burst out laughing at her friend's almost indignant expression.

"How do you manage to get away with it every time—it's not fair." Fudge gave Lilly a playful shove. "If I'd arrived late, she'd have had me cleaning all the loos in the school with a toothbrush for a month!"

They had arrived at the doorway leading out into the courtyard. On the far side Fudge could see the McDermotts' dusty station wagon parked with the front bumper up against a barrel full of blossoming Busy Lizzys. Julian was struggling with Lilly's trunk, his normally pale face red with the exertion of trying to lower it down from the back of the car without dropping it. His eyebrows were knitted in concentration and from where she was standing, Fudge could see he was muttering under his breath something Miss Brody would no doubt prefer not to hear. She held back slightly. Lilly's dad was still sitting in the car, his tousled head poking out through the window. Every now and then he would offer the gangly youth snippets of advice on how to tackle the dilemma of Lilly's trunk.

Pity. Fudge would have liked to say hello. She was particularly fond of the scatter-brained intellectual, but his son was a pain in the arse. A smart alec.

"C'mon, Fudge, we still have a sec before the gong, I just want to say goodbye." Lilly was tugging at her sleeve, but Fudge dug in her heels, deciding she didn't want one of Julian's sarcastic remarks to ruin the evening. If he spotted her brand new bosom he'd have a right old field day. She wasn't in the mood for a round of verbal volleyball with that pimple-faced neddy.

"Say hello to your dad for me, will you? I'll go on ahead and save a place for you in the queue. See you in a minute." Before Lilly had a chance to persuade her to do otherwise she turned, choosing the longer way through the old building in preference to the shortcut across the yard. Outside the dining room, small blue-uniformed groups were congregating. An excited buzz rippled from wall to wall as friends greeted each other eagerly. There were "oohs", "ahs" and "ughs" as new hairdos, figures and shoes were admired or condemned accordingly. There was no mercy. If your friends thought your new shoes were poxy, they told you so. Intuitive tact and diplomacy weren't attained until the fifth and sixth class, just in time to prevent yourself from making a lot of enemies in the outside world.

Trying to hide her shoddy college slip-ons, Fudge glanced enviously at Sarah Gibson-Smythe, who was flashing a pair of dark blue suede Kickers. *I hate your guts, Gibson*, Fudge thought to herself momentarily, before turning her mind back to Julian. They'd known and disliked each other for the last two and a half years—ever since Lilly had invited her back to their house in Ballsbridge for the half-term break.

Ten years old at the time, Fudge found the fourteen-year-old teenager positively *alien*. He was so mature, so adult—he even had a few maverick hairs on his chin. Except from a distance, she'd had absolutely no contact with teenage boys and felt because they looked so grown-up, they ought to act grown-up, too. This, of course, was a wide-spread misapprehension and, therefore, she was all the more confused when, from that very first day on, Julian made it his favourite pastime to taunt and tantalise, to scoff and sneer, shower her with sarcasm, and generally try to make her weekend visits miserable. Before she went to sleep at McDermott's house, she was forced to check in and under the bed, being terrified, and rightly so, that something prickly or slimy might be hiding there. The first time she'd sat down to the dining table, a resounding fart had broken the silence, bringing pre-dinner preliminaries to an excruciating halt. Long after the rubber "farting pillow" under the seat cushion had been discovered and Fudge's honour restored, Julian was still holding his sides laughing.

No amount of admonishment from Lilly and Mr. McDermott helped in any way to stop his antics. If anything, it only made him worse. With a flaming face and quivering lower lip, Fudge had tried to ignore him until, with Lilly's encouragement, she eventually learned to defend herself, giving as good as she got. As the years passed, her wit and eloquence developed, and it was therefore Julian's turn to be perplexed when, one day while watching a national rugby match on TV, Fudge had informed him in passing that she knew of another great match—his face, her arse. Hitching her jeans up slightly over her slim waist, she'd casually taken a glass of Cidona from the cupboard, swung it shut with her hip and left the room. Lilly reported later that Julian hadn't said another word until the game was over.

He'd been a little bit more careful after that, yet the caustic banter continued whenever they had the misfortune of being in the same room together, albeit strained and somewhat fatigued. Having learnt to turn a deaf ear, it no longer bothered Fudge very much. Far more important was the time she spent with Lilly, and nothing could ruin that.

They were best friends. The very best.

They had both arrived simultaneously on the steps of Castleglen Park three years before—nervous, homesick and bewildered—Lilly accompanied by her dad, Fudge by Auntie Dora from Kildare. Feigning nonchalance, they had surreptitiously eyed one another while the adults dealt with formalities in the reception area.

An hour later, the two girls found themselves standing side by side as they unpacked their cases in a forbidding twelve-bed dormitory. While they sorted their belongings onto the threadbare bed covers, not a word was spoken, nor did they acknowledge each other's presence in any way, both frantically fighting back the tears, their stomachs churning at the thought of spending endless weeks and months away from home. Suddenly, the suitcases half unpacked, the two girls turned and looked at each other, mouths opening and closing like fish out of water, and a second later they let fly, their faces scrunching up in anguish, snotty sobs bubbling up from the tips of their toes.

Sitting close together in the hollow of Fudge's metal military bed, they howled on one another's shoulders for a full five minutes, the rusty springs squeaking in ridiculous synchronisation to each shuddering cry until, eventually becoming aware of it, their sobs turned to gurgling snorts. When Miss Kelly (soon to be known as Smelly Kelly due to her chronic body odour) walked into the dormitory twenty minutes later to see how they were getting on, she found the two young girls bouncing up and down on the beds roaring with laughter, their eyes red and puffy. She ticked them off and made a mental note to instruct Bertie Barrett to sweet talk the local dry cleaners out of the wire coat hangers required to repair the springs now dangling down under the beds like a row of rhizome shoots.

Even at that stage, Lilly was good at making decisions and before the day was out she'd already decided on a nickname for her newfound friend.

"Finnula's *far* too long," she'd mused studiously as they marched down the stairway to the dining room. "What about 'Nula', or 'Finny'?"

"Forget it. No way I'm answering to that!"

"Ginney?"

"Uh, uh."

"Finnula Ginnane... I know! Fudge! Sweet as Fudge!"

"Isn't it a bit too sickly sweet?"

"Too late, that's what I'm calling you from now on!"

Because it was what Lilly wanted, it was what she got, and within a week the Loughrua girl was known to one and all as Finnula "Fudge" Ginnane, a name that would, one way or the other, stick to her like toffee for the rest of her life.

Later, after tea, they had finished unpacking, Lilly placing her brand new pink fluffy slippers next to Fudge's old tartan ones. Ashamed at first, Fudge tried to make excuses for her hand-me-down night-dresses and towelling, thread-snagged dressing gown, but quickly realised that Lilly not only accepted her modest background without any of the usual condescension, she genuinely couldn't give a damn about the quality or condition of Fudge's night-wear.

On the contrary, as days passed and their friendship grew, it became clear that Fudge's background, although provincial and unassuming, was a source of fascination, and even a touch of envy on Lilly's part. Stories of baking bread in the kitchen together with all the family, or helping to turn the neighbour's hay on balmy summer evenings, caused Lilly's eyes to grow wide and glazed; the vision of domestic bliss, a mother's flour-covered arms holding a child close to her warm bosom, and the image of a cosy family nest full of siblings made her broken heart constrict. She'd have sacrificed all the pink fluffy slippers in the world to experience that feeling, now lost forever, one more time.

Fudge's dad was a farmer. They lived at Birch Rise, a farm five miles out the Bullcudy road north of Loughrua in County Galway. His hair was dark brown, spattered with grey—it always had been—and was thinning a bit on the top. Strong, well-built, and just gone forty, he was not what even a ten-year-old could call really ancient, but the wind, the weather and the worry had taken a few years from him, and with them, the bounce out of his stride and the sparkle from his glance. His name, God have pity on him, was Jarleth Horace. Fudge's grandparents had a mighty sense of humour. Mercifully, everyone called him Charlie.

They had a good-sized farm, cattle, a couple of horses—including a sturdy hunter, Shanagarry—a clatter of exotic miniature chickens which shat everywhere and produced, as Dad put it, piddling little eggs the size of gobstoppers, and last but not least, a long-haired Persian cat called Sinbad that lived rough, caught mice and spat them out onto the back doorstep. The house, a rambling, box-shaped building with cracks in the walls and sagging beams in the attic, was absolute heaven. It stood in the shade of two huge horse-chestnut trees and, on windy autumn nights, the fat, rock-hard conkers could be heard bouncing off the tiles and rolling noisily into the gutters. The sound, combined with the howling wind, invariably sent the children screaming down the corridor to their parent's room where it often took half the night to convince them that leprechauns had better things to do than scuttle about the roof in hobnailed boots.

The kitchen, the heartbeat of the household, was always warm and welcoming. In the summer, the windows were thrown open letting the country breeze carry in the smell of garden herbs, wild garlic and fresh grass; in the winter, the huge range, where apple pies and soda bread were baked to golden brown, sent glowing heat throughout the room and dried the washing hanging on suspended wooden slats above. This was Mum's domain and the rest of the family (above all Dad) accepted that here, her word was law. If you dragged in clumps of earth, you got a clip on the ear; if you sat down at the table with black fingernails, you washed up alone; and if you ate out of the pot before dinner was served, you did without pudding and pity about you!

Mum wasn't slim, but not fat either. It depended on what she was wearing. With the polka-dot kitchen apron pulled tight around her she had opulent, matronly curves, a rounded belly and generous, child-bearing hips. In her grey Sunday skirt suit, however, the curves disappeared, her tall frame and broad shoulders carrying the weight well. She had strong, muscular upper arms from years of pulling calves and carting sacks of grain and, if ever a jam jar wouldn't open, one ran immediately to Mum and watched with proud admiration as she popped the lid with a flick of her wrist. But she wasn't all muscle and no brain. Mum was a great reader. In the evening, when the last batch of washing was hoisted up over the range, when Dad was sleeping in front of the telly and the younger children were in bed, she'd pull out a book borrowed from the Loughrua library and disappear into it.

"I nearly went to Galway University, you know," she'd said once. Fudge had been sitting at the kitchen table regarding her mother who, although deeply absorbed in the novel lying on her lap, hadn't turned a page for a full five minutes. Her eyes had a glassy look, her voice a certain timbre to it. She knew her mum wanted to cry.

"Why didn't you?" Fudge asked softly after a long while, afraid to break the brittle silence.

Her mother had sniffed and giggled then, blinking back the tears before they had the chance to drop. "Sure, didn't I fall in love with your Dad, silly. If I'd let him off the hook, he'd probably have married someone with a big bottom and a moustache, like Muriel McMahon from up the road. Now we couldn't have had that, could we!" They'd roared with amusement at the very thought of it, and the moment was forgotten.

She had kind features, which was normally another way of saying a *plain* face, but Mum's face really was kind; it was soft and gentle and her lips, although somewhat thin from years of being pressed together in deliberation, always promised a smile; her eyes were large and round, and friendly. Most men wouldn't have turned in the street to take a second look, but Dad, not without a tingle of jealous consternation, had noticed often enough that once a man did look into her eyes, he often had trouble looking away again.

Her hair, worn twisted up onto the top of her head and clamped firmly into place with a slide, was rich chestnut brown and had a mind of its own. As she pottered about the house, a long wavy wisp would slowly wheedle its way out and flutter about her face, yet instead of tucking it away again (which would have been a shame), she blew the tendril out of her eye at intervals with a short, sharp puff—like a locomotive letting off steam. It was a picture Fudge would carry around with her for the rest of her life: the evening sun shining through pots of parsley and chives on the windowsill and Mum bending over a bowl of cooking apples, the long strand of chestnut hair dancing jerkily up and down while she worked. Her name was Mary. Just Mary—and that's what everyone called her.

Fudge had four sisters. No brothers—not even one—and not for want of trying on Mary and Charlie's part!

Sheila was the oldest and the bossiest. Four years older than Fudge, she was Mum's right arm and had exclusive punishing rights when left to babysit. True to her nature, she never stopped to think twice when it came to effecting this privilege. She wore glasses, had a pretty, freckly face; short, wiry, dark hair; big boobs; small feet and a mole on her left cheek that she vainly termed a beauty spot.

The twins, Lizzy and Beth, were two years younger than Fudge. Mary, who never bothered too much about regular antenatal check-ups, only discovered she was to have twins five minutes before they arrived. Having only thought of one name—Elizabeth—they decided split it up.

The twins, inevitably, were identical in every way and absolutely inseparable. It didn't bother them that they weren't individual—on the contrary, one often had the impression they regretted not having been born Siamese. Stubborn and independent, they could do without anyone else and, when Fudge came to think of it, there were times when everyone else could have done without them. They had mouse-brown, wavy hair, knock knees and were able to bend their thumbs back to touch their arms.

Last, but in no way least, was Rosy, better known as "the baby" as she would be for the rest of her life. Four years younger than the twins, she was the result of Mary and Charlie wanting "a last shot at it". Not that Mary was getting too old to have children—she was thirty-four when she had Rosy and still going strong—they were just running out of bedrooms. So five children it was—all girls.

Fudge, stuck in the middle, had constantly been shuffled about. At first she'd had a room of her own. Upon arrival of the twins, she was condemned to sharing with her older sister, who consequently kicked up a fierce ruckus. Then, when Sheila turned twelve, she started getting blackheads and black moods, so Mum, deciding the older girl needed a bit of privacy, shoved Fudge back in with the twins who ganged up on her immediately. Two years later, Rosy, now too big to share a bedroom with her parents, was put in with the twins and so Fudge, well and truly fed up, ended up in a room with Sheila once again. Sheila, fourteen at the time and in the throes of puberty, went sheer apeshit at the thought of having to share a room with a ten-year-old. That was when Auntie Dora finally stepped in.

Dora was Charlie's sister and had rakes of money. She'd married a wealthy older man with a bad cough who keeled over one day at the Galway Races, leaving her a fortune. The farm was well run and Fudge's parents never had any serious difficulties, but the way things were, prices would rise and fall, one bad season would follow another, and occasionally Dora insisted on passing on a padded envelope to help make life for the Ginnane family a little more comfortable. That was how Charlie managed to afford his fox hunting, a tiny dinghy for the lake and, in the end, boarding school for Fudge.

The idea was born when, after a particularly filthy fight with her older sister, Fudge asked if she could go and live with her Auntie Dora. Mum and Dad had been shocked, and the younger girls, seeing it wasn't a joke, all burst into tears. Sheila, of course, had jumped for joy. No amount of wheedling could bring her round—Fudge remained adamant. She loved her family, even the rejoicing Sheila, but was sick of being pushed around.

A day or two later, however, she suddenly regretted her impetuosity, but the snowball was already rolling, and the more the adults thought about it, the better the idea became. Auntie Dora couldn't look after a ten-year-old child, but she knew of a great boarding school where Fudge would be able to live and learn with children of her own age. She could visit her aunt down in Kildare at the weekends and go home during the holidays. It would be a wonderfully educational experience for Fudge. All of a sudden it became an exciting project for the adults, and before the poor girl had time to blink, forms were filled out, the school uniform bought, and she was standing on the steps of Castleglen Park School for Young Ladies wearing a horrible hat and a puss on her face. Miss Ginnane had just been informed she'd be sharing a room with eleven other girls.

That was the official reason for sending her to boarding school. But underneath it all lay another one. Sheila went to the local tech and was happy there, had plenty of friends and stoically ignored the fact that she was different. That the whole family was somewhat different, if only a little bit. Fudge, however, had felt it a few times at school and although nothing ever happened which had her coming home in tears, Mary and Charlie wanted her in a school with the likes of her own.

This divergence to norm, as far as Fudge was concerned, expressed itself only in the fact that they didn't have a picture of the late John F. Kennedy next to the Pope hanging over the kitchen sideboard. They didn't bless themselves or say the Angelus, but they believed in God and said their prayers every night. The whole family went to church on Sunday—even if it was a slightly shabby one with only ten people in the congregation and dry rot in the beams. Theresa Walsh , a girl from her class, took her into the huge Loughrua Catholic church once where they'd lit a candle and genuflected, Fudge wobbling slightly until she got the hang if it. She'd been filled with awe in the face of such intricate splendour and even sensed a twinge of envy, but then they'd knelt down to say a little prayer, and Fudge realised, with her eyes closed thinking of God, she couldn't see any of it, neither the golden cherubs nor the dry rot. What she could see was in her heart and head, and it felt good.

And anyway, Loughrua was light years away from Northern Ireland, so Fudge couldn't understand why it might be of importance at all, and even years later, when she understood the history and politics, she still couldn't see why it mattered. But that's the way it was. They were proddies. And now she was going to a prim Protestant school with all its side effects.

~ * ~

The clattering of the supper gong tore Fudge out of her contemplation. She looked around for Lilly and was relieved to see her darting up the passageway. As they filed into the lengthy dining room and took their places at one of the long refectory tables, they remained silent. First grace had to be sung and the head staff seated. The minute Mrs. Oldfield's bottom hit the chair, one hundred pupils burst into excited chatter and supper began. Fudge and Lilly were positioned conveniently at the end of the last table next to the wall.

As soon as the girls on the other side were preoccupied with serving up sausages and baked beans on toast, Fudge turned to Lilly, her eyes like saucers.

"Okay, out with it! Did you, or didn't you?"

Two

They were there again—lurking in the bushes like tomcats. About four of them, down on their knees between the flowering nettles and the hairy-leafed plants with stalks that reminded Lilly of rhubarb. She could hear them scuffling around a couple of yards back from the goalposts. Every now and then a stifled snort was followed by urgent whispering and suppressed oaths.

"Shut the fuck up, will ya, ya stupid tosser—we'll ge' caught!"

"Shag off, we're quicker than any of them wagons. They haven't a hope in hell!"

"Yeh, but we don't want that Barrett wanker to start nosin' around. He knows where we live and'll be down to the Metals faster than greased snot."

Lilly listened. The Dublin accents were as thick and grainy as overnight porridge—accents evoking the forbidden. A sudden quirt of adrenaline gave rise to another feeling: rebelliousness, a longing for adventure—the scary kind.

She kicked at a tuft of loose earth behind the lines and then bent down to adjust her hockey pads, well aware that all eyes were on her backside as she did so. She fiddled with the buckles for a minute or two, hoping a practised air of unconcern would leave her audience believing she was ignorant of their oh-so-obvious presence.

Straightening up, she sauntered over to the post and pushed a tousle of blond curls out of her eyes. The hot afternoon sun made her squint. Above the expanse of green, the air was shimmering, making the walls of the school building in the distance appear to ripple. Way down at the other end of the hockey pitch, Amelda the Amazon was blowing the whistle and gesticulating wildly at the centre forward who'd seemingly taken a vicious swipe at someone's naked shins. The ball hadn't been anywhere near her goal for the last fifteen minutes and that suited Lilly fine. Two redundant backs were hovering in futile anticipation some distance away, frustrated at not being part of the action. Under the heavy protective gear, sweat was beginning to trickle down her lower back and belly. She felt like a good scratch, but knew she was being watched. That was exactly the kind of thing they were waiting for. The Teddy Boys. Bad boys. Forbidden fruit.

Under the pretence of inspecting the tattered net, Lilly turned quickly and walked to the rear of the goal. Her sudden movement caused, just as she'd hoped, a brief wave of pandemonium. Twigs snapped, undergrowth crunched, expletives were muttered.

"Hey, Johnny, get yer fat elbow out of me face, for chrissakes!"

"Shut yer cake-hole, Prof, or it'll be me boot." He snorted. "Look at yer one, pretending not to see us. Nice bit of fluff, though... oh jaysus!"

"Wha...?"

Lilly was doing optic acrobatics in an effort to peer out from under her lashes into the dense huddle of shrubs and brushwood flanking the playing fields. Rustling, pushing, snorts. Leaves were swaying back and forth, and every now and then, the sun glinted off a pair of glasses. Preoccupied with her sly observations, she had absentmindedly wrapped one index finger around a piece of netting and was trying to extricate it when a strawberry blond head shot abruptly out of the greenery. Lilly started jerkily at the unexpected sight and stumbled back a step or two, but her finger, still trapped in the thick cord, prevented a hasty retreat and she was yanked rudely forward once again.

"Hey, luv, look out! The ball's comin'!"

Lilly knew her cheeks were flaming.

"The ball! It's comin' yer way!"

Behind her, she could hear dozens of booted feet thundering down the green like a herd of stampeding buffaloes, and the brutal clacking of wood on wood as hockey sticks smashed together. Frantically, she endeavoured to release her finger that had long since turned an alarming shade of blue.

"Lillian! What are you doing, girl? Get out of the goal, LILLY!"

Amelda the Amazon was screaming from the sidelines, her cries joined by those of the rest of the team. The eyes below the strawberry blond fringe grew wide and a grubby finger stabbed the air as he pointed over Lilly's shoulder.

"Ah, feck it, luv, yer shagged now, anyway!"

Those were his last words before plunging back down into the nettles and out of sight. At the same moment she was free and catapulting backwards out of the goal, her arms flapped about her like a bird with a broken wing. Restricted by the bulky protective gear, she didn't have a hope in hell, and a second later, was flat on her back, the rock-hard hockey ball whizzing dangerously past her left ear into the goal.

She closed her eyes and groaned. This was going to need some explaining.

"Lilly, you big eejit! What *were* you doing?"

Above her, angry teammates were grouping around. Some had thrown down their sticks in disgust and were standing with hands on hip, lips pursed threateningly.

"God, McDermott, don't you know the goalie's supposed to be standing *facing* the pitch!"

Through a forest of bandy legs and knock-knees, Lilly noticed that small clusters of daisies with pink-tipped petals were clustered around the base of the goal post—tiny spots of colour sprouting up out of the trampled earth. She sighed.

"Well now, you don't say." Lilly struggled to sit up. Her bottom was as bruised as her pride, and clumps of soil were glued to the back of her head.

"Were you day-dreaming, or what?" The Amazon was leaning over her, muscular shoulders hunched up in aggravation, a line of sweaty beads dotting her upper lip.

"S'pose so, sorry. It's a hot day and the ball had been down the other end for *ages*—I must have got distracted." For some reason the last remark brought a few laughs.

The sports teacher rolled her eyes to heaven and shook her head. Pushing herself into an upright position, she glanced over at the school clock then blew the whistle, indicating the match was officially over.

"Off you go, the lot of you. Prep's in half an hour. Make sure all the sticks are put away."

Slowly, the two teams began to make their way up towards the main building, one giggling and sneering, the other grumbling cantankerously. Lilly was shaking clods of caked dirt out of her curls when Fudge sidled up. She was a left back for the "B" team.

"You were looking out for them, weren't you?"

"Looking out for who?" Lilly affected innocence.

Fudge gave her a poke. "Go on out of that, I bet you had your eyes glued to the bushes."

"Why would I do that?"

"You know bloody well why! They were there—go on, admit it!" Fudge was chuckling sarcastically, her glance wandering along the line of shrubs beyond the hockey pitch.

"Who do you mean?" Lilly wasn't giving up easily, but she now had her tongue-in-cheek.

"The Teddy Boys, of course, as if you didn't know!"

They both burst out laughing and Lilly slid her arm through her friend's.

"If you really must know, you big nosy-parker, I was having a little chat with one of them!" Lilly proudly flicked a strand of blond hair back from her face.

"You were not!"

"I was, too!"

"What did you talk about?"

"Well, obviously not politics. Actually he did most of the talking."

"What did he say?" Fudge's eyes were fixed on Lilly. She couldn't have been more astonished had Lilly told her she'd been chin-wagging with the Queen.

"Okay, to be quite honest, not a lot, but I think he fancies me. Just before he disappeared back into the nettles he looked me in the eye and said..."

"What? What?" Fudge was almost wetting her knickers with excitement.

"He said..."

"Yeh?"

"He said, 'Feck it, luv, yer shagged now anyway'!"

The pair of them collapsed into giggling shrieks of girly silliness, causing heads to turn and eyes to roll. Their chortles could still be heard when they reached the locker room five minutes later.

~ * ~

There had always been "Teddy Boys" and they had always been called "Teddy Boys", even though they had nothing in common with the original youth cult supporters of the fifties. Perhaps it was their unruly behaviour and unconstrained manner which earned them the nickname, but nobody knew exactly—nor did it really matter. If one referred to the "Teddy Boys" then everyone knew who was meant.

They were, in fact, ordinary local boys who lived on the far side of the railway lines beyond the school premises. A bunch of devil-may-care working class heroes with rough hands and even rougher Dublin accents. In the afternoon, while the girls were playing hockey or lacrosse, they would slip over the ivy-covered perimeter wall, and hidden from sight behind screens of shrubbery, spend the time dossing around, smoking fags and slapping their thighs in hilarity at the sight of so many red-faced "birds" (pronounced "burds") galloping around in short tunics. Sometimes they were particularly daring, sneaking up to within a couple of yards of the school building after sunset to throw stones at the dormitory windows. When the lights snapped on they'd scarper, guffawing loudly as menacing house staff—the likes of ferocious Smelly Kelly—shook their fists at the retreating figures.

Such events were, needless to say, wildly titillating, the girls squealing in mock fear as the first pebbles bounced off the window frames. Surrounded by a hundred young girls, ranging from homesick nine-year-olds with strange fixations to cranky, pubescent seventeen-year-olds with screaming hormones, a distraction in the form of a couple of cocky local lads, albeit greasy-haired and spotty, was a humungus adventure and one Lilly was hard set on taking advantage of. Fudge, always a tick slower off the mark was, as usual, the last one to find out about this.

"We'll nip out around the back of the gym after tea—nobody'll see us if we're quick."

"What are you talking about?"

"I'm talking about having an adventure!"

"An adventure?"

"Yeah, we're going to take a little walk along the wall."

"But that's forbidden!"

"That's what makes it exciting!"

"But what if we accidentally meet up with some of those Teddy Boys!"

Lilly crossed her eyes at Fudge in exasperation. "Isn't that the whole point of the exercise, flea brain!"

"*What*?"

"Oh, Fudge, come on! Will you close your mouth before some birds build a nest in there—it'll be great *craic*—you'll see!"

"But... but... what if they take advantage of us!"

Lilly let her pile of exercise books fall with a crash onto the prep room table. "Oh, for heaven's sake, Fudge. What do you think they're going to do? Gang rape us a couple of yards from the teachers' room window?"

"Gang wha...? But the teachers have all gone home!"

"Fudge, you really are on the ball today, d'you know that?"

"Huh?"

"Ssh! Gibbi's coming! Look, I'll meet you at the gym door after prep."

"But... but... but..."

"Put a lid on it, will you, Fudge? You're beginning to sound like an outboard engine in neutral."

Lilly plonked herself down, opened her school books and gestured at Fudge, who was still standing rooted to the spot, to do the same.

Looking back, one might say it was the first of a long line of sexual, or rather, sensual adventures the two of them were to experience together over the next few decades—not a series of lascivious escapades of debauchery, but the zigzag path of stepping stones which eventually led to sexual maturity. Most of these steps they took together, if not in body, then in spirit. It was a case of the blind leading the blind, whereby Fudge's metaphorical eyesight was even worse than Lilly's. Each obstacle, once overcome, was then discussed, analysed and evaluated—in younger years with coke and Taytos, later with pistachio nuts and bottles of cold Muscadet. Lilly, like a juicy, swollen spring bud aching to blossom was, at first, the more adventurous of the two, but then it was Fudge, who, like a late summer perennial lurking at the back of the flower bed, opened her delicate petals overnight and enjoyed a special, lasting sensuality which flourished and prospered long after others had begun to fade.

~ * ~

That evening waiting at the gym door, however, Fudge was a long way from even putting out shoots. Her stomach was churning at the very thought of stealing into the bushes for a clandestine meeting with a pack of lads from across the Metals. Lilly, on the other hand, was raring to go, and Fudge had to stifle a sarcastic remark when she noticed her friend's eyelashes almost glued together with mascara.

"This'll be great gas, Fudge—don't make such a face! We'll sneak down along the wall a hundred yards or so and if there's no sign of them we'll turn around and come back—okay? Now relax, you look as if you're about to shit a brick!"

"I *am* about to shit a brick, if you must know. Aw, Lilly, do we have to?"

Lilly didn't even bother to wait for an answer. Tossing a blond spiral of hair over her shoulder with a jerk of her head, she turned and in a flash had disappeared around the corner of the gym. Uttering a grunt of dissatisfaction Fudge, having been left without a choice, followed on her heels.

A flurry of midges rose up out of the long grass as they slipped into the gloomy, dark-leafed shrubbery. It was early evening and the sun, a glowing orange globe, hung precariously above the stone wall, ready to plunge down behind the hockey field for the night. Invisible hovering insects darted against Fudge's legs making her want to scratch mercilessly at her calves. The short summer socks offered no protection against the numerous creepy-crawlies whirring in droves about her.

To add insult to injury, an acrid smell of urine wafted up from a clump of green-yellow flowering weeds, and wrinkling her nose, Fudge wondered if it was nature's revenge or the fact that they were standing in the middle of the Teddy Boys' public convenience. The evening was warm, but a clammy dampness filled the air, causing her to perspire. Nervously, she drew her hand across her forehead noticing, as she did, that her fingers shook perceptibly.

Lilly was up ahead following a narrow path of trodden undergrowth, a sign that they weren't the first to come this way. Here and there, further evidence dotted the track—a crumpled crisp bag, cigarette butts and, worst of all, bunched-up paper hankies. Fudge shuddered when she saw them, furiously trying not to imagine what kind of hideous fluids might be lurking between the soggy folds. Once, she skidded on something that squelched succulently and, unable to contain her disgust any longer, she swore, grasping out into the prickly greenery in search for support. Righting herself, Fudge cursed again as a small trickle of blood oozed from a scratch on the back of her hand.

Swallowing her revulsion, she quickly licked the cut and, intentionally avoiding a glance at what she'd stood on, hurried after

Lilly. Shit, *shit!* How could she let herself be persuaded into such a situation? It was always the same. Lilly would start by making some crazy suggestion; Fudge would refuse adamantly for ten minutes or so before eventually yielding. She asked herself why she bothered putting up a fight at all. It would be far easier just to agree immediately and save them a lot of time and useless discussion.

Further on, Lilly had stopped and was leaning against the trunk of a sycamore tree, her unnatural stance one of affected repose. High above in the branches crows were cawing loudly—a hoarse, grating noise which jangled Fudge's nerves. They appeared to be deliberating excitedly the approach of the two out-of-place schoolgirls. Overhead, irregular chinks of blue broke through a tangle of dark, leafy limbs. The sultriness seemed to intensify by the moment, a clawing humidity radiating out of the undergrowth. The vegetation on either side of the path was spattered with globs of bird-droppings, all adding to Fudge's disgust.

"Lilly! I'm going back—I've had enough!"

The other girl widened her eyes and shook her head vigorously. Out of the corner of her mouth she hissed in Fudge's direction.

"Ssh! Come over here and shut up!"

Listening to Lilly's brusque manner and her imperative attitude towards Fudge, one might have thought the latter to be browbeaten and oppressed—a stranger would have called it bullying—but anyone who knew the girls realised that in each other they had found the perfect supplement to their own personal failings. Fudge would never learn to dominate, would never achieve that same kind of imperial charisma which Lilly exuded, but why should she even try? It wasn't her nature. She wanted and needed guidance, she sought constant confirmation that her judgement was accurate, and if it wasn't, she accepted that. While not exactly dependent on an emotional walking-frame of self-assurance, she felt happier when she had an ancillary crutch nearby. With her no-nonsense nature, Lilly led Fudge firmly and securely, but above all loyally; were Lilly ever to stop walking one step ahead, Fudge would surely lose her way.

However, just as the dark-haired country girl accepted, though often with mild protests, the other's commanding manner, so too, did the exuberant city girl accept, or rather *need*, Fudge's voluntary submissiveness. It wasn't a question of wanting to exert her will upon others, or of even wanting to satisfy the desire to merely have things her way, Lilly needed someone to direct, guide and above all *mother*. Having had the bitter experience of losing her own, she endeavoured to be strong and resolute, to follow her needs and instincts with unwavering self-confidence and, most surprisingly of all, she had developed a desire to maternally care and protect. Despite the somewhat arrogant assertiveness, Lilly would have gone to the ends of the earth to support Fudge and there wasn't a soul in the school who didn't know it. Unknown to all, however, and primarily to Lilly herself, was that, despite all the blond girl's apparent resoluteness, even then at the age of thirteen, a fatal flaw, a tiny fracture, already existed in this protective shield of self-assurance.

A flutter of wind oozed through the greenery, but far from refreshing, it simply served as an invisible conveyor belt for muggy evening air and pissy smells.

Fudge wiped a drip of sweat off her nose, leaving a bloody smudge trailing across the tip. Around the base of the tree was a small clearing, the long grass and clumps of nettles flattened to the earth. It appeared to be some kind of meeting point. Here, too, were crumpled up cigarette packets, Mars wrappers and one or two rusting beer cans.

Running her hand over the coarse bark, she noticed several initials carved roughly into the trunk, jagged scars hacked higgledy-piggledy into the wood. How romantic, she mused, momentarily forgetting her discomfort as she visualised some infatuated juvenile delinquent whittling away for hours in order to unite his initials with those of his sweetheart. *I wonder if anyone will ever do that for me.* She ran her index finger along the lines, following the turns and curves of the letters, one after the other—and then her heart fell. It wasn't two sets of initials after all, it was just one word—FUCK.

Disappointed, Fudge kicked the base of the trunk, scuffing the toe of her already worn-out shoes, annoyed that she'd let her imagination run away with her. Still, the vision of an infatuated youth lingered and she made herself believe his name to be Freddy Upton and hers, Cynthia Keegan.

"We're being watched." Gazing up into the leafy dome, Lilly mumbled in Fudge's general direction, a look of blank naivety draped across her pale features.

Fudge peered about, seeing nothing but forty shades of green.

"By what?" She scratched irritably at her hairline, which was being mercilessly savaged by an onslaught of gluttonous midges.

Lilly didn't answer. She was too busy posing. Fudge watched with fascination as her friend assumed her "I-know-I'm-being-watched-by-a-man-and-don't-want-to-let-on" stance. The shoulders went back, chest thrust up and out, back and bum curved into a Grecian bend, one leg drawn up behind her to rest on the tree trunk. Plucking some foliage from a dangling twig, she proceeded to study it intensely, her attention devoted solely to the intricate delta of leafy veins and capillaries, and all the while, through her mascara-clogged eyelashes she kept watch, her senses all pricked up like a watchdog's ears.

A rustling. A snigger. Lilly studied the leaf even harder, moistening her lips as she did so. A sneeze. Stifled snorts. Raising her eyebrows into an expression of mild surprise, Lilly at last allowed herself to glance up and let her gaze wander casually along the ivy-covered wall. To emphasise her lack of concern, she fanned herself idly with the flaccid leaf. Fudge envied her. Lilly was poised, serene. The Loughrua girl, on the other hand, was all but wetting herself, shoulders hunched up in excruciating anticipation, knees knocking.

"Howaya, girls, youse finished yer homework, have ye?"

Fudge skittered nervously, causing a burst of horsy neighing to rise up from behind a tangle of briars.

"Nuttin' to be nervous about, luv." Gales of throaty laughter.

Fudge felt her cheeks flame up as if she'd been scalded, her embarrassment heightening even more so upon noticing the cotton sausage she'd twisted tightly into the hem of her Airtex shirt.

Flustered, she tried to straighten the crinkles with the flat of her hand, resisting at the same time the urge to start nervously twisting at it all over again. Imitating Lilly's trick of feigning preoccupation with the vegetation, she pulled the top off the nearest plant, squawking loudly on discovering she'd beheaded a hairy nettle. The joviality was tumultuous. Vigorously, Fudge rubbed her stinging fingers together, tears of humiliation pricking the back of her eyelids. Gradually, the laughter petered out into sporadic chortles.

"Aw, leave off, Paul, will ya? She's only mortified."

"Don't pick on me, youse were all killin' yerslves laughin'."

"All righ', luv?"

Fudge continued to ignore them, although they had now manoeuvred themselves into a position next to an elderberry bush less than a few feet away. She stared at the blue-black berries and was suddenly somewhere else, her thoughts slipping back to their family kitchen and her mother as she cleaned and crushed the fruit they'd picked to make wine, her hands and nose stained with juices.

"We make elderberry wine on the farm." She murmured distantly, her gaze wandering over to Lilly who was still leaning against the sycamore tree.

Lilly put her hand to her face and shook her head.

Not knowing the difference between an elderberry bush and anything else with berries hanging off it, the boys stared at Fudge as if they weren't sure whether they should burst out laughing or run for it.

A second or two passed before the lads collected themselves. The one with the strawberry blond hair grinned broadly at Fudge. "Wine? Now we're talkin' business. Although I'll drink anything as long as alcohol's in it."

Fudge returned to planet earth and quite suddenly they were friends. After that, the serious flirting began.

The autumn term was saved. The monotony of boarding school routine, stretching before them like an abominable wasteland until the next half-term oasis, had suddenly been broken in the form of three unlikely characters from out of the nettles. And one of them would later supply Fudge with her first *Big F.K.*

Three

"It felt like a slimy eel—all wriggly and wet!"

"Eek, that's disgusting—you can't be serious!"

"Cross my heart 'n' swear to die, I was almost gagging 'cos his tongue was in that deep!"

Fudge studied Lilly suspiciously, her eyes squinting with scepticism. She was having her on. She had to be. That was about the most revolting thing she'd ever heard. Lilly had a way of *distorting* things, but despite the wide eyes and gleeful smirk, Fudge had a ghastly feeling that this time she was telling the truth.

"Oh yuck, you poor thing. Did you want to puke?" Fudge was running her tongue around her teeth in a cleansing manner, the vileness of it all almost perceptible in her own mouth.

"Puke? Why would I have puked? It was absolutely *divine*—couldn't get enough of it!" Lilly's eyes were sparkling.

"*No!*" Fudge's toes were almost curling backwards with repugnance. "I don't want to hear any more."

The harvest of salacious details had an abundance vastly exceeding the country girl's expectations. Lilly had, in point of fact, experienced to the full her first real kiss (the Big F.K. no less!) around the side of the Seapoint Dance Hall in Salthill a mere three weeks before. The ins and outs now coming to light had Fudge almost reeling in revulsion, and she wondered at the naivety of her thinking Lilly might need some persuasion to part with them. But the dreadfulness of it all was that she had actually seemed to enjoy it!

They were sitting side by side in the long grass in front of the wall which separated the classroom building from the hockey pitches. It was a nice place for pubertal chitchat, the kind of natter girls indulge in long after puberty transcends the menopause, and puppy fat becomes middle-age spread. It was a mild evening with a wintry bite to it—a reminder that autumn was quickly approaching. Before them, the bright green of the playing fields was being eaten up by long shadows moving slowly outwards from the high trees surrounding the perimeter. The far-off clattering of a train passing and the occasional sound of cars revving and beeping on Glenageary Road reminded them that, despite the immediate tranquillity, they were sitting on an island in middle of a busy city surrounded by a high wall.

Fudge was confused. Hadn't they talked about it all beforehand? They had agreed that a proper kiss would be soft and sensuous, a tentative meeting of tongues, the relishing of tender lips moving together in unison. Even their stance during the act had been discussed. It was decided they wouldn't assume a coy posture, bottoms sticking out in an attempt to avoid feeling something which might scare the living daylights out of them. Melting together. That was how they had described it. They would melt together, bodies cautiously joined in the comforting assurance that several layers of fabric prevented total contact. Her arms would be thrown around his neck, his resting deferentially on her hips. Caressing the back of his head affectionately was also acceptable.

Lilly's horrendous account had absolutely nothing in common with these fantasies. The young man, Lilly steadfastly claimed, was the son of a reputable Galway restaurateur, but Fudge suspected he mopped the floor at The Battered Cod chipper. He had to if he behaved like that. Slimy. He'd asked her to dance to Ronnie and the Muck Rakers' rendering of Donny Osmond's "Puppy Love" and within minutes had two of his hands up the back of her tank top, and all the rest scrambling to find a way into her elephant flares. Lilly, aware that the holiday would soon be over and with it her chances of getting "shifted", spontaneously agreed to his suggestion that they catch a quick breath of fresh air. No sooner had they reached a secluded spot between the car park and Seapoint than he had his tongue down the Dublin girl's throat and was exploring the cavities behind her tonsils. She hardly had time to think about where all his hands were, but was glad she'd implemented the old safety-pin-in-the-zipper trick, otherwise he'd have had the bell-bottoms around her ankles as quick as you can say Mary Poppins.

"He didn't feel your boobs, too, did he? I mean, you said he came from a good family." At this stage Fudge was ready to believe anything. She gazed enviously at her friend's perky rotundities, and then down at her own wide-spaced breasts.

"For God's sake, Fudge, you don't know the half of it. The smart-looking lads are the randiest runts of the lot! Bored little rich boys with as many arms as an octupus and constant stiffies. Nothing better to do with their time but sit around giving themselves hand shandies."

Stiffies? Hand shandies? Fudge was lost. What had happened to Lilly during the summer holidays? They weren't even speaking the same language any more. There was no way around it; she was going to have to ask.

"Stiffy? What exactly do you mean?"

"You know... a tent pole," Lilly replied matter-of-factly. She'd picked a blade of grass and having laid it between her thumbs was now making hooting noises by blowing on it.

"They carry tent poles around with them all the time?" The boys Lilly'd had the pleasure of encountering down in Galway certainly seemed a peculiar lot.

"Not a *real* tent pole... a horn, a hard-on!" Lilly was making a vague gesture in the vicinity of her pelvis.

"Oh, I see," Fudge replied blankly, embarrassed that it had taken so long for the penny to drop. She had unclear memories of Mum telling her about the birds and bees, and of course down on the farm she'd often enough seen bulls mounting heifers, or dogs mating with bitches. That had been purely for reproduction purposes and while she was aware that humans enjoyed sex without necessarily wanting babies, she was, nevertheless, under the impression that having a "stiffy", as Lilly so competently put it, was a physical state men reserved exclusively for wives (preferably their own) in the darkness of nuptial bedrooms. That they actually sauntered around all but brandishing the things in public was totally new to Fudge, and an idea which would need some getting used to.

"And a hand shandy?" She was now in no doubt that these young men, when indulging in "hand shandies" were not, in fact, treating themselves to nice glasses of beer mixed with lemonade.

"Jacking-off... honestly, Fudge, don't you know a thing?" Lilly snorted with laughter and stuck the blade of grass into her mouth.

"I do, of course! It's just the terms you use. If you'd stop showing off with fancy words I might know what you're talking about!" Fudge replied indignantly, at the same time frantically rummaging around in her mind in an effort to recall ever having seen either the bulls or dogs jacking off.

"Please don't tell me you haven't heard of masturbating!"

"Well, sort of... and men actually do that? Hand shandies—for no reason?"

"Yeah, they do... maybe not all the time, but sometimes." Lilly had tugged out another stalk of grass and was making the same hooting noises. Charlie had shown them that trick.

"But why?" Fudge enquired, determined to get to the bottom of it all. She wasn't going to let herself be baffled by sweeping statements which couldn't be upheld.

"Why? Well, I suppose they like the feel of it, don't they?" She pushed a stray lock of blond hair back from her brow, slightly irritated. It seemed her apparently inexhaustible cornucopia of sexual information was finally beginning to peter out.

"And how long do they do it for—a few seconds, minutes or are they at it for hours?" In the light of Lilly's irritation, Fudge was beginning to enjoy herself, but the enjoyment was limited in the face of such startling enlightenment.

"Oh, how would I know! If you'd visited me down in Salthill like you promised, you wouldn't have to be asking all these questions!"

"Aw, come on, that's not fair. You know I wanted to, but I had to help at home. We were bringing in the hay and the twins did damn all to help. I spent my time just trying to keep Rosy out of they way!"

"Yeh, but you said if we took our holidays in Galway this year, you'd be able to visit. As it was, I had to deal with all those lads on my own. You'll never get anywhere near a French kiss if you stay on the farm all the time."

"I know," Fudge acknowledged bleakly. "But if I'd been around, you wouldn't have had a hope in hell anyway!"

Both girls laughed at the idea; it was generally accepted that Lilly was by far the more attractive of the two. Even at the age of thirteen her body, despite a touch of pudginess, had reached a stage of maturity which made road workers' eyes boggle. Combined with her golden locks and mischievous blue eyes, it was evident that one day she was going to break some hearts big time. But she wasn't conceited about it; she enjoyed her looks in an appreciative manner, always wisely pointing out when complimented that her parents were responsible, and that she herself had little influence on how she'd turned out. She also had no doubt in her mind that Fudge, whose appearance was still somewhat mousy, would one day, with her help, develop into a looker. Fudge didn't mind either, that when it came to her looks she was—as always—one step behind. She had not yet really started worrying about clothes and hair and nails. That could wait.

The shadows had now devoured the last corner of green and, as dusk approached, the school building loomed up behind them, grey and menacing. Here and there, a light snapped on and from their cosy nest behind the wall the girls could see other boarders passing back and forth behind the windows, books clamped under their arms as they hurried to prep for an hour's slogging before going to bed.

Fudge shifted uncomfortably. The grass was quickly becoming damp and unpleasant under her bottom. There were still a lot of questions which remained unanswered. This smooching business, for example, had troubled Fudge immensely. If the kissing hadn't manifested itself to be the blissful act of self-abandon predicted, but a pathetic performance of slobbering spit-swapping, then why did Lilly think it was so *divine*, as she put it? Her eyes had had a kind of hungry glint in them as she related the events of that summer night round the side of the dance hall—a glint which made Fudge fiercely curious and somehow fidgety.

She glanced sideways at the blond head that was now turned away towards the darkening shrubbery behind the goalposts. Lilly leant forward and made another grassy hoot, chucking the stalk to the side when she was finished. Fudge looked at her watch. Almost half past six. In a minute the bell would ring and they'd have to make a mad dash for it if they wanted to avoid getting a ticking off from Gibbi. It didn't pay to get on the wrong side of the house mistress.

Prep was compulsory; everyone had to attend, like it or not. Once your homework was done, you were permitted to read a book, the school library sporting a careful choice of novels including, among others, *The Adventures of the Famous Five* and *The Secret Garden* for younger pupils, moving on to Agatha Christie and Catherine Gaskin. For those wishing to go the whole hog, there were one or two dog-eared copies of *War and Peace* and *The Lord of the Rings*. Anyone looking for anything juicier would have been wasting their time. While the Castleglen bookshelves held little that might cause a literary expert to sit up in surprise, there was nothing lurking in there that could lead to uncomfortable questioning on part of the pupils—questions which hard-core spinsters, such as Brody or Gibbons, would be at a loss to answer.

Miss Gibbons was responsible for Castleglen's reading matter, and also for supervising prep. Here, she governed with an iron hand, moving silently between the rows of desks, the lace-ups groaning ever so slightly under her formidable weight. Gibbi, like Brody, was of a nondescript age, and whereas an adult might have put her somewhere in her fifties, most of the schoolgirls thought her to be positively prehistoric, teetering on the brink of decrepitude with one foot in the grave and the other on a banana skin. She was carved out of a block, with thick glasses, a thick waist and thick ankles. Unshackled and free from the fetters of fashion, she was almost never seen wearing anything other than a twinset and a tweed skirt, summer or winter. She had a nest of dyed, mouse-brown, wiry hair which sat on her head like a felt beret. Her ears were always red, like she'd just emerged from under a hairdryer, and if you arrived late to prep they turned puce.

Fudge gave Lilly a dig.

"C'mon, Lil, we'll be up shit creek if we're late."

"Okay, just a minute." She was staring expectantly over at the bushes, now no more than a bundle of shadows.

"What is it?" Fudge followed her friend's intent look.

"I'm waiting for an answer."

Fudge was puzzled. "I thought I was the one with all the questions," she remarked quizzically.

"No, you big twat... from them." She gestured off to the right.

"But...?"

"Ssshh... did you hear that?" Lilly was now sitting up, alert and stiff as a ramrod.

"What?" At the same moment a familiar hooting noise rose up from the school perimeter, a hollow echo resounding over the deserted playing fields.

"Brilliant... that's it!" Fudge watched as Lilly jumped up excitedly, pulling what appeared to be a folded piece of paper out of her sleeve. She placed it in the long grass and grabbed the elbow of Fudge's jumper.

"Okay, let's go, time for prep!"

Predictably, Fudge hadn't a clue what was going on and, as usual, Lilly left her feeling as thick as a plank.

"Would it be too much to ask what's going on?" They were hurrying towards the main building. From the yard the jangling sound of the school bell announced that prep was about to begin. Lilly was still tugging Fudge along by the sleeve of her jumper.

"I'm meeting them later on, that's what!"

"You are not!"

"I am, too!"

"Where? Down there in the bushes—in the dark?"

"To start with, yeah," Lilly replied assertively.

"What do you mean, to start with?" They had reached the inner courtyard and both were panting freely, their race to beat Gibbi to the prep room now in its final stretch.

"I'll write you a note in prep. Now shut up before the whole school knows about it!"

Duly admonished, Fudge grabbed her books from a shelf and followed Lilly to a desk in the far corner, well away from Miss Gibbons' beady eye. The house mistress entered the room seconds later, tweed and nylon swishing, lace-ups groaning. There was a general bustle of activity as chairs were pulled in, books opened and pencils sharpened, but soon everyone appeared to be studying diligently, noses to the desks. The girls, flanked on either side by strategically placed piles of copies, waited until Miss Gibbons was preoccupied with correcting the English homework of her 3A pupils, among others, Lillian McDermott's—but not Fudge's. True to her character, she was in the "B" stream. Daydreaming opposite them, tubby Irene O'Neill chewed on a pencil with relish, wishing, no doubt, that it were a fat Frankfurter sausage covered in ketchup. Beside her, Sarah Gibson had slid down in her chair and was lost in biology, her blue suede feet stretched out beneath the table.

Satisfied they weren't being observed, Lilly tore a page out of her jotter and quickly scribbled a few words before furtively pushing it over to Fudge. "Sneaking out tonight" was written in an almost illegible script. The look on Fudge's face spoke volumes. Lilly grabbed the piece of paper again. "Don't worry—going after lights out." The page slid back and forth between the two friends. "You're crazy" underlined three times with four exclamation marks. "Sissy!" "You'll be expelled!" "Who's to know?" With that last scribbled statement, Lilly scrunched up the piece of paper and tossed it in the direction of a waste paper basket behind their desk, indicating that, for now, the subject was closed.

Meanwhile, Miss Gibbons had reached Lilly's copy book and was dismayed at how unsuccessfully her best pupil had converted past perfect from active to passive voice. Tut-tutting under her breath, she glanced up and searched the room. This wasn't like her at all. What had the girl been thinking? Peering over the top of her glasses, she spotted Lilly stuck away in the corner. What were they at now? Her brow ruffled as she noticed both girls pushing a sheet of paper to and fro. Opening her mouth to reprimand the two, the house mistress clamped it shut again as Lilly chucked the note towards a bin. Miss Gibbons studied the girl now bent over a world atlas, an expression of intense concentration on her face. *That child, what'll become of her? Pretty, intelligent, mad as a hatter and motherless. Always up to mischief with that mousy Loughrua girl, Finnula Ginnane, in tow.* The house mistress picked up her red felt-tipped pen and continued marking the exercises. *I'll give her another chance—this once.*

~ * ~

Later, when all the girls had left the prep room and were busy in their dormitories getting ready for bed, Miss Gibbons moved between the desks checking that no books had been forgotten. Beside the desk where Lilly and Fudge had sat, she paused, noticing a bunched up ball of paper that had apparently missed the bin and rolled up against the wall. Frowning, she leant forward and picked it up, but instead of dropping it into the basket, she instinctively proceeded to flatten it out, curious to see what had been so carelessly cast aside. The wrinkles made it difficult to read, the handwriting was a scribbled scrawl, but...

"You can leave the cleanin' up t'me, ma'am."

The rough voice startled the house mistress, causing her heart to skitter. It was Molly, the cleaning woman, armed to the teeth with buckets and mops, ready to start her rounds now that the boarders were out of the way.

"Pardon me? Oh, yes, of course... go ahead, Molly, I'm finished here." She scrunched the page up once again and, without realising she was doing so, stuffed it into her cardigan pocket where, for the moment, it was forgotten.

~ * ~

"God almighty! Have you gone completely mad or what? What's got into you?" Fudge pleaded. They were hunched over the same sink in the communal bathroom. Next door, the clatter and laughter was lessening as, one by one, their roommates settled down for the night. Lilly had it all planned.

"Ah, don't get your knickers in a twist, nobody'll know," she replied, cool as a cucumber. "I'll slip out the dining room window and round the back of the orchard. The lads will help me over the wall. Only for an hour or so—we're going to the pub."

"And how can you be so sure they'll be there?"

"Sure didn't you see me leaving a note in the grass. They signalled that it would be okay."

Fudge remembered now. All that hooting business.

"But how can you trust them? There are three of them, you're alone. What if they...?"

"Oh, Fudge! For crying out loud! They're only lads wanting a bit of fun. You've met them yourself, do they look like mad rapists to you?"

Fudge considered the boys they'd encountered once or twice under clandestine conditions down in the piss-smelling undergrowth. At eighteen, Prof, "Professor", was the oldest, but the smallest of the three. He was no taller than the girls with black, wavy, shoulder-length hair. He had slightly buck teeth and glasses like the bottoms of Coke bottles, making his eyes look as if they were set wider than his head. A young man of few words, he just watched and waited while the others did all the sweet-talking, a bland look of insouciance on his froggy face. Johnny was the red haired one. Not carrot-red, but a sandy-rust colour and, cut unevenly, it fell over one eye leaving unruly tufts standing to attention on his crown. He had a pleasant, freckle-dotted face, but one which appeared to have been scrubbed with sandpaper, and between his eyes a crater caused by chicken pox scarring slid up and down as he spoke. Paul was the hunk and, without doubt, the one who had Lilly's hormones in a smather. At seventeen (a year older than Johnny), he was tall and lanky with slim hips and no arse to speak of. His legs were like stilts starting somewhere just under his shoulder blades and ending on a pair of massive Massai warrior feet. He had twinkling eyes and an impish face surrounded by limp, chestnut-brown hair. They all came from Ballyglass, living on a small housing estate on the far side of the Metals. As for being mad rapists...

"Well, maybe not, but do you know what a rapist looks like? For all you know the one with the Coke-bottle glasses could be the Ballyglass ripper. If you ask me there's something funny about the way he just gawks all the time!"

"Ach, honest to God, stop exaggerating," Lilly retorted impatiently, squeezing a line of toothpaste onto her brush.

"Why are you so fussy about going on your own anyway?" Fudge probed, the picture of good-looking Paul still in her mind.

"Who else would go with me then?"

"Well, you could have asked me for a start," she sniffed, a hurt look crossing her features. "I can't think why you didn't."

"Okay, do you want to go with me?" Lilly glared at Fudge challengingly.

"No way!"

"I rest my case—Jeez, Fudge, how long do you think I've known you—since yesterday?" Her expression softened and she gave her friend a good-natured poke in the ribs. "Now don't worry, it'll be a cinch."

"And I suppose you're going like that?" Fudge nodded towards the baby teddy bears somersaulting all over Lilly's brushed cotton pyjamas.

"Grab a load of this!" Lilly pulled up her top to reveal a pink, tie-dyed T-shirt underneath. "I've got my bell-bottoms on, too—rolled up to the knees. And how about this for brilliant!" She unzipped her wash bag and presented it proudly. Inside were a pair of cork-soled platform sandals. "I'll change outside!"

Fudge sighed. "And haven't you forgotten you're only thirteen?"

"Now that's about the lamest argument yet. I'll be fourteen in a few weeks, and anyway, you know darn well that everyone thinks I'm at least sixteen!"

"Still too young to be going into a pub and ordering drink."

"Let that be the least of your worries."

~ * ~

But worried she was, and by the time Smelly Kelly had turned off the lights and gone, leaving a trail of BO in her wake, Fudge's stomach was churning. *Something absolutely awful is going to happen, and it'll be my fault as usual for not stopping her*, she thought bleakly. *How could Lilly burden me with all this? Some friend.*

This year, there were only four other girls in her dormitory, including Irene O'Neill, who'd fallen asleep lying on her back, mouth open. She was now making strange, gurgling noises, and if her roommates hadn't known better, they might have mistakenly thought she was being strangled. For a while, the others tossed and turned, trying to get comfortable in the yawning hollows of their school beds. Bed springs screeched intermittently in protest then all was quiet, even breathing indicating that the last of them had drifted off. In her sleep, Brenda Buckley broke wind, a sound like someone popping the lid off a beer bottle. Despite the gravity of the situation, Fudge tried not to snigger, but the involuntary wave of mirth died soon enough when she noticed Lilly slipping quietly out of bed.

"I'm going now," she whispered urgently. "If anyone misses me, say I'm hogging the loo with a dose of the squitters."

"And what if you're caught sneaking through the dining room with your wash bag tucked under your elbow?"

"Then I'll pretend I'm sleepwalking and keep going."

"Well, if you think it'll work..." Fudge couldn't share the city girl's dogged sense of self-confidence.

"Of course it'll work, now shush, I'll be back in an hour and a half at the latest—well before midnight."

"But not later... promise me! Two of us can't be having the squitters!" Fudge begged in a beseeching whisper, her bowls already feeling like jelly.

"No sweat, Fudgie-Wudgie." And then she was gone, sneaking quickly out into the dimly lit passageway with the wash bag clutched under her arm and the pink fluffy slippers padding softly as she went. Before she closed the dormitory door, there was a last, fleeting glimpse of the mass of blond curls illuminated by diffused night light.

At that moment Fudge knew that something was going to go wrong. Badly wrong.

Years later, lying alone in the darkness, she'd remember that night, remember that ephemeral image of Lilly as she slipped out the door, and the horror she had felt at that moment would come washing over her once again.

And horror it was. For a thirteen-year-old boarding school girl surrounded by rules, regulations and a contingent of rigorous house staff who spoon fed one on discipline to the point of gagging, a breach of these regulations did little to stimulate a sense of mutinous triumph, but instead, left one wallowing in a mire of moral conflict. In Ireland popping down to the local pub was as common a practise as brushing your teeth, but to climb over the high perimeter wall of Castleglen Park in order to do so was an act of such horrendous impertinence, the blatant disregard for authority being so unsurpassed in its gravity, that few would stop to think why these rules had been made in the first place—namely, for the safety of the girls.

And Fudge, at that moment, had huge misgivings regarding Lilly's safety.

She lay there, wide awake, straining to hear any movement outside, expecting at any minute the loud, scolding voice of Smelly Kelly, or worse, Gibbi's nasal bark. Her hopes suddenly soared; if caught now, Lilly would, at the worst, get a right old bollocking (as Charlie would say) and be ordered back to bed on the spot. Unfortunately, that didn't happen. Several more minutes passed without any sign of commotion and Fudge realised, in alarm, that by now her friend would be out the window and flitting through the apple trees. She continued to listen, holding her breath, afraid that the sound of her own breathing might cause her to miss something.

The old schoolhouse was making all kinds of peculiar noises she'd never really noticed before. Plumbing groaned deep in the heart of the building as a toilet was flushed; wainscoting creaked and, beneath her, something skittered helter-skelter between the floorboards, tiny claws scraping against wood in its mad dash. Although the fireplace had long since been boarded up, the odd gust of wind could be heard scurrying down the chimney accompanied by the rustle of dry leaves and twigs helplessly caught up in the draught. But soon the house settled down for the night as the sporadic rustling, scuttling and clanking gradually faded away. Now all was silent. Between a crack in the curtains, a flush of dim, yellowy light from the street lanterns down on Glenageary Road irradiated a long rectangle on the high ceiling. Every now and then, the bar of brightness would glow and fade as the headlights of cars coming up from Dun Laoghaire shone momentarily through the school gates before turning away in the direction of Ballyglass.

As she watched the moving lights, counting them like sheep, Fudge almost dozed off when, suddenly, the sound of screeching brakes and screamed oaths echoed across the school grounds. She shot up in bed, her gut seizing up into a tight hard knot. *Oh God! She's been run over!* Fudge sat there petrified, grasping the metal bed frame until her knuckles turned white. She waited, all senses alert until, a short while later, a hoot of cackled laughter together with the noisy whine of a car accelerating and driving off seeped through the trees from the street. Slowly, she relaxed, her heart thudding loudly in her chest. *I've got to stay calm,* she reproached herself, *Lilly's hardly been gone half an hour. She'll be back by eleven or so—what could possibly happen in an hour?* This thought was little comfort, but nevertheless, after a lot of shifting and turning, Fudge felt her eyelids grow heavy and within minutes she was sound asleep, her hands still clutching the hard iron frame.

~ * ~

She woke with pins and needles in her fingers and the fuzzy feeling of having forgotten something. Pushing back the blankets, she peered around, blinking in an effort to focus. The room was suffused in early morning light, barely enough for her to make out the bumpy shapes of her sleeping roommates. In the wee hours before daybreak, city noises had ceased and the excited chatter of early birds announcing the approaching dawn had not yet begun. Fudge flopped over onto her side flexing her hands, and as she did so her gaze slid over to Lilly's bed. It was empty.

And then she remembered. It all came flooding back to her in a great gush of adrenaline. The boys, the pub, the plan, the sheer madness of it all. *Don't move! Think*! She lay rigid, staring at the ceiling, afraid of waking the others. *God, where is she?*

With a start, Fudge realised that in an hour or so the school would waken up to a new day—Kelly on her reveille rounds, and kitchen staff carting plates of sliced pan to the breakfast tables. Soon the corridors would be a hive of bustling activity as sleepy-eyed pupils slouched back and forth from the bathrooms.

Her pulse quickened with excitement. Lilly would surely be down in the washroom herself, scrubbing away the gluey mascara and lipstick she'd no doubt applied the minute she was over the wall. Ever so silently, Fudge climbed out of bed and, throwing a dressing gown over her shoulders, tiptoed out of the dormitory. Nothing more than wishful thinking, her hopes dissolved moments later on discovering the bathrooms empty.

Swaying on the brink of panic, Fudge stood at the top of the wide stairway from where she had a view through the high landing window into the courtyard. Bertie Barrett's black cat slunk as soundlessly as a dark shadow across the cobblestones and out under the archway. The slightly musty smell of mildewy wallpaper and aged linoleum hung in the air. *Damn and blast her*, Fudge thought, anger not replacing, but accompanying her fear. *How could she do this to me! I'll have to find her*, she thought bitterly, knowing that the most she could do was overcome her trepidation and search the shrubbery encompassing the school grounds. *I'll never forgive her for this. Never.*

Carefully, she made her way down the stairs and along the gloomy corridor to the dining room, wincing every time the floorboards creaked. One window in the far corner was slightly ajar, revealing Lilly's exit. Leaning out, she saw to her consternation that it was a fair drop down into the orchard, but time was pressing and soon after, Fudge was on all fours in the thistles, green skid marks on the knees of her flannelette nighty.

Realising there was no going back, she pushed herself up and, after a mad sprint through the apple trees, flung herself into a protecting screen of rhododendrons. In front of her, the high bordering wall rose up, grey on grey against the pre-dawn sky. Off to the right, it continued along the side of the orchard to the groomed front lawns where the gravel driveway curved up to the front gate. To her left, the slate-coloured brickwork swept off down towards the playing fields and railway lines.

To the left it is, Fudge determined, not believing for a moment that, late or not, Lilly would be brazen enough to get back in by sauntering through the front entranceway. After a few yards, the relatively cared-for orchard greenery gave way to scruffy undergrowth and immediately Fudge was plunged into green murkiness, forced to push her way under low-lying branches and past clumps of nettles.

Blankets of clammy fog hovered over the hockey fields and rolled up over the surrounding banks of scrub in swirling ripples. She swallowed hard and, as indescribable fear began to balloon up inside her chest, she found herself whimpering piteously, the sound of her own voice contributing to her wretchedness. Every now and then she stifled a cry as heavy dew-sodden stalks whipped back against her face. The tartan slippers were soaked through and through, making her feet heavy. Despite the dank morning chill, she stopped at the small, trodden clearing to wipe a line of sweat from her brow.

And then she saw it. The flowery wash bag stuffed into a clump of ivy.

Fudge tugged at it and any flicker of hope was quenched when she saw the pink slippers inside—proof that Lilly had, indeed, not yet returned. These suspicions were confirmed a moment later when, a few feet away, she uncovered the damp bundle of somersaulting teddy bears.

Confused and frightened, Fudge pushed her way further into the fetid undergrowth until she reached the wall. There she sat down with her back to the moss- and ivy-covered stonework and stared for a very long time into space, desperately hoping that, any moment, Lilly's laughing face would appear above her. *I can't go back and pretend I don't know anything. She'll be missed. They'll ask.*

Pulling her legs up against her chest, she laid her head on her knees and cried softly. The cold and damp began to penetrate her flimsy clothing and resigning, Fudge knew she'd have to return, vaguely wondering if Lilly's whereabouts had already been established and reported to the school. Gibbi was bad, but the thought of a confrontation with Mrs. Oldfield had her quaking once again. *Maybe she's just decided to go home to Ballsbridge,* Fudge thought naively, knowing almost before the idea had crossed her mind that Mrs. Oldfield's wrath would, without any shred of a doubt, be pathetic in the face of Mr. McDermott's.

She reached down to push herself up, immediately pulling her hand away in disgust as she felt something cool and rubbery under her palm.

"Oh, damn it!" Fudge spat, wiping her hand vigorously against the front of her already grubby dressing gown. "I can't bear any more, it's all too much!" She glanced down into the long grass to determine the source of her revulsion. At that moment the world stood still.

A hand, smooth and pale, was sticking out between the long stalks, the fingers turned elegantly into the palm. Several fingernails were ragged and torn. A thin line of blood trailed from the tip of the index finger down to the knuckle where its way parted before disappearing under the wrist. Fudge, paralysed with horror, was vaguely reminded of the intricate henna designs she had once seen on an Indian girl's hands. Shaking uncontrollably, she crawled forward and shoved the grass aside.

She was lying on her back, the lush golden locks, now dull and matted, tumbled in disarray around her shoulders. She looked peaceful, serene, lips slightly parted, her head lolling to the side. Mercifully, her eyes were closed. Fudge's gaze moved down, hazily registering the slightly podgy legs thrust out in a knock-kneed manner, toes pointing inward. One sandal was missing. Although there was no doubt in her mind that the girl was dead, she reached over and took the other hand which lay, fingers spread, on her pink, tie-dyed breast. A second later, she was at last able to scream, a thin strangled squawk of terror; under the pale hand a rust-red starburst radiated out from the centre of Lilly's chest.

"Nooo..." Fudge moaned, curling up in a ball in the foliage beside her friend. "Lilly... Lilleee..."

Four

Over in Castleglen's west wing, Miss Gibbons' alarm clock jangled loudly, pulling her out of a troubled sleep. She'd been having that dream again. The Brighton one. That was the second time this week. It was all still vivid in her mind and would not, like many other dreams, fade from memory. Funny that. She'd read somewhere once that unless you related your dream to someone soon after waking, it would be forgotten by midday—and it was true. She'd tried it. This particular dream didn't want remembering, but it was the one that persistently remained in her mind to the very last detail, although she'd never told it to anyone.

She could see herself, a young girl in Brighton, proud to be old enough to wear grown-up clothes. No more pinafores or smocks. She was crunching along the pebbled beach towards the pier wearing a smart black skirt to her calves and a crisp white tailored shirt, buttoned at the neck and wrists. Although quite sure she'd never had one, in her dream she was wearing a duster hat with a scarf curtain falling over her hair. Her black, built-up shoes were polished and shining, the heels as high as a girl her age might dare. Cosmetics had disappeared from the counters, but she had a few tricks to achieve the hard, Joan Crawford lips of the day.

Pleased with herself, she turned her face to the sun. The gusty wind blowing up from France ruffled her wavy hair and tugged at her hat, almost causing her to trot. Throngs of visitors were crowding around the pavilion—a sea of bobbing heads, toffee apples and candy floss.

And then she was suddenly at the fair ground whirling round and round and round on a carousel. There was a man with black teeth sitting on the horse next to her going up and down, and up and down. "Are you on your own, little lady?" he wanted to know, and she had said not really, she was waiting for her mummy and daddy who were coming down on the train from London.

Having wanted to appear grown-up, she felt embarrassed and now he was laughing at her, saying that nobody was coming from London because bombs had fallen and the city was a heap of rubble and dust. Laughing back, she assured him it was all right, her parents were rich. They were staying at The Ritz. And he said, "not the Ritz, the blitz," and she cried "Ritz!"

"No," he laughed, "blitz!", and then she could hear the drone of a hundred bomber planes sweeping in from the continent, and the scream of sirens, and the ringing of bells, and she was going round and round and round shouting, "Mummy, Daddy, Mummy, Daddy..."

She reached over and switched off the alarm, fighting a wave of sadness that threatened to wash over her. It was still early. Plenty of time before breakfast to make one or two preparations for the first English class of the day. The thought cheered her up immensely. Today she was going to guide her students through Longfellow's *Hiawatha*—one of her favourites. A couple of stanzas off pat for homework would do the job, she decided, heaving herself out of bed. The high window offered a pleasant view across the manicured lawn and rose beds to the front entrance and the crossroads on Glenageary Road. It was a foggy morning. Cold and nasty.

Squinting, she could only just make out the wrought-iron gates at the end of the driveway. She liked to sleep with the curtains open, not for the view, but because drawn curtains reminded her of wartime and the blackout.

Miss Gibbons shuddered and pulled a powder-blue quilted bed jacket on over her winceyette nightdress, before plodding over to the sink. Flicking on the small light, she studied her reflection in the mirror. The hair net which kept her nest in place had slipped to the side during the night making her head look slightly skew whiff. Streaks of grey could be seen at the roots. *Bother*, she thought, *those girls will think I'm positively antediluvian if I don't get those give-aways touched up. Never mind, I'll wear something bright this morning, yes, my beige wool skirt and smoky pink twinset—and the dark rose beaded necklace. For Hiawatha I'll need the beads.* Pleased with her decision, she set about sorting her clothes, first tidying away the cardigan she'd left hanging over the back of the chair the evening before. Carefully, she draped the soft wool on a padded hanger and placed it in the cupboard, a frown of dissatisfaction crossing her face when she noticed the folds weren't hanging neatly. Scowling, the house mistress pulled a wad of paper out of the pocket, wondering how it had got there in the first place. Senile dementia, she construed impatiently, but then her eyes grew wide as she slowly deciphered what was written there—and remembered exactly who had written it.

~ * ~

In a stupefied state of shock Fudge didn't, at first, hear the slow swishing of something creeping through the shrubbery towards her. When the sound suddenly penetrated her senses, she realised that it— whatever it was—couldn't be more than two or three feet behind her. Miss O'Dowd, their unconventional biology teacher renowned for her rather perverse tendency to relate gruesome anecdotes to prove a point, had told the class that when being torn asunder by a lion, the victim felt no fear or pain, but fell into a state of lethargy. Mother Nature's mercy, she called it. Fudge begged for Mother Nature's mercy now. In the face of imminent danger she found herself unable to lift a finger. Instead, she turned her face to the ground, squeezed her eyes tightly shut and moaned even louder. The swishing stopped and a moment later, she felt a hand on her shoulder.

"Youse all righ', luv?"

"Huh…?" Fudge dared to open her eyelids a crack. "Please… don't hurt me…"

"What're ya on about?"

Only then did she recognise the thick Dublin accent and scruffy head of sandy red hair.

"Oh God, Johnny…" she whined, making a vague gesture towards the patch of grass nearby. "She's dead… help me!"

"Dead! Jaysus Christ!" Then his eyebrows knitted and he looked around "Em… who's dead?"

Was he blind, or feeble-minded? Couldn't he see the prostrate body splayed out in the thicket beside them, the T-shirt covered with blood?

"Li-Lilly… st-stabbed…" she stuttered, unable to control her trembling. "Look…!"

"Lilly's gone and croaked it, has she?"

He'd been crouching down beside her, but now he rolled back on his heels, laughing throatily and slapping his thigh in mirth. "That's bleedin' hilarious!" Johnny snorted, as soon as he had regained enough breath to do so.

He's mad, Fudge deduced, a raving lunatic. She slowly started pushing herself away from him. *He's murdered Lilly and now totally lost his sanity.* Her eyes darted back and forth seeking a means of escape. Johnny, still doubled over with laughter and holding his stomach, staggered over to Lilly's prone figure. He leaned forward, studied her serene face for a moment, then gave her a smart slap across the cheek. Lilly groaned.

"What…?" Fudge licked her bone-dry lips and swallowed in disbelief.

"She's only ossified." He regarded the schoolgirl's quizzical expression. "Pissed out of her noggin—totally rat-faced. We shoved her over the wall a cupla hours ago. I figured considerin' the state of her she wouldn't get very far—that's why I came back."

"But the blood, the stab wound." Fudge pointed shakily at Lilly's crimson chest.

Johnny stuck his tongue in cheek, stifling another laughing fit in deference to the country teenager's insurmountable naivety.

"Ketchup," he explained sagely. "We went for a feed of pork sausages and chips after the pub and she was so scuttered she tipped half the bottle onto her knockers."

"Half a bottle of..." Fudge murmured, feeling like the biggest idiot ever to walk on the face of the earth.

"We had to pay extra, too," he added as an afterthought. He turned back to Lilly, hiking his hipsters up a bit. "Righ', better get her sorted out if youse don't want to get serious agro."

Fudge shook herself, blinked several times in quick succession then glanced over at the limp, but very much alive form of Lillian McDermott. *Well, that little cow... I'll kill her*, was all she could think. She was *raging*, not only because of the fear and anger endured but, above all, because of the excruciating humiliation she had been forced to suffer in front of the cocky Dublin youth. Quickly, she scrabbled over to where Lilly lay and peered into her face. The blond girl was still out cold, but her lips had curled up into a woozy smirk. Johnny was patting her cheek in a feeble attempt at waking her. Fudge shoved him rudely aside.

"Let me do that," she barked, and with one swift movement, landed Lilly a good swipe across the face. She lifted her hand to get another one in when Johnny grabbed her by the wrist.

"Whoa... hey, leave over, luv, I think you've done the job."

Still seething with fury, Fudge looked down to see her best friend gazing up at her, cross-eyed and gurgling.

"Well... ha... hello Fush-wishy..." she hiccupped wetley. "Wassamadder?"

"Oh Christ, what am I going to do?" She looked at Johnny pleadingly. "You'll have to help me. I'll never get her back to the school on my own."

"Well, I can drag her by the seat of her pants as far as the orchard, sweetheart, bu' after that yer on yer own."

Fudge looked at her watch. "All right, if we hurry and she co-operates a bit, we might just make it."

Together, with a lot of shuffling and acrobatics, and much to the amusement of Lilly who cackled loudly every time she fell over, they managed to pull the pyjamas on over her clothes and slip her dirty feet into the fluffy slippers. In a commendable display of strength, Johnny then flung Lilly over his shoulder in one fluid motion. Fudge couldn't help noticing how his biceps rippled as he did so, and for a moment, she felt strangely flustered. By now the birds had begun to chirp and chatter in the trees above, mercifully obscuring Lilly's squeaks of hilarity. As one would expect, she found the whole thing bloody amusing.

"What was she drinking, anyway?" Fudge enquired, as she pushed ahead, clearing the way for Johnny and his load.

"What wasn't she drinkin', would be a better question," he replied, hardly out of breath. "She had the whole pub wrapped round her finger—everyone buyin' her drinks. Vodka 'n coke, Stag, Harvey Wallbangers... you name it, she was guzzling it."

"Harvey whats ...?"

"Harvey Wallbangers, cocktails—ladies stuff, we kinda lost track of time, then we went out for a feed. Before we knew what happened, it was three in de mornin'."

At least he had the decency to look guilty. When they had reached the cluster of rhododendrons at the end of the orchard, Johnny propped his inebriated burden up against the wall, continuing to hold her by the scruff of her neck.

"Well, luv, this is as far as I go," he said, his rubicund face breaking into a smile. "I suggest you grab her firmly under the arm and make a dash for it."

"Okay..." Fudge was unsure. She looked over toward the dining room window and was relieved to see it still ajar. As yet, nobody seemed to be around. The sunlight had slowly begun to creep over the rooftops, washing the tips of the apple trees in a yellow-pink glow. The fog was gradually dissipating, and further away cars could be heard motoring off towards Dublin and Dun Laoghaire, taking their owners to early shifts.

"Anyway... thanks, Johnny." She still felt kind of silly. "I don't know whether I should be mad at the lot of you or not."

He reached over and patted her arm. "Then don't be, sweetheart, don't be. I'll see ya around." He turned and popped back into the rhododendrons only to appear again a second later.

"Oh, and by the way, yer nighty's awful sexy." And suddenly he was gone. Merely the occasional shuddering of a branch or rustle of leaves marked his way.

Fudge flushed scarlet and sighed. *Nice fella. Pity he's bit of a gurrier.*

Johnny, deep in the bushes, was thinking about Fudge. *Nice bird. Pity she's a bit of a stuck-up bog-trotter.*

~ * ~

Miss Gibbons muttered to herself as she strained to pull the heavy-duty, roll-on girdle over her block-shaped hips.

"That girl! This is the last straw! Motherless or not, she's overstepped her mark this time, that's for sure!"

The roll-on in place, the house mistress struggled to deposit her pendulous breasts into the Playtex "Cross-your-Heart" bra, frustrated that she couldn't manoeuvre everything into position quick enough. Despite the severity of the situation, she refused to leave her room in a dressing gown, something she wouldn't do were the building threatening to burn to the ground around her.

"I was motherless myself," she mumbled bitterly. "Fatherless, too, but I had some bloody respect for authority!"

She allowed herself a little expletive under the circumstances.

All the hooks and eyes in place, she reached for the support pantyhose and proceeded to roll them up over her thick ankles. Already she was beginning to perspire.

"I've warned her a thousand times if I've warned her once—etiquette, propriety and decorum are all the ingredients crucial for getting through life, and now she's behaving like a bit of trash from the docks!" She yanked the tights up over her girdle, the waistband snapping into place just under her bosom. The whole effect made her look like a turgid Roscrea white pudding, but Miss Gibbons was oblivious to all of this.

The sun, which had peeped up over the edge of the Irish Sea, was bathing the higher up neighbourhoods of Glenageary in watery morning light. Castleglen Park was one of the first to enjoy this luxury and the house mistress could feel warmth of it on her broad back as she pulled on the twinset and hiked the wool skirt over her bottom.

"No, she's in trouble now. I've been lenient enough out of respect for her father's situation, but that poor man will just have to wake up to his daughter's antics—enough is enough!"

Prising on her brown orthopaedic lace-ups, her acrimonious muttering continued, only letting up for a moment when her double-packed waistline prevented her from breathing as she bent down to tie up her laces. Puce in the face, she stormed out into the corridor, a maverick gust of wind slamming the door loudly behind her as she went.

In the quiet of the old building, her hard-soled shoes clattered noisily on the linoleum. The west wing joined the main house at the top of a wide stairway, and there Miss Gibbons paused, the sound of her own footsteps still echoing along the passageway. Miss Kelly had not yet started her rounds, but way down in the basement a door slammed, indicating that the kitchen staff had already begun their breakfast preparations.

Gibbons turned toward the dormitories on the first floor, two on either side of the hallway, each bearing the name of well-known city streets or squares engraved on small plaques on the doors. Lillian McDermott and her accomplice, Finnula Ginnane, were in Piccadilly Circus, and if her ears weren't deceiving her, there were irksome scuffling sounds coming from that very direction. The house mistress marched purposefully towards the dormitory, forcing herself, at the same time, not to break into a trot.

"That young Miss will not get me into a fluster," she reprimanded herself and checked her stride. Maintain the dignity at all costs, her father used to say, maintain the dignity at all costs!

At the end of the T-shaped corridor, she swung to the left, listing dangerously to port like a galleon in a storm. In front of the door she stopped abruptly, disappointed she hadn't caught the malefactor on the hop. Not in the least deterred, she silently turned the doorknob and glanced into the room, her nose wrinkling slightly as a sleazy wave of stale air escaped past her. The dormitories of the second and third formers always smelt a little more pungent than others, as puberty raged and sweat glands began to kick into action.

Lilly McDermott was lying on her back snoring fitfully, the whifflings of deep sleep impossible to imitate. Miss Gibbons was irritated; surely she had heard something. In the next bed, Finnula Ginnane had the blankets tugged up to her ears, the narrow shoulders rising and falling rhythmically. As the older woman leaned over the blond pupil's tousled head, the anger went out of her. The child really did look like a sleeping angel, she thought, registering simultaneously a pleasant, sweet smell, vaguely reminiscent of oranges. Had Lilly been lucid at the time, she needn't have worried; Gibbi wouldn't have known what a Harvey Wallbanger smelt like to save her life.

Back outside in the hallway, Miss Kelly, having woken the first and second formers in Time Square and Grafton Street respectively, was surprised to see her superior coming from the direction of Piccadilly Circus. Above justification, Miss Gibbons merely nodded a terse "good morning" in passing and disappeared into the west wing. Smelly Kelly, not customarily the essence of diplomacy at the best of times, was tactful enough not to draw the house mistress's attention to the hair net dangling precariously from the back of her wiry head.

~ * ~

"I want to die."

"Good, that'll save me the bother. I was going to kill you, anyway."

"You're so mean... I feel like shite."

"Well now, my heart is only bleeding."

"Maybe you could pop down to Brody and get some liver salts."

"Maybe you could take a long walk off a short pier!"

"Fudgie-Wudgie, why so testy?"

"Piss off."

They were filing into Mrs. Devine's domestic science classes, one of the few they shared. This morning cookery was on the timetable, in general one of their favourite classes because they could eat what they'd cooked instead of school dinner, and although the girls' culinary skills left much to be desired, it was still a huge improvement on what they disdainfully referred to as "school slop".

"Now you wouldn't still be mad at me, would you?" Lilly enquired, braying loudly in a very unladylike manner. A bit too loudly, Fudge recognised uncomfortably, knowing that there must still be masses of alcohol coursing through her veins.

"You have no idea what an eejit I made of myself because of you!" Fudge snarled under her breath. "To think that in my desperation I actually phoned that rat you have the misfortune of calling your brother!"

This started Lilly snorting and chortling all over again, causing Mrs. Devine, who was busy sorting utensils at the back of the class, to peer disapprovingly over her spectacles.

Fudge was still burning with resentment and fury, the events of the morning all too fresh in her mind. How she managed to get Lilly in through the dining room window and up two flights of stairs she'd never know. Flopping around like a sack of potatoes, Lilly had gurgled, burbled, and generally done very little to make Fudge's life any bit easier, but thanks to her Kryptonian labours they managed to make it out the dining room door seconds before the first plates of wholesale sliced pan arrived up in the dumb waiter. When, on the final home stretch, the sound of Gibbi's brogues slapping on the lino could be heard thundering up the hallway, Fudge had been sorely tempted to dump the stocious heap and run for it! But luck prevailing, they succeeded in hurling themselves into bed milliseconds ahead of the house mistress, Lilly falling unconscious the instant her head hit the pillow being an extra bonus.

For once, it had paid off having to share a room with a bunch of goody-goodies; after Kelly's wake-up round they had all got up, washed and were out of the dormitory, leaving Fudge enough time to drag Lilly to a bathtub and douse her down with icy cold water for a full five minutes.

But that phone call to Julian had been a mistake—a bad mistake.

After sobering Lilly up to a level of lucidity that had led their unsuspecting fellow-students to presume she was merely exhausted, Fudge successfully guided her into the breakfast room and propped her up on a seat in the corner—well away from Oldfield's penetrating watch. For a moment, she'd even considered leaving Lilly in bed, but the risk of a roaming member of staff finding her there could have all kinds of nasty repercussions—a risk Fudge was loath to take. Thankfully, Miss Gibbons wasn't on breakfast duty that morning. For a while, Lilly had co-operated nicely, and considering half the pupils present appeared for breakfast in a state of catatonic stupor anyway, the blond girl's blank expression and hooded eyelids easily went unnoticed. It was only later when all the others had brushed their teeth and were heading for class, that Fudge began to panic again. With fifteen minutes to go before the first bell, Lilly appeared to have fallen into a trance and was lolling on her rickety bed, looking as if she'd swallowed rat repellent. In fact, her complexion had taken on such a startling shade of grey-green, that it was an understandable error for one to think she had, indeed, been poisoned. Nurturing these very suspicions, Fudge promptly decided she'd shouldered far too much responsibility as it was. The time had come for someone else to make a few decisions concerning Lilly McDermott's wellbeing for a change, and not wanting to abandon the inebriated girl without prior consultation, the obvious choice had been Julian. Without further ado, she'd scraped together the last of her pocket money, grabbed Lilly's address book, and dashed down to the pay phone near the kitchens.

Julian was a boarder at New King's College for Young Men in Monkstown and only someone with the IQ of a marshmallow would try to get hold of one of the pupils there at half past eight in the morning, yet that knowledge did little to deter Fudge.

"New King's College, good morning." Stern, but polite.

"Sorry, I know it's a bad time, but could I speak to Julian McDermott?"

"McDermott? One of the boys? Out of the question!"

"But it's urgent, otherwise I wouldn't..."

"Who's this speaking?"

"Finn... em... his sister, Lillian. It's an urgent family matter." A white lie.

A moment's consideration. "Very well then, but make it quick. He's on his way to class."

"Thanks."

In the background was a cacophony of boyish voices, some high, some low, and some breaking in the middle, above which she could hear Julian's name being called.

"Hey, McDermott, your sister's on the phone—make it snappy!"

Some clinking and rustling, and then Julian's voice.

"How do, Lilly-the-Pooh?"

"I beg your pardon?"

"Lilly?"

"Nope, sorry—Finnula."

"Fuck."

"*Lilly-the-Pooh*?"

"Just forget it, will you? What the hell do you want, or is this some kind of social call?"

"Your sister's plastered drunk, probably poisoned."

"So what?"

"I'm serious! I don't know what to do."

"Oh sure, she's been swigging Brody's cough mixture, has she?"

"No, really, she snuck out last..."

"Sneaked, pea-brain."

Let it go, Fudge thought, *let it go*. "...she *sneaked* out last night and got totally langers. She's almost comatose—what'll I do with her?"

"Sweet Jesus, Finnula! What d'you expect me to do? Beam myself over to Castleglen and hold her hand?"

"No, actually, seeing as you and your friends know all about getting pissed out of your bloody brains, I thought you might be able to give me a tip."

"What's she been drinking?" Julian sounded almost proud to be considered an authority on the subject.

"Banging Harveys."

"What?"

"Some kind of cocktail—don't ask me!"

"Oh Jesus... Harvey Wallbangers, is that all? God, you had me worried for a moment. If she'd been banging Harveys, then being drunk would be the least worrying state of affairs."

"Huh... I don't..."

"Ach, never mind—give her a sugar sandwich."

"Just a normal sugar sandwich?"

"Do you want me to spell it out for you, feather-brain?"

"Bugger you, McDermott, she's your bloody sister!"

"Ooh, we're grumpy today!"

"Thanks a bunch, you creep!"

"Any time, thunder-boobs!"

Just before she slammed down the receiver, she could hear him laughing. "Hey, lads, any of you heard of banging Harveys...?"

Fudge was writhing in embarrassment. Hearing him making fun of her was bad enough, but that last comment about her boobs was an all too blatant mockery of her undeveloped breasts, and really had been way below the belt. She was already carefully filing away that "Lilly-the-Pooh" crap for future reference.

~ * ~

"Crikey, I really do feel queasy." Lilly's chortling had stopped and she was looking decidedly bilious around the gills.

"I'm awfully sorry for your troubles," Fudge answered tartly, savouring the other girl's discomfort.

They looked up as Mrs. Devine started rapping a wooden spoon on the surface of the work unit directly in front of them.

"Right, girls, today we're going to prepare something slightly different for a change. I've laid out the ingredients here, and I'd like you all to come to the front to have a look."

Immediately, Fudge and Lilly were pushed up against the domestic science teacher's desk by a hoard of half-starved pupils who were already drooling freely at the thought of having uniform sausage and mash replaced with one of Devine's superb culinary masterpieces. As third formers, they were past Toad-in-the-Hole and bread 'n' butter pudding. This year, they'd been promised paella (without the squid please, Mrs. Devine), couscous and crème brûlée. In a country where one was successfully reared on boiled bacon with cabbage and fish fingers on Friday, such exotic dishes were only too mind-boggling for the ravenous boarding school girls.

With daintily splayed fingers, Mrs. Devine proceeded to open a plastic bag with "Tooley's Butcher Shop" printed on the front, carefully laying the contents in a row along the front of the table.

There were a couple of sniggers and a few groans.

Back in the good old days, long before people started to worry about foot and mouth disease, swine fever and BSE and were still chomping merrily away on animal offal, innards and brain, a nice stuffed cow's heart was a particularly scrumptious, festive treat. They now lay there, bluish-red and trembling two feet in front of Lilly's nose—a sight enough to make the most incorrigible of carnivores' guts quiver. Fudge only had time to realise the frightening shade of green-grey her friend's face had assumed, before hastily diving out of the line of fire.

In what was undoubtedly the most exquisite display of projectile vomiting since Linda Blair squirted bile-coloured pea soup all over her co-actors in *The Exorcist*, Lilly leaned forward across the desk and heaved what remained of three sugar sandwiches, a pork sausage and one round of chips up onto Mrs. Devine's ingredients. The teacher, paralysed by the abruptness of it all, stood wide-eyed and rigid, not even flinching for a moment when a gluey glob of semi-digested ersatz meat hit the left lens of her National Health specs.

Five

"I'm looking forward to the Halloween break."

Lilly was sitting in front of the dormitory window with a tatty bedspread draped around her shoulders. Most of the other boarders were down in the common room, leaving the two friends precious time on their own. From the window they could see through the trees and over the grey-tiled rooftops to Dun Laoghaire. In the distance the long arm of the pier was just about visible amongst a staggered forest of chimney tops and television antennas. The small chinks of Dublin Bay peeping between the buildings were dark and uninviting, all blueness sucked out by the sheet of heavy cloud hovering above. This evening, the summer appeared to have gone for good, a chilly damp flow of air having slowly, but surely, advanced from the west. Fudge shivered suddenly, feeling the cold draught which had forced its way between the joints in the window frame and was now snaking around her bare thighs. There were no such things as uniform tights; one got through the winter in long socks with blue knees and mottled legs. She pulled a chair up beside Lilly and sat down.

"Give us a corner of that," she said, tugging at the cover until the two of them were huddled underneath like a pair of refugees waiting to be gathered up by the Red Cross. A pigeon flapped onto the window ledge outside, its wings smacking noisily against the pane, sending a flutter of down zigzagging off on the wind. Fudge started then chuckled, looking automatically over at Lilly, but she was far, far away, her concentration fixed on a point beyond the horizon. She'd been filing her nails, still futilely trying to repair the damage done while scrambling over the wall days before. Now the nail file lay redundant in her lap. She looked wan and tired.

"You all right, Lil?"

"Mm…"

"Still feeling a bit the worse for wear?"

"Ah, no, it's not that…" She forced a smile. "A few pints would hardly get the better of me." Her expression went blank once again and she sighed raggedly.

Fudge picked at the corner of the bedspread and tried once more. "What is it?"

"I dunno… it's suddenly so quiet here, it makes me feel kind of… kind of…" Lilly shrugged, at a loss.

"Kind of homesick?"

"Yeah, something like that…"

"Why don't you ring your dad, or Julian, maybe that'll make you feel better."

"It wouldn't help… not really."

Fudge knew what was wrong, but felt uncomfortable, almost embarrassed, unable to find the right words of comfort in the face of the other girl's private grief. They sat in silence for a while watching the pigeon picking at its feathers with jerky, erratic movements. A second later, another one joined it on the ledge, and following a moment's confabulation, they took off together in a flurry of flapping wings. Mesmerised, the two friends stared after them as they cut a sweeping arc up above a lofty chestnut tree before turning away towards the city. It was very quiet in the room.

"I still miss her very much." Lilly's voice was barely audible.

"I know you do."

"Maybe that's why I'm so crazy."

"What do you mean?"

"Well, it's just that if I keep going, keep making funny plans, doing mad things and in between learning, learning, learning, then I won't have time to think."

"You don't want to forget, surely?"

"No, but I want to think of her in my own time and not have those memories sneaking up on me unexpectedly when I'm not ready for them... like now."

"They're good memories, aren't they?"

Lilly paused for a while. "Yes, they are, but five years is so long. I'm afraid of losing them. In a few years she'll be gone half my lifetime."

Fudge stared down at her hands, absorbing the enormity of what Lilly had just said. Half a lifetime. Half a lifetime without a mother.

The extent of it overwhelmed Lilly at that moment, too, and she turned to Fudge, eyes glistening with tears, her face crumpled up into an agonised grimace.

"Oh, Fudge, I miss her so much..."

And Fudge, forgetting her initial embarrassment, opened her arms and took the blond head onto her shoulder, holding her best friend tightly while she cried.

"I want my mummy back, Fudge, I want my mummy back."

~ * ~

There was a great clatter of clinking cups and cutlery scraping plates. A hundred girls in a sea of uniform blue chattered like machine guns in a cartridge-emptying frenzy. Halloween was approaching and with it escape from boarding school routine. At home, mothers were baking Barmbracks with rings in them and fathers were getting whacked over the knuckles with wooden spoons for wanting to pinch a slice too early. In the kitchen cupboards, bags of peanuts, hazelnuts, walnuts and those funny wrinkly Brazil nuts were waiting to be filled into bowls and placed before a crackling open fire. If you were lucky, you might lay your hands on a coconut, and even though it was probably mass cultivated on a plantation, one liked to think that a little fuzzy-haired, brown-skinned boy in a scrap of a loin cloth had shinnied up a palm tree to pick it.

In sewing class at National Schools around the country, young girls were making ghost costumes, their tongues stuck out in concentration as they toiled, while the lads huddled together hatching plans for trick or treat, genuinely hoping there'd be no treats so they might get up to all kinds of tricks. By teetering precariously on ladders, the last shiny apples were being plucked from trees and safely stored away in pantries, in the hope that a few might remain for Halloween games and pastry tarts. Logs of wood, crates, broken chairs and threadbare tires, in fact anything that would burn, were piled into heaps on fair greens countrywide for those big smelly bonfires everyone loved. Last year's spooky lanterns were brought down from attics to light up the wet and windy evenings which lay ahead. The summer gone, young and old alike craved the festivities and fun, all desperate for a stepping-stone to Christmas. In the boarders' homes, children's bedrooms, empty since the end of the summer holidays, were aired and dusted; beds were covered with crisp clean sheets, pillows puffed up and positioned.

There was excitement in the air, and the house staff felt it, too. Mrs. Oldfield's glance swept around the room, the exceeding of a certain decibel level warranting admonishment, though today she let it go, caught up in the atmosphere herself. *It will be nice to have the place to ourselves for a while,* she pondered. *Get the floors polished and the tiles properly scrubbed.*

Yet again, they'd have to bamboozle the local dry cleaners out of a box of wire hangers in order to repair all the bed springs. That was no problem, however; Carty's Corner Cleaners had always been very accommodating in the past. She would send Bertie Barrett to deal with it as soon as he'd finished raking the leaves. It was a battle every autumn trying to keep the driveway clear, but was worth it. The Castleglen park boasted the most beautiful and varied abundance of indigenous trees in the area. She smiled smugly to herself and popped another fork of macaroni cheese into her mouth before turning to Miss Gibbons, who was busy expostulating on the hazards of co-education.

A few tables away Fudge and Lilly were deep in conversation.

"Why don't you come down to Birch Rise for your birthday?" Fudge asked. They were guzzling down the selfsame macaroni cheese, struggling with the long strings of gooey cheddar that stuck to their forks.

"That'd be brillo, but Dad and Julian won't be pleased."

"Sure it's only your fourteenth birthday—nothing special about that!" Fudge rolled her eyes jokingly. "And anyway, you could celebrate twice—double presents!"

"Janey Mac, you have a point there." Lilly paused, considering the potential.

"There'll be a dance at the local hall and a monstrous great bonfire. We'll have great *craic!*"

The blond girl thought of Mary Ginnane's warm kitchen, the smell of baking bread and little Rosy's funny questions. *Why is water wet, Lilly? And why do cats miaow and not bark? And if cats did bark would it be like us speaking French?* Of course, Lilly had all the answers. After all, she was an "A"-stream third former.

"I'll have to ask Dad..."

"Ach, I'm sure he won't mind... Why don't you ask him to drive you down? He can stay for lunch and we can have a little pre-birthday party all together!" And then as a bitter afterthought. "And if you want, Julian can come, too."

"D'you think your mum would mind? The house'll be full of people."

"Go 'way, she'll be delighted. She's never met your dad before and anyway, Sheila probably won't be there. She's usually off with her friends in Galway strutting around the shopping centre handing out leaflets. Since she started studying at UCG she's all for saving tropical forests and whales, and getting rid of nuclear power and so on..."

"Oh, I see..." She didn't really, but was used to Fudge's deviations. "Well, if you think it'll be all right, I'll ask."

She had suddenly warmed to the notion; the idea of spending Halloween in their Victorian Ballsbridge house surrounded by mountains of her father's books, manuscripts and hybrid rose cuttings wasn't particularly inviting.

"Great stuff, it's all settled then!" Fudge clapped her hands together in glee, forgetting she was still clutching her fork. It didn't bother her much that she catapulted a dollop of cheese sauce onto the back of Brenda Buckley's head two tables away, or that she nearly took Lilly's eye out while she was doing it. Halloween was going to be magic!

~ * ~

They were all in jolly festive spirits as they hurtled towards the west in Michael McDermott's battered Ford Granada station wagon. It was like a ship on choppy seas surging up rises and swaying precariously around curves on dubious suspension. A calm, unassuming intellectual, Lilly's dad was an animal behind the wheel, yet took pride in the fact that he hadn't written off a vehicle so far. The girls lurched from side to side on the back seat, pleased to be freed of their uniforms and feeling the bees' knees in their own garb. Julian sat in the passenger seat, maintaining an air of bored detachment. In his final school year, he had no time or patience for the squeaks and giggles of piddling third-year pupils.

He'd greeted a mortified Fudge in passing after they had arrived at the Ballsbridge house the evening before, not resisting a raised eyebrow of ridicule. Nothing was said, although his expression revealed that the content of their phone call was still safely stowed away in his mind and would, without doubt, be exploited at will. And, indeed, it had started at breakfast when, on declining tea, Julian asked if she'd prefer a cocktail. Fudge, however, determined not to be browbeaten, courteously accepted, saying she'd love one with honey and condensed milk—just like Winnie-the-Pooh. Lilly had pursed her lips, waiting for her brother's mordant reaction to the mention of everyone's favourite teddy, and was astonished when none came. On the contrary, he was the quintessence of decorum for the rest of the meal—a rare phenomenon.

The Halloween traffic was heavy, but Lilly's dad dodged and overtook valiantly. On either side the soft flat patchwork countryside of the midlands fell away quickly. It was a cloudy day with the odd chunk of sunshine poking through. It had rained earlier and tires swished wetly on glistening roads sending great swaths of muddy water spraying into the ditch as they plunged over potholes and puddles. Ray Charles oozed out of the radio and Mr. McDermott started to hum, a wistful expression spreading across his face. The girls snickered, and Julian, deciding the music wasn't doing much for his countenance, reached out to twiddle the knob, only to be left smarting with indignation as his father batted the offending hand away in one lightning movement. Blushing furiously, he stared out the window for the rest of the journey. Fudge was near to wetting herself with delight.

Before long, they were careening down the hill, past the fair grounds and into the car-clogged main street of Loughrua where shoppers had double- and triple-parked to do some last minute errands. A while back, the typical loose stone walls had replaced neat fencing and hedgerows, conveying their arrival in County Galway.

Fudge pressed her nose against the window, anxious to see all the goings-on. After three years at Castleglen, she'd lost contact with a lot of old friends, but recognised many familiar faces as pedestrians hurried along the busy street. There was Dotty Folen hovering at the bright red doorway of her sweety shop where local children gladly parted with precious pocket money in return for gobstoppers, lollipops, sherbet, bags of Taytos, and toffees covered in powder sugar. Further along, Ned Connelly was swaying dangerously on the curb, his red-rimmed blurry gaze fixed on the gutter where the poor man earnestly believed gallons of black porter to be flowing by. Despite his miserable state, he seemed happy enough, every now and then standing stiffly to attention in order to salute a passing car. As they drove past, Fudge caught his eye and, much to Ned's joy, saluted back, prompting the bleary-eyed man to do a little jig in the imaginary river of stout. Just before they turned north onto the secondary road leading to Bullcudy and Birch Rise, Garda Doyle could be seen waving a reprimanding finger at Mrs. Poole, as in Poole's Poultry Products, whose van full of free range eggs was not only double-parked with the engine running, but obstructing the complete Galway-to-Dublin thoroughfare in both directions.

"What a bunch of bog-trotters," Julian snorted contemptuously.

Fudge chose to ignore the remark, refusing to let anything spoil the excitement of her homecoming. The withering look Michael McDermott shot his son was gratifying enough.

Mum was already standing at the front door as they finally rattled over the cattle grid and down the long driveway to the farm. She'd been just as eager as her daughter when Fudge had asked if Julian and Mr. McDermott might stay for the day before returning to Dublin. A woman whose quiet intellectual demands far surpassed those of her few acquaintances, Mary Ginnane was by no means daunted by the literary critic's impending visit; far from it—she was thrilled to bits. Fudge's dad didn't particularly mind one way or the other; Mum was the boss in the house. Flanked on either side by Lizzy and Beth, Mary waited on the doorstep. Today, her thick, wavy hair was tied together in a loose ponytail with a dark blue silk neck scarf. As usual, a long wisp had escaped and was fluttering around her face in the midday breeze. Proud not to have a totally fuddy-duddy mother, Fudge was pleased to see that instead of the standard jumper and skirt combination, she was dressed in a long, pale-blue shirt worn over a pair of navy, thin-cord slacks. A soft grey lamb's wool sweater was thrown casually across her strong shoulders.

Rosy darted out of the house, black corkscrew curls bouncing around her ears, as the Ford skidded to a halt in a shower of conkers and chestnut leaves. The front lawn had been mowed and clipped, probably for the last time before winter set in, and the flowerbeds were brimming with autumn blooms. Pink and lavender Michaelmas daisies crept around the corner of the house, while great clumps of red valerian and chrysanthemum had stubbornly colonised the side wall of the garden shed, splashing the grey natural stone with blotches of vivid colour. Behind the vegetable patch, the hedge stretching down towards the farm buildings was heavy with berries. Purple, blue and red fought for attention as sloes, blackberry, rose hip and elderberry jostled for space in a confusion of brambles and shrubs.

One by one, the travel-weary visitors clambered stiffly out onto the front drive. Very nearly forgetting to greet their sister, the twins twittered and poked each other when they saw Julian folding himself out of the car. In a household of women, it was a great novelty for them to have a young man gracing the dining room table. Fudge flew into her mother's arms, never ashamed to display her feelings when it came to family, but regretted it almost immediately when an almost imperceptible flicker of sadness crept over Lilly's features. Michael McDermott, who'd just finished unloading his daughter's weekend case out of the boot of the station wagon, hadn't failed to notice it either. But the moment passed and in a whirling bustle of giggles and gossip all the girls disappeared into the house followed by Julian, who slouched unenthusiastically after them. Mary was left standing outside on the gravel with Lilly's father, embarrassed that Fudge had omitted to make an introduction. They moved awkwardly towards each other.

With only his books and writing for comfort, the widower, having mourned his wife bitterly, had over the years grown numb and insensitive to the advances of other women. In the prime of his life at her death, and attractive in an unkempt type of way, he'd shunned the battery of batting eyelids and the pouting lips of fawning university students and pseudo-intellectual colleagues. Yet here on a farm in the heart of the verdant Irish countryside surrounded by rolling hills and miles of lonely patchwork land, stood a woman who made his heart constrict.

He'd assessed her superficially from the safety of the car as they approached, admiring her hearty, down-to-earth looks and friendly smile, and though she was no classical beauty, her solid, homely appearance, combined with a relaxed composure, was certainly appealing. But it was her eyes that took Michael by surprise as he reached out his hand to introduce himself. He'd once taken the liberty of scathingly criticising an author whose hero had plunged into the infinite blue-green sparkling depths of his heroine's eyes. That author must have known Mary Ginnane, for here they were— the blue-green sparkling depths. And more, a mellifluous wisdom, an understanding, an awareness, even a slight sadness. Although he'd never seen this woman in his life before, the moment he took her hand in his, Michael McDermott felt as if, after five long years, he was finally coming home.

At the same time, Mary Ginnane, who had a happy marriage, a caring man and a clatter of kids she'd die for, suddenly felt her heart constricting, too.

Behind them in the hallway, Rosy's squeaky voice was bombarding Lilly with questions.

"Lilly, why does Fudge always go scarlet when she looks at boys?"

"Cos boys think scarlet is a groovy colour."

"What's groovy?"

"When something isn't square."

"You mean like if it's round."

"No, more like cool."

"How can red be round and cool?"

"Well, the Loughrua lake is round and cool isn't it?"

"S'pose it is, but it isn't red!" Rosy chucked with mischievous joy. She had Lilly now.

"Course it is."

"Go 'way! I never saw a red lake!"

"Because you didn't look properly, silly."

"You're coddin' me."

"On summer evenings when the sun sinks down behind the lake, the water shimmers golden red. That's why it's called Loughrua. The red lake."

"There's no such thing as golden red."

"Yes, there is—have a look the next time the sun is setting."

"So I suppose boys would think the lake is groovy when the sun's going down."

"Yes, they would, especially if they had their arms around a girl at the time."

"Why?"

Then Fudge's voice gruffly intervening. "Rosy! Would you shut your cake hole, for crying out loud!"

"I will not! Hey, Mum..."

At that, Mary and Michael, who'd had their arms extended in a prolonged handshake, suddenly pulled apart, all of a dither. Neither of them could explain what they'd just felt, but it was suspiciously akin to the tingling shock sensation experienced when human chemistry fits. Mary tucked the lone wisp of hair self-consciously behind her ear and gestured inside.

"Come on in. I've lunch ready—you can leave Lilly's case at the bottom of the stairs. She'll take it up later."

"I hope we're not putting you out. It's very good of you to have us." He had a mellow, lilting voice.

"Not at all—make yourself at home. I'm just going to put on the kettle."

"Grand." Nervously, Michael ran his fingers through the mop of unruly salt and pepper hair, all of a sudden feeling very warm under the tweed jacket he'd thrown on in an effort to look smart. Picking up the weekend case he couldn't remember putting down, he followed Mary into the house and along the corridor to the dining room.

~ * ~

Charlie, sitting high on Shanagarry's broad back, let the reins hang loosely in his hands as the hunter trotted smartly towards the stables. They had just come over the crest of a gorse-covered hill on their way back from the Brackens, a long stretch of scruffy, uncultivated land down by the river. The area, boggy in places and dotted with thistles, ferns and huge thickets of prickly hawthorn, was also a good place to exercise the horse uninhibited by roadways or wire fencing.

He felt invigorated. It had been a magnificent morning out, Shanagarry jumping the low stone walls and splashing across brackish streams in powerful, unfaltering strides. They were a good team, Charlie rarely having to urge the hunter on. He'd only ever thrown his master once, when a startled rabbit had darted out of a warren directly beneath the great animal's hooves, causing him to rear up with a mighty whinny of fright. His rider, momentarily preoccupied with a view over the wall of Muriel McMahon's backside, which was engulfing the saddle of her bicycle in an alarming manner as she strained up the hill to Bullcudy, hardly had time to bat an eyelid before being dumped, face first, into a swampy bog hole. The hunter, having regained its composure, had plodded over to Charlie and waited patiently while the mud-covered figure pulled himself out of the mire, the wet slurping noises which accompanied his struggle obscuring a barrage of graphic expletives. Had it been possible to read the expression on Shanagarry's face, one would surely have described it as a gloating, equine grin.

The autumn sun had reached its zenith, but it was Charlie's rumbling stomach that indicated lunchtime was advancing. *Finnula will be home soon*, he thought, as he arrived at the iron gate leading to the yard, glancing, at the same time, up towards the house. Not having heard a car approach, he was surprised to see a dusty Ford Granada parked under one of the two chestnut trees, the roof already covered with leaves. What surprised him even more, however, was the sight of his wife holding another man's hand. He gripped the topmost bar, ignoring the velvet muzzle nudging his back, a strange jolt of jealousy shuddering through his gut.

From where he was standing Charlie couldn't see the man's face, only a mop of untidy hair, but Mary was smiling crookedly, and nervously hooking a loose strand of hair behind her ear—a dead give-away that she'd been caught off guard. He watched as they exchanged a few words before disappearing into the house. The vigour went out of him as abruptly as air from a balloon and, with lips pressed tightly together in disquiet, he led Shanagarry back to the stables.

~ * ~

The dining room was spick-and-span for the visitors. A tall Waterford crystal vase filled with brightly coloured dahlias was perched on the polished mahogany sideboard. Mary smiled, satisfied the extravagant wedding present could be put to use every once in a while. The girls, God love them, had been busy as bees, shining silver and hoovering the carpet. The long oak table had been pulled out to seat everyone and was now piled high with chicken sandwiches, quiche Lorraine, a platter of cold meats, two different cheeses, freshly baked whole-wheat bread and a mountain of currant scones. There was a massive pot of tea, a jug of frothy milk and orange squash for the younger children.

Starving after the long journey from the city, Fudge plonked herself down, patting the chair beside her for Lilly, at the same time taking great care to be seated at the opposite end of the table to Julian. Mum was grinning sheepishly at Mr. McDermott as she filled his cup to the brim, unaware that she'd left hardly enough room for a drop of milk. The twins were already spreading thick wads of salty butter onto the warm bread, their knives moving back and forth in perfect unison. Rosy, her nose wrinkled in repugnance, had laid open a chicken sandwich for inspection and was now dextrously picking out pieces of tomato she'd discovered lurking between the slices.

"Aren't we going to wait for Dad?" Fudge asked her mother unexpectedly, annoyed that he'd been forgotten.

Michael McDermott, who'd been reaching for a fat piece of quiche Lorraine, was left with his arm dangling mid-air, his hunger preventing him from jerking it away again.

Mum was visibly flustered. "Well certainly, normally we would, but I don't think he'd mind. He's off with Shanagarry on the Brackens and may not be back for a while."

"But didn't he know we were coming?" Fudge persisted, hurt that her father might take his time on the day she came home from boarding school.

A flush of deep red was beginning to creep out of Mary's collar and up her neck.

"Of course he did, and I'm sure he's hurrying to be here, don't worry." She turned back to Michael, whose arm was still hovering over the leek and mushroom tart. "Go on, Mr. McDermott, help yourself."

Just to be on be on the safe side, and hoping for approval, Lilly's father shot Fudge a look, but she was staring demonstratively out the window, her lower lip thrust out in a recalcitrant pout. Julian, who'd barely said a word since their arrival, hastily piped up in time to break the screaming silence that had settled over the room.

"Well, if you don't mind, Mrs. Ginnane, I'll have some of that brown bread and cheese before these two greedy guts scoff the lot!" He bobbed his eyebrows up and down at the twins who went into peels of girlish laughter, spraying whole-wheat crumbs across the table while they were at it.

Even Fudge had to smile and soon everyone was tucking in to a good feed, chatting animatedly as plans were discussed for Lilly's birthday and Halloween. On bonfire night, they would all go into Loughrua and join in the festivities on the fair green. The twins were going to dress up as witches, to which Julian sardonically remarked that it would hardly be a problem considering they were little witches anyway. That, sure enough, gave rise to another volley of breadcrumbs causing the older girls to groan superciliously at the childishness of it all.

"Just Michael," Lilly's father said softly across the table.

Mary was lost in contemplation as she mixed orange squash and water for Rosy. She was deeply ashamed to have had Fudge questioning her manners, and was thoroughly confused that, contrary to the rule, she really had forgotten her husband.

"Sorry... pardon?" She turned to her guest.

"Just call me Michael," he smiled. "It makes me feel less stodgy."

Somehow the sight of a bit of chopped leek stuck to the side of his mouth made her relax, and her face softened.

"And I'm Mary, plain old Mary—as in 'Mary, Mary quite contrary' and so on," she replied with a small laugh, hoping the nursery rhyme would suffice in way of explanation for her scattiness.

"Oh, I wouldn't call Mary plain... far from it," the art historian protested, and then he was off. "Think of all the Marys in the history of western art. They may have had different names, but they all depicted the Virgin Mary..."

And suddenly, oblivious of the limp piece of leek which had, meanwhile, made it way down to his chin, Mary Ginnane was transported away by stories of Titian's *Assunta* and the vision of the Virgin sweeping up to heaven amongst a feverish cloud of cherubs, or Giovanni Bellini's Madonna quietly praying over her sleeping child in a stony field amid herdsmen and their oxen. He was just comparing the Madonna to Leonardo da Vinci's Virgin in *The Adoration of the Kings,* when the dining room door opened and Charlie stomped in.

His glance moved from Michael to Mary and back to Michael, an action which took no more than three seconds, yet those few short moments seemed like an eternity as his wife frantically battled to assume a fitting expression of surprise and delight at Charlie's apparently premature return. He stood there in his donkey jacket and riding breeches, clearly ill-at-ease in the festive atmosphere. Mercifully, it was Fudge who saved the day.

"Dad!" She leapt up from her chair and flung herself into his arms, followed in close pursuit by Rosy, who, disregarding the fact that she'd only seen her father a few hours previously, was always on for a cuddle.

Mary used the moment to pull out a chair at the top of the table, while Michael stood to introduce himself. Not being acquainted with Charlie Ginnane, Lilly's father didn't realise that, although cordial and friendly, his manner was a touch chillier than usual; however, as the conversation moved from Renaissance Art to foaling and falling cattle prices, his mood mellowed. Lilly and Beth, eyes glued to Julian, flirted with far too much gay abandon, leaving Lilly and Fudge to debate in great detail who would wear what to the hop on Saturday night. Little Rosy went back to the job of expurgating with surgical precision any scraps of disgusting tomato still skulking under the chunks of chicken. Lunch was a roaring success.

Later, with their bellies full of scrumptious apple pie and cream, which Mary had produced just when everyone was just thinking that another morsel would make them burst, the gathering dispersed to stretch legs and encourage digestion. The girls had scattered to all corners of the house; Fudge and Lilly were busy unpacking their cases, while the twins, after much bribery and discussion, had finally agreed to do the washing up. Rosy was outside on the back doorstep annoying Sinbad, the Persian cat Charlie had brought home from the pub one night in his breast pocket, and which had the nasty habit of scaring the living daylights out of unwary visitors by appearing, when least expected, out of the border perennials. After being referred to as "that bad cat" for the first two weeks, he soon became known as Sinbad for want of a better name. Lilly's father was up in the bathroom freshening up, and Julian had offered to accompany Charlie down to the stables where Shanagarry was waiting for a good rubbing down. In addition, the gobstopper-producing excuses for chickens wanted feeding, and in the barn some loose bales of hay had to be piled.

From the living room window, Mary watched the two of them strolling along the short lane to the yard. Charlie, his shoulders slightly hunched against a sudden gust of biting October wind, was listening intently to the lanky youth. She sighed inwardly as Julian gesticulated in explanation, his large hand touching her husband ever so briefly on the arm to emphasise a point. He would have loved a son, she thought wistfully, another man around the house to share talk of horses and hay and harvesting, someone to slap on the shoulder and teach how to shave. Before they rounded the corner by the meadow gate, Charlie threw back his head and laughed, the big, throaty laugh that made his Adam's apple bob, and which was so dear to her. He was still an attractive man, a bit weather-beaten, but strong and solid, the years of physical work and fresh air chiselling his features and firming his body. Without warning, and seemingly for no reason at all, Mary suddenly caught herself longing for him.

Theirs was a happy marriage (sure hadn't she been telling herself that all day), and sex had always been good, if not ecstatic, yet in recent years a monotonous routine has stealthily enforced itself—mid-week and Sunday mornings, as sure as clockwork. Far more often than other couples of their age, she convinced herself, realising at the same time that the mid-week missionary position number had petered out a long while ago. Recently, on Sunday mornings Charlie had taken to getting up suspiciously early. It was only a question of time before the Sunday sex got the chop, too.

Mary clutched at the heavy chintz drapes as a twinge of melancholy tugged at her heartstrings. Today, she'd felt like a woman, not a housewife, or a mother with chapped hands and lines around her mouth, no, a real woman, full of emotion and desire. She'd seen his eyes, understood his glance; Michael McDermott found her attractive and she craved for this appreciation with the thirst of a withering potted plant. Almost ashamed, she registered a flush of warmth deep inside spreading to her thighs, and as her pulse quickened, she began to tremble. Involuntarily, she raised a hand to her breast, feeling the nipple harden under thin cotton.

A knock on the door caused her to jerk so violently that she almost pulled the heavy curtain down on top of herself. Michael popped his tousled head into the room.

"Am I disturbing you?"

"No... no, of course not," Mary answered uncertainly, quite sure the look on her face revealed what she'd just been thinking. "Just ruminating, as one does."

"As one does?" Michael repeated enquiringly.

"Well you know, after a good meal... surrounded by family." Instantly she bit her lip, wishing she'd saved that last remark, an action not lost on Michael, and he understood why.

"I know..." He stared at the floor for a second and then looked up, searching the room for a source of distraction.

Over in the corner, behind the oversized, loose-covered sofa, was a tall bookcase, the books stuffed willy-nilly onto the shelves, thick, thin, big, small, hard and paperbacks. He was immediately drawn towards them, as helpless as a pin to a magnet.

"May I?"

"Go ahead, feel free." Mary exhaled a silent breath of relief, glad that the awkwardness had passed. "How about a cup of coffee?"

Indifferent as to whether he wanted one or not, and without waiting for an answer, she bee-lined it to the door seeking escape, acutely aware that all the while her nipples had been prodding the inside of her shirt like a pair of conkers.

When she returned some minutes later, cool and collected, he was buried in an old, dog-eared C.S. Lewis. She smiled, knowing that was just the book she'd have recommended had he asked her opinion. She sat down in the armchair opposite him and they started to talk

Six

"You were making eyes at him!"

"I was not!"

Mary was standing in the kitchen laying the table for Lilly's birthday breakfast. The house seemed very still after the bustle of the day. It was late in the evening and the girls had gone upstairs to get ready for the night. The sound of their girlish chatter was easily swallowed up by the large old house. Exhausted, Rosy had fallen asleep on the floor in front of the range with Sinbad lying across her belly, so the twins had volunteered to put her to bed, cat hairs and all. After tea, a routine fight for the best place in front of the telly would normally ensue. Today, however, Lizzy and Beth had turned in of their own accord, eager to exchange opinions on that gorgeous hunk of a fella who'd spent the day at Birch Rise. Fudge had sniffed derogatorily at them. Were they blind as bats, or what, that they couldn't see his greasy hair and pimples?

Charlie was helping her take the good china down from the kitchen press, careful not to chip anything. *Don't mention it*, he had thought stoically, *keep a stiff upper lip*. He'd busied himself with cleaning his riding boots till they shone, and had read the Farmer's

Journal from cover to cover twice, whereby far from absorbing the text, he hadn't even been aware of the pictures. In the stillness of the evening his resoluteness had crumbled like a sandcastle in the incoming tide and he'd clomped gruffly into the kitchen.

"You were, too! Laughing over the table at him, you were! Worse than one of the girls." He was now snapping nervously at his braces.

"That's not fair and you know it! What could possible have given you the idea I was flirting?" Mary was aghast. She felt like an open book.

"I saw you outside."

"What do mean, 'outside'?"

"You were holding hands." Charlie looked at his wife challengingly, daring her to say they weren't.

"*What*?"

"Just after they arrived. I saw you from the meadow gate."

"Oh, don't be so bloody ridiculous, Charlie... we were shaking hands and probably distracted by the children. Anyway, you know the way some people forget to let go of your hand after an introduction—I hate that myself!"

"You didn't seem to be hating holding *his* hand." He searched Mary's face for a reaction, but she turned away from him, her expression concealed.

"Ach, this is stupid, I'm not going to talk about it!"

"Well I am!" Charlie was glaring now, his temper slowly rising.

Mary flung the tea towel she'd been using to dust off a china butter dish onto the scuffed wooden table.

"I wasn't flirting, all right? Mr. McDermott is an interesting man, that's all." She turned back to him then, looking her husband squarely in the face. "And I'm not a machine, I have feelings, interests... and if you don't..." She came up short, letting the words die out.

"If I don't what?"

"Ara, never mind."

"No, no, you started, now you can finish."

Mary knew once the wheedling began, he'd never let up.

"Well, there are some things I miss..." Two dots of fiery crimson had formed on her cheeks.

"It's because I don't discuss books and politics with you, isn't it? I'm completely uneducated, not good enough, plain bloody dense!"

"Oh, stop it! That's nothing but a load of Socratic irony! Do you really think I'd marry someone who wasn't intelligent—you're insulting me by claiming to be thick!" She grabbed up the tea towel again and started rubbing at the butter dish as if wanting to get rid of the glaze.

"What is it then, or are we going to beat around the bush all evening?" He looked at her inquiringly, his eyebrows curving almost to his hairline.

She hesitated a moment, uneasily biting her lower lip as she searched for the right words.

"I miss... ach, you'll think I'm being sentimental, but I miss a little gentleness."

"Am I not gentle? Am I rough with you?"

Mary studied his face. It was still tanned from hours working outside in the warm summer sunshine and an arch of grey hair had formed over his ears since the year before. Despite the Viyella shirt and the braces, it gave him a decidedly distinguished appearance. He really was an intelligent man, yet why was it that even the most astute males were total imbeciles when it came to reading between the lines of women's words?

"That's not actually what I meant—not that kind of gentleness." Oh God, was she going to have to spell it out for him? "I wish we could be together more often... in bed... like the way it used to be, on Sunday mornings."

"Oh..." Charlie started scratching the back of his weathered neck, his way of covering up awkward embarrassment. "Oh, I see..."

Mary reached out and took his hand in hers.

"You have great, strong arms, Charlie Ginnane, I'd like to feel them around me once in a while. I may no longer be the fine young thing you married, but we're not past it yet, are we?"

"D'you think I'd be jealous if we were?"

"You were jealous?"

"Wildly."

"God, I love it when you are!"

"And you're still the fine young thing I married."

"I am?"

"You are."

Taking the wisp of hair away from her eyes with the very tenderness she'd so ached for, he carefully pushed it back, letting his hand rest on her warm neck. The butter dish and china forgotten, Mary moved towards him, and the longing she'd felt earlier that day rekindled. Afraid her eagerness might scare him off like one of the nervous rabbits out on the Brackens, she held back, but Charlie pulled her to him, and encompassing her with those grand, sturdy arms, he kissed his wife as he hadn't done for years. Long and deep, and with yearning. Mary dissolved into his embrace and moments later, they were stumbling up the stairs to the bedroom, her blouse gaping open, his braces hanging loosely from the waistband of his trousers. There they made love with an abandon both believed had been lost forever. Kissing her throat, her full breasts and the soft curve of her belly, Charlie discovered his wife's body anew, and Mary opened herself willingly to him, feeling the muscles of his back undulate as he moved.

Later, glowing and spent, they lay close together in a tangle of bedclothes. The farmhouse was quiet, with only the ticking of Charlie's wind-up alarm clock penetrating the silence. Not without a trace of bashfulness, Mary believed to hear the sound of her muffled cries still echoing through the room. She cuddled up to her husband, relishing the memory of it. He'd been dozing, but now he stirred.

"Mary?"

"Yes, love."

"Can I ask you something?"

"Sure, go ahead."

"What's Socratic irony?"

~ * ~

While Charlie and Mary were making love, Michael McDermott was driving the last few miles through the city to Ballsbridge. As he passed over the Grand Canal in the direction of the RDS, his thoughts returned to Mary for the hundredth time since they'd set off from Loughrua three long hours before. He couldn't, for the life of him, get her out of his head. What was it he'd shared with her while exchanging talk of books, writers and writing? C.S. Lewis had got them conversing in low voices about life and death, about good and bad, and for the first time in years he'd spoken openly about Laura's death. About the cancer that had slowly, but surely, blossomed and spread within her, finally making submission inevitable. For a short instance, Mary had bent forward in her chair and laid a hand over his, replacing superfluous expressions of sympathy with a gesture so full of understanding that no words were necessary. More was said in those few moments of stillness than in the long-winded philosophical deliberations of his academic peers.

Shifting down a gear as they approached the dark tree-lined avenue leading to their detached house, Michael scrutinised his son who'd slithered down in his seat and was fast asleep, mouth open, knees pressed uncomfortably up against the dashboard. *I should be leaving thoughts of women and loving to the likes of him*, he mused pensively. *He's so full of life and energy, a young green sapling bursting with youth and virility, and not a dried up old plank like myself.* He didn't need a pocket calculator to work out that the years to his fiftieth birthday could be counted on one hand. But when was it too late to fall in love? His spirits suddenly soared when he remembered that C.S. Lewis had found his great love late in life, and immediately his mood plummeted again with the realisation that the author, too, had lost his wife to very same malicious, slinking disease to which Laura had ultimately succumbed.

Blocks of orange light slid past at mesmerising intervals as he steered the car down the quiet road. He still had that picture of Mary waving her farewells while they bounced off down the bumpy driveway imprinted in his mind. His last image was like the first, her standing at the front door surrounded by children, only this time Fudge and Lilly were among them. Her face was soft, her eyes laughing. Their parting handshake had been brief, their goodbyes courteous, with Charlie hovering nearby, a strange, questioning expression on his face. Yet he'd felt it again in the short second their hands had met, the same fleeting shock of static which made one's heart skitter when it hit you on a shopping centre escalator. Framed in the velvety glow of the setting sun, a sun that surely had Loughrua Lake flaming red, the whole family had waved until the Granada slowly jangled over the cattle grid and out of sight.

Michael thought of her over and over again, passing the journey in a trance. He'd guided the car through congested streets and along the busy Dublin road like a robot, not even noticing when their car was almost sideswiped while turning onto the main street in Kinnegad. Julian had given the three youths in the other vehicle the two fingers of derision, wondering at the same time why the authorities would let such an eejit behind the wheel in the first place. The said eejit flicked a wad of fuzzy hair over his shoulder and drove on, blissfully unfazed by the contemptuous gesture as he searched for a signpost to Loughrua through thick, Coke-bottle spectacles.

Shortly before midnight, when Michael pulled up in front of the garden gate, he'd made up his mind to forget it all—her face, her warmth, her understanding. He gave his son a nudge, smiling as the boy struggled to unglue his sleepy eyes and untangle his limbs. It had been a good day, but was over now and life would go on as usual. There was a manuscript waiting on the study desk to be reviewed, and a seminar on fifteenth century art to be prepared. In the middle of pulling himself out of the car Michael stopped short. Oh God, Titian's *Assunta*. He hadn't even made it to the garden gate and already he was wondering when he would see Mary Ginnane again.

~ * ~

And while Michael and Julian McDermott were driving past the Royal Dublin Society, little Rosy was surfacing from a deep kitty-cat sleep with a fierce thirst. Cat hairs had got up her nose, making it tickle. She left the comfy cosy warmth of her bed, shivering slightly when her bare feet touched the smooth wooden floor. Tonight, thank God, there were no leprechauns in hobnailed boots step-dancing on the roof, and she had no reason to be scared, yet nevertheless, tiptoeing down the dim corridor to the bathroom, she perceived a tiny flutter of anxiousness in the pit of her stomach.

Passing her parents' bedroom, she paused, wondering whether Mum would be angry if she sneaked in for a moment of reassurance. *Ah no, I'm a big girl now*, she decided as she stood staring at the closed door, her white bottom peeking cheekily over the waistband of her hand-me-down pyjamas.

Turning towards the bathroom, an unusual sound in the quietness of the night made her small heart scribble. Rosy cocked her head and listened. There it was again! A mewing sound like a cat, only deeper and throatier, coming from Mum and Dad's room. She took a step in the direction of the noise. Now she could hear panting, heavy breathing, like Shanagarry after a good gallop, only this was erratic, more hectic. Was it her father having a nightmare? She listened again. Now there was a voice, high-pitched and breathless; Mum was saying "yes" over and over again. That was strange. Yes, yes, yes. Little Rosy was all perplexed. Why would Mum be saying yes when Dad wasn't asking her any questions? She bent towards the keyhole.

"Rosy Ginnane! What are you at?" Fudge's loud whisper startled the little girl.

"N... nothing, just wanted to see if Mum was awake..."

"Why? What's wrong" The older girl took her sister by the hand to lead her back up the hallway.

"They're making funny noises." Rosy's eyes were as big as milk churn lids.

"Who?"

"Mum and Dad."

"Don't be silly, they're probably blethering in their sleep."

But as they turned to go, Fudge didn't fail to hear the soft groans behind the solid oak door and knew what it was. Flustered and confused, she fetched Rosy a glass of water and tucked the child in before fleeing to the protective haven of her own bed. Lilly was dead to the world, and just as well, too. This was not something she wanted to talk about. *Why did I have to hear that?* she thought, pressing her face into the pillow. Her head, heart, and stomach in an uproar,

Fudge fought to forget what, since her first pubescent awakenings, she'd so desperately tried to ignore. The image of a man and woman making love. Worse, the image of her own mother and father having sex.

It wasn't until years later, when she grasped the full meaning of it all, that Fudge would wish her mother might be able take her father into her arms one more time.

~ * ~

"There's someone knocking at the front door!" Mary dug Charlie in the back. "Listen!"

He'd been submerged in the delicious deep-sleep state of a man well satisfied, and wasn't prepared to surface without a fight.

"Charlie!"

"Mmm..."

"The front door, d'you hear it?"

Her husband didn't budge, instead he grunted something incoherent and flung an arm over her bosom. She lay for a moment longer, staring at the ceiling and wondering had she been dreaming herself. No, there it was again. Someone was hammering on the big brass knocker.

Mary stiffened. *He's come back*, she thought, all at once, a mixture of confusion and delight jitterbugging through her. Ever so carefully, she worked her way out from under Charlie's embrace and pulled on her indestructible quilted dressing gown, only to replace it seconds later with a black kimono Dora had brought back from an extravagant trip to Hong Kong five years before, and which had been hanging redundantly on the back of the bedroom door ever since. *Maybe they had problems with the car, or have forgotten something. No, it's far too late—after midnight, surely they'd be in Dublin by now, and anyway, they would have called.*

All these things went through Mary's mind while making her way down the stairs to the front door, yet highly unlikely as it seemed, she couldn't shake off the conviction that Michael had, indeed, returned. Mary, however, tired and confused as she was, didn't realise that this feeling was the offspring of a wish she nurtured deep in her mixed-up heart. Stopping at the hall table, she studied her reflection briefly in the large mirror hanging above it. Her hair was all over the place, falling around her face in a dark, wavy mass. Vainly, she patted and tugged at it, thinking nevertheless, that it made her look younger, less severe.

Quickly, she practised an astonished smile before moving to open the door, pausing abruptly at the carelessness of her action. And if it weren't Michael? Through the solid wood several male voices were audible, conversing in loud whispers, yet the notion that Michael and Julian were waiting on the front step eliminated any thoughts of thugs, robbers and rapists, and without further hesitation, she pulled the door open a crack.

The last thing she'd expected to see were the faces of a bespectacled frog, an imp and a boiled sweet. The three unlikely young men were, in return, more than surprised by the sight of a middle-aged, wild-haired version of Finnula Ginnane looking acutely vulnerable in a silky black kimono with what looked suspiciously like nothing underneath.

"Wh... who are you?" Mary stuttered, deciding far too late that it might have been a better idea to wake Charlie.

All eyes were riveted on the fire-spewing, multi-coloured, fork-tongued dragon snaking its way up over Mary's voluptuous hip and curving around her left breast.

"What do you want?" she persisted.

The one with the frizzy hippie cut and thick glasses managed to regain a smattering of savoir faire.

"Sorry, ma'am, I know it's late. We go' lost. Em... we're lookin' for Lilly an' Finnula. Is dis Ginnane's farm?"

"Lilly and Finnula?" Mary couldn't believe her ears. Who the blazes would be looking for the girls in the middle of the night? With Dublin accents as thick as overnight porridge, they certainly weren't locals.

"Yeah, we wanted to visit dem an' we got lost." The other two had moved into the semi-circle of light at the doorway and were looking at Mary expectantly.

"They're fast asleep. Can't you come back tomorrow?"

"Well, that's the problem, ma'am, we don't know where to stay."
Three pairs of eyes ogled anxiously at her.

Mary, annoyed now, answered brusquely. "I hardly think that's a problem the girls can solve."

"Oh, righ'... sorry, we didn't mean to bodder you."

Flicking the collars of their jackets up against the damp October night, they turned towards the rust-riddled Morris, and Fudge's mother, who wouldn't leave a rat without a roof over its head, fought against a wave of guilt. They knew the girls, as unlikely as it seemed, and deserved to be treated civilly. Pulling the skimpy silk around her she took a step forward out of the warmth of the hallway.

"Look, I can't really help with accommodation, but if you like you can stay in the barn."

The frog, the imp and the boiled sweet beamed at her.

"Janey, dat'd be bleedin' deadly!"

"Yeah, just the berries, ma'am, just the berries. We'll be no bodder at all, we have sleeping bags."

"But no cigarettes, do you hear? If I see as much as a sealed packet, I'll have my husband shove your car into the slurry pit!"

"Oh God, no way, no cigarettes in the barn or anywhere!"

"And close the gate after you!" She was regretting her bout of munificence already.

"No problem, Mrs. Ginnane, thanks a million!"

And then, after fetching a few scruffy army surplus sleeping bags out of the boot of the car, they were off, trotting briskly in the direction of the yard, afraid Finnula's mother might change her mind.

Mary stared after them. It wasn't Michael after all. What had made her think it might be, or better, what had made her want it to be him? She looked down at herself standing there, a dishevelled scarecrow in a sexy kimono. Christ Almighty! Had she gone completely over the brink? And now she'd invited a clatter of thugs to spend the night on the farm. What would she do next? Mary raised her eyes to heaven, muttered something unsavoury under her breath and returned to bed, hoping the barn wouldn't be reduced to charcoal before morning.

~ * ~

In the early hours, Fudge woke from an unsettled sleep. Unaware of her mother's nocturnal encounter, she tossed and turned, the image of her parents bathed in sweat and ecstasy refusing to leave her. Growing up was a nightmare. *Puberty* was a nightmare, she determined, and paradox as it appeared, it was an opinion that, considering parents and youths never agreed on anything, every adult with teenage children would readily support.

It had been a disappointing enlightenment to learn that the cabbage patch was impotent and that storks were unable to bring forth children, albeit in the role of a delivery service. Her mother had carefully explained it all when Fudge had first begun to question this phenomenon following several disturbingly contradictory reports on the part of her National School friends. Mary, fair play to her, had been quick to reassure her daughter that it was an altogether pleasant affair, but at the same time, omitted to inform Fudge that it also had a lot to do with panting, groaning and sweating. This disconcerting information had trickled through in her first year at Castleglen, only to be promptly suppressed.

Mum and Dad weren't like that, she decided, and anyway, they were far too old. The confirmation a short while ago, that they *were*, in fact, like *that* had shocked Fudge to the core. This, combined with her own adolescent upheaval, had plummeted her into a state of sheer confusion. Puberty was definitely the worst thing she would ever have to go through. Philosophically, she wondered what kind of hormonal Monster of Chaos was slumbering within her, waiting patiently to be born. Sticky, sweaty sex. It didn't bear thinking about. And as if that wasn't disgusting enough, there was the realisation that one day, in the not so distant future, she would probably start enjoying it, too.

Seven

Despite her state of psychological pandemonium, Fudge must have dropped off to sleep again, for when, what seemed like moments later, she sat up with a sigh of frustration, an insipid dawn glow was already creeping across her bedspread.

It was a damp, foggy morning. The central heating had not yet kicked in, and Fudge shivered as she trod softly over to the window. She was as determined as ever to enjoy her holidays, and today was Lilly's birthday. In the other bed, the blond girl was still fast asleep, the familiar beatific expression on her now fourteen-year-old face. Mum wanted to prepare a special birthday breakfast with a full fry, toasted batch loaf, presents and gift-wrapped surprises. At this point neither of them could know that the biggest surprise of all was waiting down in the barn, wrapped up in army green and out for the count. Through the curtains, Fudge admired the yellow and rust brown carpet of chestnut leaves covering the gravel drive in front of the house. If they were lucky, the sun would battle its way out and chase away the mist, bringing with it perfect birthday weather. She was just moving away from the window when she spotted the battered Morris half buried in a blanket of autumn leaves. Visitors?

This early in the morning—in a car like that? Probably a neighbour with a daybreak crisis needing to borrow equipment from her dad. She thought no more of it and leapt like a cat onto Lilly's motionless form.

Later, at breakfast, birthday greetings were made and gifts presented; cups were filled with strong black tea or hot chocolate; and plates piled with sausage, eggs, bacon, black pudding and grilled tomatoes. After Rosy had stopped making exaggerated retching noises at the sight of the latter and everyone was digging in, Mum got to the point.

"Finnula and Lillian, you have visitors."

The two girls looked up in astonishment, whereby the birthday girl seemed less surprised than her bosom friend.

"Visitors?" They answered in unison, and then Fudge remembered the Morris—whatever good the memory did. She certainly didn't know anyone with a car like that. Mum's expression was blank, as was Dad's, leading her to suspect that having visitors wasn't necessarily a good thing.

"Who are they?" She glanced over at Lilly who was studying her black pudding with a trace of a smirk.

"That's what we'd like to know." Mary glanced at Charlie. "They woke me up in the middle of the night—and are down in the barn, if you want to have a look after breakfast."

"In the barn? Why are they in the barn?" Fudge couldn't understand why her mother, the personification of social clemency, would send visitors down to the barn.

"Because that's where they stayed the night. They turned up at all hours looking for you, I was hardly going to let total strangers into the house!" Mary glared disapprovingly, yet Fudge couldn't help feeling her mother was having a good old chuckle at her.

Lilly suddenly burst out laughing. Fudge turned and stared.

"Do you know something I don't?" she enquired.

"No, no, it's nothing... really." She waved a hand in dismissal. "Just had a funny thought, that's all."

"Good for you, feel free, it's your birthday after all," Fudge answered snootily, peeved that Lilly wouldn't share the joke.

"Why don't you take them down a cup of tea. They'll probably be gasping for one," Mary intervened wisely, knowing all problems could be solved with a nice cup of Darjeeling's best. "Then you could bring your friends up to the house and introduce us."

Fudge was fairly itching with curiosity and glad of a distraction. She'd been eyeing her parents from the moment they sat down at the breakfast table, hoping she wasn't going to be imagining them naked and groaning for the full duration of the Halloween break. Although the whole thing stank suspiciously of a put-up job, the idea of mysterious guests skulking in the hay offered an amusing interlude, and was something she hoped might take her mind off less salubrious matters—for a while anyway. Her hopes were short-lived, to say the least. As luck would have it, Fudge was not to be granted the luxury of instant amnesia concerning her parents' conjugal activities. Rosy, God bless her heart, took care of that two seconds later.

"Mum?" Rosy put down her glass of milk, the white cream moustache a stark contrast to her dark curls.

"What is it, love?"

"You said the visitors woke you up."

"That's right."

"But you were already awake." She licked her milky upper lip with the tip of her pink tongue.

"I was? What makes you think that, pet?"

"Well, I was getting something to drink and I heard you talking to Dad."

"Did you now," Mary answered unconcernedly. Untrue to form, she helped herself to a second plate of egg and sausage, sublimely unaware of what her youngest daughter was getting at. Her second oldest, however, had started tensing up conspicuously in her seat.

"Yeah, you were almost shouting." Rosy took another noisy gulp from her glass.

"Is that a fact? What was I saying?" With obvious relish, Mary bit the end off a juicy pork banger.

"You were going 'yes, yes, yes'." The child was now imitating her mother in a voice which might have been Sinbad's, had the Persian been able to talk.

"I beg your pardon?" Mary's mouth, which was opening to take another bite, abruptly went slack, and Charlie, in the middle of cutting a doorstep off a loaf of soda bread, was instantly alert.

"What I wanted to know was why you'd be answering 'yes, yes, yes', when Dad wasn't asking you any questions?"

The twins hadn't the foggiest clue what Rosy was talking about and Lilly, despite all her supposed worldliness, was having trouble processing this profound enquiry, but her best friend, hyper-sensitive as she was, silently started begging the floor to open wide and gobble her up. Had she been able to see the funny side of it, Fudge might have appreciated the fact that she'd never seen her father laughing so hard in all his life.

~ * ~

The two girls were looking very trendy altogether in their flared jeans, puff sleeved shirts and tank tops as they made their way down to the yard carrying a pot of piping hot tea, mugs and a plate of generously cut slices of white bread and home-made strawberry jam. Lilly, as ever, was the height of fashion in a black patent leather belted coat Michael had given her for her birthday, while Fudge was content in a well-worn sheepskin jacket. Lilly's coat squeaked when she walked, making them chortle. Her inquisitiveness raging now, Fudge had tried unsuccessfully to prise some information out of her friend, but was waved off every time.

"Let's just wait and find out," was all the other girl said.

Outside the barn they stopped and pressed their ears to the door. A murmur of voices inside was discernible above the clucking of hens and mooing of cows.

"My back is feckin' killin' me!"

"Stop yer bleedin' complainin'. It was your shaggin' idea!"

"Well, I think I have consumption, anyway. T'was freezin' last night!"

"Jaysus, too bloody right. Would have frozen the balls off a brass monkey!"

"Hey, Prof! Your balls still there, are they?"

A cackle of laughter.

"Why're you so interested in my bollix? You queer or what?"

"That's right, bent as a banana, I am. Better not bend over to pick up the soap, the next time we're in the shower, sweetheart!"

"Bloody typical, trust you to fancy my hairy arse!"

Roars of mirth. Fudge stared at Lilly, her eyes bulging scarily in incredulity.

"I don't believe it," she mouthed. "Not the Teddy Boys!"

Lilly nodded gleefully. "C'mon, let's give them a shocker!"

With that, she made a move to shove the barn door open with her shoulder, precariously balancing the steaming tea as she did so.

"Give us a hand, will you?" In need of assistance, she turned to Fudge and was just in time to see her hightailing it out of the yard, jam sambos and all. Lilly placed the pot and mugs on the ground and sprinted after her.

"What's the problem now?"

"Are you blinking mad? The Teddy Boys, for heaven's sake—you told them where I lived!" The dark-haired girl was livid.

"Of course! They wouldn't have been able to find us if I hadn't!"

"What d'you want them here for?"

"For a bit of fun. Oh, Fudge, you can be so square at times! Come on!" Lilly tugged at the sleeve of Fudge's sheepskin.

"Can't we have fun without them?" Furious, she shook her arm free.

"Sure we can, but this is more exciting, don't you think?"

"It's the kind of excitement I can do without."

"All right, you win. I'll tell them to leave and then we can spend the afternoon making conker figures with toothpicks and collecting leaves for our scrapbooks!"

In a gesture of aggravation, Fudge kicked out at one of the said horse chestnuts that had rolled down the driveway towards the yard. She hit it squarely with the tip of her desert boot, sending it ricocheting off the barn wall.

"You can be such a cow at times!" Fudge barked.

"Moo."

"In fact, you're pretty much a cow all the time!"

"Moo."

"I should have known this morning when you put on a tank top two sizes too small that you only wanted to show off your udders—I just couldn't imagine to whom."

Lilly pulled open her coat like a flasher and wiggled her shoulders making her generous boobs bob, an action which antagonised scrawny-breasted Fudge even further. Placing the plate of sandwiches on a dented fender of her father's tractor, she reached down, and without hesitation, picked up a nice, soft ball of Shanagarry's droppings. Lilly was already retreating hastily over to the barn, shrieking over her shoulder a she went.

"Don't... Fudge... don't!"

The lads, having heard the commotion outside, yanked open the door to see what was causing it, and were just in time to see Lilly running frantically in their direction, the blond curls and ample bosom bouncing in rhythmic synchronisation. Mesmerised by the sight, none of them had time to react as the dung bomb came whizzing over her shoulder. Johnny, standing in front, took the full impact in the centre of his chest. Teetering slightly, he looked down in dismay at the brown green glob, complete with bits of grassy stubble Shanagarry had failed to digest. He looked up at the reserved country girl and gave her a crooked grin.

"Now wha' kinda welcome is that?"

"Oops," was all she could reply.

Later on, after Fudge had washed her hands in a barrel of rainwater, they were all sitting around in the barn slurping mugs of tea and exchanging banter. Lilly, needless to say, was carefree and relaxed, giving as good as she got, while Paul showered her with the kind of attention that was far more than even a birthday girl deserved. It was generally agreed that the Ginnanes would be told the lads came from the McDermotts' neighbourhood in Ballsbridge, and not a word was to be breathed about clandestine meetings in the

Castleglen Park undergrowth. Furthermore, it was understood that any reference to Lilly's nighttime antics, or her partiality to Harvey Wallbangers, would catapult them all into deep shit. Whatever happened, mum was the word.

And it *was* exciting. The thought of spending a day or two in the company of what Oldfield or Gibbons would undoubtedly describe as "unsavoury elements", was titillating beyond words, and Fudge, not without a tremor of anticipation, knew when she dared to sneak a glance at Johnny, and saw the way he was sneaking glances at her, that something was going to happen which would bring her one stepping-stone further along the way to growing up.

Charlie and Mary, while not exactly overjoyed by Fudge and Lilly's disputable choice of friends, conceded that, despite their funny Jackeen accents and raw appearance, they were polite fellas and allowed them to stay. Immediately, a temporary abode was created as patched up Lilos were dragged down from the attic and placed in a room next to the stables between coils of rope, tools, boxes of riding equipment and cans of creosote. There was mighty organisation. The girls played house, arranging extra blankets and pinching cushions from the study sofa. They fussed around, all the while aware that, outside their strict school environment, the boys observed them with different eyes. There was far more potential here than any of them had bargained for!

Especially for Fudge. It was strangely electrifying to be seen wearing something other than her uniform, as if she'd suddenly become an individual character overnight, a feeling probably only a boarding school girl could relate to. For the lads, the schoolgirls were like exotic forbidden fruits, a far cry from the brassy, bad-mouthed girls they normally hung around with, and posed a monumental challenge. Although Lilly, on that infamous evening, had not exactly presented herself as a shining example of decorous boarding school education, her countenance and articulation, like Fudge's, revealed an upbringing beyond the realms of the Teddy Boys' world. The Ping-Pong banter was full of playful reference to their respective backgrounds, Fudge being a culchie, Lilly a spoilt Ballsbridge brat, and the fellas a pack of juvenile delinquents, but the real truth was never spoken out, namely that, regardless of their fun and jokes, when all was said and done, a longstanding friendship was going to require a generous helping of social tolerance.

But there at Birch Rise, on that chilly Halloween weekend back in the seventies, they lived for a while in a cocoon where none of that mattered, not one of them realising then, how much, sadly, it might later on. Only Prof, at eighteen, was beginning to understand what it meant to come from a different world, but observing the fun and antics in his typical silent manner, he chose to ignore it, old enough to know that all too soon, they would learn to comprehend it themselves, too.

~ * ~

That evening, everyone set off for Loughrua. Rosy and the twins squashed into the Vauxhall with Mary and Charlie, leaving the boarding school girls to share the back seat of the Morris with Johnny. Charlie voiced his doubts concerning Prof's driving capabilities; however Mary, the great emissary of peace, managed to reassure her husband, by pointing out that she couldn't remember the last time she'd met more than two vehicles on the short five-mile stretch from Birch Rise to Loughrua, and anyway, with the Dublin lad's car bursting with passengers, it didn't look as if they'd get much poke out of it—forty miles an hour at a push.

As the yellow beams of the headlights cut an illuminated gash between the wobbly stone walls and brambly ditches along the road into town, Fudge could feel Johnny's knee pressing against hers. She was fascinated by the sensation—it was only a knee, after all. Yet coming from a family of seven and hardly able to remember a car journey where she wasn't squashed up against someone else, it was all the more confusing that his leg against hers should cause such turmoil. Was he intentionally putting more pressure on it than necessary, or was it the curve in the road? She couldn't be sure, but short of hanging out the window, Fudge decided to assume an attitude of innocence which, in itself, was no mean feat considering his leg felt like a live wire, making her skinny one jitter.

The fair green was thronging with eager masses dressed to the nines and hungry for excitement. Ned Connelly was absolutely reeling, his drinking habit clearly well subsidised by locals whose generosity had flourished in the heat of the festivities. Someone had given him a plastic vampire mask which would have improved his appearance no end, had he only stopped sticking his tongue out through the hole cut into the mouth. Rosy, shrouded in a white bed sheet and looking more like an angel than a ghost, clutched her mother's skirts, not knowing whether to laugh or scream. The two witches, Lizzy and Beth, trotted over to the toffee apple stand, their black pointy hats sticking up like twin peaks in the crowd. Johnny Cash droned loudly out of the loudspeakers Larry Logan's Electrics had so kindly placed at the town's disposal, and subsequently strapped to street lanterns with lengths of hairy sisal. There was a shooting stand where one could win a bunch of fake roses, and a table piled high with every type of plastic toy to be bought for under a tenner. Hazardous looking swing boats were in full flight as young men displayed their animal strength to enthralled female onlookers, and behind the candy floss cart, the carrousel of Miss Gibbons' nightmares was going round and round and round.

Mary had her arm through Charlie's in an almost unprecedented public display of affection, unusual for couples over thirty and, as a rule, unheard of if you were married, but what the hell, this was Halloween and no one gave a damn. Together with the lads, Fudge and Lilly strolled over to the huge mountain of wood and tires which two promising arsonists were feverishly trying to set alight with big balls of newspaper and generous squirts of methylated spirits, in what appeared to be an uncontrolled attack of pyromania. Garda Doyle was scurrying anxiously around the pyre in an effort to keep the enthusiastic crowds from getting their eyebrows singed off in the process. Moments later, the fire was ablaze and a great hum of "oohs" and "aahs" rose up as thick black smoke and a shower of glowing sparks spiralled up into the night sky.

Fudge sidled up to Lilly and gave her a dig.

"I have a birthday present for you."

A huge smile of relief spread across the blond girl's features. "And I thought you'd forgotten!"

"No, I just thought you deserved to be kept in suspense after the shock you gave me this morning." She handed Lilly a small box wrapped up in a pink paper serviette. "Sorry, I didn't have any birthday paper."

The look on her friend's face when she opened the package made the trouble she had gone to finding the gift weeks before, all worth while. Lilly shrieked with delight and held up the shiny charm Fudge had slipped onto a chain. It was a tiny silver cow, udder and all.

The country girl grinned broadly. "I've always said you're an old heifer, and I just wanted to make sure you wouldn't forget!"

"Jeepers, Fudge, you're the best." For once, the city girl was almost speechless, but not for long. "C'mon, let's see if we can't get a couple of shandies before we go to the dance!"

The fair green was milling with screaming waist-high ghouls, ghosts and goblins, all allowed up after bedtime to see the now roaring inferno, as the group of divergent youths made their way along the lake road to the local hall. Others were also heading in the same direction, the girls wobbling along on platform soles and the fellas in desert boots.

Loughrua's youths, while always scrambling to keep up with trends, were more often behind than ahead of it, yet tonight they'd given their best and many were tarted up in midis or minis, bell-bottoms, or wrap-around cheesecloth skirts with blouses of the same material. Most of the women, however, were still sporting the Crimplene A-lines and sling-back shoes that had become fashion history many seasons before. The men courageously dared to step out in trousers with flared legs and all of them, without exception, wore shirts with collars like albatross wings. Waves of Old Spice, Four-Seven-Eleven and the much-coveted Chanel No. 5 wafted over heads plastered down with Brylcream or backcombed up to the dizzying bouffant heights of the early sixties. For many, the hairstyles their parents had worn were grand for them, too; the long-haired, Joan Baez meets Jimmy Hendrix trend would need some getting used to.

At the door of the hall, the crowd jostled good-naturedly in order to obtain tickets, all eager to start dancing to Dicky Rock and Val Doonican hits. Once inside, as always, everyone lost their nerve, the women lining the wall on one side, the men lining the other. Only after the first fearless few had graced the dance floor, did the ice begin to break and the men, strutting back and forth like farmyard cockerels, began to survey the goods. The ladies, heads close together in an attempt to communicate over the noise of the big band, freely voiced their disapproval should any potential dancing partner fall short on requirements. These ever-so-obviously negative exchanges, combined with an accomplished glare of disparagement, never failed to send advancing youths, no matter how determined, veering off on another course at the last minute. If this approach didn't immediately succeed, then comments like "ask me sister, I'm sweatin'" or, more directly, "take a dander, will ya?" were a truly excellent deterrent.

Slowly, but surely, couples paired off and it was only when Fudge saw Lilly bopping across the floorboards with Paul, and Prof fighting his way to the mineral bar, did her guts begin to shrivel. She would die if Johnny asked her to dance, and she would die even more if he didn't. She'd been harvesting curious looks all evening from old school friends, all of them itching to know who the strangers were, and, somehow, she felt proud, even if the Dubliner standing next to her was wearing a skin-tight, turquoise shirt with the massive pointy collar resting on his shoulders. At the ticket kiosk, Fudge had heard hoity-toity Theresa Walsh as she leaned over to Pauline Sweeney.

"Who're them lads? Not from here, surely."

"Na, look at the cut of yer man, they're Jackeens, any bet."

"And not from Nob Hill, either, by the looks of things. Still, who cares, apart from the one with the swimmin' goggles, they're fine lookin' blokes."

"Jaypers, you can say that again." Pauline was smirking lasciviously in Johnny's direction.

"I wonder is Finnula Ginnane doing a line with yer one with the boiled face?"

"No idea, although with her fancy boarding school education, I would've thought she'd be a bit choosier."

"Ara, good on her, anyway," Theresa countered charitably in support of her old school pal. "She can shift him and then send him packin'. I'd do the same meself, wouldn't you?"

But Pauline's attention had moved on to the next victim. "Oh, look, there's Bridie Welsh!"

"What about her?"

"I heard she was up the pole and it wasn't by her husband!"

"Go 'way... you're takin' the mick! Not Frigid Bridget!"

"Swear to God, I heard it from..."

And then they disappeared into the ladies for a swig from their Baby Power's and an extended backcombing session.

In the meantime, Fudge could tell by the way Johnny was constantly shifting his weight from one leg to the other that he was pondering the dancing dilemma, too. If he didn't ask, she might be insulted, if he did, she might say no, but like every other man who's ever had to pluck up enough courage to ask a woman to dance knew, no risk, no fun. He wasn't too sure about this jive business, either. He'd seen none of that at the Dun Laoghaire disco and was afraid the country girl might want to have a shot at it as well. Eager as he was to get her onto the dance floor, he was damned if he was going to get talked into all that pushing, pulling and twirling. No way, he'd only make a right pig's arse of it!

He moved his weight onto the other leg yet again and started tapping his foot nervously in rhythm to the music. Still, on second, thoughts, the band was having a crack at the latest Gloria Gaynor number and not doing too badly either. She'd hardly try to jive to that, would she?

He slid an unobtrusive glance towards Fudge. She was studying the red and blue coloured lighting as it oozed up the wall, across the ceiling and down the opposite side, her outward show of bland unconcern almost conveying boredom, whereas, at the same time, her hands were wringing the corner of a cotton hanky as she might a chicken's neck. *Okay,* he decided, *I'll go for it—now or never!*

"Em, Finnula... want to dance?"

Fudge swallowed. *Praise the Lord, I thought he'd never ask.* "Grand, sure why not?"

Phew, I thought she'd tell me to take a dander.

Relieved to have overcome the first hurdle, the two teenagers stepped into the heaving throngs, all the while closely observed by Theresa Walsh and Pauline Sweeney. They had just begun to jiggle awkwardly to the strains of "Never Can Say Goodbye" when the set ended and everyone promptly disappeared off the dance floor, leaving them standing there like, as Johnny himself might have so eloquently put it, two spare pricks at a whore's wedding.

Walsh and Sweeney snickered gloatingly, Lilly and Paul chuckled triumphantly, and Prof, one elbow propped up on the mineral bar, slurped apathetically at his Claddagh orange.

"Will we stick it out?" Johnny enquired uncomfortably.

"Stick what out?"

"Wait for the next set, like." He glowered beseechingly up at the big band as they mopped their oily brows with greying towels and gulped down big mouthfuls of stout which had been smuggled in the side door from Tully's pub.

Now or never, Fudge thought. "All right."

Mortified, they grinned uneasily at each other, both desperately trying to ignore the desolate vastness of the abandoned dance floor stretching out for miles around them. Way off in the distance, Lilly caught Fudge's eye and gave her the thumbs up. Paul had his arm around her slightly podgy waist and Fudge, understanding her friend's thumbs up to be a gesture of encouragement, suddenly wondered if she'd misunderstood. A moment later, thanks be to God, the lead guitarist struck a tinny chord and the vocalist reached for the microphone. The two youths relaxed and prepared themselves to catch the beat. Another slow chord, and another—even slower.

If Fudge had known what was coming she'd have leapt from the dance floor as swiftly as a scalded cat. Such as it was, it was too late. *Dammit*, Fudge thought, her heart sinking. *A slow set. An erection section. Goodbye Gloria Gaynor, hello Andy Williams.* If only there were a few others around who might demonstrate, she'd have half an iota how to react. Johnny, his scrubbed face turning an even deeper shade of crimson, rapidly took the bull by the horns, and stepping towards Fudge, he laid his hands on her hips. After a moment's uncertainty she, in return, hooked her hands stiffly onto his shoulders and off they went, shuffling awkwardly across the forsaken expanse.

One by one, they were joined by young couples eager for a bit of necking. The erection section was a serious opportunity for a sneaky grope, a great chance to press hips together, have a tongue plunged into your ear, and to feel nipples thrusting against your shirtfront. Fudge, however, obstinately decided she wasn't going to have any of it, stringently maintaining from the chest down a distance between them in which one could roll out a coil of barbed wire. Uncannily, only minutes later, she discovered herself melting into Johnny's damp, turquoise embrace.

She cautiously breathed in his smell, the combination of Wooly's aftershave and fresh hay making her slightly woozy. More daring now, she had her hands clasped around his neck, while the sensation of his resting on the back pockets of her flares caused her skinny buttocks to tingle. By the end of the set, Fudge was hoping it would go on forever and ever. Safely surrounded by undulating teenagers, she let herself go, tentatively relishing the sensually warm feeling of being held tightly in the arms of a man, at the same time completely forgetting the ferocious hormonal monster she had been so terrified of awakening barely twenty-four hours before. With a start, she realised the dance was over and they were still clutching each other closely.

Johnny, apparently encouraged by her palpable reciprocation, had begun nuzzling at a spot just below her right ear and she was enjoying it immensely. That day, weeks before, sitting together in their grassy nest against the low wall separating the school from the hockey fields, she'd never got round to asking how Lilly could honestly have enjoyed the slobbering session around the back of Seapoint with The Battered Cod owner's son, but now, although the idea had not yet begun to merit Lilly's description (absolutely *divine!*), Fudge had to confess that, so far, the experience had been more than pleasing. Hence, she hardly hesitated for a moment when Johnny sheepishly popped the question.

"How about a bit of fresh air?" She could feel his hot breath in her hair.

"Fresh air?"

"Yep."

"Outside?"

"None in here, luv."

"Oh... all right, then."

Jeez, that was quick, the Jackeen thought, and grabbed the Loughrua girl by the hand before she had a chance to change her mind.

Fudge, thanks to Lilly's edifying disclosures, knew of course, that "how about a bit of fresh air" was merely a hackneyed euphemism for "let me stick my tongue down your throat", but felt prepared for what was to come. This evening she'd go the whole way and be done with it.

Outside, temperatures had dropped dramatically and even the heat from the crackling bonfire on the green was doing little to keep the crowds outside for long. In huddled groups they scurried off to the warmth of their own living room firesides. High above the black plumes of smoke, even darker clouds were bunching up threateningly and one after the other, the stars above them vanished from sight. The waning autumn moonlight reflecting off the soft ripples of the Loughrua waters was abruptly gobbled up by cloying blackness, and at the edge of town where street lamps no longer lit their way, Fudge and Johnny were plunged into darkness.

Over the rhythmic splashing of waves against the lakeshore, sporadic bursts of laughter could be heard echoing down from the fairground as the last few determined festival goers, warmed by greasy chips soaked in vinegar and swigs of whiskey from breast-pocket flasks, stoically ignored the frosty snap in the air and the seasonal threat of witches, ghosts and ghouls. High up in the skeletal branches above the tree-lined promenade, feathered creatures flapped and fluttered erratically as the teenagers passed by, settling again for the night when the sound of their footsteps receded around the curve of the lake. Out on the inky expanse, something surfaced noisily and thrashed restlessly for an instance before sinking once again into the watery depths.

Fudge gripped Johnny's elbow, the evil spirits and returned dead of All Hallows' Eve suddenly seeming very near. The Dublin lad took the chance to put his arm around her slight shoulders and draw her to him in a protective embrace. They didn't talk, but just plodded through the night, each preoccupied with his or her thoughts. Fudge surprised herself by wishing they might get it over and done with, yet Johnny, in all his laid-back complacency, didn't appear to be in any hurry whatsoever. Further on, they passed a couple kissing wetly on a bench, the rustle of fumbling hands under layers of winter fabric clearly perceptible. No comment was made.

From an untidy patch of woodland on the far shore, the sound of a night owl's portentous hooting was carried across the water on a chilly October breeze. The air was crisp and fresh. When finally, just before the promenade petered out into a clump of bulrushes and withering bog iris stalks, a huge black cat streaked across their path, the nervous country girl all but sprang into the Dubliner's arms, causing him to stagger dangerously towards the water's edge.

Crikey, don't look a gift horse in the mouth, Johnny decided sagely, and promptly took the blue-nosed face into his chapped hands and pressed his frozen lips against hers. Their teeth crunched alarmingly together, but soon chins and noses were organised and, determined not to make a holy show of herself, Fudge settled down to perfect what had, in the moment Johnny's tongue had hesitantly slipped into her mouth, become her first French kiss. Her first *Big F.K.* And although she still hadn't figured out why, it was, indeed, absolutely divine. But at that stage, the answer to this particular conundrum was the last thing on her mind. As for going the whole way, years later she'd scoff at her own innocence; she hadn't even come anywhere near putting half the distance behind her.

Eight

Bertie Barrett's fingers were falling off him. It was bloody freezing and he still hadn't finished dumping the pile of damp leaves he'd spent the whole afternoon raking up from the front drive of Castleglen Park. He was not exactly in what one might call an exceptionally affable frame of mind. Oldfield, her unsaid words speaking volumes, had given him one of her famous condescending looks when he'd returned from Carty's Corner Cleaners reeking of porter. He couldn't really see what the problem was. The Pier Bar was right next door to the cleaners and it had been his official lunch break anyway. Carol Carty, having provided him with a cardboard box full of wire coat hangers, hadn't hesitated at his suggestion to put up the "Out for lunch" sign and join him in one of the pub's shady alcoves for a midday snort.

Carol was great *craic*, not like those stuck-up proddies at Castleglen. Always on for a bit of fun, she was, and had massive great knockers on her to boot. Just as the young lads from Ballyglass had been mesmerised by Lilly's, so too, was Bertie Barrett by Carol's. He loved the way they jiggled and bobbed when she laughed—and that woman was always laughing. Braying, more like it, and showing a broad crescent of long yellow teeth that gave her the appearance of a donkey. But who cared? With tits like that nobody was wasting much time studying her face. What did his father, Fergus, God rest his soul, always used to say? "Son, you don't look at the mantelpiece when you're pokin' the fire."

Pearls of wisdom, Bertie reflected as he heaved the last shovel load of wet leaves and scrub into the wheelbarrow. A grand lunch break that had been, too. He checked his watch then glanced up at the sky. The sun was already beginning to set and the old school building rising up behind him was dark and silent. Over in the teacher's quarters on the first floor of the west wing a lamp winked on, the yellow square of light leaping out from the monotonous expanse of greyness. Miss Gibbons will be taking supper in her room, Bertie thought, at the same time straining to see over the rose beds and across the lawn to her window. He knew she didn't like to pull the curtains, the result of some wartime trauma, and every now and then he'd get a peek at her pottering around her bedroom.

He wasn't especially interested in getting an eyeful of the house mistress in the nip, but there was something fiercely thrilling about stealing a dekko into someone's private world for a few moments. An outside door slammed nearby, tearing him out of his reverie, and already he could hear the sound of Mrs. Oldfield's footsteps thumping across the cobblestones of the courtyard. Quickly, he threw the rake and shovel onto the mountain of leaves in the wheelbarrow and with a grunt of exertion, started pushing it towards the perimeter wall of the playing fields. In the autumn, especially, the compost heaps at the back of the orchard were overflowing with dead flowers, withered stalks and leaves. He'd get rid of this lot under the shrub border in front of the school wall, and maybe smoke a fag while he was at it. The effects of the porter were beginning to wear off and Bertie was looking forward to getting home to the nice pork and mushroom pie his mother had promised him. He was going to give Carol Carty a buzz, and with any luck, they could pick up where they'd left off at lunchtime.

A line of perspiration trickled down his back as he struggled with the overloaded barrow. The wheel was almost flat, making it virtually impossible to push the bloody thing through the long grass and banks of weeds surrounding the perfectly groomed grounds. He wanted to tip the pile well away from the hockey pitches; otherwise, sure as hell, somebody would start moaning. Up against the high stone wall amongst the ivy and nettles would be the right spot. Sweating profusely now, Bertie dumped the mound of sodden leaves and distributed them evenly with the shovel, realising before the last stubborn leaf descended that there'd be a hell of a lot of raking to do.

Minutes later, he was leaning up against the cold stone sucking greedily on an unfiltered cigarette as if it were his last. Enclosed in greenery, it was almost dark now and for a moment the gardener closed his eyes, enjoying the stillness and the delicious feeling of thick, black smoke seeping into his greying lungs. The urine-smelling vegetation didn't bother him much.

His craving for nicotine satiated, he then chucked the butt into the foliage, hitched up his trousers and grabbed the handles of the wheelbarrow. A pork and mushroom pie, a shave and Carol Carty's welcoming arms—a deadly way to end a hard working day. He gave the barrow a shove, but although empty of its load, the wretched thing wouldn't budge. Letting it fall, Bertie leant forward in search of an obstacle, squinting slightly in the advancing dimness. Probably some rubbish those young lads had left lying in the grass, he grumbled to himself, well aware that the Castleglen school perimeter was a fine hiding place for local boys up to no good. Tin cans, beer bottles and chipper bags were commonplace, and even once he found the rusting skeleton of a child's tricycle sticking up out of the nettles.

Poking around in the grass, he wasn't particularly astonished to discover an old shoe wedged up against the wheel. He picked up the offending obstruction and was amused to find it was a woman's sandal. He tittered lecherously. One of those local floozies must have been well plastered, if she'd gone and forgotten her shoe. This was hardly the kind of footwear one of the Castleglen young ladies would choose. He held it up with two fingers in the fading light. A delicate, cork-soled platform sandal. The only thing that puzzled him was that, regardless of the poor visibility and his miserable expertise on the subject of ladies' shoes, Bertie could see at a glance that this was no £5.99 item from Dunnes or Penneys. This had clearly been bought in one of those fancy boutiques on Grafton Street. He looked around swiftly, vaguely hoping he might find the other. With any luck they might fit Carol. *A good wiping off with a J-cloth, and Bob's your uncle.*

"Bertie...ee!" The shrill voice calling down from the main house made him start.

Bollix, he thought, *no peace for the wicked*, and pegging the sandal into the wheelbarrow, he pushed his way out of the bushes.

"Bertie...ee!" Mrs. Oldfield was standing on top of a small slope in front of the classroom area with her hands on her hips, the tall woman looking small and unimposing against the formidable Castleglen backdrop.

"Comin', ma'am, just clearin' away the rest of the leaves... nearly finished." He trundled up the hockey field towards her, the barrow bouncing along in front of him.

"Fine, you won't forget the bedsprings, will you? The girls will be back on Sunday." The over-anxious head mistress was biting her nails, constantly worried that all would not be to perfection.

"First thing tomorrow. No problem." He had now reached the low wall separating the playing fields from the school and was looking up the grassy slope at her. She wasn't a bad looking woman, if only she weren't so bloody nervous all the time. She nearly had her nails chewed all the way up to her knuckles. *A couple of stiff gin and tonics and a good tumble between the bed sheets would sort her out,* he decided. Immediately, however, the gardener conceded that while Carol Carty might consider him a mighty stud, he was far from being Castleglen's answer to Lady Chatterley's lover, and with that, he let his mind wander once again to the dry cleaning proprietress's breasts.

"Right then, Bertie, I'll see you in the morning." She was just turning to go when she glanced into the wheelbarrow.

"What's that?" She pointed a chewed nail down the slope.

"Sorry… what?"

"In the barrow."

"Oh, just a sandal… found it in the bushes near the Metals, I'll throw it in the skip."

Mrs. Oldfield's brow ruffled. "A sandal… a girl's sandal? Let me have a look."

Bertie wasn't about to inform the head mistress that, bearing in mind there was hardly a post-pubescent youth in Ballyglass who hadn't porked his girlfriend up against the perimeter wall, a shoe would certainly be one of the more delectable items the dense shrubbery might bring forth. Glumly, he handed it to her, figuring he could kiss his idea of finding the other goodbye.

"It's all right, Bertie, I'll take care of it." Mrs. Oldfield also hadn't failed to notice the high quality label, and this knowledge, combined with the fact that it was hardly standard uniform wear, gave rise to serious doubts. Gazing out over the Castleglen grounds towards Ballyglass, she decided she was going to get to the bottom of it.

Bertie watched her walk purposely back to the old building, the contentious sandal dangling from the ankle strap Mrs. Oldfield had hooked over her index finger. *Some poor rossie is going to get a ferocious bollacking on account of this*, he recognised too late, but deciding he couldn't do anything about it anyway, the gardener proceeded on over to the tool shed. A few minutes later, he was legging it down Glenageary Road, his salivary glands squirting juices in anticipation of pork and mushroom pie, and porking Carol Carty.

~ * ~

The discovery of the lone item of high-class footwear niggled at Mrs. Oldfield. The dark tangle of vegetation encompassing the school was a smarting bone of contention, and she'd always suspected that it offered the perfect camouflage for youngsters—boarders and locals alike—wanting to get up to mischief. She would have liked it landscaped, a reflection of the pristinely manicured front driveway, but the area was so vast the school would need an army of gardeners to keep the encroaching jungle at bay. Rumours were epidemic that some girls were indulging in underhand meetings with unsavoury elements from across the Metals. This information was congruous with her latent fears, and, if it were true, then now was the time to put this atrociously contumacious behaviour to an end, for once and for all. The Castleglen ledgers were in a sorry state, and to have one of their girls getting pregnant by some working class lout from Railway Terrace was not exactly the kind of publicity Castleglen Park School for Young Ladies needed at present time.

The hallway was dark and empty as the head mistress made her way to Miss Gibbons' quarters in the west wing. The sound of her own feet thudding along the polished floor was unnerving. Much as she enjoyed the peace and quiet of school holidays, the massive building devoid of pupils exuded an eeriness which made her skin crawl. Gibbons, who'd been nodding off when she heard the knock, was surprised to hear her superior at the door.

"Miss Gibbons, have you got a moment?"

The house mistress pushed the Reader's Digest from her lap and went to the door, grudgingly knowing she'd have to have one whether she liked it or not.

"Mrs. Oldfield! Is there a problem?" They wouldn't dream of using first names.

"You've heard the rumours, I'm sure." The tall, thin woman looked questioningly at the short, stocky one.

"Rumours, Mrs. Oldfield?"

"Yes, about some of the girls meeting... em... boys down near the Metals wall."

"Oh... yes, well, occasionally I've heard mention of..."

"What do you think of this?" the head mistress interrupted, holding the sandal up for inspection.

Miss Gibbons' forehead creased. "Well, it's not exactly my style, but tastes do tend to differ..."

"I mean where do you think I found it?" she broke in once again, slightly exasperated by Miss Gibbons' obvious unwillingness to become involved in the discussion.

"No idea."

"Down at the Metals wall—on the school side to be precise! Now I'm not Miss Marple, but one glance at the label will tell you that it wasn't lost by some woman from across the railway lines. I have the nasty suspicion that this belongs to one of our more well-heeled pupils—and I want to know to whom!"

Miss Gibbons stared balefully at the sandal, an uncomfortable feeling of foreboding creeping through her. The memory of the crumpled note she found in her twinset pocket came rushing back and with it, the image of that fair-haired girl. Rebellious, rumbustious, insubordinate and utterly motherless. Sighing inwardly, she pulled a wool shawl over her shoulders and stepped out into the hallway, knowing she couldn't go on protecting the child forever.

"Come with me."

"You know who owns it?" Mrs. Oldfield's eyebrows shot up.

"No, but we can check the lockers," the older woman answered grimly "The pupils won't have taken much home with them for the Halloween break and anyway, that's hardly a winter shoe. If the matching one is here, we should be able to find it."

Skipping Time Square and Grafton Street, where the younger children slept, the house and head mistresses started in Broadway and worked systematically through all the cupboards, fingering their way like thieves along rows of shoes and shelves of free-time clothes. Miss Gibbons, tired and disgruntled, knew in her heart they could shorten the process by going straight to locker number four in Piccadilly Circus, but felt she owed the motherless child the benefit of the doubt. And so they searched on until, twenty minutes later, they were standing in front of the aforementioned cupboard.

Mrs. Oldfield was decidedly irritable, disappointed at not having made an immediate find.

"This is the last one! If we don't come up with anything here, then you might continue on your own tomorrow—if you don't mind, that is. I do have a lot of paper work to catch up on."

Gibbi saw a spark of hope.

"Well, I can carry on alone now, if you like. It's not as if I had any other plans for the evening!" she tittered nervously, afraid her expression might give her away. "Just leave it to me!"

"Would you mind awfully?" Mrs Oldfield let her hand drop from the locker handle.

"No, no... not at all, go ahead!"

"I do feel rather guilty leaving the dirty work to you."

"No, please... I insist!"

Sadly, Miss Gibbons was a lousy actress, her eagerness awakening in Mrs. Oldfield the realisation that this woman, although renowned for her stringent perfectionism and profound respect for authority, did indeed nurture a fondness for children who shared a fate similar to her own. Without a second thought, she stepped past the house mistress and wrenched open the locker door.

It wasn't even necessary for her to bend down and search, for there, plain as day, discarded casually amongst a disarray of slippers and shoes, was the chunky designer sandal. Wordlessly, she picked it up and turned it over in her hands once or twice before checking the pupil's nameplate on the door. She read the name, nodding slowly. Lillian McDermott. This girl was in grave, grave trouble.

~ * ~

At that very instant, down at Birch Rise, greasy-haired Paul, the working class hero from No. 5, Railway Terrace, Ballyglass, was up in Ginnanes' hayloft making an impressively heroic attempt at getting his hands into the knickers of the art historian's daughter. They'd spit-swapped till their lips were bloated and raw and exchanged love bites, he'd nibbled her ear and kneaded her knockers. Now, fed up with squirming against layers of winter fabric and feeling a bit like Captain Kirk on Starship *Enterprise*, Paul was determined to go where no man had gone before him, namely straight into Lillian McDermott's aforementioned undies. If only she'd let him. Lilly was a brutal prick teaser. He'd been sporting a massive boner since their snogging session had started over an hour before, and he was feeling light-headed. There just wasn't enough blood to go round.

Next door, Fudge and Johnny, their lips equally puffed and raw, lay cuddled together in a confusion of sleeping bags and blankets on the tack room floor. For them, the kissing and necking, frenzied and all as it had been at moments, sufficed for the time being. Johnny's intuition told him that, although seemingly practised, the long, probing kiss down by the lakeside had been Fudge's first. Despite the futility of it all, and the awkward hurdle of social differences, somewhere deep in the sixteen-year-old gurrier's heart, he felt a fondness for the pale thirteen-year-old that went beyond the instinctive hormonal urge to discover and explore. Fudge was relieved, sensing she could relish this inaugural sexual contact without the usual battle of hand-batting resistance. And relish it, she did.

Mary and Charlie, sipping tea and exchanging farm gossip in the warmth from the kitchen range, were unaware of it all.

"Ara, Charlie, stop flustering," Mary had reassured her husband. "Leave the youngsters to themselves, sure what mischief can they possibly get up to out here on the farm?"

Prof had diplomatically taken a stroll up the long gravel laneway and was now sitting on the ivy-covered stone wall at the farm gate, earnestly contemplating the bright lunar crescent hanging in the sky between two semi-naked birch trees. Sinbad, on the wall beside him, was purring loudly and rubbing his arched feline back against the Dubliner's donkey jacket. Outsiders both, a touching empathy had flourished between the two hairy creatures over the past few days, each taking pleasure in the company of the other.

Despite the darkness, he pulled a tin of tobacco and cigarette papers from his pocket and, in what was a commendable display of dextrous skilfulness, proceeded to roll up a fag lined with a generous smattering of Morocco's best. Safe from disapproving glances, Prof lit up and drew in the first luxurious mouthful of sweet smoke, holding in his breath for a moment before blowing it out through his nose in short, erratic puffs. He studied the moon again, now no larger than a miserly slice of melon trapped in the autumnal night sky. The Persian had curled up in his lap, the animal's warmth and sonorous purring vibration enhancing the bespectacled man's state of cosy lethargy.

He took another puff, stifling an uncontrollable bubble of mirth which unexpectedly freed itself from the pit of his stomach, the result of some mischievous maverick memory. His attention turning yet again to the slice of melon hovering amid the birches, the young man began to ponder the meaning of life and was so lost in thought he almost failed to notice the car now pulling up at the farm gateway a few short yards away. Someone got out, and from his perch on top of the wall, he could just about discern the form of a young, short-haired woman, a mere outline in the melon's insipid light. She was leaning into the car.

"Thanks a million for the lift, Muriel, I'll be able to surprise Mum and Dad, they're not expecting me!"

They're not the only ones who are going to get a surprise, Prof thought, realising he'd hardly remain undetected when the girl passed by.

"Don't mention it, Sheila, it was grand having a wee chin wag with you. Regards to your dad... and your mother, too, of course."

"Will do."

"Are you sure you don't want me to drive you down to the house? It's fierce creepy out in the dark."

The younger woman scoffed. "No, no, that'd ruin the surprise, I'm fine. Bye now."

Shouldering a duffel bag, she waited while the car drove off before pushing open the small gate next to the cattle grid. She was only a few feet away. The shaggy cat, alert now, suddenly leapt from the Dubliner's lap and landed at Sheila's feet.

"Holy Mary Mother of God and Jesus Christ almighty...! Sinbad!" she shrieked. "You scared the life out of me! What are you up to, you big, hairy bag of guts?"

She bent down to stroke the Persian, and Prof used the moment to slip off the wall.

"He was keeping me company," he said in what he hoped was a matter-of-fact voice, aware at the same time that, whatever way he said it, his presence was going to frighten the living daylights out of her.

Her piercing scream, normally loud enough to raise Halloween's dead once again, was muffled by the banks of gorse bushes and dense hedgerows.

"Don't worry, luv, I'm just havin' a fag."

"Who the hell are you!" she yelled, her nerves jangling wildly.

"A friend of Finnula's, we're down visiting from Dublin."

"Christ, you almost gave me a bloody heart attack!"

"Sorry 'bout that, luv."

Sheila thought for a minute. "A friend of Finnula's, from Dublin? That'll be the day!"

Her pulse slowly returning to normal, she stepped towards the fuzzy-haired stranger and for a moment they regarded each other as best they could in the dimness. A scattering of stars had joined the bit of moon, offering enough illumination for initial scrutiny. Must be the older sister, Prof established, recognising the dark hair and pale Ginnane complexion. Half a head shorter than her younger sister, Sheila had cropped, wiry hair, the firm sturdy body of her mother, and a pair of wire-framed glasses on her nose.

"Well, a friend of Lilly's, too," Prof elaborated. "We drove down from Dublin to give her a birthday surprise."

"You drove down? In a car?" She squinted at him in the darkness, relaxing even more as she realised he must be about the same age as herself.

"Naw, in my Batmobile, actually, darlin'."

"I mean, aren't you a bit too old to be hanging around with thirteen-year-olds?"

"Lilly's fourteen now," he answered lamely, the effect of the joint having blunted his senses somewhat. "I offered to drive a couple of mates down. They're younger and don't have a licence."

"I see." Sheila leaned up against the wall beside him and with mild appreciation, Prof registered that, mercifully, she wasn't any taller than himself. He hated being looked down upon all the time.

"And you're the gooseberry, or what?" she continued.

The Dubliner blinked at her, insulted. "I'm not a bloody baby-snatcher! I've better things to be doing with my time."

With that, he placed the joint to his lips and sucked a luscious lungful of intoxicant into his gut. Sheila's nose twitched. She'd learnt a couple of things since she's started studying up in Galway, and one of them was how to differentiate one roll-your-own from another.

"Is that dope you're smoking?"

Still offended, Prof gave her a sneering look of scornfulness. "Now I hardly think you'd know the difference between dope and dried donkey shite."

"To hell with you, I would, too!"

"So tell me what that is." He handed her the joint challengingly.

Sheila hesitated a moment, staring at him, the moonlight glinting off their respective glasses.

"Well, I don't..."

"Just what I always say, culchies haven't a baldy clue..."

That did it. Sheila snatched the cigarette out of his hand, and ignoring the duck's arse on it, pulled a massive lung load of pungently sweet smoke down into the tips of her bogtrotter toes, reducing as she did so the length of the fag by half in one mammoth suck.

"Whooa... take it easy!" Prof called out in horror as he watched the better part of his monthly ration disappearing into the Galway girl's bronchial tubes. "There'll be none left for me!"

"Tough shit," Sheila answered nasally and slithered down into a cross-legged sitting position in the wet, thistle-dotted grass. Chuckling throatily, she handed the joint back to the aghast Dublin youth, who quickly took a blast before plonking himself down beside her. His knees popped loudly as he did so, making them suddenly snigger.

"Not bad stuff," she continued knowledgeably, reaching out for another snort.

"Only magic," he agreed, and deciding he might as well be hung for a sheep as a lamb, Prof left her to it and set about rolling up a fresh one.

"Didn't know country girls could be so deadly." He licked the paper and spat a string of tobacco off his tongue.

"You Jackeens are so conceited... think the world ends outside the Pale."

"Well, I must say, I thought I'd fallen off the edge of it when I arrived in Loughrua."

The notion of him driving out of Dublin and straight over the rim of the world threw them into hoots of laughter and by the time they were halfway into the second joint, Sheila was lying with her head on his stomach, and he with his on her duffel bag. The sound of their snorting and snickering resounding through the night had the rabbits out on the Brackens helter-skeltering fearfully into their warrens. By the third, they'd removed their glasses for a round of riotous snogging which might have led to more had Sheila, an hour later, not needed to disgorge the contents of her UCG canteen dinner into the gorse bushes.

The surprise she'd been saving for her parents didn't come until the following morning; by the time she and Prof sneaked into the Ginnane's kitchen to cook up a colossal feed of fried eggs on instant mashed potatoes and mushy Marrowfat peas, the rest of the family had long since retired for the night.

In the meantime, Captain Kirk had shamefully abandoned the inter-galactic voyage of discovery into Lillian McDermott's panties, his space rocket having prematurely ditched fuel somewhere along the Milky Way. For the city girl, it remained, thankfully, a virgin flight; for all her promiscuity, she fought to hold back, to cling onto some moral and emotional toehold, without which she might go spiralling off into space, out of control, lost and alone. Leaving Paul snoring in the hay, she crept down the loft ladder and out into the yard where she met Fudge, who, after one last parting kiss, was floating on cloud nine back to the house.

Later, cosy in their beds, they exchanged all the piquant niceties of hands and tongues and hips and lips, before finally falling into a deep, well-earned sleep. Dead to the world, neither of them heard the muffled giggles and clanking of pots in the kitchen below.

~ * ~

For Mary and Charlie it had been one of those lovely, good-old-days Sunday mornings, and when they finally arrived down for breakfast, the younger children were already sitting at the table, having helped themselves to glasses of milk and bowls of cornflakes. Everyone was in chirpy spirits, the mood only slightly dampened by the fact that today Fudge and Lilly would return to boarding school. The short Halloween break was already over, and that afternoon Charlie was going to drive them to the railway station in Athenry to catch the Dublin train to Heuston Station. From there, Michael McDermott would drive them out to Castleglen Park. The concerned parents refused to allow the girls to return to the city in Prof's rust-pitted excuse of a car and had politely declined his generous offer the day before.

They were discussing the logistical nitty-gritty when the door opened and the girls in question slouched in on slippered feet. Far from being lucid, they slipped onto their chairs and sat there, sleepy-eyed and smug. A moment later, Sheila appeared in a crumpled tracksuit wearing the same inscrutable expression.

"Sheila!" the whole family cried in unison.

Fudge sniffed. "Look what the cat dragged in."

"Now, now," Mary said, giving her second eldest a warning glance. "We'll have none of that." And then, turning to Sheila, "This is a great surprise, where did you come from?"

"I bumped into Muriel McMahon up in Galway and she offered to give me a lift home. I'll get the bus back this evening." She yawned widely and pushed her glasses onto the bridge of her nose.

"Gosh, you must have come back from town very late, we didn't hear you." Mary looked at Charlie.

"Well, yes... it was quite..." She left it at that. At eighteen, explanations were no longer obligatory. "I slept on the sofa."

"Oh, sorry about that, pet... if we'd known..."

"No problem, had a very comfortable night, actually. Slept like a log," Sheila answered as she slipped onto a chair next to Fudge and Lilly, surprising all present with her unaccustomed show of congeniality. It wasn't until the older girls were lined up in a row that Mary and Charlie noticed it. Disregarding their unkempt tousled hair and the mutual expression of sleepy, self-satisfied complacency, all three of them were flaunting puffy lips, purple love bites and puce-coloured shave burns.

Mr. and Mrs. Ginnane exchanged glances, threw their eyes to heaven, and poured themselves big cups of calming tea.

~ * ~

"Will I see you again?" Johnny enquired shyly. They were all out on the front drive saying their goodbyes.

"Well, I suppose so... you know where." Fudge answered hesitantly, referring to the Castleglen undergrowth.

He grinned reassured. "Great, I'll see ya then!"

They didn't dare exchange a farewell kiss, but gave each other a little wave and knowing looks as both cars parted ways on the main Loughrua—Bullcudy road, the boys heading for Dublin, the girls for Athenry railway station.

Later, frost-covered fields whipped by as the carriages hurtled through the deserted Sunday afternoon countryside towards the city. Now and then, a lone walker with a dog on a lead could be seen waiting patiently on a farmyard lane or side road for the Dublin train to clatter past. Once, a huddle of black-and-white Friesian dairy cows with dirty bottoms leapt away from the tracks, alarmed by the unexpected clanking din. Fields and meadows, still verdant green and lush, were surrounded by towering deciduous trees, their almost naked autumn branches dotted with untidy crow's nests and fat bunches of mistletoe. The girls, tired and deep in thought, didn't start chattering until Athlone was far behind them.

"That was the most amazing birthday ever," Lilly smirked, twisting the sliver chain around her finger. "Who would have thought we'd have so much fun down on the bog?"

Fudge gave her a dig, chuckling.

"It was brilliant, wasn't it?" she admitted readily, remembering her initial shock at the Teddy Boys' unanticipated appearance. "I can't believe they came all the way down from Dublin just to see us."

"Why wouldn't they?"

"Well, I can understand them meeting us at the school wall, just for a bit of devilment, but coming all the way down to Galway. I presumed they'd think we were... you know..."

"We were what?"

"Em... not worth visiting..."

"Huh? Why wouldn't we be worth visiting?" Lilly was looking at Fudge with an odd expression on her face.

"It's just that I thought they'd think us a bunch of... of snobs."

"They do."

Fudge stared at Lilly, crestfallen.

"What do you mean?"

"Fudge, they do. For them we'll always be a pack of Proddy snobs. They like us and we have great *craic* together, but at the end of the day, that's how they see us."

Fudge blinked. How could one birthday have so quickly catapulted Lilly into a grown up world of biased thinking?

"That's not true..."

"Look," the blond girl sat up in her seat. "How do you see them—socially speaking?"

Socially speaking? The thirteen-year-old country girl felt left behind yet again, this time intellectually.

"Well, they're fun to be with... They can't help it if their parents aren't well off."

"It has nothing to do with being rich! You told me yourself that, despite that gorgeous old house, your parents aren't exactly swimming in money. So tell me what you think, forgetting the finances."

Fudge felt cornered. "Okay, perhaps their backgrounds aren't very... very..."

"Oh, go on and say it, for Christ's sake!" Lilly was angry now, her blue eyes glittering.

"They're working class, I suppose..."

"Gurriers! In your heart you think they're a pack of yobbos!"

"What?" Fudge was near to tears. Lilly took her hand.

"We had great fun, didn't we?"

"The best I've ever had."

"See? We're culchie snobs, they're louts and we still we got on like a house on fire, so let's meet them in the bushes again next week!"

"Oh, yeah!" The dark-haired girl brightened up. "Let's!"

"Right," Lilly laughed. "Next week it is!"

~ * ~

But for Lillian McDermott, there was no next week. Not at Castleglen Park anyway. On Monday morning she was called to the head mistress's office where she was questioned by Oldfield, Gibbons and Brody, and subsequently expelled on the spot. By Monday afternoon her trunk was already packed, designer sandals and all, and Michael was driving her out through the high school gates for the very last time. Fudge was left sobbing and hysterical on the front steps.

Lilly was over the wall, and five long years were to pass before their lives would entwine once again.

Nine

Try as she might, she couldn't get the mirror clean. The mottled blotches were behind the glass and not on the surface, giving her a freckled, distorted appearance. She sighed with irritation. No wonder it had been a bargain, but at least it hid the rust-coloured water stain on the wallpaper behind.

It was late August, and summer, refusing to give up without a fight, had, if only temporarily, returned with stubborn vengeance. Outside, the air was already dancing above the ground, the smell of fumes and hot tar rising in waves from the street. The now so familiar sound of revving double-deckers, beeping horns, screeching brakes and screaming children penetrated virtually unfiltered through the mildewy walls. At the bus stop in front of the house, Fudge could see a clutter of jostling school children, all fighting to get on the bus first.

"Piss off, Murray, I was here first!" an angelic-looking, curly-haired child of about nine bellowed.

"No way! You lookin' for a belt in the puss, or wha'?"

The nine-year-old widened her eyes in mock fright. "Oh, you really have me brickin' it. If you don't shut yer gob, I'll get my brudder to shut it for you!"

"Your brudder is a stupid tosser. If he comes anywhere near me he'll get a toe in the hole from my da'!"

"If your old man isn't too langers to do it!"

"An' your ma is a goat!"

"And yours is a friggin' brasser!"

Mercifully, the bus arrived, sparing Fudge further details of this particularly eloquent adolescent exchange. The looming double-decker blocked out what little sunlight had seeped through the smog-covered window and, until the last profane child had clambered aboard, the small bed-sitter was thrown into darkness. She sat down on her bed waiting for the eclipse to pass. She wouldn't cry. She refused to! After one year of living in this flea pit, she still hadn't come anywhere near to getting used to it. Her parents had urged her to flat-share, to find something nicer, maybe a bit further up the road in Rathgar. Rathmines was flatland, full of over-priced, mould-ridden bed-sitters unscrupulous landlords rented out to unsuspecting students up from the country. If you wanted anything decent, you had to share, and the further up the road you went, the more expensive it became.

Anyway, there was nobody Fudge knew who she might consider living with. Her fellow-students at Merrion Hall Secretarial College were all dolled-up birds of prey biding time at their typewriters until a suitable up-and-coming businessman happened by. At least three from Fudge's class had dropped out, having successfully sunk their talons into unwary quarry and flown off to a cosy nest in some affluent Dublin suburb, where they were, no doubt, at this very moment, preening their feathers and sucking the victims dry.

Feeding hungry, open-mouthed chicks was the only aspect of this life which appealed to her, but to have children, you had to have a husband, and she didn't even have a boyfriend. Worse, she'd never had one—nothing that had lasted longer than two dates anyway. And worst of all, Fudge was still a virgin, so until she got that little problem out of the way, she could forget feeding chicks.

She wasn't really that mad for sex, nor did she recoil at the thought; it was simply a case of what you don't know, you don't miss.

Not much, at any rate. Occasionally, on Monday mornings when the secretarial school vultures were huddled together exchanging prurient particulars of the weekend activities, she felt more than a twinge of envy; her juvenile fear of sex had, now that she was no longer burdened with puberty, turned into plain old adult curiosity. This curiosity, on the other hand, had not been awakened by the debauched snippets of unfinished conversation in the typing pool, but was the result of unfinished feelings. More and more frequently, Fudge would awake from a bothered sleep, her body yearning to complete what had begun in some dislocated labyrinth dream, a dream of being held close, of being enveloped in a strong, fathomless embrace. She never really knew by whom, nor did it matter, the overwhelming sensation of longing making everything else irrelevant. Sightlessly, she experienced the warmth, the closeness, the sensuously clammy feeling of hot, naked skin against her own. Awake, in the dismal, pre-dawn silence of her Rathmines flatlet, Fudge would struggle to plunge back into the dream, all her senses screaming for the conclusion of what had commenced there. On such days, the normally unobtrusive Loughrua girl was the very Antichrist, her bottled-up frustration sending waves of venom rippling out to all and sundry. In short, had she possessed the knowledge of experience, or the verbal mastery to articulate it, Fudge might have admitted being as randy as a bitch in heat.

The bus having moved off, she stood up and studied herself critically in the mottled mirror. The dark hair had been cut up to her shoulders, the severe centre parting softened by a wispy fringe. She was pleased; it made her face look fuller and less chiselled. The years had added another few inches to her height and the scrawny breasts, although not exactly a shining example of voluptuous femininity, had grown from miserly bumps to praiseworthy rotundities. Straining to look over her shoulder, Fudge decided her bottom was all right, too. Stomach flat, legs slim.

It must be possible to get a man, she considered dolefully, but where? Her social life was somewhat lame, yet determined not to disappear into oblivion, she accepted any invitation which came along only, as was her fate, to find herself sandwiched on a sofa between some classmate's prospective parents-in-law, or at the best, cornered in a smoky, over-crowded room by a persistent gawky-looking gobshite with severe halitosis.

No, there had to be another way. It would be easier if she had a friend to go out with, a fellow-sufferer, someone who'd accompany her on a hunting trip through the Dublin pubs and nightclubs. Someone like Lilly.

Lilly. Not that she'd ever had to suffer from lack of boyfriends. Lilly got them all. Fudge glanced over at the postcard stuck to the front of the fridge amongst a collage of newspaper cuttings and cinema tickets. Where was she now? She hadn't heard from her former school friend for several months, the last contact being the yellowing picture postcard from Greece with a naked Greek god on the front and a coffee stain on the back. The mind-boggling message "wish you were here" left Fudge wanting to wring her neck, yet missing her even more.

Another bus pulled up and the room was pitched, yet again, into semi-darkness. The stream of schoolchildren had let up, and apart from the usual traffic noises, the flat was relatively quiet and would remain so, thankfully, until Monday came round again. At eight o'clock it started again, but at that time Fudge herself would be standing at the bus stop clutching a bag of books and shorthand pads. The double-decker hissed alarmingly and moments later, sunlight filled the room once more. It was hot and stuffy in the bed-sitter, but opening the window was useless, unless, of course, you wanted to die a gory, carbon monoxide death. There was a tiny yard out the back, and when Fudge made herself comfortable on the rickety wooden stool that served as a kitchenette chair, bedside stand and coffee table alternately, she could just about stretch out her pale legs in an effort to soak up some rare Irish sunshine. Though a far cry from an Italian patio, she'd done her best to brighten up the concrete cage with boxes of nasturtiums, yet sadly, the unexpected bout of dry weather had left the orange-yellow blossoms and long tendrils hanging limply from the top of the wall.

In Greece, the sky would be a deep, azure blue, the air fresh, the water crystal clear. Was Lilly, in that instant, sipping a glass of resin-flavoured retsina under the awning of some sleepy beachside tavern, a plate of tomato salad with goat's cheese and olives on the table in front of her, a tawny, fervent Adonis sitting opposite? *Some people have all the luck*, Fudge brooded, not without a pang of resentment, but then her last holiday had been a six-day trip to Butlins (yet again) with her parents and younger sisters over one year ago. She'd tried to protest, but relented finally, knowing Mum and Dad couldn't afford Club Med and needed a little time alone. Dad, for some reason, had been particularly anxious.

"Please, Finnula, I really want to treat your mother. The twins are old enough to look after themselves, but Rosy would love your company. She adores you."

"I know, Dad… it's just Butlins! Why Butlins, for crying out loud! We've been there about four times already! Aren't Lizzy and Beth a bit too old for it? And what about Sheila? Why am I always the one left to do the babysitting?"

"Sheila's starting a new job, I really can't ask her, and as for the twins, they love it. There are plenty of events for teenagers, discos and so on… and I can be alone with your mother…" This last part he said with a funny, distant look in his eye which made Fudge give up at last.

"Everything's all right, isn't it?" she'd asked then, a sudden stab of alarm piercing the pit of her stomach.

"Sorry, love… what?" Charlie was lost for a second, his thoughts having wandered off in another direction.

"You and Mum, is everything all right with you?"

The weathered farmer was momentarily embarrassed, forgetting his daughter was no longer a child, but an adult with grown-up worries, and a grown-up perception of human feelings. He drew a callused hand through his thinning hair, and for the first time, Fudge noticed exactly how much grey had replaced the rich, dark brown.

"Of course!" He appeared briefly startled, thrown off balance. "Why would you say that?"

"Ach, for no particular reason. I just like to think you're both happy." Now it was Fudge's turn to be flustered, amazed at her own spontaneous show of empathy.

"We are, pet... we are... Now what do you say? Will you come?"

"Well, all right, but on one condition."

"What's that?"

"That I don't have to sit through one of those afternoon shows where some gombeen in a patchwork suit spends two hours making sausage dogs out of balloons."

"It's a deal." In an uncharacteristic gesture of impulsiveness, the farmer took his daughter into his arms and held her tight.

This year she hadn't been able to afford a holiday and was aware that her parents, regardless of Auntie Dora's continuing support, were having to delve deep into their pockets to keep her in college and pay for the flea-pit flat. She could have returned to Galway after boarding school, but Mary and Charlie had insisted that Merrion Hall Secretarial College was the best, offering her an education which might get her out of the typing pool and up to the desk in front of the manager's door. With an additional smattering of PR and marketing, she'd be laughing.

So here she was in a cabbage-smelling Rathmines digs surrounded by cursing school children, screaming Dublin buses and suffocating city summer smog, while Lillian McDermott was travelling around Europe without a worry in the world, enjoying a wonderfully decadent, paid-for sabbatical year. The blond hair bleached white after weeks of Mediterranean sunshine, she'd be nut-brown, bursting with health and encircled by gorgeous willing men.

Fuck her.

In a fit of fury, Fudge pulled the postcard from the fridge door and tore it up into a thousand little pieces, the scraps of paper falling like confetti from her hands. And to hell with college today, too! The new term had only just begun, yet already the thought of those titivated, pink-nailed buzzards was making her own claws extend. *I've got to get out of here*, she decided suddenly, *get some fresh air. I'll cycle into town and sun myself on the grass in St. Stephen's Green.*

Feeling better for her having made a decision, Fudge washed herself as best she could at the chipped bed-sitter sink, pulled on a pale blue summer dress, tied a cream-coloured cotton cardigan around her waist, and slipped into a pair of flat leather sandals. A few minutes later, she struggled out of the hallway with her bicycle and down the short flight of steps to the street, banging her shin on the pedal for the umpteenth time in the process.

At the corner shop, she bought a bag of Taytos, a can of Coke and a daily newspaper, which she popped into her shoulder bag before wobbling her way through the Friday morning Dublin traffic. Gathering momentum, she sailed over the canal bridge and down Richmond Street towards the Green, her skirts flattering in the wind around her. At a road works site on the Cuffe and Harcourt Street intersection, a sunburnt young man in a string vest stuck his head out of the trench and whistled appreciatively, his worm's-eye perspective offering him a view of Fudge's thighs hidden to other passers-by. Her mood mellowed even more, and by the time she chained her bike to the park railings, Lilly, the luscious Greek men, the tomato salads and cerulean skies were forgotten.

In St. Stephen's Green, the urban clamour of hooting horns and a hundredfold car engines was muffled by the encompassing trees and bushes, the lofty branches and shrub borders with their dense screen of sooty green branches giving perfect protection against the fast-moving city stress. Here, beds of ornate flowering plants had space to blossom and grow, and out on the pond, ducks bobbed around on the murky waters. Every now and then, someone would throw a handful of breadcrumbs, causing bedlam to break loose as dozens of silky feathered gluttons flapped frantically to grab a beakful before the soggy morsels sank to the pond floor.

Fudge continued on to the centre of the park, as far away from the outside world as possible. Today, she wanted her own patch of green grass under an equally private patch of hazy blue sky. Finding the perfect place up against a row of sweet smelling flowering shrubs, she spread out her cardigan and sat down. The Merrion Hall Secretarial School was only a stone's throw away, but her conscience was crystal clear. No, she was determined to enjoy herself, to forget that she was stuck in Dublin alone while everyone else was having so much fun and doing interesting things.

Sheila had finished studying social science and was busy trying to save the world. She had a good job in Galway and whereas her work often confronted her with some of the less salubrious sides of life, it earned her enough to finance a second-hand car and a rented flat out in Claddagh. Not a bed-sitter, a real flat. With two rooms. She didn't have to go to sleep looking at dirty dishes piling up in the sink as Fudge did when college days were too long and free time too short.

The twins were going into their final year in Loughrua where, several years before, a small private school had been set up by a large Canadian mining company for their own employees and members of the local Protestant community. They'd dug in their heels at first, protesting that they wanted to stay with their friends at St. Bridget's, but as usual the grown-ups won the fight. Who knew if Charlie and Mary were really doing the girls a favour, yet they did what they felt was right. Three years after enrolment, Lizzy and Beth now had strange nasal accents, plenty of airs and graces and boyfriends called Chuck and Henry.

Sheila was incensed, accusing her parents of trying to make snobbish wasps out of her sisters. Bitter disagreements had ensued. They were good, plain country people, the all too altruistic social science student had argued, eyes flashing defiantly behind her glasses. In a land full of Catholics, it was merely some non-conformist offshoot in the intricate tangle of branches forming their family tree which had resulted in them being Protestant. Mary, picking up on her daughter's similitude, had been shocked.

"Are you trying to tell me this tree should have been pruned? The unwanted offshoot restrained, or worse, removed? You'll get yourself into trouble making sweeping statements like that, Sheila Ginnane!"

"God, Mother! How can you think such a thing! Of course not! Exactly the opposite, let it grow! What I'm saying is that it derives its nourishment from the same soil... the same earth!"

"That's what I'm doing—helping it to grow strong! There's room enough amongst all the other branches."

"I know, Mum, but stop manipulating it, let it grow as it wants!"

At this stage, Charlie, who had taken refuge behind *The Irish Times*, decided enough was enough. He looked up at his daughter.

"Sheila, if you're finished giving your lecture on gardening, you might make your mother and I a cup of tea."

Sheila, her cheeks flaming, stormed out of the room, banging the door so loudly that the china rattled in the kitchen cupboard. The farmer stared at the empty chair his daughter had left behind, then looked up at Mary.

"Did I say something wrong?"

But for all her fixed ideas, she wasn't a resentful person and, at the end of the day, whether right or wrong, the strong-minded student knew her parents only wanted all their children to be happy. The arguments finally ended, yet the occasional caustic remark thrown haphazardly into a conversation left Charlie and Mary in no doubt regarding Sheila's opinion of their views.

~ * ~

Fudge stretched out on the prickly lawn. Flushed from exertion, she enjoyed the coolness under her back, the fertile, earthy fragrance a welcome change to exhaust fumes and other city street smells. Kicking off her sandals, she pressed her feet into the freshly cut grass, relishing the sensation of slightly damp stalks thrusting up between her toes. Over on the path a white-haired old lady was tottering past, deep in earnest discourse with the fully-styled poodle pulling so impatiently at the end of its leash. Above her, an aeroplane drawing a wispy trail of vapour cut across her patch of sky, whisking passengers away across the Irish Sea to England or the Continent, or Greece, maybe.

Damn Lilly anyway! There she was again! She didn't know why she felt so disgruntled at the thought of the teenager who had once been her best friend. The girl had everything going for her, yet couldn't get her life in order. Straight "A"s in the Leaving Certificate one year before, and since then, wild excursions throughout Europe.

A postcard here, a postcard there. Everything was "far out" and "deadly", but no word of the future. Her father had done the best thing in packing her off to a boarding school near Limerick where, tucked away on the banks of the Shannon estuary, she'd managed to stay out of trouble long enough to finish her final exams. In the beginning, they'd seen each other, of course, the odd weekend or on holidays, but it wasn't the same and visits became less and less frequent. In Ballsbridge, that creep, Julian, was forever hovering in the background, his gun loaded with sarcasm, and Mr. McDermott's constant questioning concerning Mum's wellbeing got on her nerves.

Fudge wondered vaguely why he had never married again. It wasn't as if he was that ancient, and on more than one occasion she'd overheard telephone conversations with female admirers wanting to get their clutches into the intellectual widower. Once even, returning home after an evening at the pictures, she and Lilly had almost been knocked down by a tall, severe-looking middle-aged beauty in a grey skirt suit and high heels as she pounded down the front steps of the detached house, a look of fury on her face. In the hallway, tousle-headed Mr. McDermott was standing there with his dickey-bow tie at twenty-to-two, looking very much as if he'd survived a buzzard attack. He shrugged sheepishly at the girls, and when his daughter gave him the thumbs down, he merely nodded and turned towards his study.

"I knew she hadn't a bloody hope in hell," Lilly had explained later. "Dad's just not interested. I don't know why they bother."

The fact that his lack of interest in women did not apply to Mary Ginnane never, strangely enough, struck the friends as being unusual, only annoying. He was simply being polite, surely, but was it really necessary to make a lengthy report on her health, habits and reading preferences every time Fudge came to visit?

"Your mother's well, is she?"

"Yes, thanks, grand."

"That's good to hear... How's school?"

"Grand, too, Mr. McDermott."

"You've no problems with your marks then?"

"Nothing a bit of swotting won't cure."

"Good, good... and you'll be visiting your mother soon, will you?"

"In the holidays, as usual... and Dad, too, of course."

"Oh, of course, of course... Has she been getting about much?"

"Who?" Fudge was getting slightly bored by the conversation, but kept doggedly at it for the sake of good manners.

"Mary, your mum... does she get up to Galway much? Go shopping, to the library and so on?"

"Well, we have a library in Loughrua, but I suppose she pops up to Galway now and then to visit Sheila."

"Ah, that's nice... You have a library in Loughrua?"

"Not a huge one, but it keeps Mum in books."

"That's nice for her... very nice... Em... what's she reading at the moment?"

Suppressing a spasm of irritation, Fudge looked blankly at the somewhat dishevelled art historian.

"I'm sorry, Mr. McDermott, I really can't tell you. Do you want me to ask?"

Flustered, he sat up in his leather wing chair. "No, no, sorry... just my silly critic's curiosity!"

With all respect to her father, had Fudge known how much the man in front of her, after all these years, was still yearning for her mother, for Assunta, then she might have reacted a little more sympathetically; however, as it was, she hadn't a clue in the world.

~ * ~

Flopping over onto her stomach, she spread the daily newspaper out on the grass and ripped open the bag of Taytos. Nothing like a good breakfast to start the day. A small hedge bird, hoping for an offering, hopped a few feet in her direction, quickly fluttering away again at the sound of the rustling crisp bag. *Forget it, birdie*, the country girl thought as she licked the oily cheese and onion crumbs off her fingers, *try your luck at the duck pond.*

High in the sky now, the sun warmed the backs of her legs and penetrated the thin summer fabric of her dress. Ignoring the admiring glances of snappy businessmen as they hurried towards their swanky designer offices behind colourful Georgian Dublin doorways surrounding the Green, Fudge hitched the cotton dress higher up around her thighs. To hell with Lilly McDermott; their ways had parted for good, over a year ago, and life would go on without her.

Full of renewed determination, she turned the pages of the newspaper, scanning the columns for social events and party tips. What about the pictures? A nice musical? Immediately, she reprimanded herself. No, she was going to find a man, and she'd hardly do that standing in a queue listening to the buskers on O'Connell Street. Anyway, men never went to the cinema alone, unless it was one of *those* films and *they* weren't shown in Ireland—not officially at any rate. Tough luck, Linda Lovelace.

There was a *ceilí* in some Irish arts centre down on the quays, The Hibernian Chess Club's annual summer ball (Christ, look at the price of the shaggin' tickets!), and a slide show on an Arctic expedition in a North Side community hall. Adamant not to give up, Fudge considered a disco. If she turned up late and mingled well, maybe nobody would notice she'd come on her own. She had used the "my-friend's-just-gone-to-the-jacks" line more than once. You were scraping rock bottom if you had to go the disco alone. *Who cares? That's what I'll do*, she decided, suddenly excited. *I'll get myself all tarted up to the nines in something sexy, a few swigs from the Baby Power's, and then, Dublin, look out!*

Smiling to herself, she folded the paper and was just jamming it into her shoulder bag when a small ad on the back cover caught her eye. It was a short text informing readers of a lecture on Renaissance masterpieces in Trinity College that evening. It would be held by the well-known art historian Michael McDermott. Realising she's been thinking of him only a few short minutes before, a strange sense of *déjà vu* swept over her. Ach, good old Mr. McDermott. For all his inquisitive questioning he was a kind-hearted soul, and Fudge suddenly found herself missing him, too. *I could call into the lecture before going to the disco*, she thought, *just for a half an hour or so, to say hello. For old time's sake.* Yes, he'd like that. And she would, too.

Great! Her Friday evening was fully planned. It really wasn't very difficult once you put your mind to it! Later on, she'd pedal over to the street market, buy some vegetables and spuds to eat with the sausages that were threatening to go off in her fridge, and after dinner, fill herself a nice hot bath (unless, of course, some twit had gone and jammed the gas meter with foreign coins again). The cheese and onion crisps all eaten, she crumpled the greasy plastic into a ball and stuffed it into her bag along with the newspaper. Then, popping the lid on the can of Coke, Fudge took a long, refreshing drink, burped daintily into her hand, and lay down again to relish a few more precious minutes of warming sunshine before plunging into the never-ending stream of traffic which would take her over the river Liffey and down O'Connell Street to the market.

Following specks of light behind her closed eyelids, she let her body relax and soon the city clamour began to fade. Her limbs, heavy with lethargy, seemed to sink into the warm ground, and a fly, whose frenzied buzzings might have driven the most enduring of sun-worshippers to dementedness, went largely unnoticed as Fudge fell deeper and deeper into a state of glorious sluggishness.

By the time she woke, the park was milling with crowds of students and office workers who, having taken advantage of the fact that it was poet's day (Piss Off Early, Tomorrow's Saturday) were now enjoying a lazy, pre-weekend afternoon. With a start, Fudge realised she must have dozed for several hours; her legs, arms and one side of her face were sunburnt and fiery red. Succumbing to a sneaky gust of summer wind, the flimsy dress had ridden even further up her thighs while she slept, almost revealing her ravishing, polka-dotted Woolworth's underwear. A few feet away, a group of college goons were leering covetously and nudging each other.

Resisting a strong temptation to poke out her tongue, the disgruntled Galway girl picked up her bag and, trying not to wince as the hard leather scraped along the sunburnt skin, swaggered out of the park with whatever feeble scrapings of dignity she was able to salvage. Bloody gynaecology students, no doubt, she figured, already feeling sorry for the next generation of female patients. Forgetting the market, she cycled slowly back to Rathmines, for once looking forward to the cool darkness of the damp, downstairs bed-sitter.

At home, she lay down with wet tea towels draped over her scorched extremities, deciding to give the night out a miss as well. So much for making a new start, so much for resolutions, so much for finding a man. She wasn't even capable of getting through the day, God dammit! The old suburban building was quiet. Most of the other tenants were probably out and about having fun, meeting friends, finding mates! From the room next door, the strains of Neil Young could be heard emanating from the cheap mono record player her penurious college neighbour had saved so resolutely to buy. Toast, cornflakes and jumble-sale clothes for months in order to listen to *Harvest* over and over and over again. Fair enough.

On the window ledge, Fudge's tiny transistor radio stood mute and redundant, the batteries having long since grown green and powdery. What the hell, she wasn't interested in adding to the nerve-tattering mixed salad of clashing melodies which commenced every evening after tea. If her fellow tenants could only come to an agreement, but overlapping layers of Debussy, Uriah Heep, Ravi Shankar and the Clancy Brothers were hardly what one could categorise as light evening entertainment. For the moment the music was good, and it would be another hour or so before serious competition began. Outside in the hallway the pay phone jangled shrilly. She let it ring. It wasn't for her, anyway. A second later, the Neil Young fan shuffled down the corridor and a moment passed until snippets of low conversational muttering seeped under the heavy wooden door.

"You're joking! She said that... to your face? What a slut! ...With her best friend? Come on... you're bullshitting me... no way! For how long now...? And what about the other one... yeah... with the monstrous backside... no, the other one... I mean her flatmate, the one with the face like a hatful of arseholes... yep, that's the one... No, you're having me on... that's gross! Yuck! She didn't swallow it, did she?"—gagging sounds and hoots of laughter—"Talk about 'in for a penny, in for a pound'..." And on it went. On and on and on.

Charming. Fudge sighed raggedly. No, she couldn't stay here. She'd go to see Michael McDermott and then on to a disco, or a pub—anywhere! Half a tub of Pond's Cold Cream and a few aspirins would do the job. She'd been wanting a bit of colour and now she had it, albeit somewhat asymmetrical. Under the circumstances, her worries concerning the gas meter were superfluous, since the idea of anything other than ice cold water against her flaming skin was torturous, and when she clambered out of the claw-foot bath tub three quarters of an hour later, the side of her face which wasn't red, was blue. Despite her psychedelic appearance, she was feeling much better, and ignoring the expiry date on the package, she fried up the four remaining sausages lurking in the depths of her fridge before tackling the problem of what to wear. In view of her piteous condition, jeans were out of the question and short skirts had gone out of fashion, making Fudge's task of deciding what to wear relatively easy. She picked out a long, black, wrap-around skirt and dark, sleeveless polo-neck top. She was pleased with her choice. It made her look arty. Lilly would accuse her of dressing like a nun, but was it obligatory to walk around adorned in a patchwork quilt like every other student in Dublin? A natural type, the use of make-up was generally reserved for camouflaging the effects of a hard night out, or even occasional emergency repairs. This evening, the latter was on order and while it was almost impossible to hide the fact that her sunbathing efforts had gone seriously wrong, with a generous spreading of foundation the contrast was a little less startling. A touch of gloss, a sweep of mascara. Freshly washed, the dark hair framed her face in a thick mane, and in spite of her initial misgivings, the overall end result was presentable to say the least. Filled with new resolve, Fudge decided to treat herself to the bus and, soon after, she was waiting outside her doorway for the next double-decker to the city centre.

It was late, as usual, and bursting at the seams with hysterical youths eager to throw themselves into a Friday night drinking frenzy, after which they'd vomit at the bus stop on the way home and spend the following day claiming they were going to die. Amidst cheering teenagers, Fudge had to battle her way up the stairs to the top of the bus, very nearly offering her fellow passengers a private strip show by standing on the hem of her skirt in the process.

When, finally, she reached the front gates of Trinity College half an hour later, Michael McDermott's lecture had already begun, yet refusing to rush, she let her attention wander over the majestic eighteenth-century buildings and pristine lawns. It was quiet between the high grey walls now that the tourists had departed, their snapshots taken and the Book of Kells inspected. The college grounds had finally been left to the students, a few of whom now hurried past her across the front square to their rooms. To study here, Fudge thought sadly, must be a gift from heaven, and there was Lilly with her bundle of straight "A"s lolling around under Grecian skies. The solid walls were literally oozing with wisdom and learning, if only she could scrape a little off. Rounding a corner on the far side of the courtyard, she ran her hand along the rough stone surface, imagining in her typical whimsical manner, to feel the decades of knowledge embedded there. The place even smelt of intelligence, Fudge observed as she entered a silent corridor, of dusty old books, leather chairs, polished study tables, ink, chalk. She fancied she could even smell the lead from the pencils and the wood they were made of. Merrion Hall Secretarial College, in contrast, stank of Formica, board markers, Tippex and plastic disposable coffee cups.

Through a sturdy door on the left, Mr. McDermott's lilting voice was emphasising a point. When, seconds later, Fudge slipped into the room, she was surprised by the number of people gathered there, or rather the lack of them. Misled by the notion of an impressive college auditorium where a latecomer might sneak in unnoticed, she was chagrined to find this was little more than a study, and, as a result, hardly a person in the place remained unaware of her untimely entrance. Five rows of heads turned as Fudge, cringing with embarrassment, stooped along the last line of seats, stumbling, yet again, over the hem of her wrap-around as she did so. Grabbing the back of a chair for support, she muttered "shite!", her involuntary utterance resounding with unexpected clarity off the walls of the high-ceilinged chamber. Lilly's father paused for a moment, smiled, nodded a brief greeting and continued where he had left off.

His voice had a melodious, story-telling quality, a timbre one could listen to for hours, and once settled, the skirt hitched back up around her waist, Fudge found herself being caught up in tales of colour and composition, of undiscovered artists and unwavering passion, of enlightenment and religious wonder. And of Madonnas. Weeping, praying, sleeping, soaring, adoring Madonnas.

The last rays of sunlight shining through the tall windows cast a warm, rosé flush across the room. Mr. McDermott's gesticulating hands sent whirls of dust dancing hither and thither as he spoke, his actions conveying the fervour and enthusiasm of a classical conductor. With great sweeping motions, Renaissance heavens filled with a tumult of angels were depicted, and over and over again the motes swirled and plunged around him.

The rows of heads were tilted in concentration, a strange mixture of young and old. A conservatively attired, bifocaled Miss Gibbons look-alike sat stiff as a ramrod next to a slouching, pale-faced, fine art student with a wild halo of shocking red hair and a smudge of oil paint on her cheek. Smiling nostalgically at the memory of her former house mistress, Fudge let her gaze meander further along the line of seats in front.

Finally, after all other members of the audience were duly surveyed and pigeonholed, her attention turned to a young man sitting two rows ahead. A one-time "preppie", she deduced, taking in the dark blue college blazer and Oxford blue button-down. His face was turned away from her, but from what she could see of his strong jaw-line and rich, dark blond hair, he was well worth letting her mind drift briefly away from Michael's narration.

Continuing her scrutiny, Fudge began to appreciate increasingly what she saw. Strong shoulders, narrow hips, long legs that were slim yet at the same time muscular. His hands. Hands were important. She craned her neck to get a better view and when, seconds later, he shifted slightly in his chair, she was able to admire manicured fingers resting on his upper thigh. Distracted now by the thigh, her inspection intensified, and it was not until the male-model hands began to applaud did Fudge realise the lecture was over and that she'd been leaning on her neighbour's shoulder for the last five minutes of it.

Flustered, she jerked upright and began clapping with exaggerated enthusiasm, only to discover that, in the meantime everyone else had stopped. All heads turned once again, and if the mortified Galway girl hadn't been so busy pretending to look for something in her bag, she might have got a good look at the young man's face.

Still footling around in the depths her shoulder bag and feigning preoccupation, Fudge waited while the last stragglers filed out. Satisfied that the only remaining person in the room was Mr. McDermott himself, she lifted her head to greet him—and saw he wasn't alone. Worse, he was deep in lively conversation with the hunky-looking former "preppie", and whereas she normally would have leapt at the chance of becoming acquainted with a dishy guy like that, the impression left by the stumbling, delayed entrance and solo ovation had her most certainly out of the race from the start. Thoroughly cheesed off, she hiked the bag up her sunburnt arm and moved towards the exit. She'd give Mr. McDermott a ring sometime and apologise for disturbing his evening.

"Finnula! Where are you off to?" Mr. McDermott's voice rang out loudly in the empty chamber and already the click of hard-soled brogues announced his approach along the aisle.

"Oh, Mr. McDermott... sorry, I didn't want to interrupt your conversation. I was going to give you a call..." Feeling as if she'd been caught sneaking away from the scene of a crime, her discomfort was suddenly greater than before.

"Nonsense!" He laughed out loud. "And for heaven's sake, call me Michael. You're not a child any more. We're delighted to see you!"

"We? Who..." Only now did she get a proper look at the tall man standing a few feet behind the tousle-headed art historian. His laughing eyes met hers. All at once, and with unexpected force, Fudge's heart ricocheted uncontrollably around her rib cage as if catapulted out into a pinball machine. Holy Mary Mother of God!

"J... Julian!"

"That's my name, Fudgie!" His crooked smile was heavenly.

"But what happened to your s... studies?" She'd been going to say "spots", but managed to stop herself in time. "Weren't you studying somewhere?" Jesus, what a way to start a conversation with someone you haven't spoken to for years. The last time she'd seen him his face consisted mainly of a nose, but now the other features had caught up. His lankiness had turned to tallness, the broad shoulders and strong body a far cry from the gangly, adolescent awkwardness. His complexion, which four years ago had appeared not to have survived puberty, was now smooth and healthy. In short, he was bloody gorgeous, and Fudge was flabbergasted.

He drew his eyebrows together in a look of concern. "You having trouble breathing through your nose?"

"Uh...? Sorry, no... why?"

"Just wondering, 'cos you seem to have your mouth open all the time."

In response to this comment, Fudge would normally have clamped her mouth shut and then evened the score with a barbed reply, but as it was, she could do neither, her jaw feeling as though one might need a crowbar to prise it off the floor. Accordingly, retaliation on her part was not forthcoming, and Julian continued to eye her enquiringly.

"Cat got your tongue, or what?" he persisted, a smirk of recognition smeared across his features.

"Now, Julian," Michael broke in. "Stop teasing Finnula, will you never grow up—you're talking to a young lady."

"I can see that." The snappy college student stepped back, and cocking his head as a dog might do, inspected Fudge from head to toe. Those four words were the nearest thing Julian had ever come to complimenting her, not that it had ever mattered before, but now she readily accepted them as such, relieved that their first encounter in what seemed like decades would not begin with the inevitable verbal volleyball match. She gathered up her jaw and bestowed upon the two McDermotts her most winning smile.

"Gosh, it's great to see you, I was just thinking about you this afternoon... wondering what Lilly was up to."

"Lilly!" Michael exclaimed, shaking his head impatiently. "I tried to talk her into starting her studies, but I never know where she is, let alone what she's doing! As far as I know that girl is still gallivanting around the Aegean Sea. One thing is for sure, if she doesn't come home soon, I'm cutting off her allowance and for all I care she can spend the rest of her life selling bead bracelets to hippies on Lesbos!"

Julian threw a long arm over his father's slightly sloping shoulder.

"That'll be the day, Dadio, you'd crawl on your knees to Timbuktu and back for that harebrained daughter of yours!"

The older man shouldered his son playfully then turned back to Fudge, who was grinning broadly at their good-humoured banter.

"Look, why don't we all go for a meal? There's a new place off Dame Street we can try."

"Well, I don't know, I was..."

"You had other plans?" Julian interrupted, glancing down at her long slinky skirt.

"No, not really..." she answered quickly, aware the college boy would have a field day if he knew she'd planned to visit a Dublin disco of dubious sorts all on her own.

"Right then, what are we waiting for?"

The two men took an elbow each and in an instant she was sitting opposite them at the candlelit table of an arched cellar restaurant, a gilt-edge menu in her hand and a uniformed waiter hovering by her side.

~ * ~

It was a glorious evening. They wallowed in nostalgia, telling tales of respective boarding schools, of studying, of not studying, and of future plans. In the same lilting voice as his father, Julian explained that he was now studying marine biology at a university in England and proceeded with mischievous delight to relate stories of college-boy pranks and feats of heroism concerning slimy, slippery, wiggling creatures.

All at once Fudge remembered his almost unnatural affinity for frogs, worms, or scaly reptiles, in fact, any kind of fishy, aquatic vertebrate which was worth hiding under the bedclothes during her visits to Ballsbridge years before. Was this the same person? She couldn't take her eyes off him. Could this really be the pimply, sarcastic git whose very purpose in life had been to torment her? To pounce upon her weaknesses and illuminate her faults? Were those sparkling eyes the ones that had conferred upon her haughty looks of patronising condescension or abject pity? He'd worked so hard at highlighting her inadequacies and instigating inferiority. How she'd hated him for it! Had he grown up, or given up? Smiling broadly across a steaming bowl of French onion soup, his face alight with unrestrained pleasure, it was impossible to believe it was the Julian she once knew. Oh, the sarcasm was still there, but the venom had gone out of it and only the fun remained.

Deep in contemplation of a small scar blemishing the smooth skin between his left earlobe and hairline, and vaguely wondering what it might be like to nuzzle him there, she suddenly realised he was aiming a question directly at her.

"Have you seen him on the telly?"

"Um... excuse me... who?"

"Jacques Cousteau."

"Jacques Cousteau...?" The long trip back from the tiny scar beneath his ear to stark dining room reality was taking its time.

"Yes... famous for underwater exploration... the *Calypso* and so on."

"Oh... of course, what about him?"

Michael and Julian exchanged glances and chuckled.

"Sorry, I guess I'm a little tired..." she defended herself feebly, registering at the same time that starters, main course and desserts had been eaten, the wine bottle emptied, coffee drunk, and the starched waiter was floating around obsequiously in the general vicinity of Michael McDermott's shoulder with the bill on a silver tray.

"Where do you live, Finnula? Sure, we can drive you home, no bother," Michael enquired, unceremoniously slipping the servile penguin his credit card. "You're just up the road in Rathmines, aren't you?"

"Yes, but really, it's not necessary." The thought of them pulling up outside her pathetic, run-down bed-sitter filled her with shame. Knowing her luck, having been left behind by the last bus, some inebriated partygoer was probably fast asleep on her doorstep, the litter bin at the bus stop overflowing with half-eaten bags of greasy fish and vinegary chips.

"I need a bit of fresh air. I'll walk over to Nassau Street and get the bus. It's no problem, honestly."

Instinctively sensing her discomfort, Michael didn't persist.

"Well, if you're sure. I don't like to think of you out and about at this time of night."

"It's not that late, I'll be fine... I can take the last bus, it stops right at my doorstep."

Julian suddenly turned to his father. "Tell you what. You drink another cup of coffee and I'll walk over to Nassau Street with Finnula."

"Good idea! And I'll have a cigar while I'm at it!"

Before she had time to protest, he was raising his finger to the waiter and Julian was tugging at the back of her chair.

Outside, night had fallen over Dublin, and as they turned onto Dame street, the great Bank of Ireland and Trinity College buildings appeared even more imposing in the bright city lights. Alone with him now, she felt awkward, attempting to conceal her uneasiness by pointing things out in shop windows. Her hands fluttered and he nodded.

"What did you do to your arms?" he asked as they were passing the bottom of Grafton Street.

"Fell asleep in the sun, the big eejit that I am!" Fudge scoffed at her own carelessness. "In the middle of St. Stephen's Green, too! You should see my legs!"

"I did." He was smirking deviously.

"You did?"

"Yes, when you stumbled over your skirt at the lecture. I always liked that about wrap-around skirts—one wrong move and you're left virtually naked!"

"Oh, I did that on purpose. I have one or two other attention-grabbing tricks up my sleeve!"

"I bet you do. Is applauding without the rest of the audience one of them?"

"That's wicked! You haven't changed a bit." She laughed, letting him have his little victory.

"You've changed a lot, though…" They had almost reached the bus stop when he stopped unexpectedly and turned to her.

"Is that a fact?" She gave him a cocky look. "And now you're going to tell me my matchstick legs are wonderfully knock-kneed and my wit scintillating."

"No, I wanted to say that you're… well, you're beautiful and that… your legs are, too."

At that moment, both were startled. Fudge, by what Julian had said, and Julian, for having said it.

"Oops, sorry, I didn't want to embarrass you…" He was quiet now.

"No, no… I'm just not used to you being serious—you caught me by surprise." And then, an afterthought. "You were being serious, weren't you?"

"Very much so." He raised a hand to her arm and with a touch as light as a feather gently caressed the tender skin.

Fudge's throat, stomach and heart constricted all at once. The sensation was so violent she felt sure her inner convulsion was obvious to all. A few feet away a cluster of youths was waiting at one of the bus stops lining the Trinity College perimeter wall. The nightlife traffic hurled past them at breakneck speeds, screeching round the back of the university to Westland Row, or taking the corner into Kildare Street on two wheels.

Julian and Fudge were, at that moment, oblivious to all of this.

Contrary to the laws of physics and the belief that this phenomenon was exclusively reserved for Hollywood and romantic literature, the world abruptly and inexplicably stood still. His hand moved to her shoulder and Fudge knew that something unbelievable was going to happen. Something she had never thought possible. Something she wanted more than anything else at that moment. They were going to kiss. On impulse, she took a step forward and raised her face, while Julian, a full head taller, leaned his body towards her. Close together now, she could feel his warmth, smell the freshly washed shirt mingling with a trace of musk, and discern the strong pounding of his heart. And then the unbelievable happened.

"Fuckin' 'ell! What a sight for bleedin' sore eyes! Fudge Ginnane!"

The bubble burst. The warm cocoon enveloping them shattered and, whipping around, she was in time to see Paul from Railway Terrace, Ballyglass advancing upon her, as lanky and oily-haired as he had been five years before.

"Sweet Jaysus, would ya look at yerself, tits an' all!" Stepping nearer, he leered blearily at her chest and immediately Fudge recognised the sweet smell of porter off his breath. He was plastered.

"Paul..."

Julian, totally off balance, looked quizzically at the woman he'd been holding in his arms an instant before. "Do you know him?"

"Well... sort of, we..."

"Sort of! Mother o' God, that's a feckin' understatement if ever I heard one!" Paul intervened, turning to the bus stop where one or two others were quietly waiting. "Hey, Johnny, get yer arse over here, will ya? It's yer ex-girlfriend, says she sort of knows us!"

As he moved into the light of the street lantern, Fudge recognised at once the rosy complexion and sandy-red hair. "Johnny..."

"Look, who are these guys?" Julian broke in, nervously glancing from one to the other and then back to Fudge.

She didn't have a chance to reply. Paul, reeling slightly, leant forward and stifled a beery belch before continuing. "Good old Fudge, where's Lilly anyways? Haven't seen her since she nearly raped me in the hayloft!" The memory of his intergalactic voyage of discovery sent him into peals of drunken laughter.

Julian's eyes were veritably bulging out of their sockets. If the situation hadn't been so piteous, Fudge might have started laughing herself.

"Finnula! How does he know Lilly?" he gasped. "What is all this?"

"Ach, it's nothing... look..."

"Who're you, smarty pants?" Paul's attention had moved to Julian, his gaze roaming over the Oxford blue button-down and the tailored blazer.

"I'm Lilly's brother, if you must know. What...?"

The greasy-haired Ballyglass man guffawed with delight. "Johnny, look, it's yer man... her brudder." He could hardly contain himself for laughter. "He's the one who used to call her Lilly-the-Pooh!"

Johnny, sober and ashamed, stared at the ground while Paul tottered around holding his stomach. "Leave over, Paul, will ya? You're drunk. C'mon, the bus is comin'."

"Lilly-the-Pooh! What a feckin' pansy!" He was doubling up with laughter now.

The younger Ballyglass man moved forward, took Paul firmly by the arm and led him back to the bus stop. There he stopped and gave Fudge a look of apology. She took a step towards him, but already the double-decker was drawing up in a rush of hissing brakes and billowing fumes. The two men turned and clambered up the steps.

"Johnny..."

He looked back before the bus moved away.

"Johnny, I'm sorry I never..."

And then they were gone, chugging off down Nassau Street in a south-easterly direction to Dun Laoghaire and Ballyglass, but not before the dim interior lighting offered her a picture of Johnny's scrubbed face. A face full of sorrow and hurt.

Turning, she found Julian leaning against the college wall, hands thrust deeply into his blazer pockets.

"You'll never forget that, will you?"

"You don't understand, those lads..."

"No, I mean the nickname for Lilly. I suppose you told everyone about it and then you all had a good old laugh at me."

"No! That's not true! I never mentioned it to anyone! That must have been Lilly. She knew Paul quite well... for a while anyway."

"Lilly... and him?"

"Ach, look, it's not important. That was all years ago."

"For something that happened years ago, you still feel quite sorry about it. Whatever *it* was." He hadn't missed the moment that had passed between Fudge and the quiet Ballyglass man.

"Oh, Julian, please! It's nothing!"

He shrugged and glanced up the road. The Rathmines bus was swaying around the corner from College Street. "Here's your bus."

"I'm sorry about this..."

"It doesn't matter, Finnula, forget it."

They walked over to the curb together and waited for the bus, which was being delayed by a taxi picking up a passenger.

"Take care, won't you?" he said after a moment.

"I will."

"It was nice to see you."

"But... will we see each other again?" Fudge wanted to bite her tongue off, but could feel him slipping away. "What about tomorrow? For a walk?"

"Sorry, I can't. I'm going back to England tomorrow evening."

"Oh... I didn't know." The bus pulled up beside her.

"Bye."

"But..."

The bus driver was glaring impatiently out the door. "C'mon, luv, we haven't got all night."

Julian stepped aside, gave her a little wave, and began walking purposely back in the direction of the restaurant where his father was waiting.

He didn't look back once.

Ten

Oh God, oh God, oh God.

Leaning over the putrid communal toilet bowl, Fudge moaned pathetically, struggling, on the one side, to control the latest bout of dry retching and to ignore, on the other, the slimy layer of faecal grunge peeping out from under the ceramic rim. She'd been crouching on the chipped tile floor for over ten minutes and a lull was not impending. Her face, startlingly pale behind the fading sunburn, was bathed in pearls of sweat, and wisps of unruly hair were plastered to her forehead. Another spasm surged through her exhausted body and once again, grappling wildly, she heaved herself over the excrement-smelling receptacle.

Shit, shit, shit, she thought appropriately, *let me die and be done with it!* There was nothing left to throw up; why wouldn't it stop? Collapsing back against the damp wall, she closed her eyes and ran a parched tongue across her lips. Those bloody sausages! That or sunstroke, or both.

Outside in the corridor, the phone started ringing again. Where was he, the *Harvest* worshipper? *Why doesn't he answer the bloody thing? The very time it might be for me and I can't move an inch. Is there nobody else in this whole damn building?* On it went, on and on and on.

After what felt like a very long time, the ringing stopped at last, and with it the stomach cramps. Ever so slowly, afraid that any rash movement could bring on a renewed attack, Fudge pushed herself up from the floor and pulled the chain. On rubbery legs, she lurched back down the dim passageway to the bed-sitter, hoping the phone, which she had cursed moments before, would commence ringing again. She'd prayed, *begged*, all day for Julian to call, for a chance to explain, to hear his voice, to let him know it was all a horrible misunderstanding. Still dazed by the incident, she wasn't exactly sure what had disappointed him more, the idea that she'd had a fling with a Ballyglass hooligan, or the thought of her ridiculing him with regard to Lilly's nickname.

It was all a mistake! Why hadn't she just jumped off the bus and run after him—made him listen! And why did it matter so much to her anyway? What had happened at the bus stop on Nassau Street? What had passed between them? She scoffed. As if she had to ask. Fudge had nurtured a suspicion long before the bus reached St. Stephen's Green, and by the time it had crossed the canal into Rathmines it had become a certainty. She had fallen truly, madly, wildly in love with the man who had tormented her like no other. Julian McDermott. Slamming the flatlet door, she flung herself onto the bed. *I want him back! Give me another chance!* But her prayers remained unanswered and the telephone silent.

After a restless night, Fudge had plucked up the courage to call the Ballsbridge house, having first rehearsed her opening lines with exaggerated diligence. Her frustration, therefore, was great when the answering machine clicked on and the carefully practised lines were left unspoken. She'd breathed into the receiver for several seconds before leaving a stuttered, inarticulate "thank you" message for dinner the previous evening. Her disappointment turned to misery when, by three o'clock that afternoon her call had still not been returned.

It was on her way to the phone for a second attempt that the spasmodic rumbling she'd naively disregarded as love pains had culminated in a first wave of excessive vomiting. Not since Lilly's unique performance in Mrs. Devine's domestic science class at school had she experienced such an unanticipated attack, and it was during this first bombardment that the phone had begun to jangle. Her calamity rendering her helpless, she'd praised the Lord between two gagging fits when the Neil Young follower finally slouched out of his burrow in time to catch it on the tenth ring. If she thought her prayers had finally been answered, she hadn't reckoned with what happened next. Fudge's ears were surrounded by the toilet rim when the one-sided conversation reached them.

"Finnula Ginnane? Dunno... Oh, yeah, the one from number three, she's here all right—her door's open. No. I'm not sure where she is, but there's someone barfing their guts up into the jacks right now... I can hear it from here! Probably her. Crikey, she must have been stocious drunk last night by the sound of it... Will I give her a message...? No? Well, all right, if you're sure. You can try again later when she gets her noggin out of the bogs... Cheerio!" She'd even heard the rat chuckling as he made his way back to his den.

Somebody had tried, more than once, but each time she found herself debilitated, unable to let the loo seat out of her involuntary embrace. At last it had stopped—and she'd missed her chance. Not only was she a tart and a gloater, she was a lush to boot.

Fudge turned to the wall and cried. And Johnny, poor Johnny, his face stricken and hurt. After all these years. Had she been more to him than a spoilt culchie snob? Had he felt for her what she was feeling for Julian now? And had his disappointment been just as overwhelming?

She was suddenly sick of them all: of Lilly and Julian, of Paul and Johnny, of the secretarial vultures and even bloody Neil Young. Sheathing herself in a protective coat of bolshiness, Fudge finally dozed off, but in the days that followed, she simulated disregard every time the phone rang and stifled dejection when the call wasn't for her. By the end of the week she'd given up all hope, and the daily secretarial college routine settled in. She got up, washed, dressed in whatever was at hand, cycled to college in steadily dropping autumn temperatures, listened to the monotonous drone of her teacher's voice, typed sample letters and took dictation in shorthand. She studied itineraries, organised mock conferences and almost went sheer nuts before pedalling back to Rathmines in the evening. There she pulled on a pair of track suit bottoms, opened a tin of tomato soup and went to bed with Stephen King clutched to her breast.

~ * ~

As summer slowly slipped into autumn, dawn came later, dusk earlier, and when the towering city bus drew up outside her window, the bed-sitter was now plunged into inky blackness. Weekends were spent under the covers with an Aran sweater pulled over brushed cotton pyjamas and a gas heater perilously placed inches from her rickety bed. She wasn't alone all the time. Seeking refuge from the cold, a fat, grey mouse had taken up residence behind the skirting board and rebelliously ignored any efforts on Fudge's part to scare the insufferable beast away. By knocking smartly on the wooden panelling, the scraping and scratching could be temporarily suspended and so Fudge, wooden spoon in one hand, a dog-eared paperback in the other, whiled away never-ending Sunday afternoons wondering if there might be more to life.

For the time being anyway, the manhunt was put on hold. How could she have honestly believed that those fickle, incalculable, heartbreaking creatures were in any way at all capable of making life more agreeable? A man was as useless to her as a chocolate teapot, she pondered acerbically, taking another square of Cadbury's whole-nut from the family-sized bar on her lap and stuffing it into her mouth. *Maybe I could just grow fat, stop plucking my eyebrows and shaving my legs. I'll let my armpits lie fallow like those bra-burning, whale-saving, carrot-nibbling women on the Continent.* Never again would she let lip waxing cross her mind, or an Avon representative darken her doorstep.

Running an icy index finger over the smooth skin under her nose she decided, spontaneously, to grow a moustache, and that ever-infringing bikini line could gladly peep out of her panties like encroaching jungle vegetation. The blackheads which were constantly threatening to set up home in the dimples of her nostrils were welcome to settle down for good, and what refused to be dealt with by whipping a flannel across her face and two cold baths a week, could happily pick up a resident's permit for all she cared. The toenails, however, would have to be clipped; her recent show of slovenliness had caused holes to be rubbed into the tops of her cotton socks, and already her shoes felt half a size too small. The toenails were an exception. It might turn out to be a cold winter and good socks were expensive.

Fudge was so caught up in a fantasy of bodily and hygienic degeneration, and the vision of herself as the first female yeti to apply for the position of personal assistant to some yuppie business tycoon working in a plush Georgian office building, that she hardly noticed the phone in the hallway ring. Only after the rat had rapped impatiently on her door several times did she become aware of the fact she'd heard it at all. The frothy mug of hot chocolate beside her bed, and the packet of pink marshmallows on her lap, almost tempted her to ignore it, but immediately she recognised it wouldn't work. He knew she was at home; her bike stood in the corridor and light was shining out from under the doorway.

"Phone for you..." He was already shuffling his way towards the rat-hole in number two.

Damn! She'd be in trouble with the other tenants if she didn't at least put the phone back on the hook.

"All right, I'm coming." She shoved her feet into the pair of tartan slippers that had finally replaced the ones she'd plodded through the Castleglen undergrowth in. Throwing a scarf around her neck, she braved it out into the sub-zero passageway and picked up the phone, vaguely wondering which of her sisters was in dire need of advice.

"Hullo."

A strange sort of strangled squeak emitted from the receiver.

"Hello... Who's there? Rosy, is that you?"

"N... No, it's me..."

Fudge quickly recognised the seized-up sound of someone trying to talk and cry at the same time, but was at a loss as to whose voice she was listening to.

"Who's 'me'? What's wrong?" She wasn't afraid, just confused.

The voice, high-pitched and ragged, steadied long enough to make articulation possible.

"Fudge, it's Lilly... I need you!"

"Lilly! God, what is it? Where are you?"

"Dublin airport. Can... Can I come to you? I got your phone number from your mum." She sighed jerkily, the exertion of getting out a whole sentence having sucked all the energy out of her.

"But I don't understand. Why don't you go home to Ballsbridge? I live in a tiny bed-sitter..."

"Please, Fudge, *please*!" Lilly started to cry again, fat, tortured sobs.

Shocked, Fudge gripped the receiver tightly, afraid to ask what had happened, afraid of what she might hear.

"It's not your father, is it, or Julian?" An icy dart of fear stabbed the pit of her stomach.

"No... No, it's me. Oh, Fudge!" Again the choking sobs cut off her words.

"Lilly, don't cry, can't you tell me what it is?"

At the other end of the phone she could hear her old school friend snorting loudly into a handkerchief then a hoarse cough as she tried to clear her throat.

"Fudge..."

"Yes, go on. I'm listening."

"I... I'm going to die."

And then it was upon her again. That same, overwhelming feeling she'd experienced years before down by the school wall. The indescribable sensation of knowing something horrendous had occurred. Seconds turned into minutes as her world slipped into slow motion, as the hallway came rushing at her and the walls pressing in. It was the moment of shocking realisation when reality does a headstand and your stomach, a somersault. The memory of their friendship was crystal clear, the closeness still there, the bond unbroken. It was the instant you know nothing might ever be the same again, when you comprehend the clock can never be turned back.

There was silence at both ends of the line for what seemed like an eternity. Only Lilly's quiet whimpering came crackling across the miles. At last Fudge spoke. Her mouth was dry, her voice a whisper.

"Lilly… How? What's happened?"

"Breast cancer… I have breast cancer."

"Oh God, no…"

Again silence fell between them, the magnitude of it enveloping Fudge in a cloak of leaden fabric, suffocating and crushing her. She was still so *young*. Had she used up her share of living in these last few exuberant years?

"Can I come to you? Please?" Lilly's voice was urgent now.

"Of course, but why don't you want to go home…?" Then she understood. Michael didn't know yet. How could she tell him? First his wife, now his daughter. How much pain could a person bear? When did the weight of suffering become too great to carry?

"Look, can you get a taxi? Do you have enough money?"

"Not really, I could take a bus…"

"Forget that, you'll be on the road for hours. Take a taxi and I'll pay for it. Come straight here and we'll talk about everything."

Suddenly the roles had changed. Fudge was in charge. Now Lilly needed guidance and help, someone strong at her side to show her the way, to give her support and courage. Someone to accompany her through hell and, if necessary, back again. Fudge would do that.

The time crept by as she waited for Lilly to arrive, and with each minute the horror of the Lilly's nightmare ballooned into apocalyptic vastness. Images of cells dividing and multiplying with terrifyingly uncontrollable speed, her vigorous body abused by chemotherapy, the drugs and treatment causing, as well as hope, destruction and despair. With each minute the notion became more and more abominable, and when the doorbell finally rang, Fudge was shocked by the sight before her. Mentally prepared for a wan and withering apparition wracked by disease, the vision of health standing on the cracked steps of the Rathmines bed-sitter threw her fully off balance. Could cancer really be this devious? Inside, slow destruction, outside blossoming life? Confused, she quickly paid the waiting taxi with the following week's rent and steered Lilly to her room.

"I'm sorry about this..." she started, the tears beginning to fall once again.

"Don't be silly, make yourself comfortable and I'll get a cup of tea." Fudge reached for the kettle, at a loss for words. Yes, tea. All problems could be solved once you had a cup of tea in your hand. She studied the blond girl out of the corner of her eye as she lay back wearily on the rickety bed, a mountain of cushions piled up behind her. Her hips were generous under the full batik skirt, and in dark woollen tights, the long legs were muscular, but shapely. She was as voluptuous as ever, Fudge perceived, her breasts heavy, yet taut, the golden locks dropping seductively around sturdy shoulders, her complexion tanned and glowing. Only the blood-shot eyes and red-tipped nose revealed her distress. The tea made, Fudge sat down at Lilly's woolly feet.

"So tell me, when did this begin?"

The other girl sniffed and took a careful sip from the steaming mug before answering.

"About two months ago. I'm not sure when I noticed it first."

"Only two months ago...?" Fudge raised her head in surprise.

"Yes, I was in Greece, on one of the islands. It was the most glorious weather, hot sunshine, blue skies..." She paused, her glance wandering off into the distance somewhere over the top of the teacup. Fudge fancied she could hear gentle waves slopping up over honey-coloured sand, but sensed none of the rage she might have felt only hours previously.

"Go on." Fudge took one of the woolly feet in her lap and began stroking it in a comforting, motherly fashion. A fleeting smile fluttered at the corner of Lilly's mouth before her lips started to tremble once again. Even in the dimness of the dreary room her eyes glistened as tears welled up and threatened to spill over onto the bronzed cheeks.

"We were on the beach, sunbathing—topless, as usual." She snorted all of a sudden, the tea in her grasp sloshing over the bed linen. Fudge disregarded it. Tea stains on her sheets were not important at that moment.

"I was rubbing suntan oil onto my breasts when I suddenly noticed two little bumps at the side, near my armpit." Lilly swallowed deeply, forcing her voice not to quiver. "I tried to ignore it, hoping they would go away, but kept thinking of Mummy and the fact that cancer can run in the family. A few days later, I was certain."

"You had a test done on the island? A mammogram or what?"

"No... No, I didn't go to a doctor straight away."

"But something as serious as that—at your age! Why not?"

"I just knew what the diagnosis would be... I just knew it."

"So on the mainland then. Where? Athens? Did you go to a hospital? Why didn't you fly home immediately? Why—" Fudge pulled up hard; the questions tumbling out of her had caused Lilly's eyes to widen and the smooth forehead to crumple.

"Sorry, I'm just worried."

"It's okay... You see, I didn't need the confirmation of my condition then. I wanted more time."

"But it was at the early stage—the most vital time!" She bit her lip, hoping she hadn't distressed Lilly further by reminding her that an early diagnosis might save her—might have saved her. God, the futility of it all! The waste of precious time!

"It was clear to me then that it had already spread. I started getting aches in my tummy and spent a lot of time on the beach letting the warmth of the sun soothe the pain. It helped me to block out the vision of hospital beds and tubes, drips, painkillers, operations..."

Fudge was appalled. She had just lain on the beach—sunbathing! "So when were you told for definite?"

Lilly sighed. "I wasn't actually told."

"Don't tell me they sent you a letter! Of all the callous...!"

"No, I don't have a written confirmation."

Fudge began to shift around on the bed, her frustration causing her to fidget. She was clutching the other girl's foot in a vice-like grip. "So how did the doctors inform you?"

"They didn't."

"Lilly, I don't understand. You've been diagnosed with cancer which is so advanced that you are going to... that it is feared you might... might die. You've obviously had treatment. Where? When?"

"Well, I haven't actually had any treatment yet." She picked up a marshmallow and popped it into her mouth.

"No treatment?"

"Em... I haven't really been to the doctor yet, I thought I'd go tomorrow..."

"*WHAT?*"

Fudge wanted to leap upon the glowing personification of wellbeing lying comfortably on the bed before her, and strangle the very last gasp of breath out of those healthy lungs.

"Don't be angry," Lilly whimpered in a little voice. "I know I'm going to die. Mummy died and I will, too."

"We're all going to die one day, for Christ's sake! Now get off the bed and put on your shoes!" The normally calm Loughrua girl was trembling with fury.

"But it's nice and comfy here..."

"Get off the damned bed! I'm calling a taxi."

"Don't send me home. Dad'll be mad at me!"

"Home? We're going straight to the hospital. You've wasted enough time." She grabbed a coat from the back of the door and slipped into a pair of boots before turning back to the other girl. "Ah, Lilly, how could you? When was the last time you checked the lumps?"

"About three weeks ago. I've been afraid to touch myself ever since."

"Three weeks ago. Were they any worse?"

"Now that you mention it, not really, in fact..."

"Look, come on, we'll find someone who'll do an immediate mammogram and a scan—even if we have to knock on every hospital door in Dublin!"

~ * ~

No peace for the wicked, Doctor Plunkett thought to himself as he approached the two young women huddled together in the deserted waiting room. They had been so desperately persistent he'd decided it would be easier to give the patient a full examination rather than trying to persuade her to go through the right channels and make an appointment. Looking down at the pale, worried face, and the brushed cotton pyjamas sticking out under the shoddy winter coat, his heart all at once went out to her. The poor girl wouldn't sleep a wink tonight if he sent her away. He'd call Maura, his radiographer; she'd do a mammogram straight away. They'd worked together for years, yet it never ceased to horrify them when cancer was diagnosed in the very young, such as the ashen-faced girl chewing her lip a few steps away from him.

He thrust out his hand in what he trusted would be understood as a casual, friendly gesture and not a show of concerned sympathy.

"I'm Doctor Plunkett, and you're the young lady who's had a bit of a scare. Well now, don't be worrying your pretty head. I'm sure there's no cause for alarm." He took her hand in a hearty grip and started pumping it up and down vigorously. The slim fingers were icy cold, and his heart plummeted even further. This girl was not well.

"Sorry, it's not me," she said.

"I beg your pardon?"

"I'm grand... It's my friend, Lillian. I'm just keeping her company."

"Oh! Sorry about that... I thought..." His glance dropped once again to the cotton pyjamas then continued on to the young woman sitting in the next seat. Beside the dark-haired girl, she was a shining example of physical fitness; in fact, she might have just stepped out of a TV commercial for milk, or honey, or both. She even had a smudge of what looked like marshmallow on the side of her mouth. The tawny complexion blazed with healthiness, and even wrapped up in her heavy coat, he could see that she was well-nourished and strong. Still, Doctor Plunkett had been in the business long enough to know, when it came to cancer, that didn't mean a damn thing.

On closer examination, he noticed she'd been crying. Her nose was red, the startling blue eyes bloodshot. He patted the back of her sun-tanned hand.

"Now don't get yourself in a dither. Maura'll do a breast X-ray and then I'll have a wee look at you. Pop into room number two over there, and we'll have you sorted out in no time."

"Thanks, Doctor," she whispered, and made her way to the Mammography department on sturdy legs.

He turned back to Fudge. "And there's nothing I can do for you?"

"Em... No, I'm all right. Lilly gave me an awful fright, that's all. I just left the house as I was." She laughed weakly to hide her embarrassment. "I didn't want her to wait any longer."

"You did the right thing. If only everyone were as sensible as you. Now, why don't you get yourself a hot chocolate from the machine. Your friend will be back again shortly."

~ * ~

When Lilly and Doctor Plunkett appeared out of his office forty-five minutes later, there were tears pouring down her face, and seeing Fudge, she started to jump up and down, the blond corkscrews around her face bobbing rhythmically as they always did.

"I'm not going to die!" she bellowed along the sterile corridor, causing a tight-lipped nurse to stick her head out of a room and tut censoriously.

"She's really all right?" Fudge looked at Doctor Plunkett.

"Just about the healthiest breast I've seen in a long time," he answered cheerfully.

"And the lumps?"

"Hardly anything to be seen. I did a sonar scan as well, and all that came up was a bit of fatty tissue. Nothing unusual and quite definitely benign. No enlargement of lymph glands, either."

"And the abdominal pains?" She was beginning to feel like Lilly's mother.

Doctor Plunkett laughed. "Wouldn't you get a pain in your tummy at the thought of having breast cancer?"

Fudge glanced at Lilly, who had the decency to look ashamed.

"So no other tests are necessary, no biopsy?"

"None whatsoever."

Fudge turned to her friend. She wasn't sure if she wanted to smother her in kisses, or beat the living daylights out of her. Here she was, late in the evening, standing in an antibacterial hospital corridor with a duffel coat thrown over a pair of pyjamas and hardly a penny in her pocket. She'd just spent the better part of next month's rent on taxis and would now have to take a bus to Rathmines dressed to kill. No doubt the man she'd been waiting for all her life would choose a seat opposite her, and even if they did get talking, as Murphy's law would certainly have it, he'd decide he preferred winceyette daisies to brushed cotton check.

"So that's it?" Fudge asked one more time, now more than aware of her maternal manner.

"That's it." Turning to Lilly, Doctor Plunkett beamed. "Taking hereditary factors into account, it wouldn't be a bad idea to start having regular checks when you get a bit older. And watch your diet, not too much animal fat, if you can help it."

"Don't worry, I'm full of resolutions!"

"Well, don't overdo it!"

The white-haired doctor watched as the two young women bounced towards the front entrance and was relieved that, for today anyway, another life had been spared.

~ * ~

"Look at me, for cryin' out loud! Waiting for a bus in my pyjamas and it looks like it's going to start bucketing any minute!" In the face of adverse weather conditions the joy of relief was beginning to wear off, and Fudge's mood was deteriorating at an alarming rate.

"But Fudgie, I'm going to live—isn't that brilliant?"

"You'd have known that two months ago if you'd taken the time to get your arse off the beach and into a doctor's surgery."

Lilly slipped her arm through Fudge's and cuddled up close. "Fudgie-wudgie, don't be so mean."

"Well, I'm starting to feel mean. I want that taxi money back as well—and don't give me any of that 'Fudgie-wudgie' shite!"

"But I can't ask Dad, he'll want to know what it was for. I'll pay you back as soon as I can."

"Ach, forget it, will you!" Fudge glared at Lilly then at the bus stop. "What are you waiting here for? This is the stop for Rathmines."

"So?"

"So you're going to Ballsbridge. Everything's all right, you don't need me any more."

"Yes, I do."

"I don't know what for—spare me, will you?"

"We're going to share a flat together."

Fudge snorted. "Over my dead body!"

"Cos I'm starting to study—at Trinity!"

"You? Studying?" Reluctantly, Fudge turned to Lilly, curiosity getting the better of her.

"Yep. Geology!"

"Geology!" Fudge scoffed sardonically. "Why not philately, or astrology, or something which will really put you on your feet later?"

"The course is full of men."

"Aw Lilly, *come on!*"

"Swear to God, eight in ten!"

"You're serious, aren't you?" Fudge was flabbergasted.

"Dead serious. And anyway, geology sounds brainy. I fancy myself plodding through the Siberian tundra or the Australian outback gathering rock samples with some guy in a sweaty singlet and hiking boots."

"And nothing else, or what?" Already she wanted to laugh. Damn her! "Jesus, I don't believe it, the shagging tundra! Give me one good reason for wanting to share a flat with someone as mental as you."

"Because together we are going to sort out the Dublin men. You and *'moi'.*"

"What makes you think I don't have a man?" Fudge retorted indignantly.

"It's easy really. You obviously haven't shaved your legs this millennium and you have blackheads in your ears." This reply was made matter-of-factly.

"I do not!"

"Monstrous ones, believe me. I'll get to work on them as soon as we get home."

"You'd do that?"

"It has its price. I charge a quid a minute—about as much as a Dublin taxi. By the time I'm finished with your ears, you'll be owing me."

"To hell with you!"

"It's a deal then?"

A better flat, a hunting partner and a blackhead squeezer to boot. This was an offer she couldn't refuse.

"It's a deal."

By the time they had settled down on the top floor of the Rathmines bus, they were squealing with delight and hatching plans. The pockmarked man with the lazy eye sitting across the aisle wasn't the one of her dreams, but he did seem to like her nightwear. He ogled Fudge from head to toe before leaning over.

"Them is awful sexy pyjamas," he whispered hoarsely in a thick Dublin accent.

"Why, thank you very much indeed, young man," Fudge answered primly and elegantly threw one leg over the other, wondering vaguely why his statement seemed so familiar.

She was still trying to file it away when the double-decker spilled them out at Fudge's doorstep half an hour later.

Eleven

Because it was what she wanted, it was what she got. A nice cushy place at Trinity College Dublin studying geology. Michael, needless to say was thrilled at the prospect, disgusted she didn't wish to live at home, and easily persuaded when it came to sharing a flat with Fudge.

"I want to be independent," she argued.

"Lillian, you've been scuttling around Europe on your own for over a year. How much independence do you need?"

"I mean on an everyday basis."

He hadn't the foggiest idea in the world what she meant, so tried another tack.

"With Julian in England the house is empty—and it's only ten minutes from college."

"I know, but I really want to share with Fudge. I don't fancy playing gooseberry every time you have one of those badly decorated librarians home for tea! And when Julian's in the house, I'm just a maid. It would be nice to live with another woman for a change."

Oh, yes, Michael considered wistfully, his mind wandering off to the west. *Yes, it would.*

"Look, why don't the two of you move into the house here?"

"Forget it, Dad!"

"No way?"

"No way!"

"You will bring Finnula to tea every now and then?"

"I promise."

"All right then."

Lilly threw her arms around his neck and planted a doggy kiss on his cheek. "You're the best dad in the world!"

Michael McDermott swotted his daughter with the Sunday supplement he'd been reading before their conversation started. "Ara, go 'way out of that!"

~ * ~

They found themselves a two-roomed flat on the first floor of a terraced house not far from Bushy Park and were convinced they'd moved into heaven. After a year of bed-sitter gloom, Fudge was blinded by the light. When the sun rose in the morning, it shimmered through their pastel yellow, hand-sewn curtains onto high, freshly painted walls. Together, the girls did the rounds of every second-hand shop and jumble sale in town, and bought everything that was bright. Patchwork bedspreads in Greek countryside colours, cushion covers dazzling enough to make one forget the darkest of Dublin's dungeons, an Indian wall hanging in glittering kaleidoscope hues. Michael's station wagon was piled high with booty, including a sheepskin rug, posters from Lilly's room and—best of all—her stereo record player. Scouring weekend flea markets, they stocked up on Cat Stevens, Creedence Clearwater Revival and Jethro Tull. Ceramic pots were filled with dried flowers, the shelves with books. Their birthdays came and went, Fudge's landing, as it always did, slap in the middle of the Yuletide shopping rush. A few days before the festivities started, they were ready to receive male guests, and the flat was, too.

Fudge was reclining in a nest of Oxfam pillows, filing her nails.

"Lil, what are you doing over Christmas?"

"God, don't ask me. Probably the same routine as every year. Overcooked turkey, Bing Crosby and five boxes of liqueur chocolates. Ugh!" She was sitting at the small desk in the corner of their bedroom with a towel on her head and a geology book in her hand. "I hate Christmas!"

Fudge looked up. "I didn't know that—since when?"

"Since Mum died, I think."

"Oh... I'm sorry. I suppose it's difficult..." She let her voice peter out, not really knowing what she wanted to say.

Lilly unexpectedly turned to her. "I've been thinking about her a lot recently."

"Because of Christmas?"

"No, because of the cancer business."

"Your cancer business?"

"Yes. You see, at first I didn't understand what had happened to her, but now that I do..."

"It scares you."

"Fudge, it terrifies me!"

"Why? I don't see how..."

"I'm absolutely terrified of getting cancer, too. I think about it all the time. *All* the time." Having said it, a wave of panic washed over her features, the very thought turning her lovely face into a grimace of fear.

"Lilly, don't... You mustn't."

"That's why I was so hysterical. I blow everything out of proportion."

"Well, you heard what Doctor Plunkett said, you have really nothing to worry about."

"I know." She sighed and pulled the towel from her head, letting the damp curls tumble down. "I just can't help it."

"C'mon, Lilly, let's think positively. Where are all those men you were talking about?

Anxious to keep her friend's thoughts away from visions of horror, Fudge shoved herself quickly up into a sitting position. "Tell you what, why don't we have a house-warming party as soon as Christmas and New Year are over?"

Already Lilly's eyes were sparkling. "I suppose you'll be going back down to Loughrua for the holidays?"

"Only for a week or so. It's going to be mad with everyone at home!"

As quick as it came, the sparkle disappeared from Lilly's eyes once again. "Lucky you, Dad and I will probably spend Christmas Day twiddling our thumbs and watching Disney cartoons on telly."

"Julian won't be home?" It was the first time she's dared to mention his name, and even after all those months the sound of it made her heart skitter. She'd told Lilly about the lecture and the dinner, of course, but had otherwise referred to the other girl's brother as little as possible.

"I don't think so. He's been invited to some girl's parents for a few days. No doubt dead boring."

"He has a girlfriend?" Bugger it! Why did she have to ask?

"Hard to believe, isn't it?" Lilly replied with a smirk. "As far as I know he's been out with a girl from university once or twice. Probably some Sloane Square swot with a black velvet hair-band and college loafers!"

"Yuck!" Fudge felt sure Lilly would recognise the pang of sadness in her voice and hurried to change the subject.

"You could visit us down in Loughrua! Remember? Just like Halloween five years ago. My parents would love to see you!"

"No, we couldn't. You said yourself it will be mad in the house."

"Ah, come on, you know our household—everyone is welcome!"

"Do you really think so?"

"Of course! Your dad loved it the last time, didn't he? He can blather to Mum about books!" Fudge leapt up and grabbed her purse. "I'll phone right away!"

Happy to put Julian to the back of her mind, she ran down the stairs to the pay phone in her bare feet. When Mary finally answered, Fudge's toes were numb, the threadbare carpet doing little to protect her feet from the cold chill seeping up from the foundations. She was so excited at the idea of spending a festive day or two down at Birch Rise with Lilly and her father, and was so utterly convinced Mary would share their enthusiasm, that her mother's reaction took her completely by surprise.

"I'm sorry, Finnula, it's out of the question."

"Pardon?" Surely her mother had misunderstood. She explained again. Michael could drive down with Lilly, spend the day before returning to Dublin, and Lilly would take the train back a day or two later. If the worst came to the worst, she could sleep on an air bed.

"It's just not possible at the moment, love."

"Why not? It was never a problem before. You loved having visitors. I thought you liked Michael."

"I do. It's just too much work." Why did her answer sound so lame? Fudge wasn't falling for it.

"Can't we just throw a few sandwiches together? And anyway, Lilly and I will be out most of the time. We'd like to get the bus up to Galway and catch the winter sales on the twenty-seventh."

"I'm sure the shopping is better in Dublin." Mary answered blankly.

Fudge was suddenly confused and angry. What was wrong with her? Where had that frostiness in her voice come from?

"Mum, it'd only be for a day or two—what's the problem?"

"Look, I don't want to discuss this any longer. I would just prefer not to have Michael and Lilly here at the moment. I'm far too busy at this time of the year. Sorry, that's the end of it!"

It must be the menopause, Fudge deduced acidly as she trod upstairs on frozen feet. That was the first time she could ever remember her mother turning down visitors, especially if they only wanted to stay for a day or two. There had always been space in the big Ginnane house, and when every bed was occupied the attic was full of air beds and extra blankets, the fridge bursting with food, and the kitchen brimming with laughter. They'd even let the Teddy Boys sleep in the barn five years before, for heaven's sake! Her mother hadn't seen Lilly and Michael for years. Fudge had presumed she'd be thrilled. But clearly she wasn't, and it would be a long time before Fudge finally found out why.

~ * ~

Mary's hands were trembling violently when she placed the receiver in its cradle. For a long while, she just stared off into space, then she put her head in her hands and wept. Up in Dublin, Fudge would be forced to think up an excuse for Lilly, while here on Birch Rise she couldn't even think up one for herself. There was nothing in the world stopping them from coming down to Loughrua and, in fact, there was nothing that Mary wanted more—but she couldn't. She couldn't sit opposite him without touching his hand, nor walk beside him without taking his arm. It would be impossible to talk to him without looking deep into his eyes, impossible to listen without hanging on his every word. Everyone would see it, recognise it, know it. And Charlie, too. He wasn't blind, nor was he a fool, and he didn't deserve to be treated like one either. She was his life, and he, for that matter, hers. He'd given her a home and happiness, a past and a future. They'd shared the joys of parenthood and the heartbreak of it, too. Each had sworn to love and respect the other, and love and respect him, she would.

Out through the living room window, Mary watched as a single rain shower, a cold and dreary sheet of metal, moved away from Birch Rise and across the Brackens towards the hills beyond Loughrua Lake. The patchwork of fields, still vivid green in the deepest winter, were surrounded by hedgerows of dirty grey, as if autumn had sucked the very last drop of colour out of the tangle of woody briars. Only here and there, a holly bush laden with scarlet berries, or a wall of ivy, leapt out in contrast. Though the Irish never dared to share Bing Crosby's dream of a white Christmas, a fine powdering of snow lay over the distant hilltops like a greying, diaphanous tablecloth, and the sluggish, low-lying bank of cloud held the promise of more. Soon Christmas would come and go, and with it the old year making way for the new.

A new year? Another year. Not new. What was new when you were back-pedalling towards your forty-eighth birthday? When your children had found their wings and the nest was growing cold? Already the socks drying above the range no longer filled a whole row, and the number was shrinking as fast as she could blink. And when the only ones left belonged to Charlie and herself? What then?

A clutter of heifers stood crowded together on the stretch of bumpy fallow land behind the stables, their hindquarters turned towards the wind. As Mary watched them chew the cud in mesmerising monotony, the great heads dipping occasionally to tear bunches of grassy stalks from the lush green hummocks dotting the muddy ground, she wondered if animals ever felt lonely, or longed for something they couldn't have. Did they look into the future and shudder at the uncertainty of what lay ahead, or regret what might have been?

The sound of hefty winter boots clomping up the corridor made her start. A second later, Charlie appeared in the doorway behind her. Quickly, she wiped a last tear away and blinked back those threatening to come.

"All right, love? You look a bit wistful." His face was glowing from the chilly fresh air, his hair windswept. He didn't hear his wife sigh, but saw her broad shoulders rise and fall heavily.

"I was just wondering if cows ever felt lonesome."

Charlie knew not to scoff at such statements. Instead he joined her at the window and laid his hand on her waist. Together they gazed out over the yard to the fields behind.

"I wouldn't think so. Cows are gregarious animals, happy enough to be standing around all day chomping away."

"Wouldn't that be nice?"

"What then?"

"To be happy enough standing around all day. I ask myself if we humans are really blessed with all our senses, our awareness, our sentiments. Sometimes I think it would be grand not to be burdened with emotions, not to be enslaved by feelings."

As a quiver of uncertainty scurried through Charlie, he considered she might be just right. It'd be a fine thing not to know this dull weight of disquiet that settled in the depths of his stomach every time he found his wife staring blankly off across the gorse-studded countryside.

"That's a very sombre attitude altogether, Mrs. Ginnane," Charlie said, pulling Mary a little closer. "Isn't there a lot of joy in our lives?"

"There is, of course." She rested her head on his shoulder, and the weight in his stomach lifted. "And a lot to be thankful for, too."

"Indeed, there is." The farmer gave his wife a little squeeze. "I'll go and put the kettle on."

"Do that, love."

She watched as he pottered back towards the kitchen, smiling affectionately at the sight of his worn corduroy trousers sagging sadly at the seat.

In that instant, she made up her mind not to see Michael again. She hadn't cheated on her husband and never would, but her heart was doing so, and with every second spent thinking of the scatty Dubliner her guilt blossomed. They'd only seen each other a handful of times over the years since their first meeting on that long ago November day, yet each encounter released in her a flood of emotion too strong to suppress.

It had begun with a phone call thanking her for her hospitality and although pleasantries were dealt with in a matter of minutes, their conversation had lasted almost an hour. A letter followed and then another, the unspoken words between the lines filling Mary with delight and fascination. The quiet housewife had never met anyone quite like him, but swore, nevertheless, that her first reply would be the last.

Yet as weeks turned to months, their written exchanges offered not only a pleasant highlight in her daily farm routine, but on the contrary, they became an urgent necessity. With mounting excitement, Mary watched the driveway from the kitchen window, rushing anxiously to the front door when finally the postman's dung-spattered van came bouncing down the gravel lane. Afterwards, alone in her room, with Charlie out riding Shanagarry on the Brackens and the girls at school, she would first study the awkwardly scrawled address, then carefully tease open the plain envelope and let the rich abundance of words tumble out, relishing each and every one as she might a forbidden fruit.

He talked of his work, the lectures, paintings, pictures and books—always books. Everyday anecdotes became tales of adventure, simple thoughts, intricate philosophical ruminations. Mary's replies, in turn, were odysseys of exploration into the art historian's mind, venturing further than any other might dare. She foraged around in the far reaches of his contemplations, raising, with almost innocent simplicity, questions of insurmountable complexity. He fed her intellect with banquets of richness, her heart with wonder; she, on the other hand, nourished his soul with awe and understanding. For the rest of the world they were chalk and cheese, in theirs, they were kindred spirits separated by circumstance, clandestine soul mates.

A year later, they saw each other again when Mary agreed to collect Fudge in Ballsbridge, where she'd spent the first few days of the Halloween break with Lilly. Still friends despite the miles between them, they'd hatched plans to have a birthday party in McDermotts' Victorian house, inviting any Castleglen schoolmates who could guarantee to bring along eligible brothers or male friends. No pimples, greasy hair, or braces, if possible, thank you very much. When Mary nervously rang the front door bell on the morning after, it was Michael who answered. Worried she mightn't look glamorous enough in her woolly polo-necked jumper and Husky jacket, she could tell from the look on the man's face that it didn't matter a damn. They stood on the front steps for a long while smiling reticently, their hand clasped in the same prolonged handshake Charlie had observed from the yard gate twelve months before. Had he been watching now, Mary would have had considerably greater problems convincing him his imagination was playing tricks, and his fear unwarranted. What passed between Michael and Mary was plain as day.

Leaving the teenagers to clean up the party devastation, they'd walked the length of Dollymount strand and back again, only to turn around and repeat the whole process a second time. When they arrived back late in the afternoon, the girls were huffy and the mood subdued. They parted with exaggerated politeness, and contrary to Mary's expectations, Fudge refrained from making any comment during the long drive to Loughrua. At breakfast the next morning, every last salacious detail of Lilly's birthday party was reconstructed—who did what, who snogged with whom, who said what—but not one word was said about the fact that Mary had spent hours gazing out across the Irish Sea with Lilly McDermott's father. And nobody asked.

Months passed and the letters continued. Phone calls were rare, made only when the sprawling Birch Rise house was empty, the walls without ears. Then Mary would take off her apron, slip out of her shoes and curl up in the armchair opposite the bookcase, allowing herself the luxury of verbal exchange only passionate wool-gatherers and mind-travellers know best. Paradox as it may seem, her feelings for Charlie never dwindled; regardless of what had developed between herself and Michael, she knew that one man could never replace the other and vice versa. Michael was the water which let her mind blossom and grow, Charlie the earth, her toehold on life, her family, her home.

Meetings were scarce. A cup of coffee in an Athlone café six months later, a walk in Phoenix Park the following year. After that, an afternoon in the corner of Bewley's on Grafton Street in the midst of Christmas shoppers, and two very long strolls along the Salthill promenade, both while Michael was in Galway holding lectures in UCG. In five years they'd met little more than half a dozen times, but each encounter was as precious as the last. They never kissed, nor did they touch. The urgency to find a hotel hideaway suppressed and ignored; although the spark of excitement flamed each time his hand brushed hers, it was irrelevant for their relationship—a threat even. Occasionally, Michael would tuck that unruly wisp of hair behind Mary's ear, and before parting he would hold her close for a short moment while they whispered their goodbyes, she fleetingly breathing in his musky warmth and he, hers.

"Mary, love, where have you hidden the biscuits?" Charlie's voice called from the kitchen, causing her to start. The bubble of reverie burst.

"Sorry...? Oh, there are fig rolls on the top shelf of the kitchen press. I'll be with you right away."

Mary drew in a deep ragged breath, patted her hair, straightened the stripy apron with "Mum's the Best" printed on it and made her way down the hallway to the kitchen where she could hear her husband whistling, and the crackling sound of a packet of biscuits being ripped open.

Not at the same table. Not in the same house. Not together. She'd hated disappointing Fudge, and even worse, voluntarily sacrificing the chance of seeing Michael once again, but the house seething with children, the walls heavy with eyes and ears, and Charlie laden with jealous concern was a prospect she couldn't handle. One day, everything would surely get out of control, and now was the time to put an end to it.

She joined Charlie at the wooden table, and munching fig-filled biscuits, they began to discuss Sheila and the odd, fuzzy-haired Dublin man she'd apparently been doing a line with for quite some time and who nobody seemed to know anything about.

~ * ~

Fudge slammed the door so hard that the window frame rattled.

"What the hell is wrong with her?" She flung herself down on the bed and stared at the ceiling, her lips pressed into a pout. She was thoroughly pissed off.

"What is it?" Lilly looked up from an impressive looking book full of rock formations.

"Mum's too busy at Christmas to have visitors!"

"Oh."

Fudge smacked the wall angrily with the flat of her hand. "She never had too little time when the girls were younger and always screaming and making a mess! Now that they're old enough to help around the house and do most of the work, Mum's too bloody busy!"

"Maybe she'd just prefer to be alone with her family. She rarely sees you and Sheila."

"Aw, come on, Mum is always starving for visitors, I know her!"

"Look, let it go. She'll have her reasons. Now what about this party of ours?"

Fudge huffed. "And what about the men?"

With a flourish, Lilly whipped out a page of foolscap. "Okay, let's make a list. Who do you know?"

Fudge thought for a second. "Bernie."

"Bernie?"

"He's a bloke who works Saturday afternoons in the corner shop."

Lilly looked at her friend sceptically before scribbling the name on her list, but passed no remarks. "And who else?"

"That's it?"

"What do you mean, that's it?"

"I don't know anyone else—if I did, you'd know about it!" she yapped testily.

"Fudge, you've been in Dublin for a year and a half and that's all you have to offer?"

"Yep, in fact, come to think of it, I don't even know Bernie that well. Maybe you should cross him off the list."

Lilly irritably stroked the part-time shopkeeper off.

"Right," Fudge smirked. "How many do we have now?"

"Nobody."

"Mmm, that's about as many as we had a few minutes ago."

"A bit pathetic, if you ask me."

"It is, rather."

They gaped at each other for a while then Lilly shoved up her sleeves. "Okay, I'll invite all the guys from my year. They're not all God's gift to women, but there are a couple of potential candidates amongst them. You can ask some of those ornamental secretarial tarts to balance things out."

"That'll be an interesting combination!"

"Won't it just! We don't want any real competition, now do we?"

"Jeez, good thinking, Batman!"

The study book and coffee cups were pushed aside and as the list of party guests grew, goons at the bottom, hunks at the top, the disappointment of the abandoned Birch Rise visit subsided.

The last days before Christmas passed in a flurry of plans and filthy December weather, and when they parted ways for the holidays, both were already anxiously awaiting the new year. Fudge was happy to have her birthday behind her, thankful that the following year she'd be twenty. She was utterly sick of being a teenager. It was time to move on.

And time did move on. It flew. The much anticipated flat-warming party came and went in a flash, and was a greatly discussed event for months to come. There was smooching galore, spilt wine and drunken vultures. Lecherous would-be geology masters with snooty accents regressed to feeble creatures in the face of plunging cleavages and pearly painted nails. Bernie, who'd been invited anyway, arrived at three o'clock in the morning with a bottle of Blue Nun under one arm and a bubble-blowing slapper in high-heeled sandals under the other. The *craic* was mighty. Lilly did her fair share of wrestling with a bespectacled fellow-student who'd been fantasising about her in hiking boots and dungarees ever since they'd first met in The Buttery.

And Fudge? Well, as usual, she got stuck between two geezers who spent the whole night expostulating on eskers and glacial sediment. Dulling her senses on cheap wine, she was glad Julian couldn't see her, wedged securely between two pseudo-intellectual duds of boundless superficiality, a jam jar of Mosel paint stripper clutched in her hand. Fudge wondered mildly if she should take up smoking. A limp fag hanging from her lower lip would certainly complete the picture, and confirm Julian's impression of her. So near and yet so far.

Fudge observed Lilly gluttonously nibbling the Trinity student's ear as she lay on the floor between her bed and the cupboard amidst bowls of Tayto chips and peanuts that the poor man had ground into the carpet beneath them. A pang of envy scampered through her every time the wrestlers emitted alternate squeals of enthusiasm or grunts of appreciation. Thinking back to the night on Nassau Street, she asked herself if anything might have come of their encounter had events not taken such a ghastly turn for the worst. Might she ever get another chance?

He was still seeing the posh platinum blond cow with the black velvet hair-band; as it transpired, his new girlfriend was exactly as they had pictured her. College shoes, Hermés scarves, Louis Vuitton handbag. Fudge picked a bit of fluff off her jumble sale cardigan and flicked it into space. Perfectly sickening, by the sound of it. He could have her!

Downing the last of the wine and reaching for more, Mary Ginnane's daughter came to a decision ironic in its similarity to her mother's. She was going to stop thinking about that McDermott man, for once and for all! This ruling filled her with optimism. She would quit shilly-shallying through life, dithering away her precious youth between St. Stephen's Green and Bushy Park, between wisdom-spouting, smart-alec gargoyles and part-time working class heroes from corner shops.

And one thing was for sure—her virginity would have to go. It was an impediment, a restrictive shackle hampering her progression. It was impossible to move on hobbled as she was. How could she start working on any kind of decent relationship if her whole time was spent wondering whether every man who crossed her path was worthy enough of doing the deed? If she waited any longer, she might as well go and take holy orders. What good did it do waiting for Mister Right to sort her out, when chastity snatchers were only interested in looting bodies under twenty-one—twenty-two, at a push? If you were still carting your maidenhood around after that, there was something seriously wrong with you, and as a result, the poachers of purity trotted away to case another joint. Let some artful dodger plunder her body and be off with the booty! She'd sleep peacefully at night, not troubling her head with the treasures locked up in her safe. Dublin was teeming with eager pilferers; it shouldn't be any bother at all.

~ * ~

She was still trying to dump the goods long after the buds had burst open on the trees encompassing St. Stephen's Green six months later. Once again, it was Friday afternoon in the city and, as always, the early summer sunshine had enticed workers out of their sleazy offices and onto the park benches and freshly cut lawns. Fudge was sitting opposite the duck pond, her jeans rolled up to the knees, letting the insipid rays warm her startlingly white legs. Her head was bent over a college pad full of notes, a lollipop stuck in her mouth. The dark mass of unruly hair had grown, falling like a curtain on either side of her face, a protective screen from the outside world.

Every now and then, for a minute or two, she would look up and observe the ducks gliding around in pairs on the slick surface, before lowering her head once again to her books. She wasn't really concentrating on the untidy scribbles, the feet passing in front of her on the path being of greater interest. Baby feet in tiny sandals, shiny brogues and orthopaedic loafers. Further up, shapely calves, skinny sticks, bow legs and knock knees, hairy ankles and bruised shins. Slurping wetly on the caramel-flavoured sweet, Fudge contemplated the pair of brown desert boots standing on the gravel before her. Crikey, they were huge! The seam at one toe was threatening to burst open, the fettered foot fighting for freedom! She chortled behind the shield of hair.

"Finnula?" The desert boots moved a step closer. Had someone said her name? The monster feet remained where they were. A Dublin accent, broad, but timid. Had to be Bernie from the late night shop. *Jesus, spare me*, she thought, wanting to enjoy the precious college lunch break undisturbed. *Sod off and leave me alone.*

"Long time, no see." No such luck.

Impatiently pushing the swath of heavy hair behind her shoulder, Fudge glanced up, a clever Dick remark teetering on the tip of her tongue, but when she saw who was standing there, the words came to a screeching halt. Rosy-cheeked, scrubbed and as large as life, there he stood. A blast from the past. The sandy red hair sticking up in a boyish cow's lick, the grey eyes nervously expectant, questioning. Ballyglass Johnny. Fudge frowned, not due to the fact that his unannounced appearance was in any way inopportune, but because her stomach had done an unanticipated flip at the sight of his crooked smile. For a while she was caught off guard, her mouth open in a slightly unbalanced "o", the lollipop hanging loosely from the inside of her cheek. When it slipped out of her mouth she failed to notice the summer breeze which coiled a wisp of rebellious hair around the gummy stick and tugged it from her grasp.

"Am I bodderin' you?" he ventured, the strawberry blond eyebrows knitting together quizzically.

"No... No, not at all. I'm just surprised to see you."

He thrust his hand self-consciously into his trouser pockets, glanced indecisively at the park bench beside Fudge, then up the busy pathway towards the park gates. Stay or run was written all over the young man's face. Fudge put him out of his misery by patting the seat beside her, but not before stealthily checking that none of the Merrion Hall secretarial buzzards were circling nearby, an instinctive reaction she immediately hated herself for.

"C'mon, sit down, or are you in a hurry?" she asked tactfully, giving him an avenue of escape should the impression he wanted to stay transpire to be naive presumptuousness.

"No, I'm on my lunch break." Relaxing a little, he settled down beside her in a laid-back pose, the ankle of one leg resting on the knee of the other. Over a black tee-shirt, he was wearing a faded jeans jacket, the collar flicked up at the back. He smiled a crooked, James Dean smile—or what he probably hoped was one.

"Been yonks, hasn't it?"

"Ages, not counting last year, of course." The words were out before she could stop them. Christ! When would she learn to think and then speak?

"Oh, righ', sorry about that... I was only mortified. Paul's a head case. Langers, he was."

"Mm, quite."

"He yer boyfriend? Lilly's brudder?" Was it her imagination, or did the inquiring look reveal more than the mere social exchange it was surely meant to be?

"Nope, that didn't work out."

"Pity, but you used to hate him anyways, righ'?" He smirked at the idea of it, unaware that his remark was cutting through Fudge like glass. "Hope Paul had nuttin' to do with it." Johnny continued to grin broadly, sublimely ignorant of the fact that it had everything to do with it. Everything.

"No… Em, are you working in the city now, or what?" she quickly added, having sworn not to waste any more precious thoughts on Julian McDermott and desperate to steer him onto another course.

"Sometimes. I work for an express delivery service out in Blackrock."

"Not one of those hair-raising white van drivers who rule the inner city streets and give lily-livered women drivers heart tremors?" Fudge bantered with a chortle, feebly endeavouring to inject the conversation with jocularity.

"Exactly one of those."

Shit. Fudge, cringing at her stupidity, gave him an apologetic look, but Johnny, less awkward now, was still smiling.

"Peachy job, actually. Out 'n' about all day, better than bein' stuck on an assembly line, or on the dole. None of us made it very far."

"Oh… and Paul?"

"When he's not chasing birds, he's packin' boxes in a biscuit factory." Johnny's expression was neutral. She couldn't tell whether he thought having a job packaging custard creams was good or not, and decided not to ask.

"And Prof…?"

"Ha! Good old Prof. We didn't call him 'Professor' for nuttin', ya know. Got himself a real snazzy number workin' for a computer company floggin' word processors, software an' so on. No flies on him!"

"So he's a sales rep. Goodness, he must be well into his twenties now—ancient really. Did he ever get married?" Fudge tittered inwardly at the memory of the short, bespectacled man with the froggy eyes and curly hair, wondering at the same time what kind of girl would go for him.

"Na, not yet. Haven't seen him for ages, either. Works down the country a lot. Come to think of it, as far as I know, he's doing a line with a Galway girl."

"A Galway girl! I thought we were all ignorant culchies!"

"You are, too!" He laughed, completely at ease now. "But this one has brains—got a college degree an' all, if I'm to believe what my local barman tells me!"

"Well, fair play to him. A culchie with brains—who would have thought of that!" They both had a giggle then fell silent for a while. An obese duck heaved itself out of the pond and waddled cautiously towards Johnny's bread-coloured desert boots, ignoring on its quest for food the stream of hurrying legs marching smartly back to their office desks. Fascinated, Fudge watched as glistening pearls of water rolled like mercury from the silken back, leaving a dark chain of droplets snaking across the path. In a flash, the watery trail was trampled into the ground, and what existed a moment before was gone already. The duck, establishing that the pair of feet in front of the park bench offered little in the way of sustenance, turned mechanically and zigzagged its way back to the water's edge.

"A pity we never saw each other again." Johnny was staring out across the pond.

"Yes, I know... Did you hear that Lilly got kicked out of Castleglen?"

"Yeah, we got it from Bertie Barrett. Hope it wasn't our fault."

"No, Lilly was always getting away with murder. It had to happen one day." Fudge fiddled nervously with the copy books on her lap, suddenly aware of how silly she must look with the jeans rolled up her startlingly white shins. "We're sharing a flat near Bushy Park now."

"No way! What's she doin'?"

"Geology—at Trinity. Don't ask me why."

"Geology! What the hell does she want with geology?"

"My very words."

She expected him to ask what she was doing, but he didn't. A silence settled between them once again and after a minute Johnny looked at this watch. Turning to Fudge he opened his mouth, then closed it again. A moment passed, and when neither of them said anything, he stood up and shoved his hands back into the trouser pockets.

"Well, I'd better go—still got a few rounds to do."

"Yeh, have to get going myself." Fudge held up her books. "Secretarial course."

Johnny nodded, smiling. A secretarial course wasn't as scary as geology, but then again, he hadn't seen the vultures. Shifting uneasily from one foot to the other, he hovered a second longer.

"Righ', maybe we'll bump into each other again."

"Maybe, who knows."

"See ya 'round."

"Bye."

He turned and walked away in the direction of the park gates. Fudge watched him go, his unruly, straw-coloured hair jutting up in the throngs passing through St. Stephen's Green. She sighed. There was something about the man that always made her feel a little sad, which made her want to say sorry and, strangely enough, made her want to take him in her comforting arms. He had a nice, perky little arse, too, she observed just before he disappeared round a curve in the path.

She remained on the bench for a while daydreaming, the books on her lap forgotten. Lunch break over, the flow of feet passing along had slackened, the midday bustle diminishing. A tired looking, middle-aged woman with two bulging carrier bags in her hands and smoker's rings under her eyes shuffled by, and soon after that, a businessman going at a trot, his stripy tie flapping over his shoulder, a disconcerted look on his face. *He'll be needing an excuse for his boss*, Fudge thought as the man veered off around the duck pond towards Leeson Street and out of sight. When she looked back the desert boots were there on the path before her once again. The same ones, with the seam threatening to burst open at the toe.

"Would ya like to go out for a drink tonight?"

"What...?" Fudge lifted her head in surprise. Plunging his hands nervously in and out of his pockets, Johnny had her fixed with a questioning glance.

"I thought we could have a drink together..."

"A drink...?"

"Or whatever."

"Em... okay, sure. Why not?"

"Magic. In town?"

"Well, we could meet halfway. Ballsbridge, or somewhere."

"Grand, the pub down from the RDS? Normal pub—nuttin' trendy."

"Okay."

"Eight o'clock?"

"Fine."

"Deadly, see ya later."

"See you."

He turned to leave then stopped. "Em... You might want to take that lollipop out of yer hair first."

"Of course... Bye." He was long gone by time she realised what he'd said.

~ * ~

"You're what?"

"Having a drink with Johnny later on."

Lilly went into hoots of laughter and fell back on the quilt, pounding the bed with her feet.

"I don't believe you—that's hilarious!"

"What's so hilarious about it?" Fudge felt slightly peeved. She knew exactly what her friend was thinking.

"Well, you know... Johnny! Where are you going to meet? The Shelbourne Hotel?" That sent her into further gales of hilarity.

Fudge said nothing. She picked up her wash bag and twenty pence for the meter and headed stony-faced to the bathroom, refraining from slamming the flat door behind her as she went. When she returned forty-five minutes later, bathed and manicured, she was heaving with wrath. Lilly looked remorseful.

"Sorry, Fudge, there's nothing wrong with Johnny, I didn't mean to put him down."

"I know exactly what you're thinking! Johnny—and Paul—were good enough for you when you were bored at school! Have you forgotten the hayloft—the Loughrua dance?"

"That was only a bit of fun, we weren't looking for boyfriends."

"Does that mean that every man I go out with now has to be the potential father of my unborn children!"

"Of course not, but it's nice to build up a certain social circle of friends..."

"Social fecking circles! Don't talk to me about social circles! What good has it done me? Where are all those eligible students with horsy backgrounds and stashes of dough? Those friends of yours from Trinity either bore me to tears, or disappear after two dates! It's all very well for you, you've had your fair share of boyfriends! Do you have to worry about ending up on the shelf? Go on, take your pick! There are enough men sniffing around at our doorstep, but never for me! Never for me! They're all the same, those college dicks with Dalkey accents. I hate them all... Do you hear me? I hate them! And your brother, too!"

Fudge flung her wash bag onto a chair and missed, the contents spilling out onto the floor in a shambles of tubes and bottles, powders and paints, shaving contraptions and manicuring utensils. Lilly peered at the welter of cosmetics strewn across the carpet then at Fudge, whose freshly washed hair was hanging around her fuming face in long, limp rat's tails.

"I'm sorry, Fudge, I didn't meant to..."

"Look, forget it, will you? It's just a drink, okay?"

"You'll say I was asking for him?"

"I will."

Later, after the disgruntled Loughrua girl had departed, leaving a swath of flowery perfume floating in the air, Lilly asked herself how

Julian had managed to pop into their discussion and what he had to do with Fudge's wrath, anyway.

~ * ~

At quarter past eight the Ballsbridge pub was still quiet, but already a hazy sheet of cigarette smoke hovered beneath the low ceiling. A row of male heads at the bar turned as she pushed her way in through the heavy swing doors, quickly returning to the line of pints before them after a brief scrutiny of the goods was completed and classified as acceptable, though not of superior quality. A few couples sat dotted around the lounge, heads together in conversation.

A young girl in dizzyingly elevated stiletto heels and brittle, chemically bleached hair tottered from the bar to an alcove grasping a vodka and white lemonade in blood-red claws. The stretch boob-tube was as flat as a board and the hips boyishly narrow. *Fourteen if she's a day*, Fudge decided sceptically, remembering the escapade over the wall which consequently led to Lilly's expulsion from Castleglen. The peroxide blond girl-child hardly belonged in a boarding school for young ladies, but surely somewhere her parents were at home happily watching telly believing their daughter to be upstairs listening to records, or at a friend's house doing homework.

The barman appeared unconcerned, yet given the fact that he himself hardly looked any older than the girl, and thus unlikely to have teenage children of his own, his indifference wasn't surprising. The strife of parenthood was an abstract phenomenon hovering beyond the borderline of their awareness. A singularity of life lying in wait for another generation, not theirs. *Well then,* Fudge mused, not without a touch of gloating righteousness, *they were going to get the surprise of their lives one day.*

Moving between the tables and lounge stools, she squinted down the length of the room, deciding to turn on her heels if Johnny wasn't there. She'd purposely arrived fifteen minutes late and detested nothing more than sitting alone in a pub with everyone around placing bets on the chances of her being stood up or not. Already regulars were eyeing her as they might a greyhound prior to a race, and judging by their expressions, the stakes weren't overwhelming.

Feck this for a lark, she thought suddenly, and was turning to flee when she heard someone call her name.

"Finnula, over here." Johnny's sandy head popped over the low wooden partition of a dimly lit alcove, a toothy smile wrapped around his blushing face. "Thought for a minute you weren't comin'," he said, clearly relieved.

Equally relieved, but gracefully hiding it, Fudge slipped out of her jacket and sat down opposite him. "Sorry—the bus, as usual."

They gawped awkwardly at each other for a while, both waiting for the stroke of inspiration that would help them on their way to witty, carefree conversation. As always, inspiration took its time in coming, giving her the opportunity for a nippy once-over. She liked what she saw: the bashful face, the cornfield hair, the faded blue jeans and meticulously ironed white shirt all emphasising the spatter of summer freckles marching across the bridge of his nose.

"What'll ya have to drink?" he asked, the freckles rippling as he spoke.

"A Stag, thanks."

As he walked over to the bar, she suddenly became aware of a flutter of excitement scuttling around the pit of her stomach once again. Was it the nostalgic memory of her first kiss? The air of secrecy which electrified their meeting? Was it the uncertainty of how the evening might develop, or simply the fact that in the well-fitting jeans his arse looked perfectly irresistible?

By the time he came back with the drinks, the tiny fluttering had become wild flapping, and Fudge hurriedly downed half her glass of cider in a futile attempt to drench it. Her concerns were unfounded; before her glass was empty they were deep in animated discourse and Johnny was sitting next to, rather than opposite her. That long ago Halloween was relived in every tiny detail, the barn, the dance, the lakeside promenade, the kiss. Above all, the kiss. Two Stags later, Fudge was wallowing up to her ears in romantic reminiscence.

"It was my first, you know."

"Go 'way, yer takin' the mick!"

"No, honest to God, my first French kiss."

"Janey, I thought you'd been years at it!"

"Well, that's what I wanted you to think."

They chortled at the idea and moved a little closer. A while later, he laid the arm, which had been stretched casually along the back of the seat, across her shoulder, and throwing caution to the wind, Fudge decided to enjoy every wicked moment of it. All of a sudden, the scent of plain soap and shaving cream penetrated her slightly cider-dulled senses, promptly hurtling her into a time warp where the far-off fragrance of saddle wax and freshly turned hay filled her with nostalgic yearning, and later, with plain old animal longing.

She didn't want to blame it on the cider, and it wasn't the bout of wistfulness. The huffy recalcitrance she'd felt as she left the Rathgar flat had lingered somewhere in the corner of her mind, but it wasn't that either. Nor was it the memory of the gushing geology would-be studs with mouths full of hot potatoes and their brains in their Y-fronts. And it wasn't Julian. The coward. First spouting words of appeasing flatter then scuttling off with his tail between his legs at the first nasty disagreeability.

There was, in fact, absolutely nothing whatsoever she could blame it on, and as it was, there didn't have to be; Fudge never for one moment regretted a thing, and later, waiting for the last bus, it was the reserved country girl who hinted they might go back to his flat for a cup of proverbial coffee. The question of how she would return to Rathgar was not posed for fear it might require answering.

They sat on the top of the 7A double-decker, right up at the front with a panorama view of Dublin Bay as the ageing vehicle lurched and swayed its way down the coast. Like a pearly necklace, a glimmering crescent of neon lights separated the city from the inky blackness of the Irish Sea. Only now and then, pinpoints of light moving sluggishly along the horizon revealed that out there ships were labouring through the night towards a safe harbour.

Japers, Fudge thought a trifle woozily, all at once terrified of her own courage, *I hope I get myself safely docked tonight!* She was unexpectedly alert, wildly grasping the naive notion that this might remain a social visit. Observing his reflection in the windscreen, and the way his eyebrows were knitting slightly, causing a pair of inverted commas to appear above his nose, she realised he was probably thinking the very same thing. The poor man was clearly under pressure to perform. Had she taken leave of her senses? If she told him she was a virgin, he'd throw her off the bus in Blackrock and it would take her hours to walk home. *Better not tell him*, she considered incisively, *I won't get far in these high heels.*

A moment later, he caught her watching him and the inverted commas disappeared temporarily. Nervously, he took her hand, wishing he were back in the warm, protective womb of the Ballsbridge pub. Closing time had come too soon and once ejected out into the mild June night, there was no going back. They were on their own. The banter came harder, the bonhomie as bothersome as plodding through ankle-deep muck in oversized Wellingtons.

Johnny, in turn, tried to sneak a look at Finnula's reflection in the window before them. She was deep in thought, the dark head lowered as she contemplated her high-heeled shoes. He relaxed somewhat. If her footwear was all she had to worry about, then there was no reason for him to be getting his knickers in a twist. Still, for some reason he was terrified. The bus listed dangerously towards the curb as it pulled up in front of the shopping centre and for a moment they were thrown together. In that instant the last remnants of doubt dissolved. They looked at each other and laughed, both silently conceding that one didn't take the last bus from Ballsbridge to Dun Laoghaire on a Friday night for the sake of a cup of Nescafé.

Johnny didn't live in Ballyglass any more, he explained as he fiddled with the door lock of a squat little building in a residential cul-de-sac two minutes away from the main shopping street. He'd long since given up trying to make his father understand that he was far too old to catch a clip on the ear for coming home late. Each explanation had earned him another swatting, and the day Johnny came home with his first pay package was the day he moved out.

Three feet back from the house wall, a chipped iron railing any child could easily vault did its utmost to keep the outside world at bay. Tufts of fluffy green moss spewed out of the gutter clogging the rusty drainpipe which slanted precariously away from wall. A scraggly network of dappled ivy clawed its way across the pebbledash and up around the chimney stack where the woody tentacles threatened to prise the slate tiles from the slightly sagging roof.

The small bed-sitter in the basement, however, was clean and comfortably furnished, albeit in a typically bachelor manner—no frills, no pernickety paraphernalia, no fussy fittings. Mercifully, the bed was made, a blue and green checked plaid rug neatly draped over the hollow-backed construction. A disarray of greying sheets, socks skulking under chairs and underpants soaking in the sink would have sent her sprinting back to Rathgar in the very highest of high heels.

They stood gawkily in the middle of the room for a long time saying nothing until, without warning, a slow, slithering snake of tension rose its head between them and threatened to gobble up the fragile ease they'd so painstakingly managed to establish.

"The coffee!" Johnny almost shouted, fighting for composure. This scenario had not been rehearsed, his expectations for the evening having been long since exceeded when Fudge nodded happily in acceptance of a third Stag. That she'd end up wide-eyed and inclined in his flea-pit pad was way beyond what he might ever have dared to bargain for. Yet here she was, and to make matters worse, his vigorously practised countenance of savoir faire was crumbling hard and fast.

"I'd love that," Fudge breathed.

"Luv wha'?" His heart scribbled. Was he going to have to start performing already?

"A cup of coffee." She blinked at him, bewildered.

"Oh, righ'... Milk, sugar?"

"Anything."

She sat down on the bed and watched as he pottered back and forth, opening and closing cupboards, laying out matching mugs, sniffing the milk and filling the sugar bowl. Lilly would have had him spread-eagled two minutes inside the door. "No bloody messing around," she'd said in answer to one of Fudge's insistent queries regarding the whole virginity-losing business. "Make up your mind, tonight's the night, and then just get on with it." Lilly spoke with the expertise of one who loses her maidenhood on a daily basis, when in fact, she'd only mislaid it once and had little interest in ever finding it again. If Fudge remembered correctly, her flatmate had purposely disposed of her innocence in the sand dunes at Brittas beach the summer after her seventeenth birthday, later rewarding her accomplice with a bag of oleaginous chips and two portions of cod for his troubles.

"Get yourself well plastered," she'd advised sagely. "But don't mix your drinks—wouldn't want to woof your cookies in the middle of it!"

"Enchanting," Fudge commented. "What happened to romance?"

"Oh, fuck that. There's plenty of time for romance when you know what you're doing. The main thing is to get it in—and out again, of course."

"In and out."

"Precisely. Wham bam, thank you, ma'am."

"I see... Does it hurt?"

"S'pose it's a bit like getting your shins bashed in a good hockey match. You don't feel the pain if you're having fun." Lilly replied learnedly. "And anyway, if you're pissed out of your noggin you won't notice a thing."

Even then, Fudge had viewed her best friend's advice with considerable scepticism and when, a few minutes later, Johnny asked if she'd like a shot of anything in the coffee, she fearlessly declined. The problem didn't lie in her lack of experience, but more in the undoubted wealth of his, yet when she noticed his fingers trembling as he placed the mug on the bedside table, the Galway girl knew everything would be all right. She had her reasons for being anxious and he, quite evidently, his. They were quits.

It was long after midnight before either of them began to relax. In the cosy crater of Johnny's bachelor bed they lay entwined, gravity pressing them together like nature's helping hand. Flitting to and fro in time, Fudge's senses were filled with the saddle soap and straw of Birch Rise's tack room one minute, and the coffee and cotton smells of the small Dun Laoghaire flat the next. The same man, almost six years later, but this time their bodies were no longer separated by layers of scratchy winter clothing or timid adolescent reservation. Now they lay skin to skin, breath to breath, the barriers down, inhibitions cast aside.

For an "uncouth element" as Miss Gibbons would have put it, he was surprisingly tender, and any covert discriminatory thoughts concerning his worthiness rapidly slipped away leaving only the conviction that what they were doing was right. His kisses were soft, his touch light, and as their embrace became more passionate Fudge let instinct take over. Every unrehearsed gesture was smooth and flowing, a spontaneous choreography of intertwining limbs, each movement, sensual intuition. As he moved above her, she clasped him tightly, anticipation and eagerness creating an exhilarating mixture of emotions that startled her in their intensity, and when at last the moment came, when the short, sharp pain swiftly eased, taking with it the burden of virginity, she let her body soar.

"Don't be such a bloody dreamer! An orgasm is absolutely out of the question first time," Lilly had remarked with her usual air of proficiency. "You can forget that to start with."

In an absurd moment of intoxicating headiness the words scurried through Fudge's mind, making her want to laugh, to scream! She was on a roller coaster surging upwards with dizzying speed, hurtling aloft, and high up, teetering on the crest of something indescribably exquisite, she did shout, a loud, throaty outburst of pleasure, before plunging down the other side in a rush of physical and emotional recklessness.

Some time passed before she registered the ticking of the bedside alarm clock, the dripping of a leaking tap, the roughness of over-starched bed linen against her thigh, and Johnny's warm breathing in her ear. *Jeepers*, she thought giddily, *it never felt like that at Butlins.*

All of a sudden she wanted to bawl her eyes out, and if the former boarding school girl had known anything at all about *la petite mort* and its fickle intricacies, then she'd have realised that this was a perfectly common occurrence, just as normal as the fact that Johnny, like most of his post-coital peers, had fallen fast asleep and was now beginning to emit nasal whifflings of deep satisfaction.

In the wee hours of the morning, just before her left leg ceased to exist under the weight of his body, and the first rays of watery Saturday morning light were cutting through the chipped iron railings in front of the basement window, Fudge finally dared to extricate herself from Johnny's clinch. He mumbled incoherently, flopped over onto his back and opened a gluey eye.

"Mornin' luv." The sandy hair stood away in all directions like a halo of straw. "Where ya goin'?"

"Nowhere... The loo, shower. Don't mind me." Fudge felt around in the mound of clothes next to the bed, her nakedness startlingly obvious in daytime reality.

The haystack mop snuggled up close, the freckled nose against her breast. "Sorry 'bout that... em... just-in-time method, not very romantic," he gurgled sleepily.

The freshly deflowered country girl hadn't the foggiest idea what he meant, but found out seconds later when she pulled a tee-shirt down over her belly. Her nose creased into a wrinkle of mild distaste. Charming, she thought, realising at the same time that she, in fact, would have a lot more explaining to do than he, and fiddling self-consciously with the corner of the stiffly starched bed sheet, an appropriate approach was engineered.

"Johnny?"

"Hmm..." He was drifting off again.

"Who does your laundry?"

One eye unglued again and fixed her inquiringly. "Me mother. Why?"

"That mightn't be a good idea... Em..."

"You worried she'll get in the forensic experts, or wha'?" He sniggered into Fudge's armpit.

"No... It's just that I am—*was*—a virgin and..."

"You were a virgin? When?"

"Yesterday."

He thought about that for a moment. "And you're not today?"

"No... not unless I dreamt it all." She smirked coyly at him.

Johnny went alarmingly pale and then puce as he exploded into a stomach-clutching fit of hysterical guffawing.

"Sweet mother of jaysus!" he bellowed heartily. "An' I thought you'd forgotten to take yer tights off!"

At that, Fudge likewise collapsed into a seizure of frenzied laughter, and later, after a feed of burnt toast, two cups of stewed tea and a freezing cold shower, they took up where they had left off the night before.

Twelve

Fudge waddled slightly splay-legged into the Rathgar flat early Sunday afternoon with dark circles under her eyes, her tee-shirt on inside out and a smile of worldly contentment smeared all over her face. Lilly was not amused.

"You could have called, at least," she barked before Fudge had time to close the flat door.

"Since when do I have to report to you? Can't remember you ever signing out prior to one of your three day foraging trips through Trinity Hall."

"I don't forage, thank you very much."

The Galway girl kicked off her high heels, dropped into one of the threadbare armchairs positioned before the redundant fireplace and closed her eyes. The smirk of satisfaction remained spread across the pale freckled features. She felt gloriously, deliciously, voluptuously female and it would take more than Lilly's snottiness to faze her.

"Where were you anyway?"

"Butlins."

"Don't be so damn stupid. Are you drunk?"

"Nope."

"What were you doing?" Lilly's curiosity was rampant.

"Getting my shins bashed in a hockey match."

A moment passed before the penny dropped and immediately the testiness disappeared from her voice. "Finnula Ginnane, you did not!"

"Did, too."

"With him? With Ballyglass Johnny? All the way?"

"All the way and back again—several times. And I don't regret a second of it!"

"Oh, my God, oh, my God!" Lilly was already dragging the second armchair over to the first. "You filthy little tart! Tell me everything— all the ins and outs!"

And Fudge did, in every detail, the craving to relive it all opening the floodgates to her own private world. She told of the double-decker passing along the twinkling necklace of lights separating the city from the stygian Irish Sea, of the simple bachelor flat tidy enough to make any mother's heart bleed, of the cups of coffee left to grow cold on the sloping bedside table, of their nervousness, his gentleness, and of the fact that lying intertwined, skin to skin, it no longer mattered where they came from or where they were going.

Her eyes still closed, Fudge talked about tarry tea in the tiny hours of the morning and the wishy-washy June sunlight as it tiptoed through the black iron railings, over the bumpy hillside landscape of jumbled bedclothes, and across the smooth plain of their naked backs. When finally, lost in the fresh, tangible memory of it all, Fudge recounted the reckless roller coaster rush, she failed to notice the blank facade of envy which had crept into Lilly's expression. The glimmer of mischievous curiosity sputtered and died; for all her promiscuous adventures in the arms of Dublin's up-and-coming social elite, Lilly bitterly missed the tender intimacy her friend had known in the gloomy confines of Ballyglass Johnny's Dun Laoghaire bed-sitter.

"And now?"

"Now what?"

"Are you seeing him again?"

"Maybe I will, maybe I won't." Fudge's secretive smile was serene.

"So it was just a nice bit of good old smutty sex. A virginity-removing bonk, so to speak."

"Honestly, Lilly! No, it wasn't!" Fudge thought for a minute, her forehead wrinkling. "Perhaps we both wanted to follow up on something special we started on the Loughrua promenade years ago."

Lilly made a gagging noise. "How moving. Excuse me, but I don't feel any urgent desire to follow up on the hayloft petting session I had with greasy-haired Paul!" She struggled to keep the sting of envy out of her voice.

Puzzled, Fudge regarded her friend. "You don't have to, Lilly, you don't have to."

The shrill jangle of the front door bell broke the mounting tension and both girls jumped instinctively to their feet.

"Who the hell is that on Sunday afternoon." Fudge said, rushing to the bay window overlooking the quiet suburban street.

"My visitors!" Lilly piped before clattering out of the flat towards the stairs. "Could you throw the kettle on?"

"You're expecting visitors?" But already the other girl was halfway to the front door and a moment later excited chattering could be heard in the hallway. Oh God, some college nobs stopping by for afternoon tea. That was all she needed. Fudge vaguely wondered if Lilly wasn't putting on display the kind of company she felt her flatmate should be keeping. *Well, let her. They won't impress me!* She slithered rebelliously down into the armchair, her bare feet up on the coffee table and arms folded over her belly in a pose of slovenly indifference. *They can make their own shagging tea!*

Outside the flat door a woman's West Brit voice chirped exclamations of sycophantic enthusiasm.

"How wonderful to meet you. Gosh, you're *sooo* kind to have us. I *would* hate to put you out."

Jesus, this one appeared to be a particularly hard-core, top-drawer anglophile. Her treacly amicability was enough to give any snowman heartburn, and as the door swung open Fudge could feel a bout of indigestion coming on. Lilly bounced into the room first, her eyes sparkling.

"Surprise, surprise!" she cheeped piercingly, stepping aside to let her guests enter.

Fudge blinked. A walking, talking porcelain doll glided across the carpet, hips swaying in a practised Paris catwalk swagger. Her face, frighteningly artificial in its unblemished, pristine purity was emphasised by the ice-blond hair swept back in a painfully tight, fully controlled ponytail. The rapidly advancing outstretched hand was infuriatingly slender and hung in a slightly dislocated fashion from an anorexic wrist, almost as if the weight of the slimline gold bracelet was too much to bear. A slate-grey silk top and pearly earrings set off the green-blue iceberg eyes; the never-ending length of her pedigree legs were accentuated by punctiliously ironed black slacks. Never in all her life had Fudge felt more like a tinker's dog than at that moment. She remained slouched in the armchair, mechanically raising her arm to reciprocate the damp "dead fish" handshake.

"Hi, I'm Millicent," the ash-blond automaton exhaled. "I'm *sooo* pleased to meet you. Finnula, am I right? I've heard *sooo* much about you."

Who the f...? Smiling vacantly, Fudge struggled to place the woman. Millicent? Hardly a name she would forget. Was she supposed to know her? Hoping for assistance, she swivelled a glance in the direction of her flatmate, who was busy embracing the ice queen's companion with her usual exaggerated exuberance. When Lilly finally disentangled herself, allowing the man to step into the room, Fudge's lopsided grin slithered off the side of her face, the expression remaining there leaving no doubt whatsoever as to what she thought of Lilly's surprise.

"Hello, Finnula, you don't mind us stopping by, do you?" Julian McDermott was looking down at her from lofty heights. "Lilly insisted we visit."

"Oh God, no... I'm absolutely thrilled," she oozed, not without a touch of sarcasm. "Your sister might have had the decency to warn me though."

"Don't mind us, we're just passing through." His eyes flickered over the back-to-front tee-shirt, tousled hair and dark-ringed eyes. Albeit untrue to form, he thankfully abstained from making any comment, his features remaining tactfully blank.

Why now? Why not next week, next month, or never? Afraid to move for fear the scent of the weekend's lovemaking she felt so sure was emanating from every pore might waft up into the air between them, she observed the Englishwoman's sleek elegance, her fragile beauty, her grace. A stinging spark of fury sprung up within her. The bitch. No wonder her fancied her, with that cold "dead fish" handshake any marine biologist would die for. *Is she like a dead fish in bed, too?*

As if she could somehow read her roommate's thought, Lilly broke in. "I thought it would be a nice surprise. You two haven't seen each other for ages. Now, tea or coffee?"

"Just don't expect me to make it!" Fudge suddenly yapped, the words spilling out involuntarily. Millicent's smooth brow furrowed fretfully, her air of sang-froid ruffled.

Julian turned to Lilly. "Look, maybe this wasn't a good idea—just barging in."

"You're not barging in—I invited you, remember? And anyway, it's not as if you're a complete stranger, for heaven's sake!" Lilly glared at Fudge. "You don't have to be so bloody bad-mannered—he's my brother!"

"I know who the fuck he is! I just don't feel like socialising!" She could feel the situation getting horribly out of control, yet was utterly helpless to stop it. Those words weren't her own—they couldn't be! The arctic beauty began to wring her hands and look pleadingly at Julian. Lilly was beginning to fume.

"Jesus, why are you in such a filthy humour?" she bristled. "I would have thought your wild fling might have cheered you up a bit, but you're as frustrated as ever!"

Fudge leapt to her feet. "Go on! Why don't you give them all the bloody particulars of my private life while you're at it?"

"What private life, you hypocrite! You didn't bother to spare me all the juicy details of your sordid weekend antics! Why so demure all of a sudden?"

"You cow! How could you? I'd only just got in the door... I wasn't ready for this!"

Julian took Millicent's hand and steered the fretting woman towards the stairway. "Listen, I'm sorry. This really isn't the right time for a visit." Once again, he cautiously regarded Fudge's back-to-front tee-shirt, a look the incensed country girl didn't neglect to register. "I didn't realise you'd just come home."

"Now look what you've done!" Lilly was virtually screeching. "You're acting like a bloody commoner, Fudge! I wouldn't have thought a couple of nights shacked up with one could turn you into a pleb so quickly!"

"You rotten bitch!"

Fudge's explosion of profanity already had the neighbours across the street running to their windows. The icy blonde emitted a squeak of distress and scurried down the stairs, leaving Julian hovering in the flat doorway.

"Em... Girls, come on," he ventured, but was immediately cut off as Fudge turned upon him.

"Why don't you piss off, Julian? You're great at legging it off every time the situation starts getting a little unpleasant. What are you waiting for? Was there something your sister forgot to mention? Oh, of course! She omitted to explain I spent the whole night getting my brains fucked out by a van driver in a seedy cellar bed-sitter!" She paused for breath, her whole body trembling with rage and the horror of what she'd just said.

Julian took a step towards her. "Finnula... I'm sorry, I didn't realise..."

"No, you didn't realise, and you still don't realise. Now, sod off, for Christ's sake, and take that frosty ornament with you. Jesus, Millicent! That name is unreal, I bet you call her *Milli-the-Pooh*!"

The flicker of understanding, which had softened Julian's features a moment before, suddenly disappeared, his expression freezing solid. He stared impassively at the seething, dark-haired woman for a long while then left without a word.

Lilly started to cry. Outside, a car door slammed and after what seemed an eternity, the sound of an engine starting severed the Sunday afternoon residential street silence, and with it the spell of inertia that had seized Fudge's limbs. She went to the bedroom and pulled a case from the top of the cupboard.

"What are you doing?" Lilly appeared in the doorway, the blue eyes puffy and red, the chubby cheeks blotchy.

"I'm going home."

"Home?"

"To Birch Rise."

"What about college?"

"The term's nearly finished. I'll think of some excuse." Fudge's voice was cold, neutral.

"And when are you coming back?"

"I don't know."

"And what about me?"

"Don't make me answer that question."

~ * ~

Two hours later, Fudge was huddled against the window of the Dublin to Galway express, her head leaning on the hard glass as the train hurtled towards the west and away from a catastrophic mess of emotions. With every patch of green that whipped by, the events repeated themselves, each disastrous moment blinking past like endless celluloid frames of a low-budget movie spilling out of an exhausted projector, and when the heap of horrendous film material reached its peak, she recalled Johnny and the feel of his skin against hers, the laughs, the burnt toast, Butlins. They had been lovers, but were not in love. Infatuated, maybe. Was there a word for it at all? He knew it, she knew it. Johnny longed to escape from his world, she from hers, yet only for a while, their roots, like an unseen magnet, pulling them back to an environment, to a slot in life's community where each sensed he or she belonged.

The weekend had been a private adventure, a clandestine quest, both cautiously squeezing through the invisible bars of their own circumstantial playpen. The two days in Dun Laoghaire weren't to be the last. It had been a mad, romantic splurge, and if Fudge hadn't lost her heart a year before, she might have lost it that weekend in the comforting hollow of Ballyglass Johnny's sagging bachelor bed.

And there it was again! The admission, the confirmation. She still loved that McDermott wretch! The horrific scene had been all her fault, every vile minute of it! She'd wanted it—needed it, as a release for her stifled frustration. That woman! Her pristine perfection, the poise, the composure. Oh God, how could she have lost her temper like that, yelling and cursing? She'd wanted to beat him around the face, to kick and scratch and scream. What a pure, unmitigated fool she was!

As the train approached Athlone, they passed an untidy plot of unused land where a scattering of young children tomfooled hither and thither in the slowly sinking summer sun. A small girl with bruised knees and large round eyes stared trance-like at the row of lurching carriages as they clattered by, studying with obvious consternation the anonymous faces behind the flashing glass. Had she just seen her own face there? Had she found in the features of one of the passengers an expression as transparent as an open window through which she'd glimpsed into her own future, and discovered there something which left her heart as bruised as her knees?

They came then, the tears, surging to the surface and spilling down over Fudge's pale cheeks in a steady stream of wretchedness. She let them fall, her gaze unwavering as she stared out over the dusky, rolling countryside.

"You all right, dear?"

Fudge blinked several times in quick succession and focused on the elderly lady sitting opposite. The woman leaned forward, her wrinkled hand patting Fudge's arm in a motherly gesture. She was wearing, despite the warmth of the stuffy carriage, a hat that appeared to have been sat on more than once, and beneath it, a look of abject pity.

"Don't be sad," she said. "Everything will work out, you'll see."

"I'm not so sure," Fudge mumbled nasally.

"If you want it enough, it will." Her voice was full of conviction. It was a simple statement leaving no room for doubt. She hadn't asked the unhappy, dark-haired girl who the tears were for, and why should she? Hadn't she shed enough of them herself as a young girl, God knows? Life was a tightrope walk, the way impossibly long, firm ground often far beneath, yet if you kept your balance and didn't look down, you got there in the end.

~ * ~

It was dark by the time she arrived at the front gates of Birch Rise, the pitch blackness and vast silence of the nighttime countryside enveloping her in the cloak of solace she had so greatly craved after the bustling brightness of the city. Mikey Boland, the chief ticket man and whistle blower at Athenry railway station, had organised a lift for Fudge in a flash, charging out onto the car park as the small spattering of travellers were being met by family and friends. He'd known Charlie Ginnane's daughter ever since he'd first seen her on the platform, sitting on a boarding school trunk in a smart blue uniform, a one-way ticket to Dublin clutched in her fist and a shimmer of apprehension in her eyes. There was an awfully queer look in her eyes this evening, too, Mikey had thought while he watched her leaving the station squashed between the two excited Finlay youths who'd been picked up by their parents after a weekend in Meath and were now on their way back to Bullcudy. *Hope she's not gone and gotten herself into trouble up in Dublin,* he mused briefly as he trotted back to his post, the whistle that hung around his thick neck jumping up and down on his chest with each stride.

Back on the farm, Fudge stood alone on the gravel driveway, staring up into the endless starry night sky, the bitter-sweet smell of gorse, turf smoke and rich soil filling her with a rush of childhood memories. She closed her eyes, letting her senses wallow in the luxury of it all for a few, precious moments. A deep purring sound broke through the nocturnal stillness, and a second later, the outline of the shaggy-coated Persian cat slinking out of the long grass became visible. Smiling, Fudge reached down and stroked the rotund body as it circled her legs.

"Sinbad, old fella, were you waiting for me?" she whispered, allowing her hand to run over the smooth coat of silver-grey hair before picking up her case and continuing on to the farmhouse, the cat padding faithfully ahead. There were lights shining from nearly every window, illuminating the massive dome of chestnut leaves arching out over the roof on either side of the house like a protective shield. Mum would be in the kitchen folding socks, Dad in the living room, his nose in *The Farmers' Journal*, Rosy and the twins upstairs listening to records and talking about boys. Lovely, uncomplicated happy lives. If only she knew.

Fudge tapped on the back door before entering, so as not to make Mary jump. As predicted, she was standing at the table taking dry washing down from the wooden frame above the range, and through the window Fudge saw her glance up in surprise. She'd been deep in thought as usual, far away from Birch Rise in a special place of her own and it took a second to register her daughter hovering in the doorway.

"Finnula! What...?" The older woman was shocked and delighted in one, the long wisp of dusky hair floating back from her face as she rushed to embrace her second born.

Fudge hugged her mother tightly. "I needed to come home for a while," she mumbled into the soft, woollen shoulder. "I couldn't stand Dublin any longer."

"Oh, pet, what's wrong?" Her very presence, although soothing, caused a knot of misery to form once again in Fudge's chest.

"It's nothing, I'm just tired of the noise, the people..."

Mary took a step back and looked right into her daughter's eyes, sensing, as only a mother can, an anguish which had little to do with people and noise.

"Love, what is it?"

"Oh, Mum... It's just..." God damn it! Fudge pressed her lips together in a grimace of despair. She couldn't stop it! Damn! Damn!

"Tell me. Let it out... Is it a man?"

Fudge nodded jerkily, still hopelessly trying to stem the flow.

"Who... why?" her mother urged gently.

And then it was out. At long last, she put into words the jumble of feelings that had accompanied her for more than a year.

"He's making my life miserable! Just when I think everything is okay, he pops back onto the scene. Doesn't he know what he's doing? Doesn't he know how he's torturing me?"

"I don't understand. Who?"

"That bloody McDermott bastard!" Fudge spat. "Why doesn't he stay behind his books?"

The cogs and wheels running Mary's world ground to a halt in an instant. She stood riveted to the spot, her face a mask of disbelief.

"Oh God, Finnula, how do you know...?"

"What do you mean, how do I know? Just when I think he's out of my life, he worms his way back in again!"

"You saw him recently?" Mary's mouth was dry, her stomach churning.

"Recently?" Fudge snorted through her tears. "He visited us this afternoon with his girlfriend! A snooty, stuck-up painted doll! Of all the bloody cheek!"

The older woman grasped the back of a kitchen chair as a wave of lightheadedness washed over her.

"He... He has a girlfriend?"

"A student... Millicent. You should see her!"

Mary sat down then, her knees all but buckling, and for the first time Fudge noticed how pale her mother had suddenly become.

"Mum! I'm sorry, I didn't mean to upset you. I shouldn't have said anything. Are you all right?"

Mary couldn't answer. A girlfriend. One of his students. How could he? She hadn't asked him to wait, had never expected him to. He knew she couldn't leave Charlie, didn't want to, and never would, but hearing those words from Finnula had wrenched a gaping hole in her heart. Michael and another woman—a young woman. Why hadn't he told her? Warned her? *Jesus, I'm such an idiot,* she thought bitterly, *an ageing old fool! Why did I have to see him again? Why couldn't I have stuck to the promise I made to myself? How could I have let him creep back into my life only to do this* And how had Finnula found out about their relationship? Her mind was reeling with questions. Why, why, why?

"What's wrong, Mum?"

Mary focused on her daughter and saw the alarm there. "What did you say, love?" she whispered.

"Why are you so pale all of a sudden? I didn't want to worry you. I'll be all right."

"But how did you know? You... You won't say anything to your father, will you? Please, let me deal with it."

Fudge, the tears trying quickly now that her torment had been voiced, viewed her mother quizzically.

"I hardly think Dad'll be bothered about my boyfriend problems. There's nothing to deal with."

Mary swallowed hard. "Your boyfriend problems? What have they got to do with Michael McDermott?"

"Michael? You mean Julian... I'm talking about Julian."

An electric shock of realisation and relief bolted through Mary, almost lifting her out of the seat. "Julian, of course, I meant Julian—a slip of the tongue." She blinked at her daughter. "And you've fallen for him?"

"Head over heels." Fudge moaned. "But I've made the most godawful mess of it all. He'll never want to look at me again!"

"Why don't you tell me about it?" The dazed housewife got up and walked shakily to the range to fetch the kettle, stopping halfway there.

"Do you know what? Let's have a gin and tonic!"

"A gin and tonic! Mum, that's wicked!"

"Who cares—purely medicinal. I think a small one is what you need!" She headed for the kitchen press and fetched two glasses, hoping her daughter wouldn't notice as she poured a double measure for herself.

~ * ~

Years later, when Fudge began to put the jigsaw puzzle together, she would find a few more missing pieces in the conversation she'd had with her mother that night. But for now she was home, safe within the reassuring boundaries of the farm and her family.

The days sailed by—lazy, countryside days spent nestled in the cradle of contentment that was Birch Rise. Like a cat curled in the hollow of its mistress's soft lap, Fudge relished each wonderful minute. She slept deeply, getting up when the late morning sunlight finally managed to penetrate the dense curtain of lush green chestnut leaves in front of the bedroom window. Surfacing from potpourri dreams filled with familiar faces, she would hear the back door slamming as Charlie arrived home from his farm rounds and the low murmur of conversation in the kitchen below.

The huge house was virtually empty until four o'clock in the afternoon when Rosy returned from school, the stillness a luxury Fudge gladly took advantage of. Hours were spent in the cavernous living room armchair re-reading books she'd devoured as a child. At midday, after a lunch of fresh batch loaf and hunks of yellow cheddar eaten out on the lawn, she stretched out in the sunshine and let the farm fragrances soothe her troubled heart.

The meadow sloping away towards the Brackens was a lush carpet of buttercups, daisies and beds of juicy clover. Acres of verdant green rolled away on all sides, and the hedgerows, a dismal grey tangle of spiky growth in the winter, were now exploding with colour and life. Bindweed, honeysuckle and dog roses cascaded in a sweet-smelling waterfall of foliage, while in the shade beneath the trees mauve foxgloves thwarted the gloom. Out along the driveway, banks of wildflowers were in bloom, pushing their way up between clumps of feathery fox-tail grass and purple tufted vetch. Tall oxeye daisies nodded gently in a mild breeze and in the air above, fat bumblebees and red admirals, giddy with the succulence of it all, careened drunkenly from one delicious blossom to the next.

Off towards the west and the Atlantic Ocean, stacks of heavy cloud holding the promise of rain graciously kept their distance, leaving the skies above Loughrua azure, a startling backdrop for the house martin parents that were flitting back and forth as they collected mud for their nests. Wafting out through the open back door, melodious strains of mellow orchestral music came from the kitchen radio, and every now and then, the jingle of cutlery and clink of china enhanced the atmosphere of calming, homely contentment. Birch Rise was a garrison for Fudge's peace of mind, a refuge.

When Rosy came home from school, they lay on their stomachs in the grass, Fudge answering, as best she could, the multitude of obscure questions her younger sister had accumulated over the months. The queries posed by the curly-haired nymphet—a teenager herself now—no longer concerned the colour of Loughrua Lake or the wetness of it, but were hesitant, sisterly probings into the enigma of what went on above and below the belts of male adolescents. Fudge, suddenly feeling somewhat of an authority, when only just, advised and enlightened to the best of her ability, the memories of Castleglen and Lilly's teachings crystal clear in her mind.

"Have you been shifted yet?" Fudge asked, giving Rosy a conspiratorial glance.

"Of course I have!" the young girl replied indignantly. "Loads of times!"

"And did you like it? Being kissed, I mean."

"A spit-swapper or a normal peck?"

"Well, the real thing, you know—tongues and all."

"It's all right, I suppose. A bit messy if it's someone like Muriel McMahon's son, Brian. He leaves a trail across your face like a snail, yuck!"

"I see." Fudge smiled inwardly, thinking of Johnny's first kiss.

"Fudge?"

"Hmm."

"What do I do if someone wants to grope and I don't?"

"Then you don't. It's quite simple."

"And if I sort of want it?" Rosy ventured cautiously.

"Up your jumper, or what?"

"Yeh, grabbing my boobs and so on."

"First of all, you never let anyone *grab* your boobs. Tenderly touch them at the very most—but outside your bra."

"Not inside?"

"Are we talking about someone you've known for a while? Do you mean at the pictures, or round the back of the dance hall and the like?"

"For example."

"Hmm, that's a difficult one, Rosy. I would say you don't let anyone do anything you don't want—and only if you feel you really want it, and think you're old enough. Don't be afraid to tell them to keep their paws off!"

"Even if it's Martin Morgan? He's gorgeous!"

"*Especially* if it's Martin Morgan! God Almighty, Rosy! 'Morgan the Organ'! He's far too old! You deserve a clip on the ear even thinking about it!"

"All the girls are mad for him," she countered with a pout.

"You're not all the girls. You're special."

"Go on, what's so special about me?"

"You're my little sister."

"Oh... Fair enough. That's an argument, I suppose."

Later in the day, the twins arrived home from their Canadian-Irish private school tennis classes, their faces still glistening with perspiration and full of excited chatter. Lizzy had dumped Chuck, which meant Henry's days were numbered, too, and anyway, Bob and Dick were waiting off court to pick up where the other two would-be Mounties had left off, namely, still far too many sets, games and matches away from the white frilly tennis knickers.

Mary was in her element, glowing with maternal pride as she observed the jumble of laughing girls sprawled together on the lawn in the early evening rays. If only Sheila were here, she pondered, it would be like old times. The whole family together. Rosy asking her questions; the twins gabbling in unison, each shouting louder than the other to be heard; Finnula, the go-between, answering pubescent queries while fighting to keep the peace; and Sheila, grown-up Sheila from the age of twelve adamantly protesting against the injustices of social, racial, and sexist inequality, as well as the cataclysmic state of our natural, political and economic environment. Charlie serenely observed from the sidelines, a lopsided grin of utter satisfaction on his windswept face, a cockerel fluffing his feathers in a yard full of clucking hens. Every now and then, his gaze met Mary's and a look of acknowledgement would pass between them. They'd done all right.

Fudge spent the rest of the summer at Birch Rise. A week or so after she arrived, the school holidays began and suddenly the farm was a hive of activity. There was a helter-skelter of jobs she longed to throw herself into. The stunted Bantam chickens Charlie insisted on keeping needed to be fed, the stables mucked out and Shanagarry groomed. Bales of straw were waiting to be scattered and, sadly, the slurry couldn't shovel itself any more than cows could count, earmark or dose themselves.

Early in the morning she often accompanied her father as he walked the land, checking walls and fences and accounting for each and every farm animal. Sometimes, they'd take a detour through the Brackens just for the pleasure of it, squelching across boggy ditches overflowing with pungent-smelling meadowsweet and great clusters of wild watercress. Occasionally, a rabbit stuck its twitching nose out of a warren before disappearing as fast as it came, the fluffy tail a downy flash of white as it plunged back into the earthy cavern. Resting a callused hand on his daughter's shoulder, Charlie sometimes pointed out a shimmering dragonfly as it flitted over the surface of a watery patch, or a thrush's nest hidden amongst the furze. In his caring touch, Fudge sensed an urgency in him to preserve these fleeting moments, to tighten the family bonds that threatened to slacken with the years, a desire to clutch his children to his breast knowing that, before long, even little Rosy would spread her wings and fly.

"We'll always be there for you, Dad," she said suddenly early one morning as they skirted a scruffy hillock studded with clumps of purple-flowering cotton thistle.

A light drizzle had fallen briefly during the night and the damp grass made their black Wellingtons shine.

"I know that, pet, but you have your own lives now. Another few years and you'll all be scattered around Ireland, far away from Birch Rise."

"I would have thought you'd be happy to get rid of us!" Fudge joked, not missing the twinge of sadness in her father's voice. "You'll have time for yourselves at last—just you and Mum."

"That's what I'm afraid of!"

"What? Being alone with Mum?" She laughed out loud and gave him a saucy look. "Now, why would you be afraid of Mum?"

Charlie didn't laugh. Instead he stopped and stared down across the meadow towards the house where Mary was standing alone in the kitchen, her apron and hands covered in flour as she baked fresh bread for the hay-makers.

"Will I be enough for her when all you girls have gone?" he said out of the blue, his eyes still fixed on the image of his wife working beside the range. Fudge hesitated a few steps behind her father. He was a man who rarely showed strong emotions, his personal fears and feelings safely stowed away in a corner somewhere. His unexpected statement worried her.

"Dad, what a strange thing to say! You're everything to her. She was here long before we arrived and she'll be here after we've gone, too."

"Will she, Finnula?"

"Don't say that! What's got into you? She loves you and always has—any fool can see that!"

"I know, but does she love me enough?"

Fudge took her father by the arm, his sudden outburst sending the fear of God scampering through her gut.

"Stop it! Do you honestly think she's going to run off with the postman, or the butcher, or what? How can you think anyone can give her more than you have? This is her home, you're her family... For crying out loud, Mum will be fifty in a few years!"

Charlie laughed half-heartedly. "Ach, Finnula, you may think I'm a weather-beaten old codger who knows nothing about romance, but one day you'll realise, when it comes to falling in love, it doesn't matter a damn whether you're fifteen or fifty." He grinned awkwardly at his daughter, ashamed at having selfishly unburdened his concerns upon her young shoulders. "Now come on, the hay-makers will be here soon and there are a mountain of sandwiches to be made!"

Together, they plodded back towards the yard, the warm sun drying the long grass and taking the moist shine from their boots. Charlie smiled reassuringly. It was one of those everything-will-be-all-right smiles which, in her childhood, had chased away many a thunder cloud of doubt, yet now did little to disperse the tiny puff of worry hovering at the back of Fudge's mind. By mid-afternoon, however, when haymaking was in full swing with the clanking agricultural machinery farting and chugging its way up and down the pasture, the disquieting conversation was all but forgotten.

~ * ~

Everyone had to pitch in. The neighbouring farm lads, red-faced and shy, ogled the Ginnane girls from under their sweaty brows. The twins minced teasingly along the long rows of freshly cut grass, far too fashionably dressed for the pastoral chores. The weather, mercifully, was holding up, so Fudge and Mary dragged the long kitchen table out onto the lawn where it was piled high with fruit cake, raspberry jam sandwiches, whole-wheat scones and trays of sausages. Inside, the kettle was kept boiling all day as gallons of tea disappeared down hot, thirsty throats, while outside jugs of cool orange squash were left to grow warm.

The air was full of boisterous laughter, barked instructions, butterflies, bees and a multitude of buzzing insects intoxicated by the ripe, juicy sappiness of the meadow harvest. Over the higgledy-piggledy stone walls, heavy-eyed cows observed the goings-on with disinterested apathy, even the luscious feast of newly cut grass heaping up before them doing little to excite their state of trance-like lethargy. In the middle of it all, the furry Persian cat slunk back and forth, the silver-grey back undulating silently through the long stalks as he preyed on frightened field mice frantically escaping from the mechanical, smoke-belching monster looming ahead.

Late in the evening, while Fudge was slouched on the living room sofa, her limbs leaden from the day's work, and her mind luxuriously blank, Johnny phoned. Was she all right, he wanted to know, the concern in his voice sincere. They talked for a long time then, his strong lilting Dublin accent strangely out of place and alien deep in the Irish countryside.

Without mentioning Julian, Fudge poured out her heart and he listened patiently, his intermittent murmuring of understanding reassuring her he was still at the other end of the line. "I know, luv... that's terrible, that is. Don't bother yer head, sweetheart..."

And when Fudge finally grew tired of talking, he told her about his work, the driving, the city, the gobshites he delivered his parcels to, the latest soccer results. They teased each other, she calling him a football hooligan, he fondly referring to her as a hay-making, bog-trotting brat. At that, they laughed long and hard and promised to meet again. When Fudge finally placed the phone back in the cradle, she felt as if life could go on at last. She would return to Dublin after the summer, finish college, and start creating a future, let come what may. And there was Lilly. She would have to talk to Lilly, but not now. Soon.

Weeks later, when the hay was turned and stacked, and the long meadow as stubbly as a vagabond's chin, Sheila came home, prancing unexpectedly into the kitchen as if she'd only stepped out on an errand. They were complete again, the whole Ginnane family, a laughing, shrieking, quarrelling bundle squashed around the wooden table. Mary was in heaven. Inwardly, Fudge rejoiced as she caught her parents exchanging proud, meaningful looks. Every now and then, they would touch each other, he laying an arm across her shoulder as they stood before the range, she resting a hand on his as they sat together in front of the TV. At such times, Charlie's eyes glimmered with contentment, and observing them, one would never believe for a minute that even the tiniest flicker of doubt had ever lingered there. Fudge mentally packed, parcelled and stowed away these shared moments, realising they would become more and more precious with every day that passed.

Sleeping arrangements were reshuffled, the older girls sharing a room for the first time in years. At bedtime, they stood awkwardly back to back, an uncanny shyness preventing them from stripping off in the natural, carefree manner of their childhood. As children, they'd run together naked and squealing across the lawn, Mary in hot pursuit armed with a garden hose. They weren't strangers now, but time had forced an invisible wedge of modesty between them, a wedge both flippantly pretended to ignore. Only after the light was out and the milky moonlight sent leafy shadows scrabbling across the ceiling, did they hesitantly begin to talk about more than jobs, fashion and city life.

"Why're you home, Finn?"

"Got a bit stressed out up in Dublin."

"College?" Sheila sounded sleepy and mellow.

"Not really... Other things."

"Men, then."

"Sort of."

"Do you have a boyfriend?"

"Not a steady one—a good friend."

"I see... Doesn't sound like a bad arrangement, actually."

They were quiet for a while, Fudge admiring the social worker's calming manner. Interested, but not probing. How they had fought as children, and now years later, her voice was full of patience, a voice practised in reassuring the distressed and needy, a voice which awakened trust, gave hope.

"And you, Sheila? Mum said you have a boyfriend."

"Hmm."

"So tell me about him. You haven't brought him home yet?"

"Not yet, he's quite busy—away on business a lot."

"A business man? Not one of your social working colleagues?"

"In sales—doing all right," Sheila answered, smiling.

"Wow, that's a contrast. Where's he from? Galway?"

"Dublin, as a matter of fact." There was a trace of mirth in her sister's answer that Fudge couldn't place.

"A Dubliner! You're fierce hedgy altogether. What's his name?"

"I'm not being hedgy, I just haven't had a chance to introduce him to the family. His name's Danny."

"Danny from Dublin."

"Yep."

"And where did you meet him? At the Seapoint Dance Hall, any bet."

"No, he was on holidays. I met him on my way home one evening."

"And you're happy with him?"

"Blissfully."

"You're really in love—the real thing, like?"

"Hook, line and sinker!" Sheila laughed out loud, a gurgling, secretive laugh which petered out as cloud nine transported the Ginnane girl off to the Land of Nod.

The next day they threw the tarpaulin off the Mirror dinghy in the yard, and with Sheila at the wheel, the girls towed the trailer the few short miles down to the lake and spent the whole day sailing.

A stiff breeze swept down from the hills behind Loughrua, carrying Fudge and Sheila smartly across the waters. The surface was green-grey and choppy, the foam-crested waves slapping against the bows of the little vessel in small explosions. The sky was a changing landscape of scudding clouds, and intermittently, brief showers chased the young sailors across to the far shores and back again, drenching their bright red plastic jackets in lukewarm rain. When the two girls finally tied up at the wooden pier, they were bursting with exhilaration, the dark Ginnane locks plastered flat around their excited faces, water running off sunburnt noses.

On the way home they stopped off for fish and chips at The Little Chef on the main street. The takeaway was full of youngsters, a meeting place where they whiled away their summer holiday evenings. These teenagers didn't fly off with their parents on package tours to Spain and Italy, but stayed at home to help run farms and family businesses. At the most they might take a week on a crowded campsite in Connemara, or visit relatives in England, the journey across to Hollyhead on a ferry full of reeling construction site workers being the greatest adventure of all.

Sheila popped another greasy chip into her mouth and washed it down with a massive gulp of Club orange. She was quiet, and behind the steamed up spectacles it was hard to know what she was thinking. Fudge eyed her older sister. She could tell by the way the other woman was absent-mindedly picking the batter off her cod that she wanted to say something. There was a cryptic twist to her smile, an air of hesitation in her manner.

"C'mon, out with it, you're driving me spare!" Fudge said at last.

"What d'you mean?" Sheila asked innocently, the furtive smile still tickling the corner of her mouth.

"We may have lost contact over the years, but you're still my sister. I can tell you're bursting to get something off your shoulders."

Grinning broadly now, Sheila pushed the wire-framed glasses up her nose.

"It's Danny. He's moving to Galway."

"Well, that's fantastic! Why so secretive?"

"We'd like to move together."

"Move together? In Galway! Holy Mary Mother of God, Sheila, you haven't a hope in hell!" Fudge exclaimed exaggerating her Irish accent. "We're in Catholic Ireland in case you haven't forgotten. You'd be living in sin, girl! You'd have to pretend you're married. Dad'll have your guts for garters!"

"Actually, we didn't want to pretend."

"You don't mean...?"

"Yes, I do."

Fudge let out a shriek of disbelief, causing an elderly man at the next table to slop half a glass of lemonade up his nose. Several heads turned.

"Married! You're going to get married? Jeepers, I can't believe it!"

"Sssh! You don't have to tell the whole of Loughrua! Mum and Dad don't know yet!"

Fudge leaned across the table. "Sheila, they haven't even met him yet—none of us have. Isn't it about time?"

The older girl shifted uncomfortably in her plastic seat. "Well, you have actually..."

"What?"

"....met him. It was years ago. Mum and Dad won't remember him—the girls won't, either."

"But I will?"

"You might." Sheila was torturing her sister with obvious delight.

"Oh, Sheila, who is he, for cryin' out loud?"

"Danny, Danny Scully, I told you. Look, he's coming to visit tomorrow. You'll see him then."

She started clearing away the chip bags and paper serviettes, indicating that, for now, the subject was closed.

If Fudge hadn't been so fond of her sister, she might well have throttled her. Instead, she promised not to breathe a word and spent the rest of the evening picking through her brains with a fine comb. Danny. Was he the one she'd seen handing out leaflets together with Sheila at the Galway shopping centre two years ago? No, he'd been a UCG student. Or the fella who had picked her up for the Christmas party? No, he'd had a girlfriend waiting in the car. A childhood friend, then, someone from National School. Had they scrambled over walls together, scratched their knees and played marbles? Maybe he'd moved to Dublin later. It was no use; she hadn't the foggiest idea in the whole world who Sheila's mysterious fiancé might be and decided, like the rest of the family, to just wait and see.

At the three o'clock the next day, seven pairs of eyes were peeping around curtains as a nearly new Cortina bounced down the driveway. Mary and Charlie, who'd taken up position at the kitchen window, nodded their approval. With a car like that, the young man must have a fairly decent job, they thought simultaneously, both knowing that when it came to choosing her friends, Sheila, with her huge heart and philanthropic attitude, had never really reached for the skies. *Let's hope her bloody benevolence keeps her in bread and butter*, Charlie had once commented in a moment of uncharitable crankiness, a remark which had him eating humble pie for a week.

"Be careful, Charlie, he'll see us." She nudged her husband away from the window when the young man pulled up in front of the house and got out. The curious parents glanced at each other and grinned. Thanks be to God, this wasn't one of those radical, world-saving, pot-smoking lay-abouts in faded jeans, happily living off tax-payers' money and promising the stars. But he wasn't Steve McQueen, either, Mary silently decided, immediately wanting to smack herself on the hand for even thinking it as she watched her eldest daughter rush across the driveway and into the strange man's arms. He was dressed smartly in casual slacks and a blue and white striped business shirt open at the collar.

Watching them from the window, she was amused to see that, like Sheila, Danny wore a similar pair of wire-framed glasses and had dark, curly hair. Above a slightly goofy face, his frizzy locks, however, were cut into the very short-back-and-sides style the girls themselves had so mockingly used to scorn. No taller than Sheila, his arm was stretched awkwardly over her shoulder as they walked to the front door, but Mary and Charlie were satisfied. They could see genuine love and tenderness there, a mischievous, conspiratorial twinkle in their eyes, and knew, had he arrived on a bicycle and looked like Quasimodo, they would have welcomed him all the same.

From her position at the living room window Fudge couldn't see much but was sure she'd never seen this guy before. Sheila had to be mistaken. He looked all right, a bit square, not at all what she'd expected, yet they were obviously bonkers about each other and that was the main thing. Upstairs, at the bedroom window, Lizzy and Beth were making gagging noises.

"He's yucky! Has Sheila gone mad?"

"And a Cortina, not exactly all the rage. A bit gicky—look at his hair!"

"Oh, gross, they're smooching!"

"Far out! He's just banged his specs into hers, how mortifying!"

Rosy, who'd remained silent until now, turned to her sisters. "You're really mean! Not everyone is interested in pea-brained Canadian rugby players! I think he's quite cute, actually. Kind of Mr. Magoo-ish. A young one."

"Mr. Magoo-ish?"

"Well, sort of."

The twins raised their eyes to heaven and returned to their posts behind the curtains.

Fudge waited until everyone was settled in the living room and Mary was passing around tea and currant buns before she came downstairs. She didn't want the poor man to feel overwhelmed by the stampede of inquisitive Ginnanes, a prospect which most, having the choice, would gladly exchange for an onslaught of North American buffalo. Danny, however, had come up smiling and was now sitting serenely next to his girlfriend on the sofa, the rest of the family forming a ring of spectators around them. Sheila tugged his elbow when her sister walked into the room.

"Danny, here's Finnula. She's down from Dublin for the summer."

Danny politely stood up and stretched out his hand in greeting. As she took it, she searched his face again. There was something about his stature, that mysterious smile. She could tell by the sparkle behind his spectacles that he was having a good old laugh, but for the love of her, she didn't know why.

"Nice to see you," he said, the Dublin accent clearly evident. A prickle of recognition. Who was he? She'd kill Sheila for this.

Once seated, Fudge began to munch on a sticky bun, her full mouth relieving her of formal conversation and giving her the chance to continue her scrutiny. Danny? Dublin? She was biting into her second pastry when he turned to her.

"So when are you going back to Dublin, Fudge?"

Fudge? She'd been introduced as Finnula. How did…? A massive flood of recognition surged through her, causing her throat to constrict and the mouthful of sticky bun she'd been about to swallow to catapult out across the coffee table in a shower of currants and crumbs. Fudge, to hide her laughter, launched into a cleverly staged coughing fit and fled from the room.

She was still holding her sides when Sheila joined her in the kitchen five minutes later.

"I gather you've copped on." The older girl's face was questioning. "Are you going to tell me I've gone nuts?"

"God, no… I'm delighted for you, it's just…" Fudge shook her head and dabbed a tear of mirth from the corner of her eye. "Who would have thought… It seems my past keeps catching up with me all the time—even here at Birch Rise. In the bosom of my family! I thought I'd hit a time warp. Honestly, you really pulled the wool over my eyes."

"No, I didn't, I said you'd met him before and that he was from Dublin."

"But you said his name was Danny."

"It is. Danny Scully, better known to his friends as 'Prof'."

"Sheila, you're evil! I thought you met him on the way home—while he was on holidays in Galway."

"*County* Galway. The holiday was at Birch Rise and he scared the shit out of me up at the front gate."

"But that was years ago!"

"A letter here, a phone call there, the odd visit. We kept the kettle simmering over the years, but when he turned up last September with short-back-and-sides and a Cortina, I was a gonner! My kettle's been whistling ever since!"

They collapsed into hoots of hilarity. The conversation with Johnny in St. Stephen's Green suddenly came back to her. Floggin' word processors and doing a line with a Galway girl, one with brains, he'd answered when Fudge had enquired about Prof. Theoretically, she'd known for weeks. Prof from Ballyglass, the silent, intellectual Teddy Boy. Now Prof the salesman, her future brother-in-law and proof that if destiny set its mind on something, one hadn't a hope in hell of changing it. Providence would take its course, and if you didn't like it, tough shit.

In this case, however, Sheila was quite obviously satisfied with what fate had dropped into her lap, her infectious happiness spreading to the whole family, and when, during a man-to-man conversation in the study, Danny formally asked Charlie for his daughter's hand, the somewhat flustered farmer told the Dubliner he could gladly take it, and good luck to him, too.

One bottle of champagne and several bottles of wine later, the dazed parents, in the privacy of their bedroom, discussed the fact that a Catholic computer wheeler-dealer was hardly the man they had hoped might take over Birch Rise one day. Ah well, they agreed finally, Sheila was happy, and catching an eligible Protestant in rural Ireland was like finding a needle in a proverbial haystack, and anyway, judging by the way things were developing, it was fairly likely the zealous salesman would one day earn far more money with his hand in computers then he ever might with it up a calving cow's backside.

The next morning, seriously hung over after an evening of celebrating, and clearly the worse for wear, Fudge phoned Lilly.

"Hi, Lil, it's me," she slurred slightly, ball bearings crashing relentlessly around in her head.

"Humph."

"Is that, 'hello, lovely to hear from you'?"

"No, its 'you have the bloody cheek'."

"Aww, Lil, don't be mad at me anymore. Come on." Fudge smiled to herself. Funny to be doing the wheedling for a change.

"You just shagged off and left me here on my own without even calling once! What do you want?"

"Will you have me back? Please?"

"Go and get stuffed!"

"Aw, Lilly, come on, like old times... Okay?"

"No way. I'm looking for a new flatmate."

"Please?"

"No, no, no! Forget it! Shag off!"

"Plee-ease?"

"Over my dead body!"

"See you Monday, okay?"

"Okay."

Thirteen

The six-foot, pear-shaped man with the size eleven shoes and a balding head slammed down the phone with such force that the office girls jumped in their seats with fright. They were well used to it, but occasionally his explosions of wrath managed to catch them unawares.

"Those wankers!" he bellowed at nobody in particular. "I'll have their knackers if that consignment isn't on my doorstep at nine o'clock sharp tomorrow morning. Pox artists, the lot of them!"

Skids Curry was in the motoring business and the undisputed master of the known Irish spare parts universe. There wasn't a man in Ireland with motor oil on his hands who didn't know the beefy giant from Drumcondra. He was the king of his trade, doing business over, under and beside the counter, on the street or even behind the potted plant, if necessary. He kept everyone happy—the tax payers, tax collectors, tax dodgers, taxi drivers and his overtaxed secretaries. His books were pristine and not, as some slanderers maintained, because there was nothing in them. Every invoice was meticulous, listing items, units and reference numbers, and if one did happen to slip down the back of his desk, or into the bin by mistake, it was a hardly any reason to get one's knickers in a twist.

His name was as famous as the man himself, though nobody quite knew how he managed to get it. Some claimed it had to do with his hazardous driving skills and last-minute braking technique, while others put it down to his somewhat slippery business approach. Particularly bad mouths amongst the competition even claimed he'd been branded with the name way back in his youth after team mates found his Y-fronts lying crotch up in the sports locker room. Their maliciousness knowing no bounds, they even went as far as maintaining he'd originally been christened Curry Skids as a result, a rumour which had a decisively negative effect on the dealer's mood for weeks after these filthy lies reached his ears.

Finnula Ginnane was his private assistant, crusader of concord, counsellor, coffee maker (when the other girls made it, it tasted crap), and shrewd navigator, having never failed to manoeuvre a way out, on the rare occasions Curry's Car Parts had managed to get itself well and truly up shit creek without a paddle. Renowned for her skill and dexterity, she had been approached more than once by executives in swish suits and yellow ties making her lucrative job offers which included private offices, company cars and excessive holidays, but Fudge remained steadfast.

What started out as a two-week temping stint had become a full time job and an adventure she was loath to give up voluntarily. She'd worked for Skids for over four years, through thick and thin, ups and downs, and could not recall ever having a dull moment. Between juggling appointments with customers, dates with women and diverse social commitments, it was Fudge's task to remember his mother's birthday, bet on his favourite horses and warn him well in advance should any business documents suddenly and inexplicably require shredding. In short, Fudge had become an indispensable component in the Skids Curry empire, her job keeping him out of trouble and her in real leather shoes, smart skirt suits and a car with four side windows.

There were two other girls in the office. Gráinne had the fastest fingers north of the Liffey, her supersonic typing speed all but unbeatable, and that on a huge ribbon typewriter she so tenderly referred to as "The Brute". The row of shiny trophies glistening on the shelf behind her desk was proof of the pudding. The only things she could bat quicker than the keys were her eyelids, but, regrettably, there were no competitions for that.

She worked together with Kathleen (who insisted on being called Kitty), the likeable, bird-brained filing clerk and court jester, a woman whose strength lay in her ability to talk the hind legs off a donkey, an invaluable asset allowing dicey paperwork and other corpora delicti to disappear into the shredder before unannounced officials got a word in long enough to ask for the files. She wore tight tops with yawning cleavages and flimsy, flowery skirts which got stuck in her bottom every time she stood up. It invariably took two trips to the filing cabinet and back before the slinky fabric managed to finally extricate itself from her grasping buttocks, a process which kept the aforementioned officials mesmerised for minutes, and thus increased precious shredding time significantly.

Despite his gruff, somewhat direct manner, the girls thought their boss was the berries, his offensive remarks rolling off them like water off a duck's back.

"…Gráinne, sweetheart, take a couple of quid out of the petty cash and buy yerself some new perfume—that one makes you smell like a hoor's handbag."

"Thanks, Skids, but you should've thought of that before you gave it to me for Christmas…"

"… and Kitty, will ya get yer skirt out of yer arse, yer chewin' on it again."

"I wouldn't have to if you gave me a decent lunch break…"

"… Finnula, you give me mother bleedin' carnations for her birthday again, and I'll wrap them around yer scrawny neck."

"Sorry, Skids, you said the cheapest would do…"

Not that he was a completely insensitive man; on the contrary, should he ever spot a glint in the eyes of his girls that indicated he'd overstepped his mark, he'd pull an oil-smeared bundle of crumpled notes from the depths of his baggy trouser pockets, instructing them all to get the hell out of the office and not come back until they'd consumed several mollifying measures of vodka and lemonade at Kearney's Arms, a few generous rounds of Asian chow at The Lion's Paw, and a nice slushy matinée down on O'Connell Street. It did wonders for the work morale and by the time the credits were rolling up the screen, all was forgiven.

On this particular day Fudge was dying of heartburn. Skids had made the mistake of saying Kitty's boyfriend was a decent bloke even if he did have a face like a hatful of arseholes, a comment that had cost him a five-course Peking duck midday meal. The sweet and sour orange sauce had been wreaking havoc with her digestive system ever since. She was downing her last two Rennies with a glass of milk when the phone rang.

"Curry's Car Parts, good afternoon." Fudge stifled a burp.

"Hi, it's me." Lilly's chirpiness was not quite as exuberant as accustomed.

"Hi, Lil, what's up? Have you put a pick through your foot again, or what?"

"Ha, ha."

"Problems with the invisible man?"

"Oh, come on, don't start in on me about Jack. You know he's a busy man."

A busy, married man with two kids and a rich wife, Fudge thought acidly, biting back a scathing remark. They'd been through it all a hundred times before, but Lilly was in seventh heaven and resolute in her belief that the handsome consulting engineer would one day be hers. The two had met up in the Wicklow Mountains while working together on a geological project, Lilly claiming she'd skidded down a field of loose scree and straight into his arms. It had been love at first sight. The fact that he was almost fifteen years older and married with two kids did not deter her for a moment. They were meant for each other. That had been over six months ago and Fudge hadn't clapped eyes on the man once.

"I can hardly bring him back here, can I?" Lilly argued when Fudge suggested she invite him to their flat for a drink. They had moved once again and were back in Rathmines in a three-roomed flat looking out onto a residential street lined with slightly sooty cherry trees. The bedrooms were barely big enough to swing a cat in; however, at least each had their own private room, an extravagance they decided working girls deserved. In retrospect, Fudge wondered whether it was worth it. If Lilly wasn't off gallivanting somewhere, they spent most of their time together on the lumpy sofa in their modest living room, where they inevitably dozed off long before the late news flickered across the rented TV.

"Why not? This may not be a luxury penthouse, but we're not exactly living in student squalor any more. When I think of all the work we put into it!" Fudge was indignant. A lot of time and money had been spent turning the flat into a home, giving it a sense of permanency. Framed pictures replaced dog-eared posters, fresh flowers instead of dried. They'd forked out a mint on two tall silver candleholders for the mantelpiece and a huge, intricately-framed flea market mirror to catch the light slanting in from the shady street. Patchwork and batik had made way for cream-coloured throws and cushions in country hues. A tall bookcase displayed the hard and paperback books collected over the years together, most of them belonging to Fudge and sad evidence of her paltry social life. In the corner, a small glass cabinet stocked with brandy, port and wine stood waiting for the guests who seldom came. Looking around one could tell they were no longer teenage students, but two young women with a sense of style, women in their mid-twenties teetering on the top of a hill which would take them freewheeling into their thirties, the downhill ride gathering further momentum with every passing year.

"Ach, you know what I mean. It's awkward, the three of us sitting together gawping at each other, but you'll meet him soon, I promise."

To this day Fudge hadn't met him and, to be honest, wasn't particularly interested anymore. The relationship was taking its toll on Lilly's nerves even if the bouncing blonde would never admit it.

She'd been looking wan recently, and was lethargic, irritable. Fudge took another gulp of milk.

"Okay, I won't mention Jack. So what's up?"

"I'm not well," she said hesitantly. "I need to see a doctor. Will you come with me?"

"Oh… Of course, do you want me to call the surgery in Rathmines?" Knowing the idea of anyone in a white coat caused a line of pearly sweat to appear on her best friend's brow, Fudge didn't hesitate for a moment. "Is it this bug going round?"

"No, I need to see Doctor Plunkett."

"Oh, Lilly, not again. Are you sure? You've been mistaken so many times and you always get yourself into a fierce state!"

"I can't help it, Fudge, I have pains again. If I don't see him I won't have a moment's peace."

And I won't, either, Fudge thought with a sigh. This was the fourth time in the last five years. The fourth cancer scare. Lilly was obsessed by her fear of the disease. It clung to her like an invisible cloak, throwing a shadow over her healthy young life. Every mole or blemish was scrutinised with bated breath, every bewildering twinge of discomfort became a dart of anxiety, every unfamiliar undulation under her skin a cause for alarm. She'd read specialist books and journals, tried transcendental meditation and even hypnotism. Nothing worked. In Lilly's mind, her fate was sealed. Cancer would get her in the end, and no amount of persuasion could convince her otherwise. Yet she had learned to live with it in her way. If Doctor Plunkett was nearby, she could keep the monster at bay.

"Don't worry, I'll give him a call. We'll meet at the surgery, okay?"

"Fine… Fudge?"

"Yeh?"

"I don't know what I'd do without you."

~ * ~

It was lashing out of the heavens as they walked up the steps of the doctor's surgery, the fickle April weather making a mockery of them, sun one minute, torrential rainfall the next. Lilly had already been waiting in the mud-spattered company station wagon when Fudge arrived, the familiar look of dread twisting her features, her eyes as overcast as the skies. In an hour they'd be out of here, relieved, giggling and heading for the next pub, yet for now there was no point in telling Lilly that. No point at all.

Doctor Plunkett was patient, understanding, and not one bit surprised when the two girls had turned up at his doorstep hardly a year after that first encounter at the hospital. He'd recognised it immediately, the blond girl's inexplicable fear, the steadfast conviction that death had pointed its bony finger at her. Since then, they'd appeared regularly and each time, mercifully, he'd been able to relieve the tortured girl's anguish, for a while, anyway. Such a lovely, healthy person, he thought as he walked with her down the hall to his office, if only she could stop worrying her pretty head.

Fudge stood up and went to the window. She'd read all the magazines on the table, shuddering slightly at the thought of how many licked fingers had turned the pages. It was taking ages this time. Usually Doctor Plunkett had her examined and reassured within half an hour. Outside, it was getting dark, the wet asphalt avenue glistening in the light of the street lanterns.

Glancing at her watch for the umpteenth time, she started walking restlessly to and fro, following the same threadbare path in the trodden carpet that other concerned patients had taken before her. She was getting angry. That shithead Jack should be here now, pacing the room, sharing Lilly's anxieties. Bastard. Probably at home in front of the telly with his arm around the gorgeous wife he had absolutely no intention of leaving, his two sweet children at his feet. *He* was making Lilly sick—not the thought of cancer. The empty promises, the waiting hours, an uncertain future. She'd gladly give him a piece of her mind, Fudge thought. Egoistic rat!

When Doctor Plunkett and his patient finally emerged from the office, she had worked herself into a rage, but the look on Lilly's face told her that maybe, after all, Jack alone wasn't responsible for Lilly's poorly condition. It was something else. Something serious. No false alarm this time. The doctor's expression was grave, his arm resting on his ailing charge's shoulder in a protective, fatherly fashion. Fudge could see she'd been crying, yet was struggling to remain calm, her lips firmly pressed into a stoic, crooked smile. She stood before them with bated breath, afraid to ask.

"Shall I...?" Doctor Plunkett looked at Lilly, who nodded jerkily in return.

"Well," he started hesitantly. "I've given Lillian a thorough examination and even without further tests, I can safely say there's nothing that might actually support her fears..."

Fudge relaxed, her shoulders falling noticeably.

"...however, I did discover the reason for her discomfort, her bouts of faintness. She's rather anaemic, needs iron... You see, she's..."

"Oh Christ, Fudge! I'm pregnant!" Lilly suddenly found her voice, a long drawn out wail of distress. "Knocked up! Up the bloody spout!"

"Quite." Doctor Plunkett confirmed.

That bloody bastard, Jack! His fault, after all. In that moment, it didn't dawn on Fudge that Lilly could be held to blame in any way whatsoever. *Damn him! He takes her heart and gets her pregnant in a country where there are no laws allowing divorce and even fewer for abortion. Beautiful, Skids would say, fucking beautiful!*

She clenched her fists and fought back the barrage of oaths. "Right, Lilly, now don't worry, we'll work this out."

"Work this out! With a coat hanger, or what!" the inconsolable woman moaned. "Oh, Jesus, this is a disaster!"

"There's a solution for everything. One step at a time."

Doctor Plunkett accompanied them out onto the street. He'd scribbled the address of an unofficial counsellor on a piece of paper, promising his support if there was anything at all he could do for them. Before the young women drove off in Fudge's car, leaving Lilly's parked outside the surgery, the slightly perplexed man urged them not to be hasty. It was early days yet.

The city centre was clogged with evening traffic as the little car steered its way down O'Connell Street and over the Liffey to the South Side. For the first mile or so, they sat in silence, staring blindly out at the blur of bright shop fronts slipping slowly by. It had started to rain again, the merciless sheets distorting shape and form, diffusing light and turning the world outside into a wishy-washy impressionist painting. The sounds of hooting horns, the whistling of bus brakes and the clatter of running feet were all drowned by aggressive drumming on the car roof and the monotonous slapping of windscreen wipers.

Like sitting in an aquarium with the water outside, Fudge considered bleakly as they waited at a pedestrian crossing. Even the passers-by had taken on a bizarre, fish-like appearance, skin and clothes slick with wetness, mouths opening and closing as they gulped for air in the suffocating, watery deluge. On the street in front of them, a young mother was struggling to manoeuvre a pram with a buckled wheel up onto the pavement with one hand, while clutching a drenched and screaming toddler with the other. Her words were lost, carried away as fast as the litter that hurtled along the overflowing gutter, but observing the hectic facial movement and wide-open eyes, Fudge could literally feel the exasperated barrage of expletives. She glanced over at Lilly who was silently watching the pitiful scene, her face a mask of horror as she watched the mother—a symbol of her own future—wrench the pram up onto the footpath and disappear off down the quays, the whimpering child in tow.

"I can't," she whispered hoarsely. "I can't have a baby. Not now."

"It seems you don't have much choice, Lilly."

"Maybe..." She sighed heavily and pushed a limp blond corkscrew behind her ear. "Maybe I'll lose it."

"I wouldn't reckon on it, and anyway, that's a terrible thought. Look, what about Jack, won't he support you?"

"Of course! He loves me... He said so! The timing is just bad. Very bad."

"And if you readjust your timing? I mean, if he really loves you..."

"I don't know." She hesitated, suddenly seeing the potential.

"You could just push all your plans forward a bit."

"Yes... Yes, you're right." Her voice gained confidence. "He said he was going to leave his wife. Maybe it's about time."

Oh dear, Fudge reflected dourly, *I wouldn't reckon on that, either.* The idea, however, perked Lilly up immensely and by the time they crossed the canal into Rathmines, she was subconsciously stroking her belly.

"He'll be surprised, shocked even, but delighted. I'm sure. He told me he'd love to have children with me one day!"

Ha! Did he now? One day? That'll be the day the Sahara freezes over and the camels come skating home. These suspicions Fudge kept to herself, not wanting to threaten Lilly's new-found, yet brittle, self-assurance. She desperately needed the buoyancy to carry her through the stormy waters ahead.

"Do you want to give him a ring?" she said instead. "I'll go to my room if he'd like to call round. You can have a chat in private."

"No... No, I can't ring him at home. I mean, it's too late. I'll call him in the morning." A shadow fell once again. Of course. The wife and children. One had to show consideration. Damn him to hell!

Later, wearing pyjamas and towelling dressing gowns, the two friends curled up on the sofa with mugs of milky cocoa. They didn't speak for a long while, both peering silently into their cups as if hoping to find a brighter and more promising future swirling round and round in the creamy, hot chocolate depths.

A baby. Fudge knew what that meant. Giving up your job, putting your social life on hold, changing nappies, puke on your shoulder, oozing breasts, flabby stomach, sleepless nights, the responsibility, the fears—and the joy. She'd seen that, too. The sheer and utter elation of holding one's own flesh and blood cradled in caring arms, of breathing in the sweet, powdery baby fragrances, feeling the soft, downy hair against one's cheek. The longing had come rushing over her two years before when Sheila and Danny had had their first child, a plump, rosy bundle with a shock of black hair so startling that people did a double take when passing the pram. What a commotion there had been at Birch Rise!

"Another woman to annoy me!" Charlie had bellowed proudly as he lit up a fat Cuban cigar. "Is there no peace for the wicked, at all?"

Mary, almost forgetting the child was not her own and only there to visit, had immediately cleared a space on the drying frame for nappies and babygrows, and when, at the weekend, the sound of vigorous baby's cries reverberated through the old farmhouse, she was in heaven. Sarah, who the twins called "siren" on account of her healthy screams, would grow up wallowing in love, surrounded by a clatter of doting aunts and concerned grandparents. But what was to become of Lilly's baby? Illegitimate, a bastard child born out of wedlock and, as Fudge feared, fatherless, too. Michael McDermott would support them surely, yet what kind of a life lay in store? And how long would it be before Lilly's quirky, gregarious nature drove the single mother back to a life of parties, pubs and discos, leaving the child alone with its grandfather? The Heidi of Ballsbridge.

"I'll always be here if you need me." Fudge said all of a sudden, reaching out to pat Lilly's hand. "You never have to feel alone, you know that."

"I know, but everything will be all right. Jack will take care of me, you'll see." A rose-coloured glow of conviction had changed her appearance; the tears had tried, the sparkle returned to her eyes. "I'll ring him at the office, first thing."

"Do that. Take the day off. I'll be at work and you can have the flat to yourselves. Talk everything over."

Lilly nodded bravely, and moments later their thoughts reverted to the cocoa cups and the chocolate crystal ball floating within.

Neither of them slept a wink that night.

Late as a result, when Fudge finally left for work the following morning, Lilly was already up and dressed to the nines, her hair freshly washed, her make-up impeccable. In the pastel green, scoop-necked pullover and hip-hugging skirt, she was the very picture of voluptuousness. A ripe plum bursting with new life. She'd been to the shop, and next to a plateful of fresh rolls and rock buns, a huge vase brimming with bright tulips decorated their modest dining table. The delicious smell of freshly percolated coffee wafted out of the kitchenette. Fudge looked at Lilly quizzically.

"Can I presume this isn't for me?"

Her flatmate smiled timorously. "Jack's coming over. He'll be here soon. I've... I've told him. I couldn't wait!"

"You've told him! Gosh, that was quick!"

"I caught him just as he was arriving at the office—he still had his coat on!"

"And what did he say?"

"Wow."

"Wow?"

"He said, 'Wow, this is a surprise!'" Lilly giggled nervously. "That's good, isn't it?"

"Well, em... I suppose so, I mean, he didn't say 'shit, this is a bloody disaster', did he?"

"No... And when I asked him, he said he'd be right over. He just had one or two things to clarify with his secretary."

"Good, I'm glad. It's a start."

Lilly rushed to the mirror, studied herself from all sides and teased a lock of hair over her forehead.

"I don't look fat, do I? You can't see anything yet?"

Fudge snorted. "Lilly, your baby is a pea-sized bundle of dividing cells—will you stop fussing! Your tits are massive, though, positively vulgar. Jack'll go wild!"

Lilly laughed and pushed her friend towards the door. "Go on, get out of here before he arrives. You're cramping my style!"

During the night the black clouds had dispersed, and outside the sun was shining, warming the air and causing fat buds on the row of cherry trees lining the road to burst open like popcorn, the pastel pink blossoms glowing vividly in the grey suburban street. Springtime. Pathetic fallacy. Everything budding, blooming, sprouting.

Driving away, Fudge waved at Lilly who was standing in the doorway, but the expectant mother didn't wave back. She was too busy searching the junction at the end of the road as she waited for the father of her child to appear around the corner.

~ * ~

At one o'clock the phone rang on Fudge's desk.

"He hasn't arrived yet." Lilly's voice was hollow with fear.

"Oh dear. Have you tried the office?"

"His secretary said he went out about an hour ago."

"Well then, don't worry, he'll be on his way."

"Fudge, his office is only fifteen minutes away!"

"Then he's off buying flowers, or a bottle of bubbly—or both! He's probably stuck in the long queue at Dunne's—Murphy's Law!" The excuse sounded feeble, pathetic.

"What'll I do?"

"Wait, of course. I bet he's at the traffic lights on the main road this very minute."

"D'you really think so?"

"Yeah," Fudge answered with as much fervour as she could muster under the piteous circumstances.

"Okay, I'll put the kettle on again."

At three o'clock she phoned for a second time in floods of tears. The voice was the same strangled squeak she'd heard so many times.

"He never came! Oh God, I want to kill myself!"

Fudged breathed deeply. How she'd hoped her suspicions could have been unfounded.

"Lilly, try to keep calm, I'm sure there's an explanation. Did you try to call him again?"

"That snooty bitch of a secretary said he was off on business for the day—I don't believe her!"

"Maybe something urgent cropped up, I'm sure..."

"Am I not urgent? I rang him first," Lilly wailed indignantly.

"You're right. Look, I'm sure he'll call..."

"Maybe he's had an accident, been seriously injured—or killed!" The despairing woman's voice reached a feverish pitch.

No such bloody luck, Fudge grumbled silently in a moment of fury. Fate would not be so gracious. She struggled not to lose her temper.

"Someone would call you if he had, wouldn't they?"

"Who? His wife? Nobody knows about us—only you!"

Oh sweet Jesus. This springtime nightmare was blossoming nicely, too.

"Fudge, could you...? Would you...?"

"What?"

"Would you ring his home later on, give him a message? You're good on the phone, if his wife answers you could pretend you're someone from the company."

"But you could do that, too."

"No, no, I couldn't. I'm far too emotional just now. If you would just tell him to call me as soon as possible."

"I don't know…"

"Please."

It seemed they spent their lives begging each other to do things. Fudge sighed in resignation.

"Oh, all right, I'll be home at five, but I'm sure he'll have been in touch by then." She put down the phone knowing in her heart of hearts that, this time, the shit had really hit the fan big time.

The inner city traffic chaos stubbornly refusing to let Fudge out of it possessive clutches, it was nearly half five when she finally squeezed into a parking space at the far end of the residential street. *I hope that bastard has called*, she thought as she trotted up the front steps, her gaze hurriedly sweeping over the other parked cars on either side of the road. Most of them were familiar, but none looked like it might belong to a successful consulting engineer with a wealthy spouse. Wishful thinking.

Prepared for the worst, the pathetic heap of wretchedness lying in a foetal position on the rug in front of the sofa still managed to take her by surprise. The heap was mewing like a tiny kitten with a lousy cold. Fudge crouched down beside her flatmate and stroked the tousled head.

"He never called, huh?"

The confusion of blond curls shook.

"Shit… Right, you want me to call him?"

Lilly pushed herself up into a sitting position. Her eyes were hugely swollen, a delta of mascara fanning out across the blotchy cheeks like a hideous tribal war mask. A profusion of bunched and tattered tissues lay spread about the floor around her. She grasped Fudge's sleeve with trembling fingers.

"I can't believe this is happening to me. He sounded fine on the phone—a little gunked perhaps, but not really mad or anything. He was relatively calm actually."

"Hmm, and you're sure he said he'd be right over?"

"Positive. I was so relieved."

"Right, then we should try to reach him at home just to be sure nothing's happened to him for a start."

Fudge had to fight back the burning desire to rattle off a long list of horrific things she hoped might have happened to him in the meantime.

"You don't mind?"

"Don't worry, these kind of phone calls are part of my job—leave it to me. Where's the number?"

Lilly handed her the bit of folded paper she'd fished out of the corner of her purse. Reaching for the phone, Fudge studied the name, address and number. The Bay Mews, Killiney. Upmarket prick. She dialled and waited. The telephone rang out for a long time before someone finally answered. Expecting a woman, she was momentarily confused when a man's deep voice spoke.

"Hello." Not more.

"Good evening, my name's Fin... Francis. Might I be speaking to Jack... Em..." Jesus wept! She didn't even know the man's surname. She searched the piece of paper in her hand. "Mon... Montig..." Lilly's handwriting was illegible.

"...Montague, yes, speaking. What is it?" Composed, collected, clammy and related to Romeo, too.

"Well..." She hadn't done her homework on this scenario. "A mutual friend asked me to call. I think you should ring her."

"I beg your pardon. I don't think I quite understand."

"You were to visit her this morning, but didn't turn up. She's rather upset."

"I had no appointments, if I'm not greatly mistaken." His equanimity didn't fail him for an instant. In the background Fudge could hear a high-pitched female voice calling, "Dinner, darling," and decided to get to the point before his Châteauxbriand started to congeal.

"Mister Montague, would you please phone Lilly this evening?"

"I'm afraid I really don't know who you're talking about." He was calm, self-assured and in complete control.

"Lilly! Lillian McDermott, your girlfriend! She needs you now and you know it!" Fudge had to stop herself from shouting.

"I'm sorry, Miss... um... Francis, but I've never heard the name before in my life."

"What...?" Click. The phone went dead. As she replaced the receiver, she could see Lilly's reflection in the mirror over the sideboard. She was startlingly pale, trance-like, swaying on the verge of total shock, as though her world had gone into the slow lane, the early evening sounds of passing cars and barking dogs having been sucked out of the vacuum in which she found herself trapped, leaving only ominous silence behind.

"What... What went wrong?" she asked at last.

"I'm not sure. I think his wife was listening. He couldn't speak."

"Do you think he'll get in touch?" That tiny flame of hope was still there, faltering and frail.

"Maybe." And all at once, Fudge couldn't bear it any longer. She took Lilly's icy cold hands in hers. "Lilly, you have to forget him."

"No... No, the baby..."

"Perhaps he loves you, but he won't leave his family—ever!"

"You can't know!"

"No, listen to me! He won't leave them and I don't think he'll contact you again. I'm sorry..."

"But... But..."

"You have to be strong now. I'll help you through this."

"I can't..."

"You can!" Fudge held Lilly's shoulders firmly.

"No... No..." The blond woman moaned weakly.

"You don't need him. It's over."

~ * ~

A few days after that, a hastily addressed envelope fell through the letterbox. In that second, all the hope came flooding back once again and, for a short moment, the deep crease of worry furrowing the pregnant woman's forehead softened. But only for an instant. A minute later she placed the contents of the envelope on the table in front of Fudge, went to her room and locked the door. Several crisp hundred-pound bank notes lay fanned out like a hand of cards on the dark wooden surface. Instantly, she knew who it was from, and what it was for. Blood money. It stank, making Fudge recoil.

It was late in the evening before Lilly came into the living room and sat down in the nest of country-coloured cushions. Her face was blank, devoid of emotion. She stared at the notes on the table while she spoke.

"Fudge, I have to go to England."

"Are you sure? You should think about this carefully."

"There's nothing to think about. I just want to get it over and done with."

"Maybe you should talk to someone. I still have that note from Doctor Plunkett."

"No, I've decided."

"Why don't you wait a while?"

"It has to be done, Fudge. I'll do it with or without your help. I need some addresses."

"Leave that to me."

"Thanks." Lilly stood up and walked to the table where she paused before returning to her bedroom. "Fudge, would you take care of the money? I can't touch it."

~ * ~

"Skids, I need some addresses—quickly, if possible." She was standing in front of her boss's desk, having first carefully closed the door to the front office where the girls were busy discussing the previous evening's quiz show. Fudge fixed him with a challenging look.

"What kinda addresses?"

"In England—clinics—you know what I mean."

"What the hell makes you think I'd know anything about clinics in England!"

"With all respect, boss, but don't bullshit me. This is an emergency. I'm the one who screens your women and makes up stories to keep the wife happy. You know everyone and everything—and I think you know the address of a clinic in England."

"You up the pole, or what?"

"Not me, a friend."

"Ha! That's what they all say. Now, c'mon, Finnula, get back to work." He waved a beefy hand at her.

"Skids, don't force me to remind you of Maggie Rourke—eighteen years old if she was a day. What was she doing visiting her aunt in London a week after college term began? Huh? You should know, you had her driven to the ferry, remember? I had to pay the taxi from petty cash."

"Talkin' dirty to me is one thing, Miss Ginnane, but now you're treadin' on awfully dangerous ground. Don't you like your job?"

"An address, Mister Curry."

The pear-shaped man shook his balding head and pulled a well-fingered and frayed business card from his wallet.

"You didn't get that from me, d'ya hear?"

"Get what?" Fudge answered, slipping the card into her jacket pocket.

"Get out of here!"

"Thanks, Skids, you're a dote." She blew the scowling man a kiss as she made her way to the door.

~ * ~

The following Thursday the two women were looking for a seat on the car ferry to Hollyhead where they would catch the boat train down to London. As usual, Fudge had made all the arrangements, organising appointments, booking tickets and bending Skid's arm backward for two days off work. Nodding towards her flat belly, he'd glared suspiciously at her.

"You sure there's nuttin' in there?"

"Nothing that hasn't been there all the time."

"Humph... Well, just make sure you're back to work on Monday, or I'll shag you out on your ear!"

"Nine o'clock sharp!"

"Eight o'clock, if you don't mind, madam."

"Janey mac, Skids, you're a slave driver!"

Fudge and Lilly found a place with a view towards the stern of the ship from where they could see the long arm of Dun Laoghaire pier receding into the distance behind them. Automatically, they had both searched the crest of the hill up behind Glenageary hoping to catch a nostalgic glimpse of Castleglen Park, but a foggy blanket of haze stretched along the coastline towards Dalkey, obscuring their vision. It was all so long ago, the musty school corridors, the smell of waxed linoleum, the tightly corseted Miss Gibbons, farting Brenda Buckley. And the night Lilly went over the wall. Tomorrow, she would stand before another wall, the biggest hurdle of all, and Fudge was there to help her over. Yet what was waiting for her on the other side? Regret, guilt, sorrow? A picture of what might have been? A relinquished chance and the horrible realisation that a snippet of her soul had been irrevocably extinguished?

The boat had reached open waters, heaving and crunching over the undulating swell of the Irish Sea. The horizon was barely distinguishable, dissolving without a transition into the leaden sky that spread away on all sides, unbroken and monotonous. Occasionally, lurching over the massive wake, a fishing vessel chugged by, dwarfed and insignificant beside the looming multi-storey ferry. The deckhands were tiny figures struggling with sheaths of slick trawling nets

Nearby, the lounge was open and already rows of ruddy-faced workers in donkey jackets were balancing their pints at the bar. Every now and then, one of them would glance over and wink, or with unmistakable gestures, endeavour to entice the young women over for a drink. Fudge rolled her eyes and turned to the window.

Lilly, always on for a flirt as a rule, wasn't even aware of their existence. She was far, far away, staring unwaveringly out across the rising and falling expanse. They didn't talk, but sat in silence, the time passing as laboriously as the endless sea miles, and when the smell of smoke and beer became too strong, the rolling of the ship unbearable, and the men's advances too obnoxious, the two friends walked the decks, their jackets pulled tightly up around their ears as a biting, salty wind whipped over the railings and along the empty gangways.

It was late at night when they eventually arrived at the small family Bed and Breakfast tucked away in a suburb of London where every house on the street looked identical. Skids, God bless him, had sidled up to Fudge's desk the previous evening and handed her the pile of documents she'd given him to sign earlier that day. The number of Biddy Flanagan's B & B on Victoria Road fell out from between the sheets before the beefy giant had time to retreat.

"She'll see you right," he'd mumbled bashfully. "Her husband owes me for a pair of grease-nippled male-ended ball joints."

"A pair of grease-nippled male-ended ball joints?"

"And a drive shaft."

"Thanks, Skids, you're a gem."

Her boss coughed and tugged his bulging tweed waistcoat into position before abruptly remembering his superiority. He pointed a pork sausage finger at his PA.

"Don't even dream of legging it out of here until the last quotation has been faxed, d'you hear me, Miss?"

"You drive a hard bargain, boss," Fudge answered with a grin. "I'll see what I can do."

"Humph," Skids answered in his usual eloquent manner, signifying that the subject was closed and forgotten.

Fussing around in her floral dressing gown, Biddy Flanagan apologised profusely as she filled up two hot water bottles and shoved them under the mountainous bed-quilts. Even before she'd fluffed the pillows and drawn the curtains, the two younger Irish women were falling asleep on their feet.

An instant later, it seemed, the alarm clock was ringing and Lilly was dashing madly to the toilet, the wave of morning sickness relieving her of the greasy corned-beef sandwich the landlady had so persuasively insisted on serving up minutes before they'd collapsed into bed. It would be a long day, Fudge knew, every second stretching into perpetuity, every minute tortuously eternal.

At the breakfast table, Lilly pushed the rubbery dollop of scrambled egg away from her and leaned forward.

"Would it look like me, do you think?" she whispered, afraid Biddy might be lurking somewhere behind the door.

"It? The baby? Oh, Lilly, don't!" Fudge put down her tea and heaved a sigh. "You're torturing yourself!" *And me*, she thought, miserably.

Over and over again, visions of little Sarah gurgling happily in her pram flashed through her mind. The gleam of pride shining from Sheila's eyes, the family sharing her happiness. There it was again, the pang of envy, the longing. A child. A family of her own. She'd never really wanted to study, never wanted a career, nor felt the slightest desire to keep up with the new power-seeking, bra-burning academic Amazons the universities were churning out by the hundreds. Maybe she had something in common with the secretarial college vultures after all.

She felt it now more than ever: a housewife and mother was what Fudge, in her heart of hearts, had ever wanted to be. Perhaps if she hadn't been so critical, viewing every man she met as a potential candidate, a sperm donor and provider, and furtively testing his paternal assets while, at the same time, building maternal castles in the sky. She'd had her chances, but none were right for the job, all dismally falling short of fitting the bill. Or had she scared them off with her eagerness? One or the other, who knows? Anyone capable of glimpsing into the far reaches of Fudge's heart, however, would know there was something else standing in her way, but even she herself did not have the courage to look that far. Relationships remained brief, petering out into sporadic evenings spent in silence in front of the telly, usually his.

And then there'd always been Johnny, sometimes a lover, sometimes a listener, hovering somewhere in the background when she, yet again, needed to escape from her world, or for that matter, he from his. Until last year. He'd called one evening just as Fudge, in a fit of frustration, had been rummaging through the fridge looking for something sweet and fattening.

"Johnny, what's up? You lusting after my bod again?" she bantered, tucking the phone under her chin in order to pull the lid off a carton of raspberry ripple.

"Jaysus, Finnula, always thinkin' of smut, you are!"

"Look who's talking! But now that you mention it, I do have a hankering for something sweet..."

Johnny didn't leap to the bait; instead he hummed and hawed for a while before getting to the point.

"Em... Finnula... You know I had a sort of a girlfriend?"

"Yeah, Jacqueline, wasn't it?"

"Well, it's like this..."

"Don't tell me I'm not the centre of your universe anymore." Fudge chuckled; their borderlines were clearly defined, jokes like this allowed.

"Actually, she has a bun in the oven."

A pang of envy took her by surprise. "Yours?"

"Yep."

"Oops."

"We're getting married..."

Fudge swallowed, faltering briefly before continuing the banter, and hoping he hadn't noticed. "So you're no longer number fifty on my puny list of lovers?"

"'Fraid not." A wistful timbre that picked up hurriedly. "But if you ever need a good thrashing you can give me a shout. You're not mad at me, are you?"

"Ach, Johnny, sad maybe, not mad. I'll miss your rotten sense of humour, but I suppose this day had to come, life moves on."

"S'pose so, pity though, you're great *craic*!"

"Take care. You'll be a good husband, won't you?"

"Cross me heart."

"And a great father?"

"No sweat!"

She'd been overtaken once more. While she plodded along in the slow lane, everyone else was galloping ahead with their lives, one way or the other, good or bad. She seemed to be the only one not getting anywhere. Like a hamster on a treadmill.

The sound of Biddy Flanagan clearing away plates at the next table tore her out of her contemplation. Passing on her way back to the kitchen, she pursed her lips in a momentary pout of displeasure at the sight of Lilly's untouched plate.

"Eat up, deary, you'll be needing your strength. I'll bring another pot of tea."

Lilly paled visibly. Biddy, an expatriate with a huge heart, wasn't an eejit and knew exactly what the young women were doing in London. It was always the same, they arrived pale and anxious, usually with a friend, and left shocked and confused, but never, as one might have thought, relieved and pleased. When the dining room door thudded closed behind the landlady, Lilly leant forward again.

"It might be a little girl."

"What difference does it make? You have to stop thinking about it!"

"They say that at eight weeks the heart is already beating."

"Stop it! Stop it!" Fudge felt her throat constricting. She was suddenly so sick of it all. Sick of guiding Lilly through hell and back, fed up with sharing her anguish and suffering, of being an emotional crutch.

"Look, you've made up your mind. You didn't want to think about it—refused advice!" Fudge snapped. "It's too bloody late now, this afternoon it'll be all over!"

"All over." A tear slid down Lilly's cheek. She sat perfectly still, letting it fall.

Biddy Flanagan popped her head around the door, frowned disapprovingly and disappeared back into the kitchen. Ashamed, Fudge stared down at her trembling hands. "I'm sorry, this isn't easy for me either. I didn't mean..."

"No... My fault."

They said little else until they arrived at the clinic, a squat, grey building situated three tube stations from Flanagan's B & B. The nurses were cheery and business-like, the patients glassy-eyed and dazed. In the waiting room a young man in a bomber jacket and a pair of Doc Martins sat clutching the hand of an even younger girl whose jaw was grinding away nervously on a mouthful of neon pink chewing gum. Opposite, a chubby, bewildered teenager sat bolt upright next to her equally bewildered mother. In the corner, hidden behind a daily editorial, a middle-aged woman in a tweed suit and support pantyhose squinted blindly at the paper through horn-rimmed glasses, sadly unaware she holding it upside down.

And then it was Lilly's turn. A rigidly pressed and bleached nurse accompanied the two Irishwomen to a small room where Lilly was instructed to change into an open-backed hospital garment.

"That's fierce sexy," Fudge commented dryly as she watched her friend clamber up onto a narrow gurney, her white bottom flashing briefly before she had time to settle.

She laughed weakly. "Don't talk about sex at a time like this. What do you think got me into this mess?" An instant later her smile vanished. "I'm not making a mistake, am I, Fudge?"

"How can we know whether anything we ever decide to do is a mistake or not? Sometimes we just have to make decisions—even if we don't want to."

"And if someone took the responsibility of making a decision for you?"

"Well, I'd put my foot down if it concerned me. I think I'd want a say in the matter, wouldn't you?"

"And if you couldn't?"

"Couldn't what?"

"Couldn't have a say in the matter."

"You mean if I were ill, injured, or unconscious?"

"...or a foetus."

Fudge sucked in her breath, shocked.

Lilly looked at her with wide eyes. "Don't you think this baby wants to live?"

"Lilly, it's not really a baby yet."

"When exactly does a foetus become a baby?" Lilly's voice was becoming increasingly agitated. "When does it begin to think, to feel!"

"Ssh, calm down."

"Can it hear us now, discussing its life?"

"I... I don't know..."

The starched nurse came into the room and started pushing the gurney towards the door. Lilly's eyes were darting back and forth like a caged animal's.

"Fudge! Don't go away!"

"Sorry, love," the nurse said with an air of superiority. "Your friend can't come with you. She can visit later."

"But... But..."

"Off we go now."

Trance-like, Fudge watched as the hospital gurney receded quickly down the brightly lit corridor, its unoiled wheels screaming loudly in sympathetic protest. Lilly's eyes were blinking frantically under the blinding white neon lighting, her hands grasping the hard metal frame in a vice-like grip.

"Fudge! Can it think?" she called just before the heavy doors leading to the operating theatre swung open to engulf her. "Can it feel...?"

Fudge stood riveted to the spot, the palm of her hand pressed to her mouth as the swing doors snapped shut once again, amputating Lilly's cries. *Sweet Jesus, what have we done?* The busy passageway seemed suddenly silent, the squeaking of hurrying rubber-soled shoes on linoleum and the rumbling of hospital trolleys very far away. Off in the distance a hollow, breathy intercom voice ordered Doctor Jones to the reception, and somewhere near the main entrance on orderly was yapping directives. In the nurses' station a phone was ringing.

And then she heard it. A loudly barked command, forceful and determined.

"*STOP!*"

Then again.

"*Stop*! Let me out of here!"

A moment later, Lilly exploded through the swing doors, the green hospital gown flapping up around her naked thighs as she galloped barefooted along the corridor, her hair streaming back in a wild, golden mane.

"Grab my clothes, quick!" she screamed, half laughing, half crying. "We're bunking out of here—all three of us!"

"What?"

"You heard me, get a move on!"

"But the ab—"

"Forget it, Fudge, we're going to have a baby!"

"We?"

"Yes! We're going to have this baby—together—you and me!" She shrieked with delight, and Fudge found herself shrieking, too, vaguely aware, nevertheless, that this decision had been made for her, and she hadn't an ice-cube's hope in hell of changing it.

Fourteen

While Finnula Ginnane was contemplating an ice-cube's chances of surviving Lucifer's fiery inferno, her mother, Mary, was going through a hell of her own.

She couldn't believe it. A pair of ageing fuddy-duddies, as Rosy would say, and they were still at it. Their relationship, over the years, had waxed and waned with the regularity of a lunar cycle, the intensity of it as variable and capricious as earthly seasonal changes. As she'd slipped inexorably over the borderline into her fifties, the winter of inner turmoil had been bitter and long, and with it, the harsh realisation that even the greatest emotion of all could not stop the clock. The icy cloak of advancing time had put springtime on hold and kept feelings checked. Yet these feelings flourished, hardly noticeable initially, like the first blade of coarse Siberian grass pushing its way up through the snow-covered plains. And Mary, looking at herself in the bathroom mirror, was tired of feeling like one of those prehistoric mammoth cows plodding wearily back from winter grazing at the foot of the Alps to spend the ice-age summer on the vast northern pampas. That's what it felt like—trudging laboriously across life's tundra.

She splashed her face with a handful of icy cold water in an effort to wash away the unexpected wave of dejection. Exaggerating again, as usual. Mammoth cow, indeed! *Pull yourself together, woman,* she thought suddenly. *Here you are, loved by two men despite the web of crow's feet next to your eyes and the slightly thickening waistline—and still complaining! Isn't that something to be proud of—even if it is throwing a spanner in life's works?* Two men, three lives, a mixed salad of feelings.

Yet after all these years it was still there, the flutter of unexpected excitement, the giddy anticipation, the temptation. She sighed heavily. Strange, she was good at containing feelings, at exercising willpower, suppressing a laugh or bridling anger, but what did one do to stop the dart of emotion triggered off by a certain name, a face, a voice? Mary thought she had it under control, especially after Sarah was born. At weekends, when the young family came down from the city, her life was full again, the house alive with girlish laughs, the living room strewn with toys. The empty places at the dining room table were filled once more, the kitchen churning out meals for eight. Grandparents now, there was a reawakened closeness in her relationship to Charlie, a shared pride, a sense of belonging. Until that day she found herself standing alone at the window looking out across the distant Loughrua hills, she'd been sure her happiness was complete.

It had started on a Monday when the rambling farmhouse was quiet. Sheila's family had returned to Galway and the girls were at school. She'd been watching Charlie as he slowly followed the trail across the stubbly winter meadow on his early morning rounds, the collar of his wax jacket turned up against a shroud of persistent drizzle. It started as a tiny prickle of nostalgia, a wistful memory, a lone thought, then slowly, but surely, it began to spread and strengthen until it had become, as it had a thousand times before, a fully-fledged feeling of incompleteness and wanting. Turning, her eyes automatically searched the high bookcase for the dog-eared C.S. Lewis. It had been over a year since they'd last spoken, a brief, awkward telephone conversation made from a phone box in

Loughrua. No, she couldn't meet him, she'd explained soberly, not now. He'd noticed it then, the determination in her voice, the will power. Her life was whole again, his presence always a threat, and Michael knew he had to let her go.

In a way Mary had been relieved to put an end to it, throwing herself into her role as a grandmother, the doyenne of the Ginnane family, the mother hen clucking with bustling pride as she gathered her flock around her. This flock was more than just family; it was a human screen protecting her from sentimental intrusion, and it had worked, too. For weeks, since that first lone twinge of nostalgia had penetrated her consciousness, she'd tried, as best she could, to ignore the relentless trickle of emotion slowly seeping through, occasionally throwing a sandbag of resolve onto the dam in the hope of stemming the ever-increasing flow.

Until now. With Sheila's phone call that morning, it had finally burst, the unanticipated flood bowling her over in an instant. It was Friday and the two women were making plans for the weekend. Between snippets of gossip, baby talk and lamentations over the price of nappies, she'd mentioned the UCG lecture.

"I see Lillian McDermott's father is in town," Sheila piped casually. "Haven't you met him?"

"Yes... a few times," Mary answered, wondering if Sheila could sense her heart tightening.

"He has a lecture on something or other up at the college. Is he an art expert, or what?"

"Something like that..."

And the talk moved on to puréed vegetable dinners and whether she should take Sarah's soother away from her or not.

"It'll ruin her teeth," the young mother complained. "And anyway, she's far too old for it."

Far too old for it. That was the last bit of the conversation Mary had absorbed. Far too old for it.

Now, standing at the bathroom sink, the mirror mockingly confirmed her suspicions. Too old for it, yet still attractive. Her figure was womanly, curvaceous and still under control, the dark chestnut locks speckled with grey, but thick, her shoulders straight. And deep inside was that feeling the mirror couldn't reflect, a feeling resistant to age. A murmur in her mind that cried "never to old!" He wouldn't call her, she knew. There was no point hoping. It was over; she had seen to that.

Mechanically, she began to pull a brush through her hair, slowly combing the same strand over and over again. He'd be staying at the Ardmore Hotel, as always, in a room decorated in rose-patterned chintz and a view out over the gardens. If he had time, he would drive out to Silver Strand and walk along the sandy beach. She could see him in her mind's eye, the tousled, greying hair fluttering around his face in the Atlantic breeze, his gaze searching the ocean swell where it joined the horizon.

Mary switched the brush to her other hand and started tugging it through her hair once again, this time more vigorously. Just a walk. One walk with him along a lonely beach, maybe take his hand and talk for a while. Not more. That would be all. It would be enough. She glanced at her watch. It was almost midday. Michael would be sitting in his hotel room preparing the evening lecture, checking the slides, writing an article, the telephone next to his elbow. With a start, Mary realised she was clutching the hairbrush so tightly her knuckles had turned white, and her skull was numb from hectic combing.

Damn! Damn! A year. She hadn't seen him for a year. All she wanted was an hour. One hour with Michael. It wouldn't hurt anyone. One hour. And all at once, her legs were carrying her down the stairs to the living room where the telephone stood on the sideboard. The Ardmore Hotel. With trembling fingers she turned the pages of the business directory until the number jumped up at her, begging for attention. She reached for the receiver twice, each time pulling her hand away and wiping it nervously on the side of her slacks. Then Mary made up her mind.

~ * ~

Outside the back door, Charlie was grunting with the exertion of taking off his heavy green Wellingtons. His hands were cold, but his body steamed with perspiration. The spring weather had brought with it a confusion of temperatures enough to drive any farmer sheer mad, yet he was in good form, Ireland's seasonal quirks insufficient to dampen his mood. He lined the huge muddy boots up next to a tiny pair of bright red ones, and smiling to himself, he padded into the kitchen on thick-knit woollen feet, his thoughts wandering to Sarah and how such a small bundle of gurgling humanity had changed their lives.

They were whole again—he could feel it. The moments of uncertainty he'd sensed time and again during the previous years had passed. The bond had tightened. It was almost noon and he was tired, hungry, but happy. The house was silent, only the crackling of wood burning in the range was perceptible, and every now and then the plinking of water from a leaking tap. Mary would be upstairs somewhere making beds, or stacking clothes in the hot press.

Wearily, he put the kettle on to boil and sat down at the long wooden table, straining ever so slightly to catch his breath. Lord, he'd have to watch himself, he thought, running a hand over his brow. He wasn't the youngest anymore, a fact which had occurred to him an hour before when he'd feebly tried to vault a stone wall out on the Brackens, the action leaving him flat on his face in the wet grass on the other side and his heart thumping erratically. His pride was intact, the stone wall flattened.

The unexpected fall had given him a fright, but he was fine. He'd had worse scares in his past, that's for sure. Charlie sniggered to himself remembering the long ago vision of Muriel McMahon's backside engulfing the saddle of her bike as she laboured up the lane towards Bullcudy. He'd survived that scare, hadn't he? After lunch, he'd ride out on Shanagarry and build up the wall again, but first, a rest and a bite to eat.

A moment later, the kettle was whistling urgently and Charlie wished he didn't have to get up to take it off the range. Where was that wife of his, anyway? He listened again for the sound of her footsteps and hearing nothing, heaved himself up to wet the tea. *She'll be nestled in the corner of an armchair with that latest bestseller wrapped around her ears,* he thought affectionately. Mary and her books. Yet again, when he considered Muriel McMahon's passion for crocheting and the way their house was coming down with acrylic tea-cosies, cushion covers and antimacassars, Charlie realised it could be a lot worse. Inwardly, he was proud. He'd married a wonderful, intelligent, well-read woman, the mother of their children and now granny to boot.

He placed two cups of tea and a packet of gingernut biscuits on a tray and pushed his way out into the corridor, his socked feet shuffling silently over the carpeted floor. Approaching the living room, he began to distinguish a murmuring monologue and for a moment his brow ruffled. Visitors? Was one of the girls home early? No, she'd be on the phone nattering away to beat the band about babies, bottles and chapped bottoms. Books and babies, her favourite subjects. The door was slightly ajar and, as he drew near, he saw her head bent over the receiver, the familiar wisp of stray hair falling over her forehead. The expression on her face made him stop and, hovering uncertainly, Charlie waited in the darkness of the shadowy hallway.

"It's been such a long time…" Mary was saying, the wistful urgency in her voice making Charlie's heart flutter with unease.

"We shouldn't, I know." Conspiratorial, hesitant. "Maybe just an hour or so…"

The farmer's shoulders sagged. He knew his wife and recognised that this was no conversation between female friends surreptitiously plotting a shopping spree, nor a confidential plan for afternoon tea on the sly.

"I understand, it's so difficult," she continued. "If only I knew what to do…"

Charlie's hands began to quiver and instinctively he tightened his grip on the tray, afraid the cups might rattle. His breathing was shallow, strained.

"I feel terrible, too, but…" The words faded momentarily as Mary turned her head towards the window overlooking the garden. "Ach, Michael," she sighed, and suddenly there it was. The verification. Just as he'd suspected. That McDermott man was still lurking in the background like an animal of prey waiting to spring.

Charlie had seen the sparkle in his wife's eyes many years before when they'd first welcomed the art historian into the house as their guest, and in later years suspected there might be a friendship he knew nothing about, a friendship tugging at the bonds of their marriage. It was an unspoken subject and it seemed that Mary had resisted temptation, showing her husband time and time again that her heart was with him at Birch Rise. His doubts had faded, disappearing at last when little Sarah arrived, bringing a new sense of purpose to their lives, strengthening and deepening their relationship once again. How happy he'd been in recent months. And now this. This man was trying to get in the way, luring his wife into a trap of enticement. Thankfully, it never occurred to Charlie for a moment that Mary might have initiated the telephone conversation he was unwillingly being forced to overhear. A poor comfort.

"All right, then. We could meet at the hotel." Her resolution was crumbling. She was slipping away. "A walk on the beach... Silver Strand? Yes, yes... Fine."

Her voice had softened to a whisper, but already Charlie had heard enough and was retreating quietly back down the passageway to the kitchen. With trance-like robotic movements, he went to the back door, pulled on his Wellingtons, threw his damp wax jacket over his shoulder and slipped noiselessly out into the chilling veil of incessant drizzle.

~ * ~

Mary was all of a dither. It was done now; they'd arranged to meet. Two o'clock in Galway. She paced uneasily up and down in front of the fireplace. What had she done? Was she mad? What would she wear? This last bizarre thought scurried through her head, causing an involuntary snort of nervous laughter to bubble up inside. Feeling as giddy as a teenager, Mary, had she been able, would have taken the steps two at a time as she rushed upstairs to tear apart her wardrobe. It was nippy outside. Where was it, that soft charcoal cashmere pullover she always claimed was too expensive for a farmhouse kitchen? It camouflaged her slightly chunky middle-aged waist nicely—and under it, the pale-blue and white checked shirt with the small round collar. Fresh, young. And jeans! By God, she'd wear jeans today! The twins were constantly trying to bamboozle her into putting them on, claiming they made her look girlish, less "mumsy". *You'll have me looking like mutton dressed as lamb*, she'd protested, vainly knowing they were right. Today, she'd gladly take their sartorial advice. *To hell with middle-aged modesty! Jeans, it is!*

Three quarters of an hour later, freshly made up and feeling like she'd bathed in the fountain of youth, Mrs. Ginnane hurried into the kitchen. Where was Charlie? He usually turned up at the back door at midday looking for lunch. It was almost one o'clock and there was no sign of him. She didn't want to go traipsing down to the yard in her good shoes.

Growing nervous again, she walked over to the window, her forehead wrinkling at the sight of the cups and gingernut biscuits sitting on the draining board untouched. A milky skin had formed on the surface of the cold tea. Her mind full of other things, Mary shrugged and searched the laneway leading to the stables. She didn't want to just disappear off, or leave a note. That wasn't her way.

A glimpse at the kitchen clock told her that she'd have to leave soon if she were to be at the Ardmore Hotel on time. Once again, she looked up and down the lane and then, heaving a sigh of edgy irritation, pulled on a wool jacket and left the house through the back door, grimly kissing the gloss on her shiny leather shoes goodbye. As she turned the corner of the house, Mary was suddenly surprised to see Charlie riding Shanagarry out of the yard, his shoulders bunched up against a cutting springtime breeze, his chin lowered onto his chest.

"Charlie!"

Her husband appeared to glance her way, but then continued on, urging the huge hunter through the iron gate and into the meadow.

"Charlie! Will you wait a minute?" Mary cried, hurrying along the muddy lane.

He stopped then and waited, letting the old horse drop its head to graze. His wife climbed onto the first rung of the gate in an effort to avoid the quagmire of churned soil beneath.

"Are you not having any lunch today, love?" she asked.

"Not today, Mary." His voice was hollow, dull.

"You're not hungry?" A prickle of guilt stabbed the pit of Mary's stomach.

He shook his head.

"I see... Em... Look, I have to go to Galway for an hour or so, do you need anything?" She held her breath. He wouldn't ask what she wanted to do in the city; he never did, presuming, as always, she was off to bury herself in a bookshop, or visit Sarah. In most cases he was right.

"No, I don't need anything."

"You're sure? I'll be passing the hardware shop." How could she know that what her husband needed most just then was not for sale on the shelf between nails and screws and pop rivets?

He shook his head once more and turned Shanagarry towards the Brackens, allowing the hunter to find its own way across the new growth of spring grass. Mary watched him for a long moment before heading back to the house. He wasn't himself, she could tell, and immediately the stab of guilt became more piercing, yet beneath it, the longing for Michael remained. She wanted to scream and shout, to wrench out the turmoil of feelings which was throwing her life out of alignment.

How could she love Charlie as she did, and still crave for Michael's company? There was no room in her life for wanton adventures, for clandestine meetings and stolen phone calls. Could there not be an end to it for once and for all? As she reversed the car out onto the driveway, Mary began to feel herself teetering on the brink of am immense decision, a final decision. One last meeting with Michael and no more. No sooner had the idea crossed her mind than she felt like a hypocrite. God, how often had she made that promise in past years. Three, four, five times? Probably more.

Slowly, Mary steered around the curve of the front driveway and up the lane towards the front gate. Automatically, she searched the stretch of pasture off to her right hoping to catch a glimpse of Charlie once more before she turned the corner. The distant form of horse and rider could be seen slowly plodding up the flank of a soft incline behind which the scruffy span of gorse-covered land spread out towards Loughrua.

She'd never really liked him riding out on the Brackens. It was full of rabbit warrens, boggy ditches and grassy hummocks, each obstacle posing a hazard should the ageing hunter misjudge its stride. But Charlie loved it: the rough, lonely landscape, the unrestrained marshland oozing with the fragrance of fresh soil and turf, and above all, the peace and quiet. Outlined against the overcast sky, he appeared very small, a forsaken figure lost in contemplation. Alone.

Approaching the farm entranceway, it suddenly came to her like a flash of lightening, and clutching the steering wheel, she slammed on the brakes. The car slithered to a standstill just inside the Birch Rise gateway. No, she wouldn't! She couldn't! One last meeting— always one last meeting! What kind of an insufferable traitor was she? She could trivialise her relationship to Michael as much as she wanted, the truth was one word—betrayal. To see him a last time would be deceitful and two-faced.

There was no other way; she'd put an end to this hypocritical farce for good. *Here is my home, my life*, Mary thought savagely, *I won't risk it for an hour or so of selfish excitement. If he cares enough for me, he'll understand.* Instantly, she reached a decision. She would leave Michael waiting today, but only today. In the future he must never, ever wait for her again.

~ * ~

Nearing the crest of the incline, Charlie felt dazed, the weight of disappointment unbearable. He'd been grasping the reins so tightly that his hands were stiff and, little by little, a dull numbness had crept into his arm. He shifted in the saddle and flexed his muscles. Why hadn't he stopped, or at least confronted her? Was he a coward, afraid she would protest, afraid she might say something he didn't wish to hear?

The drizzling rainfall had finally ceased and on the horizon a small chink of blue sky appeared beneath the hazy blanket of cloud. Around him, bright April green sloped away on all sides, the grassy expanse interspersed with clumps of pastel yellow primroses and cowslips. Further on, where the meadow became moorland, the gorse was blossoming in glorious clouds of vivid colour, the vaguely coconut scent pungent and heavy.

Charlie saw none of this, his gaze fixed on a point far off in the distance. The weariness he'd felt earlier that day had become crushing lethargy, his energy barely sufficing to encourage the great horse onwards. Just before they began their descent towards the Brackens, the farmer, as always, turned in his saddle to view the land. From the crest of the hill the farm spread away in front of him. Off to the south, the huddle of farmyard buildings separated the long vegetable garden from the grazing fields, where sleepy Friesian cows stood in docile rumination. Ahead, the main house rose tall and solid, the chestnut trees towering up on either side like watchful sentinels protecting the very core of Birch Rise. He let his eyes sweep along the curve of the front driveway, and up the gravel laneway, following the path Mary had taken some minutes before.

A pang of surprise shot through him at the sight of her car standing at the gate, the two front wheels on the cattle grid. The brake lights were flashing bright red, a lurid contrast to the surrounding country hues. Pulling up the reins with a jerk, Charlie's heart pounded, a tiny spark of hope causing his pulse to race. All of a sudden, the rear lights went out and for a moment he believed she would continue on, but then, as quickly as they had extinguished, the glowing red lit up once again.

The spark of hope grew stronger, and when a short while later, the car had not yet moved out onto the road, it became a feeble, sputtering flame. *Come home, Mary! Come home*! He could feel it. She was struggling to make a decision and Charlie knew, deep in his heart, that this choice would be a final one. Holding his breath, he watched and waited. The old horse snorted and shook its mighty head, sending a fine spray of droplets showering out from the wet mane. Willowy plumes of vapour wafted up from the sleek brown equine coat, the warm flanks rising and falling rhythmically. Overhead, a swallow plunged and soared across the pasture, relishing the few weak rays of sunshine that had gradually penetrated the dull leaden skies.

Several minutes passed, then the gleaming brake lights flickered out yet again. Soon after that, the car reversed a short way back from the entranceway and came to a halt on the grassy verge. The driver's door opened and Mary stepped out onto the gravel. Leaning against the bonnet, she lowered her head as if reflecting upon the clump of nodding daffodils springing up out of the grass at her feet. Then she looked up, her eyes fixed on the top of the rise where Charlie sat observing her. Immediately, Mary leapt up and hurried over the lane to the pasture, pushing a way through the soaking, shin-deep stalks in long, resolute strides, a broad smile spreading across her baffled features. Clambering over the loose stone wall separating them, she began to wave, then laugh, tripping and stumbling as she dropped down on the other side.

At first her husband merely watched, taking in the sight with the same eagerness as one would the first rays of sunlight peeping over the arctic horizon after many long months of darkness. Then he began to nudge Shanagarry down the slope, leisurely at first, but soon with ever increasing impatience. As the hunter broke into a labouring trot, Charlie's heart began to flutter erratically in his chest, a fat blue-bottle trapped in a jam jar, buzzing frantically to and fro. A feeling of indescribable happiness flooded over him as his wife drew near. She was still chuckling, shaking her head in mirth at her awkward clumsiness, the knees of her jeans covered in green stains.

They were barely fifty feet apart when, without warning, the laugh that had been bubbling up within Charlie unexpectedly caught in his throat. Small points of light danced before his eyes and his breathing grew arduous. He felt no pain, only a bewildering pressure under his rib cage, a sensation the farmer couldn't remember ever having experienced before in his life. Slumping forward, a strange look of bafflement crossed his face, then try as he might, he found himself unable to grasp the horse's solid neck for support. Far, far away, he could hear Mary calling his name over and over again, and suddenly he was lying in the drenched grass, the rich earthy scent of soil rising about him, and she was cradling his head. He felt the soft wool of her pullover and the warmth of her hand stroking his brow.

"Charlie! Are you hurt? What happened?" Her voice was frantic. "What is it..?"

"I'm tired, Mary, very tired." His breath was coming in small, erratic bursts, every lungful of air drawn an immense struggle.

"Oh God, I have to get help, Charlie, don't move...!"

"Mary, stop... Stay here with me..."

"You need a doctor straight away... I'll..."

"No... No... Don't leave me, stay here," he repeated urgently. Already the periphery of his vision was growing cloudy and dark. Mary was crying openly now, her face twisted in panic.

"It's alright, love, I'm here with you... I'm here..."

"Mary..."

"Ssh, don't talk."

"Mary..." With immeasurable effort, her husband raised his hand to hers.

"What is it... What...?"

"...love you, Mary Ginnane..."

"Oh God, Charlie, I love you, too... So much, so very much..." She pressed her tear-stained face against his, and as the cloudy darkness suddenly turned into a blinding tunnel of white light, Charlie was acutely aware of his wife's strong arms holding him tightly, of the sweet fragrance of her thick hair falling across his cheek, and the gentle touch of her breath against his skin.

~ * ~

The phone was ringing when Fudge and Lilly fell into the flat laden down with parcels, boxes and carrier bags. They'd gone utterly berserk, buying outrageously priced maternity gear, baby clothes and enough cuddly toys to fill the window ledge in the expecting mother's bedroom. From the Dun Laoghaire ferry port, they'd gone straight to the city centre and splurged out on a three-course lunch in a trendy Grafton Street pub before systematically working their way through every shopping arcade between St. Stephens Green and Henry Street. The lunatic idea of having the baby together had ballooned into heady madness, and feeling pregnant herself, Fudge experienced for the first time in years a giddy excitement and satisfying sense of purpose.

"Get it, Lilly, will you?" she called when the jangling ring of the telephone refused to cease. "I'm still trying to disentangle myself from all these packages and parcels!"

"Jeepers, I hope it isn't Dad or Julian, I don't know how they're going to take this baby bombshell! They'll slaughter me!"

She was still tittering when she lifted the receiver to her ear and chirped a cheery hello. An instant later her expression froze and, for a moment, Fudge thought that bastard Jack had called, but then Lilly held the phone towards her.

"It's for you... Sheila."

"What's up?" Fudge quizzically searched her friend's sombre face hoping for an answer, but Lilly merely shook her head.

In the months that followed, Fudge tried time and time again to remember the conversation she'd had with her sister that Saturday evening, yet to no avail; the dialogue, as if never spoken, was totally deleted from her mind. Her first recollection after the news was of Lilly taking her by the arm and leading her to the sofa.

"Fudge! Jesus, what's happened?"

"It's Dad..." Fudge's mouth was completely dry, the words sticking in her throat. "He's had a heart attack."

"Oh Christ, no! Not Charlie! Look, I'll drive you straight down to the hospital. Where is he? The Galway Regional...?"

"No... No, you don't understand..."

"What then?"

The words seemed abstract, alien.

"Lilly, he's dead... He died yesterday, when we were in London."

"Oh Fudge...!"

"While we were in the clinic..." Fudge added numbly, the tears burning her eyes.

This bitter twist in the path of providence was to be, bizarre as it seems, a strange comfort to Fudge in the coming years. On that April day, separated by hundreds of miles and the stormy Irish sea, one life was lost, while another was being saved, a life which all too soon would become, as her father's had been, an inextricable part of Fudge's own.

~ * ~

Charlie Ginnane was buried in the scrubby, slightly unkempt protestant graveyard in Loughrua. It was a short, straightforward ceremony, just as the unassuming farmer would have wanted. No pomp, no fuss. Friends and acquaintances crowded in through the narrow church gateway to pay their last respects, while Mary, still stunned and speechless, stood flanked on either side by Auntie Dora and the five Ginnane sisters. And later, all alone, while her daughters waited beyond the wrought iron railings, she knelt down amongst the profusion of blossoming floral wreaths and silently whispered her husband farewell.

Fifteen

"You have to poke your pelvis forward a bit."

"Christ! It was a poke that got me into this state to start with!"

"Come on, you're not doing it right. Look, watch me."

Hitching up the skirt of her grey business suit, Fudge stretched out on the rug and began to demonstrate, the sight of the high-heeled PA grunting and puffing, her legs drawn up at the knees and the slender hips thrust forward, sending Lilly into hoots of hilarity. A glossy gynaecological guide jam-packed with graphic high-colour photographs lay on the floor beside her.

"I can't possibly do that! If I lie down you'll have to hire a crane to get me back on my feet. I feel like a bloody hippopotamus!" the pregnant woman wailed.

"Now that you mention it..." Fudge pushed herself up into a sitting position and studied her flatmate's mountainously extended belly, the awe-inspiring protuberance making all other extremities appear puny and dwarfed. "...You sure you're not having twins?"

"Not unless there's another baby lurking under my armpit somewhere."

"It wouldn't be the first time a twin has been overlooked. Think of Lizzy and Beth."

"No way," Lilly protested as she rubbed a podgy finger over the button-shaped protrusion of her naval. "There's only one bun in this here oven."

"Well, don't say I didn't warn you."

"Anyway, I had enough trouble persuading Julian to be a godfather—if he thought there were two he'd resign. Some family I have!"

"You have a great family. Any other father would have disinherited you, the disgrace to the neighbourhood that you are! Personally speaking, you deserve to be burnt at the stake for throwing everyone into such a state of confusion—above all me!"

"Oh, go on, you love it! You're worse than a fussing mother-in-law!"

"It just so happens I promised your father I'd make sure you acted like a halfways responsible human being during this pregnancy—and it's a promise I intend to keep."

"And I appreciate it, Mammy."

Fudge lay back on the rug and stared at the ceiling, her gaze following the outline of a yellowing water stain which had appeared soon after that torrential downpour almost eight months ago. On the day Doctor Plunkett had told Lilly she was expecting a child. With mixed feelings she remembered the afternoon two weeks after Charlie had died when Lilly decided to prepare her own father for the worst.

"I've been putting off telling him," Lilly confessed nervously one morning. "He'll think I've messed up my future and worry that I won't look after myself properly."

"I said I'd help you. That hasn't changed," Fudge answered soberly. The shock of her father's death had taken all the sparkle out of her, the memory of him still far too fresh. The hurt was persistent, a blunt, niggling ache.

"But things have changed now, I couldn't expect you to..."

"No, I want to. It'll help me take my mind off things. Danny and Sheila are sorting everything out on the farm, I need some kind of distraction. Ring Michael up and let him know you're making a granddad out of him. He'll notice it sooner or later."

"You're right. Tell you what, let's drive out to Ballsbridge. The house will be a mess because he's been away lecturing for a few weeks, but it'll be a nice surprise."

Fudge snorted weakly. "A nice surprise? Now that's what I call an understatement!"

It was May already, and as they zigzagged through Rathmines and east along the murky canal towards Ballsbridge, both women failed to notice how abruptly the city had burst into life, the grey suburban streets dotted with lofty trees bearing conspicuously bright green crowns of freshly unfolded leaves. Here and there, window boxes brimming with white and red geraniums heroically thwarted the rush hour smog, and in residential front gardens proud house owners busied about, raking, hoeing and weeding like there was no tomorrow.

"He won't mind us just dropping in like this, will he?" Fudge asked as they neared the tall detached house, noticing at the same time that the downstairs curtains were only partially drawn.

"Of course not! It's hardly as if we're strangers expecting regally-fitting hospitality. He'll be out the back tending to his precious roses, any bet?"

But he wasn't. Instead, he was sitting alone in the corner of his loose-covered sofa when the two young women unexpectedly appeared in the living room doorway, making the poor man jump.

"Sorry, Dad, I thought you'd hear us coming in. I didn't mean to startle you."

"Lilly! Don't worry, pet, I was off with the birds, as usual. Don't mind me." A barely perceptible flicker of consternation swept over his features when he saw Fudge, but vanished a second later.

"Finnula! Well, this is a surprise, I must say... Em, come in." He glanced over at his daughter. "Love, would you rustle up some coffee and cake? You know where everything is."

He didn't have to ask twice. Lilly was gone in a flash, leaping at the chance to postpone the dreaded confrontation. Fudge sat down in the leather wing chair next to an old mahogany desk.

"I haven't seen you for ages," Michael was saying, nervously shuffling a pile of well-thumbed journals on the coffee table before him. "How've you been? Well, I hope."

Fudge stared blankly at the tousle-headed historian. He wouldn't know about Charlie. How could he? She hadn't visited the Ballsbridge house for months, and since Doctor Plunkett's enlightening revelation nearly three weeks before, Lilly had been avoiding her father like the plague. She sighed and plucked at a loose thread in the hem of her skirt.

"I'm afraid not. My dad..." She would never get accustomed to saying it, each word leaving a bitter aftertaste. "My dad died unexpectedly two weeks ago... A sudden heart attack."

She'd been staring at her lap for several long seconds before she realised that Michael hadn't responded. While not expecting an exaggerated show of compassion, his obvious silence was unnerving.

She glanced up at the older man sitting opposite. His face was ashen, and the hands still clutching the stack of magazines he'd been in the process of tidying away began to tremble markedly. For a moment his mouth worked feebly in a desperate attempt at articulation then gave up. Rising stiffly from the sofa, Michael dropped the journals onto the floor at his feet and quickly left the room.

Fudge was shaken, Michael McDermott's reaction throwing her fully off balance. He'd only ever met Charlie once, as far as she could recollect, and that over ten years before. Her father's death couldn't possibly touch him deeply enough to justify his apparent shock. Or was it the memory of losing his wife? Had Fudge's statement awakened in him a sadness too great to suppress?

The room was gloomy, the rust-red walls and dark mahogany catapulting her into another time. She wished Lilly would return from the kitchen. The air was oppressive, the quietness of the house increasing her feeling of discomfort. Anxiously, she looked about, her eyes coming to rest on the dusky wooden desk next to the armchair where a bundle of letters lay scattered on the polished surface. Old letters. Michael must have been reading them shortly before they'd arrived. The pages looked thumbed, the paper no longer crisp, but worn from constant re-reading.

Fudge leaned over the side of the chair to get a better look and immediately regretted her inquisitive intrusion, a dart of guilt tickling her conscience. They were no doubt letters from his wife, private personal exchanges from another life when Lilly's parents were young and in love.

It came to her then that the source of Michael's sorrow lay here on the desk, his unpredicted flight from the room the result of unleashed emotions. Resisting closer inspection, Fudge looked away, yet before she did, a sense of recognition caused her to pause. The handwriting. Uncanny, although unable to read the contents from her position in the tall wing chair, she clearly identified the long, drawn-out sloping script as that of her own mother. She had to be mistaken, of course, but the similarity was astonishing, the same familiar, slanting style that filled the ledgers at Birch Rise and hundreds of lovingly written pages collected over the years at Castleglen. No, it was a coincidence, undoubtedly, but bewildering that both her and Lilly's mother should have the same handwriting. She was still pondering upon the congruence of it when her friend bustled into the room.

"Where's he gone, then?" she asked, surprised by her father's absence.

"I don't know. I told him about Dad and he just suddenly left the room. Look, Lilly, I really don't think you should break the news today after all, he appears terribly upset about something."

"He was grand a moment ago."

"It seemed to come over him all of a sudden, he was..." Her words petered out as Michael materialised in the doorway once again, his Beethovian hair framing a face stricken with anguish.

"Dad..." Lilly started, rushing to his side. "What's wrong?"

Fighting for composure, he raised his hand in a confused, fluttering gesture and looked at Fudge. "I'm all right... I didn't mean to alarm you, you'll think me very rude."

"No, of course not..." For an uncomfortable moment, she thought Lilly's father was going to embrace her, but instead, he took her hand, paternally patting the back of it.

"I'm so sorry, so very, very sorry," he said, his voice full of heartfelt commiseration.

~ * ~

Under the circumstances, Lilly had wisely put off revealing her delicate condition, finally dropping the bombshell during a roast beef and Yorkshire pudding dinner a few weeks later when Julian was home for a short family visit. Fudge had graciously declined the invitation to join them. There were some things better done alone.

Needless to say, the McDermotts were shell-shocked, but confronted with Lilly's contagious exuberance the looming prospect of unemployment, the lack of a supportive husband and worse still, the resulting disgrace the unmarried mother would surely harvest suddenly all became petty trivialities, peripheral nitty-gritty of no urgent importance. And then there was Fudge, Lilly assured them as she shovelled a second helping of mashed potatoes onto her plate. Fudge was going to help. They'd juggle jobs, share sleepless nights and pull straws when the child's nappy was full to the brim.

"The neighbours will think you're lesbians, of course," Julian had commented dryly. "A pair of dykes living in sin!"

"Julian!" Michael's fork hovered halfway to his mouth as he shot his son a warning glance.

"We're very much heterosexual, thank you very much. What d'you think got me in this situation—immaculate conception?"

"And Finnula? Is she doing a line with anyone?" the marine biologist asked casually, keeping his eyes purposely on the food.

"Well, not at the moment. She's a bit picky."

"That's not the impression she tried to give me that Sunday up in Rathgar."

"You actually remember that?" Lilly looked at her brother enquiringly, rejoicing when two pink spots of embarrassment appeared on his handsome cheeks. "And while we're on the subject, what happened to Millicent, anyway?" she continued. "You seem pretty bloody picky yourself."

"If I were you, sister dear, I'd mind my own business and concentrate on that tadpole of yours."

And they had. The days turned to weeks, the weeks to months and just as Lilly was getting used to balancing her protruding belly, labour day was almost upon them. Fudge demonstrated the pelvic thrust one more time, knowing the antenatal acrobatics would hardly do the mother-to-be any good at this late stage, but Lilly needed diversion. She'd been driving Fudge round the bend, moaning and groaning ad infinitum about leg cramps, incontinence, raging heartburn and the notion of post-birth haemorrhoids. In horror, she had screamed at the sight of close-up educational snapshots of gaping vaginal apertures, sticky crowning heads, quivering blubbery placentas, vibrant purple stretch marks and bulging varicose veins.

"Where the hell did you get that monstrous rubbish!" Lilly had howled, tossing the hard-backed testimony of childbirth into the bin.

"A present from Skids, probably trying to teach us a lesson. He almost went through the roof when I suggested flexitime."

"Jesus wept!"

The final days were spent packing and unpacking the hospital suitcase, choosing names, or just gawping at Lillian McDermott's ever-expanding girth as one would a balloon threatening to burst, and when, one December evening in the middle of the Midnight Movie something did in fact rupture, the two flustered women were mightily relieved to establish it was only Lilly's membranes.

"Oh, fuck it," she'd remarked articulately as the warm amniotic fluid dribbled down the inside of her thigh to form a soggy puddle in the hollow of the sofa. "I've gone and wet my knickers."

While Gary Grant chattered energetically in the background, they sat paralysed, silently observing the slow-spreading stain as it crept outwardly in a perfect radius around the Dublin woman's corpulent form. When the realisation of what had happened gradually began to dawn on them, all hell broke loose. Scampering helter-skelter like scared bunnies seeking refuge, Fudge and Lilly criss-crossed willy-nilly throughout the flat, donning winter coats, grabbing bags, searching for car keys and generally not getting anywhere. In a last minute wave of panic, the expecting mother suddenly stopped at the front door, her bulky form heaving with exertion.

"Fudge... wait, I can't!"

"Get a move on, will you? Or do you want to hatch in the middle of the street?"

"No, no... I've decided I don't want to have it after all!" she panted as the first contraction compelled her to grab the front railings for support. "I'd... I'd prefer not to go through with it!"

Throwing the hospital suitcase into the boot of the car, Fudge struggled to remain unruffled. "Lilly, I'm concerned about your timing. It might well be that it's a little too late to turn back."

"Oh, bugger it," Lilly squealed, making her mounting pain clearly evident to the surrounding sleepy neighbourhood. "That's what I was afraid of."

Huffing and puffing, with golf-ball eyes bulging out of their sockets, Lilly writhed in the passenger seat as they raced through the Dublin city centre towards the maternity hospital. Once or twice they were forced to stop at traffic lights, the sight of the squirming woman's deranged gyrations scaring the living daylights out of other motorists waiting nearby.

"Tell Skids he can shove those baby books up his arse!" she screamed after another wave of contractions had her hanging from sun visor. "So much for the birth process taking up to fourteen hours! Unless I'm mistaken, I'm sitting on this infant's head!"

"Shut up and stop exaggerating! You'll make me crash the bloody car! Just keep your legs crossed!"

As it happened, for once the pregnant woman was right. By the time they'd reached the front entrance the pressing contractions had set in and birth was imminent. Screeching to a halt, Fudge left the car parked precariously with one wheel up on the curb, and dashed into the hospital where she accosted the first member of staff to cross her path. When they got back to Lilly, they found her kneeling on the car seat facing the rear, her arms hugging the headrest in a grizzly bear grip.

"It's coming! Sweet mother of God, it's coming!" she screamed hysterically as the first capillaries in her globular eyeballs began to give way. "I can feel it!"

Forgetting the wet icy-cold plaster stones, the woman fell to her knees on the pavement beside the open car door and began peering under Lilly's smocked dress, much to the consternation of an elderly male visitor who happened to be passing by with a Christmas poinsettia in one hand and a box of Quality Street in the other. A second later, the nurse's eyes were almost as wide as Lilly's, who, meanwhile, in a desperate attempt at relieving the pain, had pressed her face into the back of the seat and shoved her beamy bottom up against the glove compartment. Muffled by the upholstery, her screeches now sounded less like a stuck pig's. The gurgling grunts, on the other hand, couldn't be compared with anything known to mankind..

"Oh, deary me," the elderly hospital employee exclaimed, glancing at Fudge. "Lovey, would you trot to the reception and tell them we need a midwife out on the front steps sort of snappy. I can't promise we'll get this young lady up to the delivery room in time."

"Ah, Christ! I knew it," Fudge yapped, resisting the temptation to stamp her foot. "She's going to make a mess of my car covers, isn't she?"

"Not to worry, lovey, vomit's a lot worse. Now you better hurry along."

As it turned out, the midwife might just as well have saved herself the sprint down from the third floor; when she arrived at the scene, out of breath and perspiring, Lilly was reclining splay-legged and pale. Her helper squatted nearby, a pink, mewing bundle wrapped in a hospital overcoat clasped to her chest.

"Heavens above, Shirley! Don't tell me you delivered that baby on your own!" the matronly midwife gasped.

"Actually, ma'am, I didn't have much choice!"

"Well, good for you, I suppose that's one of the hazards of working in a maternity hospital. You'll put me out of a job yet!"

Fudge looked from the midwife to Shirley, who shrugged apologetically and nodded towards a bucket and mop standing abandoned in the foyer.

"Sorry, lovey, I'm only the cleaning lady, you didn't give me much of a chance to explain, but if you have any problems with the stains on yer car seat, let me know. Haven't come across one that's got the better of me yet!"

Lilly, having regained lucidity just in time to absorb this last snippet of conversation, rolled her eyes to the starry Dublin night sky. "Holy cow, Fudge, you deserve a medal, I swear to God."

In a brisk no-nonsense manner, the midwife went about her business and soon after, the young mother was whisked away on a hospital gurney, her newborn daughter pressed to her breast. Fudge trotted along beside them, feeling as euphoric as had she given birth herself. Lilly was crooning sublimely.

"A girl, a little girl... Oh, Fudge, we have a little girl," she breathed dreamily. "Isn't she divine?"

"She's perfect, absolutely perfect. Lilly, we did it, we actually did it!"

The orderly pushing the gurney eyed the two women sceptically and, as Julian had so astutely predicted, came to a firm conclusion. *A pair of bleedin' lesers*, he thought with a sigh, *what's Ireland coming to, at all, at all?* The mother probably raped some poor, unsuspecting bloke and wrung the last drop of sperm out of him. Still, in all fairness, he couldn't remember a couple having shown that much emotion in donks. Touching, it was.

~ * ~

Late in the night, after all the paraphernalia of childbirth had been snipped, stitched, swashed down and soothed, Lilly came up with a name for her new-born.

"Polly?" Fudge retorted. "We can't call her that. Polly is the prefix for paint primer, or putty, or something out of a hardware shop. Give the snapper a break, will you?"

"Aw, c'mon, Polly's gorgeous, a little old-fashioned and romantic, but sweet, a nursery rhyme name."

"It's a crack-filler, believe me. Birch Rise is full of the stuff, and anyway, she won't be a baby all her life. One day she'll be forty!"

"Okay, I'm going to call her Attracta." Lilly pouted mulishly. "... or Philomena..."

"Now, now, let's not be hasty. Polly, you said? Mm, it's beginning to sound better already. Polly McDermott. I suppose I could live with a godchild named after do-it-yourself builder's mix."

And all of a sudden, they couldn't imagine the tiny, sleeping form lying between them on the hospital bed as anything other than Polly. The baby, a podgy, blue-eyed child with a downy fuzz of blond-red hair, was the spitting image of her mother, a merciful gift of nature sparing Lilly the memory of the father every time she looked upon her daughter's face. His name hadn't been mentioned once during the pregnancy, but now Fudge took the plunge.

"What about Jack, will you tell him?"

"Jack who?" Lilly smiled, as she stroked her baby's soft velvety head. "You don't mean that shit who wanted me to abort, do you?"

"You're over him then?"

"You can say that again!" She paused for a moment, a pucker of melancholy passing over her glowing features. "One day Polly will want to know, of course. I suppose for her sake I'll have to contact him, but not yet. I won't let anything spoil this moment."

"Nothing could."

After that, mother and godmother fell silent, gaping wide-eyed like a pair of mesmerised half-wits at the miraculous wonder of evolution burping wetly on the quilt before them.

~ * ~

The responsibility of godmotherhood weighed heavily on Fudge's shoulders, a burden she bore as gladly as the Santa carrying his sack of toys in the Switzer's Christmas display on Grafton Street. This analogy had occurred to her as she motored around College Green on her way to work the following Monday morning, her eyes automatically drawn to the bright Yuletide fairy lights, seasonal decorations and shop shelves cascading with toys of every description. She was going to be late this morning, Fudge registered while waiting at the same traffic lights near the Liffey where that poor young mother had so bitterly struggled with the bockety-wheeled pram eight months before.

For once, Skids would just have to go and have his hernia. Right now, she had more important things to do. It was a freezing cold morning, the milder weather that the Atlantic gulf stream generally brought to many parts of Ireland having given up its battle against adverse elements somewhere over Ballinasloe. Rooftops were covered in a white, icy sugar coating and the faces of pedestrians hurrying by were shrouded in the frosty clouds of their own breathing. Blue-kneed schoolchildren waiting at bus stops had their hands stuffed up their blazer sleeves and wore stripy scarves wrapped around their heads to shield them from the biting gusts slicing up the river from the Dublin port docks.

The lights turned green, and five minute later, Fudge was pulling into a parking space in front of the old maternity hospital building on the North Side. She'd only stay five minutes, long enough to bring Polly a present. It had caught her eye in a toy shop two weeks previously, and she'd been keeping it well-hidden in her wardrobe ever since. Now the time was right. Michael had spent most of the afternoon with his daughter and granddaughter the day before, so Fudge had waited, wanting Lilly to open the parcel when they were all on their own.

As she struggled with the huge packet, her high-heeled shoes slithered about on the icy tarmac, the short grey skirt offering little protection against the cutting north wind whistling around her long, shapely legs. If she'd any chance of appeasing her boss at all, then it was in the figure-hugging tailored suit. She'd just about made it up to the front entrance without doing the splits when someone called her name. Turning, her heart lurched at the sight of Polly's uncle loping gracefully across the frozen car park, his long-fingered hands holding the collar of his jacket closed at the neck. Her heart sinking, she peered down at the huge bulky parcel, vainly hoping it might evaporate into thin air, but her wish was not to be granted, and already he was reaching to take it from her.

"Finnula! Long time no see. Goodness, this is a coincidence... Here let me help you with that."

Without protest, she allowed Polly's present to slip from her hands into his. He chuckled at the weight of it.

"What have you got here, then? Spoiling our godchild, are you?"

Fudge, deliberately ignoring his question, smiled thinly. "Hello, Julian."

He was looking strikingly attractive, as usual, the dark blond hair curling slightly over a thick-knit turtleneck sweater, the muscular thighs hard under a pair of faded blue jeans. Wind-swept, brawny. He might have stepped off a Norwegian fishing vessel, she considered fleetingly as she studied his face, the barely perceptible web of fine lines around his eyes revealing his almost thirty years. She'd noticed his glance flickering over her on approach and was relieved that, this time, she was looking good, the excitement of the past days giving her complexion a new glow. Her full, shoulder-length hair had been dramatically swept up into a neat chignon, her outfit crisp and elegant. They'd met once or twice over the years since the Rathgar flat disaster, but only briefly, always hovering on the front door steps, or on the street outside the house, Fudge's ongoing acute embarrassment causing her to flee any time he called by to see his sister, her constant evasion preventing the awakening of slumbering emotions. Now, he'd caught her on the hop once again.

"You're here early," she said. "I'm on my way to work myself. Can't be sure if they'll let us see her at this early hour." They were still standing at the hospital entrance, and Fudge could feel her nose turning blue.

Wedging the parcel under one arm, Julian took her elbow and guided her in through the swing doors, his touch sending a shower of collywobbles jitterbugging through her stomach.

"I'm heading down to a place near Westport myself. I have a job in a marine laboratory there," he explained. "Thought I'd try my luck here before I hit the road. I'm dead curious to see what that bird-brained sister of mine has managed to produce!"

They passed along the brightly lit corridor. Every now and then, a nurse squeaked by in uniform shoes, but nobody paid the attractive couple much attention. Lilly was breast-feeding Polly when they poked their heads around the door.

"Julian!" the young mother piped a little too gleefully, causing the baby to jerk upwards in a natural reflex of fright, but pressed against the warmth of her mother's turgescent breast, the moment was instantly forgotten.

"My goodness, what have you got there, Jul?" Lilly whispered, hers eyes alighting eagerly upon the massive package. "Can't remember the last time you brought me a present, you stingy dog!"

"Actually, it's not from me and not for you," he laughed, placing the parcel on the floor. "It's from Finnula for Polly. True to form, I've just brought my scintillating self."

"It's nothing much," Fudge broke in, trying to kick the gift-wrapped monstrosity under the bed. "Just a toy, we'll look at it later. So, how did you sleep..."

Lilly's curiosity was unbridled. "*What is it*? C'mon, let me see!"

"Ach, no... Later. Julian doesn't have much time, he came especially to see you and Polly."

The young mother wasn't to be distracted that easily. She disconnected the slumbering child from her nipple, buttoned up her nighty and placed the infant in her brother's arms. Julian's glance searched the ceiling.

"Jesus, Lilly, why is it that breast-feeding mothers forget the meaning of the word modesty? Can you not keep your oozing boobs out of sight?" He then glanced down at the bundle cradled in the crook of his arm and instantly the disquieting vision of his sister's mammary eye-opener lost all importance.

"Good grief," he uttered, his mischievous face softening into an expression which tugged at Fudge's heartstrings. "How did you do it? She's beautiful!"

"I'm not just a pretty face, you know," she responded haughtily. "And now I want to see what's in that mysterious looking parcel..."

She was leaning dangerously over the side of the hospital bed in an attempt to locate the object of her inquisitiveness.

"Please, Lilly, let's open it later when we have time. Polly's sleeping anyway." Fudge was clearly agitated.

"With all respect, unless it's a King-Kong-sized seeping breast, Polly won't give a damn. Now come on…"

"Yeah," Julian broke in. "Now you've got me all curious, too!"

"It's a teddy, just an ordinary teddy bear—that's all."

"Oh, great, I love teddy bears!" Lilly had extricated the parcel from under the bed and was tearing it open with exaggerated gusto.

Shit, bugger and damn. Fudge stared at the floor. Already she could feel her cheeks flaming. How could she have been so bloody stupid! She'd done it again. Any hopes she'd ever had of exonerating herself in Julian's eyes were about to be dashed. He would think she'd done it on purpose, an underhand endeavour to rile him, a pathetic retribution for unreciprocated love. The rustling of paper stopped and Fudge knew they were staring at it. She concentrated feverishly on her high-heels. A moment passed, then Lilly gasped.

"Oh, Fudge! This is fabulous, absolutely fabulous! Polly will love it. Julian, look, our favourite—remember?"

Deeply ashamed, Fudge glanced up apologetically and, knowing there was no escape, looked Julian squarely in the face. At first, a cloud of surprised confusion scudded over his features, then a twinkle appeared in his eye accompanied by an involuntary twitch of mirth. A second later he was hooting with laughter, causing the poor child on his bobbing lap to squirm in her sleep.

"Winnie-the-Pooh! A huge, child-sized Pooh bear! Really, Finnula, you're absolutely evil, will you never stop twisting the knife?"

"I'm sorry… No, really, it has nothing to do with… well, you know. I just happened to see it in a shop window. I didn't mean to…"

His mirth was contagious, and soon she was laughing, too, the hilarity chasing away the awkward reservation that had so doggedly dampened their few brief encounters over the years. Suddenly, just as one does when a worrying splinter is removed, Fudge felt a sense of relief. It was out. The thorn was out. Perhaps, at long last, they could be friends again. Lilly looked from one to the other, and while she hadn't really understood the knife-twisting remark, she felt the touch of underlying hostility had finally lifted and decided, for once, to keep her fat gob shut.

Ten minutes later, a scowling head nurse turfed them out on their ears, but before parting Fudge and Julian stood for a while in the warmth of the hospital foyer.

"I heard about your dad," he said after a moment's silence. "I'm so sorry. It must have been a great shock for you all."

"Yes... Yes, it was. It's been hard on Mum. For some time we thought she wouldn't get over it—not that she ever will, really—but things are slowly picking up. Danny and Sheila were a great support, selling off cattle and some grazing land to take the burden off her. The horses had to go, too, of course."

"And the twins, Rosy...?"

"Fudge smiled. "The Ginnane women have the West under control. Lizzy and Beth, inseparable as usual, are working for the mining company's head office in Ballinasloe, and Rosy, for all her quizzical curiosity, is learning to be a florist in Loughrua!"

"Your mother's not lonely?"

"Well, the house is bursting at the seams over the weekend, but during the week it's almost empty. Just Rosy and Mum. It's hard to know what she's thinking. She doesn't like to talk about it."

"Loneliness is a terrible thing." Julian said suddenly, revealing a show of wistfulness Fudge had never seen in him before. There seemed to be a question hovering on the tip of his tongue, she felt sure, but all of a sudden he changed the subject.

"You're looking great—this your working gear?" he said, giving her a playful once-over.

"God, no. I dress like this all the time!" Fudge knew those give-away splodges of crimson were flushing her normally pale cheeks. She'd never learnt to control it and was helpless to do so now. "Speaking of work, my boss will have my guts for garters. I really have to go."

Julian glanced at his watch. "Me to. I have a long drive ahead."

"Yes."

"Quite."

"Hmm"

Each waited for the other to leave and when, finally, both simultaneously made a move, they ended up getting wedged in the heavy swing doors, her body firmly pressed up against his. Completely off guard, Julian wrapped his strong arm around Fudge's waist and for half an eternity they remained locked in a tight embrace, half inside and half outside the hospital entrance. Eternity ended when a red-nosed, pot-bellied doctor with a stethoscope swinging from his neck coughed diplomatically, indicating he wanted to get out of the freezing cold.

The spell was broken. Having disentangled themselves, Julian walked Fudge to her car, his hand hovering at her back should her high-heeled shoes suddenly lose control on the icy surface.

"I'll see you at the christening, then, I suppose."

"Yes, duty calls…"

"Indeed," she answered limply.

"Em, look, if you're at Birch Rise give me a call. I could pop down from Westport. Maybe we could have lunch together, discuss godparental duties, or whatever."

"That would be nice," Fudge breathed, not daring to hope.

"Grand." He handed her a business card with a leaping salmon printed in the corner. "You can get me here."

"Okay, good… Great." *Take it easy, don't scare him off. Stay cool.*

"Bye then, Finnula."

"See you."

He turned and walked a little too briskly across the frozen car park, swaggering slightly as one does when being watched. Two steps away from his station wagon, he slipped and instinctively grabbed the wing mirror, almost breaking it off in the process. Stifling a hysterical laugh, Finnula Ginnane jumped into her car and slowly set off towards Curry's Car Parts. As she inched her way through early rush hour smog, Skids' PA felt high as a kite, way up above it all, as if she'd suddenly and miraculously learnt how to fly.

Sixteen

It was half past eight in the morning and Lilly still hadn't returned. *I'll wring her bloody neck,* Fudge decided as she paced up and down the living room with Polly on her arm. Skids Curry's generosity was great, but not boundless. *This time I'll lose my job for sure! Damn her!*

"Stop fussing!" Lilly had chirped before disappearing out the doorway dressed to kill. "I'll be home by midnight!"

Well, damn you, Cinderella! Fudge's wrath was, to put it mildly, all-embracing, every grievance working its way to the surface like a purulent pimple screaming for release.

They'd had it all planned to the last piddling detail, and as long as both stuck to their side of the bargain, it worked, too. Lilly had hung geology on the nail and taken up a post as a receptionist in an inner city hotel, while she had persuaded Skids into letting her work flexitime. When one started early, the other started late, Fudge making up for lost time by staying in the office long after hours. On Lilly's evening shifts, they reversed the whole process. With a little financial support from Michael, they'd managed to juggle their time in such a way that they were never required to fall back on the services of a child-minder. They'd arrogantly claimed they could do it, and do it they would, both innocently believing two mothers ought to be enough for such a little child. More and more frequently, however, Fudge wondered if they were really doing the right thing. Were they turning Polly into a ping-pong baby, showering her with motherly love that bounced at her from two different directions? Were they causing some irreparable confusion in that little mind? A topsy-turvy land where daddies didn't exist? And now this. Coming from Lilly's side of the net the ball had once again fallen short, and Fudge, alone, was expected to save the game. As if to confirm her god-mum's disapproval, Polly hiccuped loudly and woofed a dollop of curdled milk onto the shoulder of Fudge's blazer.

"Ah, crikey, Pol, not over my working clothes!" She sighed and walked to the kitchen to fetch a J-cloth, glancing at the wall clock on the way.

It was now quarter to nine. Skids was going to go apeshit. Why hadn't she put her foot down the minute she'd noticed Lilly tarting herself up the evening before, twittering and humming in such a way that Fudge knew she wouldn't be back before the clock struck twelve? It had started as soon as she got her figure back. First one night out—and why not—but later it became two or three. Businessmen stopping over at the Trinity Court Hotel were immediately attracted to the bubbly blonde, and now, seven months on, Lilly suddenly found herself sitting on an exceedingly productive goldmine of male admirers.

"Japers, you don't look a gift horse in the mouth," she'd exclaimed when her distrustful flatmate had expressed misgivings. "Most of these guys have real money—they're not all posers looking for a bonk."

"Is that what you're after?"

"A bonk?"

"No, you eejit, the money."

"Not necessarily," Lilly sniffed. "But it's hardly what I would call a disadvantage."

"You realise most of them are married? You've been through this before."

"Not all of them, I do my homework!"

"And they know you have a baby daughter?"

"First things, first. Fudge."

"Christ, Lilly! You're heading for trouble again, I can feel it!"

"Ach, stop fussing!"

Time and again, Fudge had asked herself why she even bothered. She could easily move out and get a place of her own. Nothing was stopping her—not even her sense of loyalty. Yet whenever she was about to reach for a suitcase, Fudge remembered not only Polly, but all those little things that made Lilly special. The shared cups of drinking cocoa, the teenage memories, the occasions—seldom as they were—when Lilly had surprised her with her favourite evening meal, or breakfast with fresh croissants. But above all there was the realisation: if the tables were turned, Lilly would surely do the same for her.

Pushing aside these thoughts, Fudge finally dialled Michael's number. Much and all as she loved Polly, she wasn't prepared to lose her job as a result of Lilly's lack of responsibility. He'd be raging with his daughter, of course, but it wasn't her problem, she decided stubbornly. For once she couldn't give a shit. She would drop Polly off with her grandfather in Ballsbridge and head on to work. Wedging the receiver under her chin, she shifted the child onto her other hip while the phone rang out unanswered. Sensing her godmother's agitation, the baby began to whimper, the rosy-cheeked face scrunching up fretfully. Desperate now, Fudge was about to dial again when the front door banged open and Lilly stumbled into the flat.

"Fr... friggin' top sh... shtep," she slurred fuzzily. "Always fall over it." Her blond hair was unkempt and wild, the corkscrews sticking out in all directions, the normally flawlessly applied make-up smudged, a long smear of cherry-red lipstick pulling the side of her mouth down into a macabre grimace. There was a gaping hole in the knee of her sheer nylon stockings. In short, she looked like something the cat coughed up.

"Haalloo, Polly-wolly," she squealed gratingly, finally noticing her daughter clutching the other woman's neck. "Come to Mumsy…"

Fudge was horror-struck. "Don't you dare touch her!" she said, instinctively raising a protective hand to the child's head. "You're pissed out of your skull! How *could you*?"

"Ara, don't be so sht… shtuffy." Lilly kicked off her patent leather sandals and flopped onto the sofa. "Jus' a little tipsy, tha's all."

"A little tipsy! You're bloody stocious!"

"C'mon, gimme Polly, you can go to work." She stretched out her arms towards the baby, but by now the silvery-blue-powdered eyelids were beginning to droop.

"Lilly! I can't leave her with you! Have you gone completely mental?"

"Gimme Polly," she repeated with dramatic forcefulness, the tone of her voice causing the fuzzy-haired tot to clasp even more tightly at Fudge's neck.

"No way! Jesus, Lilly! I can't!" She grabbed Polly's bag of baby gear, a blanket and a bottle. "There's no way I can leave Polly here with you. Sorry, she's coming with me."

Expecting bitter protest, the frazzled working woman glanced hurriedly over her shoulder as she struggled out the front door. Hardly half a minute had passed, yet the baby's mother was already fast asleep, a yellow waterfall of hair cascading over the side of the sofa, her arms and legs splayed haphazardly in an awkward, discarded rag-doll fashion. From her open mouth a tiny glistening trail of dribble was slowly beginning to creep across the smooth, flushed cheek.

~ * ~

Skids hit the bloody roof.

"Get that thing outa here!" he bellowed when he caught his PA trying to sneak the child into a back room.

"It's not a *thing*, boss, it's a baby."

"I don't care what the hell it is, Miss Ginnane, remove it from my premises on the double!" The round face had turned purple and the veins on his neck were standing out rigidly, threatening to pop.

"Just an hour or two… Look, she's dozing off already. By lunchtime I'll have a solution. I swear to God, you won't notice she's here."

Mr. Curry snorted derisively. "This is a spare parts business and not a shaggin' babysitting service. You have more important work to do."

"I'll do it, Skids, honest—and overtime."

"Jumped up Jesus, you can't expect me to…"

"Please, an hour or two." Fudge looked at her boss beseechingly, and perhaps it was the sight of Polly's sleeping chubby-cheeked cherub face, but for a second he mellowed.

"An hour, d'you hear me? One peep and it's out on its arse!"

"She. It's a 'she'."

"Humph." Skids spun about and stormed back to his office, resisting, she noticed, the urge to slam the door shut with a bang.

With the baby blanket, Fudge made a cosy nest between two filing cabinets in the back room where she laid the child to sleep. Leaving the door ajar, the PA settled down at her desk and within minutes was up to her ears in itineraries, order forms, complaints and schedules. Every now and then, Skids appeared from his office with a bit of paperwork for one of the girls, each time throwing a filthy glance at the gap in the filing room door. Gráinne and Kitty tittered with delight. It was a right panic working for Curry Car Parts.

By midday, Skids' secretary was gradually starting to relax. She'd conquered a fair bit of backlog work, kept a pack of unpleasant hounds at bay and managed a few menial tasks on the side. Satisfied the situation was under control, she was just making her way back from the photocopier down the hall when it dawned on her that Polly must be ravenous, and was surprised the hungry mite hadn't begun to fret.

In the main office she listened at the filing room door; however, all was silent. Too silent, she considered with a tickle of apprehension. Normally, the baby should be screeching for tucker at this stage of the day. Uneasily, she looked over at her colleagues, who were deeply engrossed in their duties, Gráinne's fingers flying hell for leather over the keyboard and Kitty sorting folders onto a shelf, her skirt stuck in her bottom, as always. Holding her breath, Fudge pushed the door open and tiptoed over to the bundle between the tall metal cabinets. For a second, she was perplexed, then her heart lurched violently as she realised the nest was empty.

"Polly!" she whispered urgently, peering back and forth into the dusty corners. *The tiny thing can't just crawl off,* she thought nervously, *she's only just started making those funny swimming motions, pushing herself up onto podgy limbs, but not getting anywhere.* An uncomfortable feeling of unease skulked through the pit of her stomach. Where was the baby? Fudge rushed back into the outer office and found the other two women staring at her, tongue in cheek.

"What's going on? *Where's Polly?*"

Gráinne pressed her lips together to stifle a laugh and nodded towards their boss's door.

"What? He hasn't!" Fudge barked. "I'll kill him..."

Without as much as a perfunctory rap on her superior's door, the overtaxed personal assistant barged into the room, a torrent of blasphemous accusations at the ready. At the last minute, she checked her fire. The massive Drumcondra man was on all fours on the plush carpeted floor, the knees of his checked golfing trousers hitched up to reveal a pair of yellow socks. In front of him, Polly was squeaking with glee as Skids manoeuvred a convoy of Matchbox lorries around the hilly terrain of her short plump legs.

"Brumm, brumm," the managing director of Curry Car Parts was growling deeply, while steering the container truck up the mountain path of the child's shin, prematurely screeching to a halt on her knee at the sight of his approaching secretary. Polly was so ecstatic that great slimy strings of drool were dripping off her dimpled chin. Mr. Curry leapt to his feet and coughed uncomfortably.

"Dropped me pencil..." he waffled, at the same time dusting off a chequered knee and tugging the cuffs of his shirt from under the sleeves of the tight-fitting jacket. He jerked a thumb in Polly's direction.

"It was grumblin' a bit. You were off up the hallway and... Anyway, you can remove it now, it's beginning to leak."

"Jeepers, Skids, thanks, you're a real..."

Skids raised a hand in objection. "Say no more. Off with you now, the pair of you. Shoo!"

Scooping up the burbling tot, Fudge carefully stepped over the Matchbox truck convoy and headed for the door.

~ * ~

Lilly McDermott was wallowing in abject remorsefulness when her flatmate and daughter arrived home that afternoon.

"God, I feel like such a shit," she wailed later, knocking back her third glass of fizzy liver salts. "I don't know what got into me."

Fudge was standing at the kitchen sink pouring warm milk onto a rusk. She heaved a sigh of frustration.

"Lilly, I'm not Polly's mother, you are. Don't think I'm saying this to get out of helping, but the poor thing needs you."

"What do mean by 'the poor thing'? She gets lashings of love, and anyway, I need a life away from nappies and bottles occasionally!" the blond woman whinged.

"For Christ's sake! Do you think I don't?"

"You can go out whenever you want, I'm not stopping you!"

"Ach, you know I hate going to pubs on my own... Makes me feel like a tart."

"We could leave Polly with Michael and go out together."

"No," Fudge broke in adamantly. "No, we won't start that, she's too young."

"What about the girls from the office, you could have a night out with them."

"Actually, I was thinking of driving down to Birch Rise this weekend." Fudge tied a bib around Polly's neck and settled down in front of the high chair.

"To Birch Rise? This weekend?"

"Yep, I want to see Mum." She was embarrassed to reveal the real reason for wanting to go down to the West, afraid the other woman might laugh.

"Oh..." A look of dismay crossed the young mother's face. "I was hoping to..."

This time Fudge was steadfast. "No, you're staying here with your daughter, understand?"

"And if you came back on Saturday evening...?"

"Lilly, no!"

"Oh, all right." Insulted, Lilly strutted into the living room and flicked on the TV, leaving her friend to feed the baby alone.

The following day Fudge took the plunge. Pulling the business card out of her purse, she studied it for a long time before reaching for the phone. They hadn't talked since their brief encounter at the maternity hospital. Not really. He'd called the flat, of course, enquiring after Polly, but with Lilly in the background, their conversations remained short exchanges of repartee, both unsure what the other was thinking—a kind of verbal hopscotch, each afraid of treading on a crack which might abruptly catapult them out of the game. She glanced about the office before dialling the number. It was lunchtime. Gráinne and Kitty were down at Kearney's Arms murdering an Irish stew, and Skids was off playing a few rounds of arm-twisting business golf. The place was empty.

When the phone began to ring out, she could feel her hands grow damp, and the cluster of butterflies gingerly stretching their wings deep in her gut suddenly began to flutter haphazardly up into her chest.

"Hello," a man sung lightheartedly down the line, taking her by surprise.

"Julian?"

"Finnula?"

Fudge smiled. He'd recognised her voice at once. That was good.

"Are you down in Galway?" he continued, and Fudge immediately relaxed. He sounded eager. That was good, too. Very good.

"No, not yet. I was thinking of driving down tomorrow... See the family, and so on."

"That'll be nice."

"Er... Yes." She hesitated a moment. Wasn't this his cue? "I thought perhaps, if you weren't working..." Why was he making this so difficult? Was he up to his old games?

"At the weekend, no... I'm off Saturday and Sunday, actually."

"Well, maybe we could meet for lunch or something."

"...or something?" Julian repeated with a chortle. Fudge suppressed a sigh. Funny how well she knew him, this stranger.

"A chat, a walk—whatever. It's a bit of a drive out to Loughrua. We could meet halfway."

"Halfway sounds good, if you don't mind."

She hadn't really expected him to insist on driving the whole way, had she? "Grand, no problem. Look, what about Oughterard, or Maam Cross? The weather will be glorious, if they haven't lied to us, that is. I'd love to see Connemara again."

"Maam Cross sounds fine, on Saturday?"

"One o'clock."

"No problem."

Why did it somehow sound as if he were doing her a favour? "Great. See you then."

"Saturday, one o'clock, fine."

"Good, ah... Bye then." Fudge replaced the receiver feeling quite convinced she'd made the most wojus dog's dinner of it.

Still, what the hell. They had a date, a kind of one anyway. Just the two of them, alone in the Connemara vastness, in the distance the purple slopes of the Twelve Bens, and all around wild, untidy moorland, gushing brooks, deep black loughs and byway banks of towering rhododendron.

One of those rare summer days had been forecasted, hot and sunny, the heat subdued by a southerly breeze carrying the invigorating scent of salty seas, flowering heather, fuchsia, montbretia and the ever-present tang of matured peat. One of those days when you wanted to throw yourself face-down in a bed of spongy woodland moss and breath in the lushness of it all, to shut out the clatter of so-called civilisation and let nature's blanket of tranquility settle upon you, to press your ear to the warm ground and listen to Mother Earth's steady heartbeat pulsating in time to your own.

It would be magical, the kind of day Finnula had been romanticising about for the last ten years, and as the weekend drew near, she began to count the seconds of every incessant minute separating her from that carefully nurtured dream.

~ * ~

She started having doubts five miles outside the Dublin city limits. It was Friday evening, and Fudge had impatiently blasphemed and cursed her way through one hour of mounting stop-and-go weekend traffic. Could she really trust Lilly alone with Polly, she wondered, immediately hating herself for even letting such a preposterous thought cross her mind. How could she dare to believe for a moment that Lilly wasn't capable of looking after her own child, her own flesh and blood? It was Fudge's own stupid fault that more and more often she found herself dealing with chores that clearly fell into her flatmate's list of tasks. The mischievously manipulative blonde had expressed it precisely. One didn't look a gift horse in the mouth, and when it came to Polly's needs, the doting godmother had always been just that little bit too eager to oblige.

How she loved that child and the time spent together in cosy twosomeness, the tubby form draped languorously across her stomach as they lay nestled in the depths of the living room sofa listening to melancholy soul music deep into sleepless nights; the walks through Dublin suburban patches of green, Fudge pointing out cats and dogs and budding blossoms to the bright-eyed little girl, and all the while bursting with pride as passers-by smiled broodingly at what they believed to be mother and child.

It would have to stop. Already Polly was confused, her round eyes darting indecisively from one woman to the other whenever a situation called for comforting arms. One day, Lilly would meet a caring man, settle down and start a life of her own, and as unlikely as it seemed in this phase of new found freedom and extroversion, that day might be tomorrow, or even the next. After that, Fudge would merely be Auntie Finnula, the visiting godmother, the one who handed out padded envelopes on birthdays and slipped you some matinée money on the sly. Not more. If she weren't careful she might end up being the maiden aunt, one of those fussy, prying spinsters who smelt of compact powder and greasy lipstick and constantly demanded updating on first steps, first teeth, budding breasts and pubescent pimples. If anything at all, she wanted to be Polly's friend and could only achieve that by relaxing her grasp, and allowing the poor mite to find its way.

In Maynooth she resisted the temptation to stop at a phone box for one last reassuring call, and did the same in Kinnegad. However, by the time she'd reached Athlone, Fudge found herself searching for a suitable place to send up smoke signals. A decade down the road, Ireland would become the Celtic Tiger of computer technology, but in the mid-eighties the luxury of a personal mobile phone was, for many, still science fiction. Falling into this category, Fudge was forced to sneak past the pointy-nosed receptionist of a town-centre hotel on her quest for a public telephone. Lilly, understandably enough, was indignant.

"I thought you'd be enjoying pastoral bliss by now. What's up?"

"Nothing, just ringing to say hello."

"Fudge, that's a load of crap. You're checking up on me, aren't you?"

"No, I'm not, honest."

"Good, then hello and goodbye."

"Polly asleep, is she?"

"No, she's sitting in the corner playing with a packet of razor blades, and I'm laying into my fifth gin and tonic."

"Okay, okay, I get the message. Say 'night, night' for me."

"Will do, see you Sunday."

"Bye."

Fudge was kicking herself in the backside the rest of the way down to Loughrua. Of course, Polly was safe in her mother's care. There was absolutely nothing to worry about. Absolutely nothing.

The sun was setting when she passed through the Birch Rise gates and clattered over the cattle grid. The far-off horizon leaked deep blood red like a gaping wound in the dusky mid-summer sky. Red sky at night, she thought smugly as the car lurched the last few pot-holed yards down the gravel driveway. Through a chink in the front room curtains a neat slice of light penetrated the growing darkness. Mary was alone for a change. The twins, a pair of grown-up lanky bean stalks with well-paying office jobs, were off on a Costa Brava package holiday escorted by their present pickings from the Canadian mining company, Ted and Craig, whilst Rosy, thirsty for adventure, was in Galway for a spot of disco-hopping with a colleague from the flower shop. She'd spend the night there with Sheila's family, all driving down to Birch Rise the following day in order to catch Fudge for a late breakfast before she set off to Maam Cross. It would be nice to have Mum to herself for once, to chat about Polly and exchange women's talk, to just enjoy being a girl again, greedily lapping up maternal affection and childhood memories.

Mary was waiting in the living room, the chestnut grey-speckled head bent over a library hardback, her reading glasses balanced on the end of her nose, and in that split second before the older woman glanced up, Fudge's heart wept. Was it a devious trick of the light, or had her mother shrunk? The tall, strong-armed woman, who had popped the lids on many an unyielding jam jar with the mere flick of her wrist, suddenly appeared diminutive and fragile, as if Charlie's death had left a yawning cavity behind, an emotional soufflé threatening to crumple.

"Hi, Mum," Fudge whispered. "I'm home."

Taking the spectacles from her nose, Mary straightened in the armchair and smiled, that same old smile of welcome that accompanied every homecoming and, if only for a moment, brought a sparkle back into her lustreless eyes.

"Hello, pet, you're late... A lot of traffic?"

"The usual slog—got caught up in that awful Athlone bottleneck." She bent down and gave her mother a hug, soaking up the familiar, sweet-smelling homeliness.

"Do you want some supper? There's shepherd's pie in the oven. I could fetch..."

"No, stay where you are. I'll just change into something a little more comfortable. How about a glass of wine? I brought a bottle with me—it'll go down well with a decent portion of gossip!"

Mary sighed and leant back into the cushions.

"Sounds grand to me."

They talked late into the evening, Fudge on the floor, sitting cross-legged and relaxed in a baggy sweat shirt and track suit pants, her back leaning against the old sofa, a glass of chianti and a plate of cheddar chunks on the coffee table beside her. Mary listened to her daughter recounting tales of Polly McDermott's development, those precious pockets of time, the monthly milestones which grew farther and farther apart the older a child became. The first real smile, those funny verbal utterances that might be words, but aren't, the wonder of clutching fingers and chubby pedalling legs, the worries of colic and gripe. And while she was talking, Fudge, in turn, studied her mother's face, absorbing the melancholy in those still captivating blue-green eyes, the eyes that once challenged passers-by to take a second look.

She was slimmer, her figure almost girlish in a pale-blue cotton shirtdress and navy cardigan. Her hair was shorter, cut above the shoulders, but still unruly and thick, refusing to be reined into a standard middle-aged hairdo, the soft, grey-streaked curls falling naturally this way and that about her wan features. Though almost brittle in appearance, Mary would always be the anchor of the Ginnane family, a focal point, their home.

In that moment, Fudge began to understand Lilly's restlessness, and how the flirtatious, extrovert blonde was drifting aimlessly across life's rolling swell, slithering recklessly over the crest of one wave after the other, constantly seeking a haven, an anchor of her own to offer safekeeping when the tugging of invisible underwater currents become too strong, and the threat of being swept away into the unknown too great. Out of the blue, the memory of Lilly sitting on the rickety boarding school bed at the dormitory window came to mind, her gaze fixed on a point far beyond the slate grey Irish sea, her expression one of fathomless misery, and those words, *I miss her... I miss her so much.*

The memory was so vivid, the lucidity so startling, that Fudge stopped mid-sentence and, leaning forward, firmly grasped her mother's hand, the desire to physically feel her presence surprisingly overpowering.

Mary started. "Goodness, you gave me a fright! What is it, pet?"

"Sorry, nothing... Just a wave of silliness." She laughed to hide her embarrassment. "It's good to be home."

Mary smiled and stroked her daughter's hand in return. "Ach, Finnula, what would I do without the lot of you?" As if fighting off a bothersome twinge of unhappiness, she sat herself up in the armchair and busily straightened the skirt of her dress. "So you're off gallivanting tomorrow?"

Fudge's eyes glimmered excitedly. "That's right, and you'll never guess who I'm meeting out at Maam Cross for lunch... and maybe more." She popped her eyebrows up and down impishly.

"By the look on your face it has to be a man."

"The most divine specimen alive, to be precise."

"Surely not Sean Connery...?"

Fudge snorted. "Okay, the second most divine fella! Julian McDermott!"

"Julian... Julian McDe..." Mary's words faded, the very name opening the jagged wound of gnawing guilt, a wound that inflamed anew with every bittersweet memory. "Who would have thought," she continued weakly. "After all these years. He's back from England, then?"

"Since last year. He's working up near Westport now. Honestly, Mum, I don't know what it is, but I'm all of a dither! When I think of how he drove me to dementia as a teenager, and now..."

"Love works in funny ways, pet... It is love, I presume?"

The younger women nodded bashfully. "I don't really know what he feels, but there's something there, all right." She laughed suddenly, an impulsive release of excitement. "Crikey! If Lilly only knew! We're Polly's godparents!"

Mary struggled to share her daughter's enthusiasm, yet the pain was too great, fate's ironic twist too much to bear. Straining slightly, she stood up.

"Finnula, I'm awfully tired all of a sudden. Don't be offended if I take myself off to bed, will you?" She caressed her daughter's wavy dark hair. "I'm happy for you, love, I really am. Good luck tomorrow."

Unexpectedly, Fudge found herself sitting alone in the dimly lit room, her eyes fixed on the open doorway, through which Mary had passed an instant before. She was bewildered. What was this hurt she had seen in her mother's face? It was a different one, not the pain of Charlie's death, more an overlying layer of guilt and confusion. But why? Perhaps she disliked Julian and couldn't bring herself to say it, yet that was impossible; they'd only had one, brief encounter all those years ago. Did it have something to do with Lilly's mad-hatter disorder, their commitment to Polly? With abrupt clarity, it dawned on her that the very name McDermott always seemed to cast a shadow of wistful perplexity across Mary's face. What was it? Why? Irritated and unsure, Fudge pondered these things as she finished off the last drops of wine, then, switching out the lamp, slowly made her way up the old familiar stairway to the cosy comfort of her childhood bedroom.

~ * ~

Later, Mary, her mind a tangled jumble of disquieting memories, sat on the side of the lumpy double bed she had shared with her husband for so many years. For a long while, she just stared at the empty space beside her, at the slight hollow in the ageing mattress where even now Charlie's presence could be felt, his strong, well-built form resting against a mountain of pillows, a pair of reading glasses on his nose, and the Farmer's Journal on the quilt in front of him. He was still there, in every corner of every room, when she poured the tea in the morning and locked up the house at night. Three times a day she would wait for his shuffling steps at the back door, the familiar grunt of exertion as he struggled out of the huge

Wellington boots. Occasionally, alone in front a TV show, Mary would glance instinctively towards his armchair expecting some scathing comment of criticism, or snort of amusement, each time his absence taking her by surprise. Why couldn't she let him go? Let his restless spirit move on? In those last moments of Charlie's life, as he lay with his head cradled in her lap, the weary farmer had felt his wife's love. Mary had sensed, too, that in that instant of precious understanding he had found peace with himself. Now she had to come to peace with herself, to loosen the last ties, to clean the slate and start afresh.

Moving to the great wooden chest at the opposite side of the room, Mary reached into the back of a bottom drawer and took out a bundle of letters from under a neatly folded pile of nightdresses. Slowly, she leafed through each one, her fingers brushing fleetingly over the jagged handwriting, and fighting the desire to look inside, finally placed them on her bedside table. *Tomorrow*, she said to herself resolutely, *I'll do it tomorrow.*

~ * ~

Fudge couldn't remember ever having spent so much time putting on make-up, doing her hair or choosing an outfit, and when ultimately, a decision of mediocre satisfaction had been reached, her pulse was racing, her nerves in tatters. To add insult to injury, in the middle of it all Sheila and Danny arrived down from Galway with Rosy and little Sarah in tow. The house, a sleepy cocoon of early morning peacefulness moments before, became a humming hive of pattering feet and relentless, laughing chatter.

Her younger sister's usual bombardment of questions hit her the second Fudge walked into the kitchen.

"Wow! You look like the bee's knees and spider's ankles. What's the occasion?" Rosy piped inquisitively. "Meeting someone?"

"For lunch, if you must know."

"Man, woman, young, old, good-looking, rich?" Mercifully, she'd learnt to condense her interrogatives in order to save time.

"Man, gorgeous, none of your business." Fudge poured herself a glass of milk and pulled Sarah onto her knee. "Hello, Sausage."

"Not a sausage!" the toddler squealed shrilly.

"You are, too!" The doting aunt playfully tweaked her niece's nose and smiled over at Mary, who was standing by the window surveying her family. She looked tired and contemplative, alone with her thoughts amidst the ruckus of happy merriment.

"So who is it, huh?" Rosy broke in, her nosiness unbridled. "I'll find out anyway."

Fudge gave up. "Lilly's brother, Julian. We're just having lunch together."

"Him! Go away! Weren't you always moaning and groaning about that bloke? I thought you hated his guts. And now you fancy him, or what?"

"That's what I'm going to find out."

When eventually Rosy's inquisition began to flag, the breakfast table was cleared and scrubbed, and the hands of the clock were marching steadily towards midday. After a few cosmetic repairs and a final twirl in front of the mirror, Fudge went out to the front lawn where Mary was sitting with Sarah on a red plaid rug. By now the sun was high in the sky, and as the rich, tangy scent of freshly mowed grass reached her nose, Fudge felt even more convinced that today, at last, her dream really would come true.

"I'd better be off," she said, bending down to peck her mother on the cheek. "I'll give you a call if I'm late."

"It's all right, sure aren't you grown up now?" Mary touched her daughter's arm before she turned to leave. "Be happy, love... whatever happens."

"I will, Mum, I will. I promise."

For once, the Saturday morning traffic was in her favour, the customary Galway city congestion lessening, graciously allowing Fudge to reach Oughterard by midday. Travelling inland away from cooling coastal breezes, she was forced to wind down the window as she passed through Moycullen, leaving the glittering blue expanse of Lough Corrib off to her right. The holiday season was in now full swing and a constant stream of vehicles with strange foreign number plates and overflowing roof racks trundled along ahead. Away from the main thoroughfare the lonely moors would be as peaceful as ever, the narrow bog roads and lake-studded wetlands a perfect backdrop for this idyllic day. Already, the pungent aroma of newly cut turf was causing her heart to thump and her grasp on the steering wheel tightened.

When finally, just outside Oughterard, a lurching camping van with a row of red-cheeked faces at the rear window kindly pulled into a lay-by, the whole breathtaking panorama of Connemara unfolded before her. Up ahead in the distance, outlined against flawless azure, the craggy slopes of the Twelve Bens and the Maumturk Mountains swept majestically up to meet the sky.

On either side huge mounds of stacked peat flanked the road, the black, hairy clods defying all laws of gravity as these listing walls leant inquisitively towards the passing holidaymakers. Far less curious were the lone sheep with mud-caked rears and coloured markings, as they sauntered light-footed and fancy-free into the path of oncoming traffic. Often, surprised motorists had to swerve violently, releasing badly secured suitcases from the roofs racks, an action that sent luggage hurtling over the grassy verge or into depths of some wayside lough. Today, they generously chose to graze on the cooler nearby slopes, the heat of the sticky asphalt making suicidal strolls along the white dotted line an uncomfortable undertaking.

It was shortly before one o'clock when Fudge pulled up outside the pub at Maam Cross. A German tourist coach had disgorged several dozen elderly tourists who were now wandering aimlessly back and forth across the wilderness crossroads, their hi-tech cameras aimed at anything vaguely exuding bucolic Irish auras. She searched the few cars parked randomly in the tarred bay, but couldn't spot Julian's station wagon among them. A pity. She hated being the first one to arrive for a date, but inevitably managed to do so every time.

After the muggy heat of the car, the countryside freshness was welcoming, and throwing a light cotton cardigan over her bare shoulders, she started to stroll northwards out along the green, daisy-dotted roadside away from the intersection, hoping to meet him as he approached. Further on, the air rippled hazily above the hard surface and soon the unaccustomed warmth became oppressive. Tying the cardigan around her waist, she sat down on a mossy hillock and let the light wind cool her arms. High above, a small bird warbled shrilly, hovered for a moment then flew on, plunging and soaring gracefully in long, drawn-out loops.

Fudge checked her watch and once again searched the narrow road up ahead. It was twenty past one already. She sighed, irritated, but curbed her impatience, reminding herself that punctuality was a question of good luck when travelling longer distances through the Irish province.

It was unusually peaceful for a summer Saturday afternoon, the busy traffic sticking to the east-west Galway-to-Clifden route. Only occasionally a local motored by, waving a friendly greeting in passing. Ten minutes later, stoically ignoring the bothering dart of anxious exasperation, she stood up, brushed off the seat of her jeans and wandered slowly back towards Maam Cross, all the while firmly believing to hear the sound of a car bouncing up the bumpy road behind her. Yet this belief remained a figment of her imagination, and when at last she arrived back at the car park, only a rust-ridden tractor and two cyclists had passed.

At quarter to two, Fudge went into the pub and ordered a glass of Cidona, at the same time enquiring if anyone had called and left a message. Sorry, deary, no call, no message. Damn! Agitated and fidgety, Fudge took her drink outside, and leaning against the low window-ledge, she began to stare at the curve of the road leading northwards in the hope that the very act of concentration might make Julian and his station wagon materialise out of nowhere. Taking small sips, she succeeded in making the now lukewarm apple drink last half an hour. Having dribbled the last drop out of the glass, Fudge decided to ring home. Perhaps he'd chosen to contact her mother at Birch Rise—although heaven only knew why. He must realise she'd be waiting here at a junction in the middle of nowhere, twiddling her thumbs.

Mary answered after two rings. Today, there was a particularly gloomy timbre to her voice.

"Mum, it's me. Julian didn't call by any chance?"

"No... Has he not turned up?"

"Not yet. I wonder what's happened."

Mary paused for a moment, the fleeting memory of a failed meeting hurrying through her head. "Have you tried to call him?"

"I only have a work number, there'll be nobody there at the weekend."

"Oh dear, I'm sure there's a good explanation."

"God, I hope so... He wouldn't just stand me up, would he?" She hadn't wanted the notion to cross her mind, but it had nestled there nicely nevertheless.

"Ach, of course not. He probably has a flat tyre. I'd wait another twenty minutes or so before coming home."

"Twenty minute? Ten, maybe..."

Fudge, hating herself for her gullibility, waited, in fact, another hour. She paced the road, counted sheep and ate a bag of salt and vinegar Taytos before the truth ultimately set in. Even as she pulled away from the lonely Connemara intersection well after half past three in the afternoon, she kept her eyes fixed on the rear view mirror in the unlikely case a miracle should occur. When, at last, the small group of buildings vanished around a bend in the road, and the last-minute wonder failed to transpire, she finally conceded that her rendezvous had flopped miserably, and the carefully cherished dream was nothing more than a proverbial sandcastle in the sky.

For the first few miles of the return journey, she successfully kept the tears at bay, forcing herself to focus on a whole series of plausible explanations, yet manoeuvring the car through rows of double-parked vehicles in Oughterard, she eventually let them fall.

~ * ~

At the same time, a crow flying in a north-westerly direction over swampy marshes and uncombed hillsides would have crossed high above the lonely road between Maam Cross and Kilmeelicken in Joyce's Country and spied a handsome, dark-blond man as he tried to disentangle the rapidly stiffening carcass of a suicidal ewe from the front radiator of his station wagon.

It was a truly pitiful sight, the widening pool of water mingling with the victim's blood to create a greasy red puddle in the middle of the remote Connemara roadway. The curved horns curling around the sheep's black face had become so ensnared in the front grille that it was a long time before the beast could finally be dragged onto the soft shoulder. As it turned out, the man might have saved himself the bother; the car was, for the time being anyway, far beyond repair.

Giving the dangling bumper a furious kick with the tip of his boot, Julian McDermott bellowed an unsavoury expletive into the tranquil Irish countryside and slowly began the long march back to the next telephone five miles away.

~ * ~

Cringing at the idea of her sister's probing queries, Fudge was relieved to see that Danny's car was not parked beneath the chestnut tree when she pulled up in front of the farmhouse early that evening. *On a day like this they'll all be down at the lake and, with any luck, Rosy will be with them*, she thought ungenerously. Her hopes were confirmed some minutes later while walking through the seemingly abandoned building. Blinded by the bright sunshine outside, Fudge blinked as she searched one room after another, surprised that even Mary appeared to have taken flight. In the kitchen the fire in the range was out and, despite the warm ruffling of evening air sneaking past the gap in an open window, the very heart of the Ginnane household felt strangely cold and inhospitable.

Pouring herself a glass of water from the tap she remained at the sink and closed her eyes, hoping the barely perceptible draught might clear her mind. Her senses numb with disappointment, it was some time before she became aware of the bittersweet smell of burning. Turning back to the range she checked again that the fire was out, remembering that on windy days maverick gusts often carried wafts of smoke in through open doors and windows from the chimney outside. Today, however, all the hearths were cleaned and bare, the summer sun sufficient to warm the depths of the dark old house.

Concerned, Fudge stepped outside the back door, briefly checked the path curving around to the front driveway, then walked towards the vegetable garden. Further on, by the brambly hedgerow that meandered down to the farmyard, billowing grey smoke rose up in irregular plumes. Who on earth would be burning newspapers on a glorious evening like this? It was a regular chore; cardboard boxes, papers, or anything either too big or evil-smelling to be put in the range was incinerated in a large rusty barrel at the end of the garden. As children, they had loved helping, everyone screaming and quibbling about who should throw the last pile into the mesmerising orange flames. Drawing near, she could see Mary standing away from the heat with a small bundle of papers in her hand. Her eyes fixed rigidly on the fire, she made no move to destroy them, but merely stood there staring blankly. Curious now, Fudge wandered along the path between heads of cabbage and walls of brightly flowering sweet pea. Not until she was almost at her mother's side did the older woman become aware of her daughter's presence. Flinching noticeably, her mouth opened in surprise then shut again, an action vaguely reminiscent of a ventriloquist's dummy.

"You all right, Mum?"

"I... I... Finnula, you're home already. Don't tell me he didn't turn up!"

Fudge shook her head. "Nope... I just gave up waiting."

"Ah, love, I'm sorry. But there'll be a good reason, I'm sure."

"Maybe..." Sighing, the younger woman shrugged, her eyes falling to the papers in her mother's grasp. "What are you doing? Are they letters?"

Mary looked down at her hands and then back up at Fudge, as if wondering herself how the collection of envelopes could possibly come to be there. "No... Nothing special, just cleaning out some old things." She took a step towards the fire.

"Wait, let me have a look," Fudge broke in. "They're not our old letters from Castleglen, are they?" She moved to her mother's side and tried to reach for the bundle.

"No!" With unexpected assertion, her mother pulled away. "They're... They're from your father, please..."

"Mum! Don't! You can't burn them!" In a sudden rush of panic she began to tug at Mary's arm and for a moment mother and daughter struggled frantically for possession of the letters. Suddenly, the older woman capitulated, and uttering a gasp of despair she released her clutch, allowing the envelopes to fall in a shower about them. Fudge stared at the faded white papers scattered across the grass, but even before she had time to focus on the unfamiliar, jerky scrawl another realisation hit her; in all those years together, according to her mother not even at the height of courtship, had Charlie ever written Mary one single letter. "He's not what you'd call a great writer," their mother had joked a thousand times. "In fact I'm not even sure what his handwriting looks like!" The five Ginnane girls had found the idea hilarious, accusing Mary of pulling their legs. Now, raising her eyes, Fudge watched the older woman collapse to her knees, the skirts of her summer dress ballooning outwards as she sank back in the grass, then, pressing work-weary hands to her face, she began to cry, the deep sobs of wretchedness causing the strong shoulders to shake.

Fudge, greatly shocked and confused, dropped to the ground and without hesitation, drew Mary into her arms.

"Ssh, Mum, tell me what happened." She was rocking the other woman like a child; mother became daughter, the daughter, a mother.

"Oh God, Finnula, you'll hate me... Hate me!"

"I never could, you know that. Is it because of the letters?"

The dark grey-speckled head nodded briefly, the tear-streaked face still hidden behind her hands. "I did an awful thing..."

For an instant Fudge's stomach constricted, afraid of what she was about to hear. "What can be so awful?"

"I... I had a friend... a man friend."

It all seemed ludicrous, yet the younger woman's suspicions deepened and her heart sank. "You mean a... a lover?" Crestfallen, she glanced at the envelopes strewn before them, some of which had tumbled along the garden path.

Mary's head immediately jerked upwards, the red-rimmed eyes wide with alarm. "No, no, not a lover... never, not once... a friend, a special friend."

Relieved, Fudge's embrace relaxed. "That's not a sin, Mum. Why was that wrong?"

"I kept it a secret from your father—from everyone—for years."

"For years..." The idea was astonishing. How blind had they been? "But if he was only a friend?"

"We had an unusual friendship and only met occasionally. We wrote, talked on the phone. Ach, Finnula, I cheated on your father and he knew it—felt it!"

Fudge held her mother away and looked deeply into those startling blue eyes. "But you loved Dad all those years?"

"Deeply, he was part of me, and always will be. I was more dissatisfied with myself."

"Don't you think he sensed that?"

"I think I hurt him, but at the end he felt it, I'm sure. He knew how much I cared for him." Through the tears a small smile creased the corner of her mouth. "Yes, Finnula, he knew."

"Then that's all that matters now. He'd already forgiven you, don't you see? And he would want you to be happy now."

Wearily, Mary pushed her hair away from her face. All at once, in the mellow light created by the long shadow of the lofty hedgerow, she seemed at peace, as if with those last stinging tears a crippling burden had been lifted. Simultaneously, both women surveyed the letters spread haphazardly about the vegetable patch. Fudge picked up the nearest one, and when Mary didn't protest, she studied the handwriting with a crooked smile.

"He's got a wicked scrawl, whoever he is, this cryptic friend of yours." She was about to turn it over in her hand when her glance flickered over the postmark. Dublin.

In that strange, surrealistic moment, the pieces of an intricate puzzle suddenly fell into place. The surge of understanding was almost dizzying, like a runaway train hurtling through a tunnel towards the light. The well-thumbed letters on Michael's desk. It was as clear as day. All from *her* mother, not Lilly's. Mary's confused reaction when she had poured her heart out about Julian, and before that, the long walk along Dollymount Strand. Abruptly, those long-lost memories arose as the engine of her mind sputtered into action. Further back again, there was Lilly's fourteenth birthday at Birch Rise, the stolen glances, the girlish smiles. And Michael himself, persistently inquiring about Mary's health, hobbies and habits every time she called round to the McDermott's house for Sunday tea, and finally, on that mysterious May afternoon in the stillness of the art historian's living room, the stricken look upon hearing the news of Charlie's death. The scatty intellect must truly love her mother, Fudge reflected sadly; in his reaction there had been no spark of hope that Mary might now be free, only the awareness of how she must be suffering, and in that instant, he had felt her pain.

Fudge looked up at her mother. "It's Michael, isn't it? Lilly's dad."

Mary nodded. "I'm sorry..." she whispered.

"No, there's no need."

At a loss for words, they just stared at each other for a long moment, before suddenly, created by a random thought, a minuscule bubble of absurdity wormed its way through the mountain of melancholy and began to make the corner of Fudge's mouth twitch.

"Those bloody McDermotts!" she whooped unexpectedly. "What have they done to our lives?"

The ludicrous congruence of it all slowly started to dawn on Mary, and fighting off an attack of infectious laughter, she pressed a hand to her mouth. "Oh God, Finnula..."

Her daughter was guffawing openly now. "Mother and daughter, father and son—and to add insult to injury, Lilly and Polly to boot! How ensnared can two families be?"

Laughing and crying, crying and laughing, the two women lay back in the cool grass amongst curly cabbage and carrots, while all around them dozens of faded envelopes fluttered about in the soft, summer evening wind.

They were still lying there when the rest of the family arrived home sunburnt and exhausted after a day splashing around in the waters of Loughrua Lake. Observing mother and daughter from the corner of the house, the others shook their heads and very astutely decided not to pass any remarks.

~ * ~

After bedtime, Fudge crept into Mary's room and sat down on the end of the quilted bed where she'd taken refuge from leprechauns in hobnailed boots so many years before. Her mother put down the library book and smiled.

"Well, did he call?"

The younger woman rolled her eyes. "He managed to murder a sheep on the way to Maam Cross. The car was banjaxed and the next phone a five mile march away."

"You're joking—and now?"

"We'll see each other at the christening in a few weeks. He's promised to take the train, so nothing can go wrong!"

"It'll work out, you'll see." Mary patted her daughter's knee. "Now off to bed with you."

Fudge remained seated. "Mum…"

"What is it?"

"You're coming to the christening, aren't you?"

"I don't think so, love. I… I don't know Lilly that well, I wouldn't like to…"

"It's because of Michael, isn't it? He'll be there."

Mary stared down at her hands. "I'm afraid, Finnula, I hurt him, too."

"Mum, I think he loves you. I can see it now. He was never interested in other women no matter how hard Lilly tried to pair him off. He was waiting for you."

"I told him not to…"

"You can't tell someone's heart what to do. Come to the christening, please?"

Mary shook her head. "I can't… your father…"

"Listen, Mum, I think at times Dad really was afraid of losing you, but in the end he realised how much he meant to you. He wouldn't want you to be lonely now."

"I don't know…"

"Think about it." Fudge kissed her mother goodnight and returned to her own bed where very soon she was dreaming of Connemara slopes, crystal clear skies, curly cabbage and cryptic puzzles.

Seventeen

The christening congregation had already gathered in the small Wicklow chapel and was waiting patiently for the ceremony to begin, while outside Lilly was leaning against a cornerstone battling against another wave of wooziness. She was startlingly pale, the insipid pastel yellow pencil dress and matching blazer doing little to enhance her complexion.

"Jesus, I feel crap," she groaned. "Couldn't we just cancel the whole thing?"

"For heaven's sake, Lilly, try and pull yourself together. We've put it off long enough. Soon Polly will be old enough to toddle up the aisle herself. Now, come on."

On that morning, the godmother was not of a particularly sanguine disposition. She'd gone to vast lengths organising everything—church, invitations, food—and was determined that today, of all days, Polly's mother wasn't going to let her down.

"It's not my fault," the blond woman whined. "Somebody must have put something in my drink."

Checking her temper in front of the child, Fudge grabbed Lilly under the arm with her free hand, at the same time fighting to keep the nine-month-old tot balanced on her hip.

"Don't use that excuse on me! I've heard it once too often. You just guzzled far too much booze as usual! Now get going, Lilly... Please!"

The ceremony was short, the tiny chapel barely large enough for the small group of friends and family who had come to celebrate Polly's baptism and naming. Michael and Julian were seated next to them in the front row and, further back, feeling positively alien in the close confines of the small church, Skids sat stiffly between Gráinne and Kitty, who were looking like dynamite in the latest autumn creations. One elderly man in a brown tweed suit and yellow waistcoat had innocently seated himself behind the latter, and was so flustered by the sight of the secretary's skirts retreating between her buttocks every time she stood up from praying, that afterwards, had an inquisitive passer-by asked, the baffled man wouldn't have been in a position to say whether he'd just attended a christening, wedding or memorial service. Across the aisle, Sheila and Danny flanked a wriggling Sarah, and behind them, a handful of colleagues from Trinity Court Hotel filled the second pew, all of them looking as pale and hungover as Lilly herself. A scattering of local churchgoers, especially women, dotted the remaining few benches, their permed heads straining to get a look at the gurgling child. Mary wasn't in the congregation.

"I'm not ready to see him," she'd explained to Fudge the week before. "You'll think it cowardly, but I need more time."

"I just want the best for you, Mum. Michael would be a companion, a friend."

"I know, love... Maybe soon."

They'd left it at that, and shortly before the service began, while the cluster of guests were still standing around in the crisp September morning air exchanging gossip, Fudge took Michael aside. The art historian, fidgety and obviously ill at ease, had searched the faces as everyone arrived, his shoulders sagging perceptibly when the person he sought most failed to appear. With Polly squirming on her arm, Fudge beat about the bush for several awkward seconds before eventually talking turkey.

"Michael, my mother won't be coming today."

His bushy eyebrows drew together in consternation. "Ah, I see." Rocking on his heels, he clasped his hands nervously behind his back. "What a shame. It would have been nice to see her again." He coughed and glanced away.

"It's all right."

"Sorry?" His gaze returned to Fudge. "I don't..."

"I'm aware you both had a... a special friendship. We talked about it, just Mum and I, the others don't know—and don't need to know." She gave him a wistful, omniscient look.

Suddenly, his lower lip trembled and for a horrible moment she thought he was going to cry, but then he pressed his mouth into a thin line and stared down at his shoes.

"I'm sorry, Finnula. I hope you don't think badly of me. Your mother and I, well... She's a very remarkable woman."

"I know." She gave him a smile of assurance. "Michael, she needs some time, but maybe one day soon..."

"You mean...?" A sparkle abruptly lit up his dull grey eyes.

She nodded. "I think so."

After that his step was a tick lighter and while an air of disappointment remained, the deep furrow of concern had vanished from his brow.

Fortunately, despite all misgivings, the christening took place without any disasters. Polly only squeaked in surprise when the cool water was splashed on her head, Sarah refrained from galloping along the aisle, Skids managed not to fall asleep and the greatest miracle of all was Lilly. White in the face and green at the gills, she battled heroically against apparent waves of nausea and succeeded in surviving the service without vomiting into the font.

Julian, with whom Fudge was only able to exchange a few obligatory words of greeting on arrival, turned out to be an exemplary godfather, cradling Polly in the crook of his arm for the better part of the ceremony. She had trouble keeping her eyes off him, the picture of Lilly's brother holding the child with such ease playing havoc with her imagination.

The setting was perfect. Nestled in a small valley, the surrounding forested slopes sent a shower of golden-yellow autumn leaves down upon them as they left the church and, nearby, the icy waters of a small woodland brook leapfrogged over moss-covered stones and scrubwood before disappearing under a humped-back stone bridge, and on towards the endless depths of Glendalough. Lilly had spotted it on a rare Sunday afternoon outing when the summer city smog had driven them out into the Wicklow mountains in search of fresh country air. For the first time in many months the two friends had been in perfect agreement. This was it.

Later, the modest christening party gathered in the cosy tea rooms of a village hotel for a feast of scones, sandwiches and cake. Lilly, after a quick medicinal visit to the bar, had cured herself by means of the hair of the dog and was deep in animated chatter with Gráinne and Kitty. Skids and Michael, as unlikely a pair as one could imagine, hit it off immediately and before the afternoon was out, the tousle-headed historian had shaken hands on a deal which pronounced him proud owner of a new exhaust pipe, two drive shafts and an alternator.

Polly, baptised, named and exhausted from all the excitement, was fast asleep in her pram. Alone at last, Fudge and Julian wandered into the antiquated hotel conservatory where snaking Mediterranean plants in Tuscany pots stood amongst enamel pails of petal-shedding geraniums and African violets. Her nervousness accentuated by the smell of steamy humus-rich soil, Fudge felt the palms of her hands grow damp. She giggled nervously.

"We certainly made a hames of things out in Connemara, didn't we?"

Julian shook his head. "We? It was entirely my fault. I was driving a bit too fast when the damn creature suddenly materialised in front of my car. Neither of us had a hope in hell."

"At least you weren't hurt, that's the main thing."

They stood side by side looking out through the glass doors and across a wide, steeply sloping lawn that ended at a small copse a hundreds yards away. Clumps of brightly blossoming dahlias jutted up obstinately amongst slowly fading autumn foliage.

"I'd like to make up for it," Julian said, giving the silent dark-haired woman a sideways glance. "What about dinner tomorrow evening? I've taken a day off work and don't have to be back until Tuesday.

While Fudge's stomach busily turned cartwheels, on the outside she remained poised. "Why not?" she smiled. "I'd like that."

"We could go to that restaurant off Dame Street, remember?" He jerked one eyebrow up in a manner which turned her knees to jelly.

"Fine, sounds great." She risked looking into his eyes, a quick, challenging glimpse.

The corner of Julian's mouth hitched up into an all too familiar roguish smirk. "And afterwards I could walk you to the bus."

They both laughed then, the vision of that bizarre scene on Nassau street many years before abruptly springing to mind. They were still lost in the memory of that brief and rudely terminated embrace when a piercing shriek coming from the tea room next door caused them to jump. A second later Polly began to cry.

"Jesus," Julian uttered. "What the hell...?" He took a step towards the door, but Fudge laid a reassuring hand on his arm.

"You've never heard your sister laughing after a drink or two?" she asked almost sadly.

"What?"

Sure enough, the heart-stopping squeal was followed by a wave of staccato braying, and a moment later Gráinne and Kitty's voices joined the explosion of hilarity.

Julian shot a glance at his watch. "She's started drinking already?"

Fudge sighed. "She was out partying yesterday, I don't think she really stopped."

"You're joking. On the night before the christening?" He walked over to the door of the tea room. Lilly was reclining lazily in a floral-covered armchair with what looked like a gin and tonic clasped in her hand. Nearby, Michael was pacing up and down between the tables with Polly on his arm. Every now and then, he would stop and observe his daughter, the deep furrow of concern marring his features once again.

"Finnula, is she often like this?" Julian enquired anxiously.

She nodded hesitantly. "I'm afraid so. You know she's always been a little wild, but lately…"

"Why didn't you say anything? Call me?"

"I hoped it was only a phase… Her new job, colleagues and so on…" She shook her head helplessly. "Julian, I'm beginning to think she needs help, I'm worried about her—and Polly, too."

"Good God, that bad?" His face paled.

"Maybe not yet, but it could be." Fudge hesitated for a moment, her gaze moving to the huddle of trees at the bottom of the garden. A light gust rustled through the branches, sending a flurry of gold-rust leaves zigzagging onto the grass. "I think her problems lie deeper."

"What do you mean?" Julian took her arm and they moved to the great glass doors leading to the lawn.

"For a long time Lilly has been constantly worrying about getting cancer. She's perfectly healthy, but can't really believe it. I have to accompany her to the doctor once or twice a year—every time she has a scare. It's a phobia and seems to be getting worse." Fudge suddenly turned to Lilly's brother. "She's very unhappy, I think she just tries to cover it up with all this wild living, she…" She stopped, afraid to open old wounds.

"Tell me."

"I may be wrong, I suspect she hoped being a mother would help her get over losing her own—and it hasn't."

"We'll never forget Mum, of course, but she died so long ago."

"At a time Lilly needed her most. I don't think she ever really got over it and misses her every single day."

"Oh God, Finnula… I didn't know." Julian raised a hand to cover his face. "What can we do?"

Wearily, Fudge tucked a lock of hair behind her ear. "I tried to suggest therapy recently and she went sheer berserk—nearly threw me out of the flat! At this rate she'll hardly hold her job much longer and I'm terrified of leaving her alone with Polly. I know it's an awful thing to say, and she'd never do her child any intentional harm, but if she slipped, or fell into a deep sleep... "

"Perhaps if I talked to her?"

"No, she'll get angry. Look, I'm going to take a week or so off work. We'll spend some time together and maybe I can persuade her to reconsider therapy. Don't worry Michael with this just yet."

Julian suddenly drew Fudge towards him. "Why are you doing this for her? When are you going to get on with your own life? I've never met such a selfless person."

"Lilly has been part of my life since we first turned up on the school steps at Castleglen together, and Polly... I can't imagine a life without her."

Without warning, Julian raised a slender finger and pensively traced a line along the curve of Fudge's cheek.

"Waz goin' on here!" The unexpected slurred utterance making them start, the godparents jumped apart, embarrassed. Lilly was standing in the doorway, a beaming, crooked smile plastered across her features. "Jul! You weren't making a pass at Polly's god-mum, were you?" The idea threw her into a fit of throaty hysterics and she grabbed the doorframe for support.

Julian went to his sister, laid a fraternal arm across her shoulder and gently steered the cackling woman towards the nearest cup of strong black coffee. He glanced over his shoulder as he went. "I'll pick you up at the flat at seven thirty tomorrow evening. That okay?"

Fudge smiled and, forgetting her composure, nodded as eagerly as a child being offered a bar of chocolate.

~ * ~

In comparison, however, to the disappointment a child might feel should a promised bar of chocolate suddenly be whipped away again, Fudge's feeling of frustration was overwhelming when the following evening her second rendezvous with Julian fell flat.

On arriving home late on Monday afternoon, full of excited anticipation and ready to propel herself into the full beauty program, she found Lilly lying curled up like a prawn on the sofa clutching her stomach. Polly was spread-eagled in the playpen fast asleep, the red dummy pumping up and down in her little mouth as she dreamed. Fudge drew a baby blanket over the blond-haired cherubic form before going to Lilly's side. The other woman had been crying, her tears forming wet splotches on the cushion under her head.

"I'm sorry..." she whispered faintly. Her voice was scratchy and dry.

"What for?" Fudge pushed a swath of curly hair back from her friend's forehead.

"For being such a shit, for letting you down, being a rotten mother... a lush... having pains all the time."

"Ssh, don't exaggerate. We'll get through this, you just have to let me help you. Have you got another stomach ache?"

Lilly nodded. "Just a little one, don't worry about..." She winced noticeably, unable to finish the sentence.

"I'll get a hot water bottle and an aspirin." On her way to the kitchen she looked at the clock and although there was plenty of time before Julian was due to arrive, already she felt her heart sinking. In such a deeply depressed state Lilly could not be left alone, and as if to confirm her fears, when she returned to the sofa a minute later, the other woman was crying softly into the crook of her arm once again.

Fudge stroked her back. "I'm taking a week off work. Why don't you do the same? We'll go to Brittas Bay and show Polly the sand dunes—and the zoo, she hasn't been to Dublin zoo yet. What do you think?"

Lilly snuffled nasally, her face still hidden. "I'm going to try, Fudge, I really am. Starting tomorrow."

"Great! We'll make one of our famous plans, and should even start thinking about a Halloween party for your birthday!"

For a moment, the despairing woman brightened up, yet a mere instant later, her shoulders began to shudder once more. "I can't..."

"Oh, Lilly, don't cry. Please don't cry!"

And for the first time in years, almost as if she'd overheard the conversation with Julian the previous day, Lilly put her deepest feelings into words. "I miss her, Fudge, I miss Mummy so much."

"I know, but she's with you all the time, I'm sure..."

Unexpectedly, the grieving woman looked up. "It's not enough, *I* need to be with *her*!"

"I don't understand..."

"At times like this, I feel I want to go to her... to join her wherever she is."

It took several long seconds for the magnitude of Lilly's statement to sink in, and when it did, Fudge, in a moment of awful comprehension, understood that everything that had gone before—the drink, the pain, the sadness—was all only the tip of a brittle iceberg.

When Julian turned up at the flat shortly before half past, Fudge stepped out onto the front step and sat down, inviting him to do the same. Hesitating momentarily, the tall man hitched up the knees of his neatly pressed trousers and squatted down beside her. Dressed for an evening out in a smart city centre restaurant, he was looking squeaky clean and impeccably groomed in a navy blazer and pale blue cotton shirt, his appearance making Fudge's decision all the more bitter.

"Lilly's not well," she said wearily. "I'll have to stay here, sorry."

Julian gave her a worried look. "Has she been...?"

"No, she's just terribly depressed."

"We could have dinner here altogether. Why don't you let me fetch some Chinese food? It might cheer her up."

Fudge shook her head. "I don't think she'd want you to see her like this. She's always afraid of worrying the family. You won't mention it?"

"Not if you don't want me to, but something should be done, Finnula."

"We're taking time off. She's going to try."

They were silent for a short time, each contemplating the long line of cherry trees flanking both sides of the quiet Rathmines street. Rush hour was over and most residents were already at home seating themselves down to a standard weekday supper. Every now and then, a straggler coming home late from work walked swiftly past, the idea of a cosy evening in front of the telly more interesting then the dejected couple crouching on the top steps of house number thirty-one.

"I wish there was something I could do." Julian said after a while. "You're taking all the weight onto your shoulders."

Fudge shrugged. "I'm not some kind of martyr. It's for Polly, too. I love that child so much."

Her own outburst of emotion catching her off guard, she swiftly turned her head away in an effort to hide the flush of embarrassment. Feigning exaggerated interest in a tatty stray dog that had stopped in the middle of the street to scratch its ear, she almost jumped when Julian rested his hand upon hers. With fingers intertwined, they sat in silence for several minutes before Fudge dared to glimpse into his eyes, and in that instant her almost adolescent coyness vanished abruptly.

Afterwards, Fudge asked herself who had actually made the first move, but could only recall his soft lips touching hers, tenderly at first, then with ever increasing eagerness. At the same time, she felt his arms encircling her and instinctively reciprocated his embrace, gently locking her hands behind his strong neck. It might have been only a minute, or even less, yet had the two young lads on bicycles not ridden by at that moment, their kiss would surely have lasted forever.

"Hey, Mister!" the red-haired freckle-faced youngster bellowed. "Get yer tongue ou' of yer wan!"

His greasy-haired buddy uttered a piercing, free-hand wolf whistle, and before Julian and Fudge had time to pull apart, the boys were standing on the pedals and racing off down the avenue at top speed, their raucous guffaws causing faces to appear between net curtains on both sides of the street.

Reluctant to let go, they held each other tightly long after the lads had disappeared around the corner of the intersection, Fudge unashamedly relishing the feeling of his body pressed against hers.

"Will there ever be time for us, do you think?" His voice was pensive, almost sad.

"We're so far apart," she whispered. "Maybe, one day..."

Puzzled, Julian suddenly sat back and studied the dark-haired woman's face. "Maybe, *one day*?" he said dully. "Any idea when 'one day' might be?"

"No, I didn't mean it like that. It's just that you're working so far away, and at the moment with Lilly I can't…"

The marine biologist stood up and straightened his jacket. "Sorry, it seems I jumped to conclusions. I gather you're not interested in getting involved."

"Julian, please, you don't understand. It's just that…" She tried to reach for his hand, but he was already descending the steps to the street. On the pavement he hesitated and looked back towards her.

"Finnula, I really appreciate what you're doing, however, you have your own future to think of, too. I can be here if my sister needs me, and there's a very lonely man waiting in an empty house in Ballsbridge. You don't have to sacrifice yourself all the time—unless you're using it as an excuse to keep other people at bay. It's not as if I'm not willing to make sacrifices myself, but you can't put your life on the back-burner—or me, either."

He turned and walked down the avenue to his car. The scenario, so startlingly reminiscent of that awful evening on Nassau Street many years before, threw Fudge into a eerie time warp and before she had a chance to react, he had started the engine and was moving away in the direction of the canal and the main Dublin-to-Galway thoroughfare which would take him out towards the west.

Bloody men. Bloody men and their bloated egos! Filled with fury, Fudge leapt to her feet. Grabbing a ceramic pot of wilting geraniums from the window-ledge next to the door, she drew on all her resources and hurled it down the street at the receding station wagon. The pot exploded in the middle of the road, the rust-brown shards of clay whizzing like shrapnel across the asphalt surface.

"Sod off, Julian McDermott!" she roared at the top of her voice, indifferent to the spattering of gleeful spectators who no longer deigned it necessary to conceal their blatant curiosity behind living room curtains. "*Sod off!*"

~ * ~

Brittas Bay was freezing cold, the stiff September breeze whipping spirals of sand up into the scrunched-up faces of the three intrepid day-trippers. *That peroxide cow from the weather slot would wet her knickers laughing if she saw us now*, Fudge thought mordantly, at the same time conceding the poor woman could hardly be held responsible for the fact that the gaily heralded Irish-Indian summer had failed to transpire. To give her credit, the day had started well, razor-sharp rays of sunshine beckoning gullible sun-seekers out into the early autumn morning, and falling for it, the threesome, armed with plastic buckets, spades and packed lunches, had set off for what promised to be an afternoon romping in the dunes and building sandcastles.

With a dart of consternation, Fudge had observed the bank of grey cloud hulking on the western horizon and, sure enough, before they'd passed Greystones, the treetops were beginning to thrash about, causing flurries of dried leaves to somersault across the dual carriageway ahead. All things considered, Fudge chose to ignore the all too conspicuous meteorological threat and instead began to sing. "Off we go to Brittas on a sunny day, off we go to Brittas laughing all the way..." Polly screeched with delight, drumming her pudgy legs against the baby seat. Lilly, endeavouring to share her daughter's joy, soon joined in, sadly capitulating after two lines.

"Sorry, Fudge, singing in the car always makes me feel a little queasy." She eyed Polly's red bucket at her feet and pressed her lips together.

At the beach at last, the final chunks of blue sky had been engulfed by greater forces, and although the rain graciously held back, the wind chose to hitch up to a level on the Beaufort scale which sufficed to flatten the tall, spiky expanses of resilient dune grass. With the hoods of their windcheaters firmly tied under their chins, and Polly's woolly hat tugged down to the tip of her nose, Fudge and Lilly struggled towards the Irish sea, dragging the baby buggy behind them. When finally, separated from the water by a mere twenty yards, a ferocious clap of thunder shook the heavens, they grudgingly admitted defeat and took to their heels.

Later, in Dilly's Doughnut Bar, the two women slurped hot tea, while Polly blissfully plastered her face with sticky raspberry pastry filling.

"So much for our excursion," Lilly snorted as she lifted the cup to her lips, her fingers trembling ever so slightly. "Still, we tried."

Fudge smiled. "All is not lost. There's Powerscourt, the zoo, the botanical gardens…"

"Anywhere we won't get our arses frozen off?" The blond woman snorted and handed her daughter another piece of doughnut.

"We could go home, turn up the heating, and have a picnic on the living room floor."

"That's the most sensible suggestion I've heard all day."

The two women laughed, and almost as if she could understand, little Polly joined in, too.

The return journey to Rathmines was far more harmonious, and for a while it was like old times, inventing stupid jokes, pointing out strange-looking pedestrians, commenting lasciviously on muscular road workers' backsides and generally forgetting what had driven them out into the inhospitable tempest in the first place.

That evening, sitting on a plaid rug on the floor in front of the TV, all three watched as the yellow-haired weather girl apologetically ventured a further, timorous prophecy of fabulous early autumn conditions. To the country's relief, her courageous forecast turned out to be true.

For seven wonderful days the two women escorted Polly from one attraction to the other, fed the ducks in St. Stephen's Green, visited gardens, picnicked at Powerscourt and Glendalough, collected shells at Dollymount, lurched the whole way to Bray and back again on the top of a double-decker bus, ate hamburgers at Captain America's and visited Michael in Ballsbridge. For a while, Fudge dared to believe that, at last, Lilly's crippling cloak of depression and fear had slowly begun to slip from her friend's shoulders. Without a tiny pang of jealousy, she watched as mother and daughter discovered each other anew, the two blond, curly heads bent close together while they explored brightly coloured picture books from cover to cover over and over again, and later, at bedtime, Lilly took Polly into her arms and, gazing into those tired green-blue eyes, cradled her until she slept.

When work called once again in early October, Fudge returned home each day with bated breath, anxious the old routine and corresponding temptation might upset Lilly's determined, but fragile, equilibrium. They continued to visit Michael regularly, occasionally leaving Polly in her grandfather's care and treating themselves to a decadent afternoon's shopping, or the odd evening out. After three more weeks, she gradually started to relax and with each passing day became more and more confident that the battle had been won. Far more important, however, than Fudge's belief that her friend's anxiety and hopelessness had been conquered was, in fact, Lilly's own conviction. Understanding at last, that her sorrow was not in her heart, but in her head, she too, soon began to hope that the final hurdle had ultimately been crossed, and was therefore all the more bewildered when, early one morning shortly after before her twenty-seventh birthday, she perceived a dull, throbbing ache under her left arm.

Terrified by the awesome power of one's subconscious mind, she sat clutching the side of the bed, knowing the pain was, as on every other previous occasion, a figment of her own self-destroying imagination. Not this time, she swore bitterly. Not this time! She had made a pledge, one she would not break! Throwing on her dressing gown, she glanced down at Polly's sleeping form before padding into the kitchen on bare feet. Fudge was up, dressed, and ready to start work early in order to be home again in time for Lilly's late shift at the Trinity Court hotel. Fresh coffee was busy percolating on the cooker.

"Mmm, real coffee," Lilly chirped, bravely hiding her anxiety. "What ever happened to the plain old cuppa tea?"

Fudge grinned and pulled two monstrous sticky currant buns out of a paper bag. "We've deserved it. Come on, let's tuck into this lot before that tadpole of yours raises the roof."

"Don't worry, any bet she'll wait until you've gone to work and I'm settling down for another zizz."

Giggling like the two silly schoolgirls they used to be, both women flopped down onto the sofa and launched into a scrumptiously calorie-loaded, nutritionally lethal breakfast.

An hour later, while Polly sucked greedily on her bottle, Lilly continued to suppress a rising wave of panic. What if, just this once, it wasn't a false alarm, a physical expression of her paranoia, but something real? Staring into her daughter's chubby-cheeked face, she frantically tried to wipe out the old familiar vision of creeping cancerous growths and death-bringing tumours. *Go away*, she wanted to scream, *go away*! The little girl, sensing her mother's tension, stiffened for a moment then carried on drinking, drawing the milky mixture in hungry draughts. By mid-morning, Lilly couldn't stand it any longer. Without even bothering to call first, she bundled the child into the car and drove straight to Ballsbridge, where Michael was just settling down at his desk to write a report.

"What's the rush?" The art historian peered over the top of his glasses as Lilly heaved his granddaughter onto his lap.

"Please, Dad, just this once, don't ask." She took Polly's face in her hands and placed a wet kiss on her nose. "I won't be long, honest."

"But..." A second after the front door slammed behind her, the confused child began to howl.

~ * ~

Calmly, as he had so many times before, Doctor Plunkett went through the motions, carrying out the examination with the mandatory thoroughness required to quench his troubled patient's fears. Afterwards, he placed his hands on Lilly's shoulders and fixed her with a long, hard look.

"Lillian, you've lost some weight, I see, but otherwise you're perfectly healthy."

Lilly nodded slowly then, lowering her head, she began to cry. This time, however, they were no longer tears of relief, but of shame.

"I tried, I really did…"A salty trail snaked along the side of her nose. The doctor pulled up a chair and sat down, forgetting for a moment that the front room full of waiting patients.

"We've talked about this before. I know you don't want to, but maybe it's time you talked to somebody else, somebody who can help you better than I can." He looked at her anguished face, remembering the night he first met her down at the hospital, and after that, the regular visits. One moment depression, the next elation—a roller coaster of emotional torture.

Lilly sniffed and looked up. "It's getting better, honestly. Knowing it's all in my mind helps."

"But realising that hasn't stopped the symptoms, the pains."

"I came on my own today," she smiled thinly. "Without Finnula… All on my own."

Doctor Plunkett immediately understood the importance of what the young woman was saying. "That's good, Lillian, it's a first step in the right direction. You can do it if you try—and with some help."

"No… I can do it alone!" Lilly broke in, her voice filled with new determination. "I want to do it alone!"

The white-haired doctor patted her hand and stood up. "Then you will, Lillian. You will."

On her way to the door, Lilly turned. "Thanks, Doctor Plunkett, for everything."

The older man smiled and nodded; yet deep in his heart he had the odd feeling he wouldn't be seeing Lillian McDermott again, and while, under the circumstances that should have been a good thing, it somehow made him very, very sad.

Driving away from the surgery near Fairview Park, Lilly drew in a deep breath of resolution. A new sense of euphoria had settled upon her, not the usual feeling of reprieve experienced on countless occasions subsequent to her visits to Doctor Plunkett, but a huge surge of mounting confidence. In a way, she felt like an abandoned bird in a world of walking creatures which, by chance, suddenly discovers its wings, and unable to comprehend it can really fly, begins to flap around experimentally, with bewildered caution at first, and then with ever-increasing self-assurance. *I'll do it!* she thought to herself as she crunched down a gear and revved around the corner in the direction of the Liffey, *I'll do it on my own!*

Moving away from the park, Lilly flicked down the sun visor. It was one of those rare autumn days when the late October sun, having reached its zenith, was still low in the sky, blinding motorists heading south. Midday traffic had already clogged the city centre access streets, making progress cumbersome. She glanced at her watch and searched the road up ahead, realising she would need the better part of an hour to get to Ballsbridge, if not longer. In the vain hope of finding an easier way across the river, Lilly spontaneously swung a left and soon found herself zigzagging back and forth through a complex network of shabby Dublin back streets the south-side woman had never seen before in her life.

Her elation soon gave way to aggravation, and by the time she'd reversed out of two dead-ends, Lilly had begun to swear profusely. Nervously pressing the accelerator, she whipped past boarded-up shops, derelict buildings and huge, hulking warehouses. At intervals, massive container trucks and delivery vans thundered past, leaving little more than a hair's breadth between her vehicle and theirs. With escalating anxiety, she drove on, hoping the dizzying one-way system would eventually bring her back to the main city centre route. When, moments later, the sun glistened off an expanse of water, Lilly put her foot to the ground. The Liffey. Up ahead she could turn right onto the quays and drive along the river towards O'Connell Bridge less than a mile away. Satisfied she'd regained her bearings at last, her surprise was all the greater when the road opened out onto an alien stretch of unfamiliar dock-land. Jerking her head right and left, the confused woman frantically tried to locate a recognisable landmark.

Here, the air was full of diesel fumes and the smell of warm tar, the metallic rusty odour of scrap yards and shipbuilding intensifying her inexplicable fear. Desperate to escape from this unforeseen nightmare, Lilly tore the steering wheel around in a hectic attempt to manoeuvre the car into a U-turn. Halfway across the road the noon sun flashed brightly off a high storehouse window, and for a second, she was completely blinded, the white light forcing her eyes shut. It was one of those moments when everything glides into a surrealistic time warp, when control is lost and all actions are intuitive and beyond influence. Even the hollow warning blast of the container lorry's horn seemed far away and unreal, the slithering, sideways motion strangely dreamlike.

Gathering momentum, the car bounced off a curb and abruptly shot forwards. In those few short seconds before impact, Lilly calmly watched with growing fascination as the light dancing over the surface of the harbour waters rose up to meet her. Sinking slowly into the underwater gloom, she felt the cold wetness rushing up to envelope her in an icy grasp. Far away, a voice sounding very much like her own began to call out. "Mummy... Mummy, help me..."

While salty estuary waters surged up her nostrils and down her throat, Lilly suddenly felt a warm hand take hers in a good solid grip. Strangely devoid of any desire to breathe, she forced her eyes open and peered into the swirling murkiness. There she was, sitting peacefully nearby, a comforting smile of assurance spreading across her serene face.

"It's all right, pet, I'm here. There's nothing to be afraid of, nothing at all."

"Mummy..." Lilly leaned towards the other woman's open arms, and experienced once again, after so many long years, the joy of sinking into her mother's comforting embrace.

~ * ~

Fudge had just thrown the last sealed envelope into the out tray and was putting on her jacket, eager to get home, when the Gardaí called. Although, outwardly, she remained curiously calm, confirming efficiently that she and Lillian McDermott did indeed live at the same address, and were close friends, a ballooning wave of horror rose up within her, erupting the instant she replaced the receiver in its cradle. Putting her head in her hands, she let out a low, animal groan of shocked disbelief which brought Skids running to her side.

"Christ Almighty, Finnula! What's goin' on?"

"Oh God, Skids... It's Lilly, her car went off the docks."

"Off the docks! Sweet Jesus, she's not...?"

Wide-eyed, Gráinne and Kitty stood rooted to the spot, their hands pressed to their mouths in alarm.

Fudge grabbed the phone and began to dial Michael's number. "She's in hospital—in intensive care. They wouldn't say any more."

"And the wee one... Polly?"

"She wasn't found, the baby seat was empty, the straps open. Oh God, Skids..." Her fingers were shaking violently as she waited for Lilly's father to answer, her face ashen grey. A second later, Michael's soft voice crackled over the line, and to Fudge's overwhelming relief, a child's gurgling chatter was perceptible in the background.

"Michael!" she almost shouted. "Is that Polly?"

"Yes, she's here with me, Lilly had an errand to do."

The mixture of tension and relief too much to bear, Fudge abruptly exploded into tears. "Michael... Michael, come quickly, something awful has happened!"

~ * ~

It was late at night before they were allowed to see her. Julian, despite Michael's protests, had dropped everything and driven to Dublin at a breakneck speed, hurtling dangerously along a criss-cross of swiftly darkening country roads. When he finally rushed through the swing doors into the hallway outside the intensive care unit, he found Fudge slumped on a hard plastic chair with Polly asleep in a pushchair beside her. Having no more tears to shed, she seemed stunned and trance-like, barely reacting when Lilly's brother sat down and took her hand.

"Where's Dad?" he whispered quietly as if the very sound of his voice might tip the scales between life and death.

Fudge glanced towards a closed doorway at the end of the corridor. "He's with her now."

"Will we be allowed in?"

"I think so. She's in a coma. The doctors don't know…" Fudge's throat tightened, strangling her words. "Oh God, it's all my fault!"

Julian wrapped his arm around the tormented woman's shoulders and drew her to him. "Don't say that."

"But I promised to help. Why didn't I recognise the signs?"

"What signs.?"

"There were moments…" Fudge had said too much, gone too far. "Ach, nothing."

His hand, as icy cold as hers, tightened its grasp. "Tell me."

"She missed her… your mother so much. At times I think she wanted to be with her."

"What do you mean?"

"To… To go to her."

Julian sat up straight, his eyes searching hers. "You mean Lilly tried to take her life?"

"I… maybe… oh Jesus, I should have helped her!"

Julian shook his head violently. "No! It was an accident!" He grabbed Fudge's shoulders and forced her to look at him. "An accident. I've already spoken to the Gardaí. She lost control of her car trying to do a U-turn. A lorry driver witnessed it all. Finnula, it wasn't your fault!"

Nearby, Polly mumbled incoherently in her sleep, raising one heavy eyelid in a lizard-like motion, before slipping back to the Land of Nod.

Julian, seeing Fudge flinch, immediately relaxed his iron grip. "I'm sorry…"

Falling silent, they sat staring at the sterile linoleum, each lost in memories of their own. Deep in the heart of the spread-out hospital building, a phone began to ring, the far-off, incessant jangling echoing shrilly along empty corridors and stairwells. Outside, the city was still alive, the muffled sounds of hooting horns and nighttime laughter rising up from the street beyond the front gates. Once, exuding an aura of experienced efficiency, a night nurse swished hurriedly by, her face a mask of concerned preoccupation.

The heavy door at the end of the passageway bounced shut behind her and suddenly everything seemed quieter than beforehand.

"I'm sorry for driving away, too," Julian added softly. "I don't know what got into me—it was childish. Selfish. I suppose I thought I could sweep you off your feet."

"It's okay. I... I threw a geranium at you."

"... and missed by miles, I know."

"Oh."

Shortly before midnight, Fudge felt her eyelids begin to droop, and drained of energy, she let her head fall onto Julian's shoulder. As she dozed off into a shallow restless sleep, she vaguely registered the weight of his head gently resting against hers.

That's how Michael found them when he emerged from Intensive Care some time later, and had the circumstances been less tragic, his heart would surely have soared at the sight of Polly's godparents slumbering in such tender intimacy, and drawn comfort from it. Julian heard his father's steps first, and jolted up out of a confused, troubled dream.

"You can see her now." Michael's glance moved to Fudge, who, having woken up, was now running trembling fingers nervously through her uncombed hair. "Both of you," he added. "A nurse will keep an eye on Polly."

Father, brother and friend approached the dimly lit hospital room and though inwardly prepared, Fudge was shocked by the rows of monitor screens and intricate network of intertwining tubes and cables. Pale but unmarked, Lilly lay motionless under starched linen, as peaceful and apparently untroubled as if she were taking an afternoon nap on the living room sofa.

"She's only sleeping, surely," Fudge said unexpectedly, overcome by the feeling that a good tug on Lilly's ear might wake her.

Grimly, Michael shook his head. "No, she's in a coma. Her... Her chances aren't good." Julian, until that moment the hope-giving comforter, abruptly crumpled onto the edge of the bed, and unable to hide his despair any longer, moaned piteously. "Lilly, come back, please... come back."

His father, who had so courageously battled to maintain composure for so long, sank down opposite him and, together with his son, suddenly allowed his grief to overflow. Fudge looked from father to son, and then to Lilly.

"No!" The determination in her voice caused the two men to look up. "Don't! She wouldn't want it! Look at her, she's not suffering, look at her face!"

Framed by a mane of golden curls, the porcelain features were tranquil, her mouth, it seemed, curved into the trace of a smile. For a long while, they just stared at her lovely face, soaking up the very peacefulness Lilly so vainly sought in her restless lifetime.

"Yes..." Michael said. "I can feel it... She's happy."

And then it happened. Hardly any more perceptible than the quivering of a tiny insect's gossamer wings at first, but then more noticeably, the blond woman's eyelids began to flutter. Each believing it to be a roguish trick of nature, nothing was said until, ever so slowly, Lilly opened her eyes. Michael quickly moved to his daughter's side, while Julian sat back holding his breath.

"Lilly, love... We're all here with you." The older man forced his speech to remain calm. "Polly, too."

Her mouth moved, yet the words were too faint to hear. Michael leant a little closer.

"Daddy, it's wonderful!" Her utterance was breathy, excited. Julian and Fudge exchanged bewildered looks. "Mummy's here, too..."

"Oh, love." Michael's eyes brimmed with tears.

"You won't be sad, will you?"

"Why...? I don't understand..." her father stuttered, completely at a loss.

"I want to stay here with her. You won't be sad?" Lilly repeated, her words fading into a barely audible whisper.

Michael looked at Julian and tenderly stroked his daughter's hair. "No, my pet. We won't be sad, I promise... We promise..."

Then for a moment, Lilly looked past the two men at Fudge and smiled, her eyes twinkling impishly as the two friends gazed in silence at each other.

An instant later, Lillian McDermott slipped away, and was gone.

~ * ~

Mary surfaced from a strange, lonely sleep to the far-away jingling of a telephone. Taking a moment to realise it was their own, she slipped into her dressing gown, swearing to go sheer mad if it were some young lad looking for Rosy. In the living room, she switched on a table lamp and squinted at the clock on the mantelpiece. Christ. Three o'clock. With a tingle of apprehension, she reached for the receiver and was surprised to hear Finnula's sombre voice.

"Mum... Can you come to Dublin? Michael needs you."

Two Years Later

Wiping his wet hands on the sides of his trousers, Julian came into the living room, pausing at the doorway to take in the sight of Finnula and Polly huddled close together in the yawning hollow of the old sofa, a photo album lying open on their knees and the log fire crackling in front if them. The little girl, however, was staring bravely at the huge window where a stormy autumn wind had suddenly hurled a conker at the glass pane.

The blond head turned towards him. "S'not a lep... leprechaun, Daddy, only a conker."

"*It's* not." Fudge corrected the child.

"Snot's easier to say, isn't it, Poppit?" Ignoring the reprimanding look on his wife's face, he slipped down onto the sofa beside them and close together, they watched as a sudden shower of sparks spluttered from a piece of fresh firewood and spiralled up the chimney.

"Thanks for helping me with the dishes," Fudge yawned. "I'm shattered."

"Sure you have me well trained." Julian grinned and glanced at Polly. "Shouldn't you be in bed?"

"Uh, uh." She shook her head vigorously, causing the corkscrews to dance.

Fudge raised a knowing eyebrow in Julian's direction and with one great scoop he swung the little girl up onto his shoulders, heaved himself up off the couch, and galloped up the stairs. Enjoying a few precious moments to herself, she leaned back into the cushions and closed her eyes. Birch Rise was a family home once again, and while not exactly as Charlie might have imagined it, she knew her father would have been pleased. The stables, lovingly renovated and completely revamped, had been turned into Julian's private world full of microscopes, aquariums, computer technology and shelves of jars brimming with disgusting, slimy things. Some of his time was still spent in Westport, but most of it on the farm, and if all went well, he would soon take up a position in a marine institute in Galway. Just as well, she thought, tweezing a thick, man-sized woollen sock out from between the sofa cushions; she didn't necessarily need a man under her feet during the day.

Following them upstairs, Fudge winged the offensive article of clothing into the laundry basket as she passed the bathroom and joined Julian in Polly's bedroom. The little girl was hiding under the quilt.

"You're not afraid of that wind, are you?" She stuck her hand beneath the sheets and tickled the child's tummy playfully.

"Nope!" The pixie-faced child popped up and giggled. "My angel-mummy's here!" Julian and Fudge followed Polly's gaze to the photograph on the bedside table and smiled. Lilly's laughing face surrounded by a glimmering shroud of unruly honey-coloured locks had, indeed, an astonishingly angelic quality. Spoiling themselves, more than the child, with several further minutes of stories and fun, they finally turned out the light and called it a day.

"Phew! What a bundle!" Julian gasped as he crawled under the covers of their own big double bed some time later.

"You don't mean me by any chance, do you?"

He snorted and pulled Fudge onto his broad chest. "No way, you're only a skinny rake. I think I'll have to fatten you up a bit." He shot her a saucy look. "If I haven't already…"

Fudge swatted her husband. "You're awful, honestly."

"Speaking of fattening you up, how about a dirty weekend out in Connemara somewhere?"

"Sounds good to me, even if we're more than two years late... What about Polly?"

"Maybe Dad and Mary would like to come down to Birch Rise for a few days. Your mum might like to get away from the Ballsbridge house for a change."

"Are you joking? She's in her element in Dublin, surrounded by libraries, bookshops, theatres and then, of course, there are her studies. She's taking her first exams soon."

Julian laughed. "She's an amazing woman."

"Who bagged herself a wonderful man."

"They're happy together, aren't they?"

"Ridiculously."

They cuddled together, just staring at the ceiling and enjoying the cosiness.

"Finnula, maybe Sheila and Danny might..."

"Julian!"

"What?"

"Would you stop calling me 'Finnula' all the time, for crying out loud, it sounds so formal!"

"Oh please, don't make me say 'Fudge'. I always found that a bit... well... sickly sweet. What do you suggest?"

"Ach, who cares, anything. Just... just..." His wife suddenly erupted into hysterical hoots of laughter.

"Just... what?" He gazed at her as if she'd completely taken leave of her senses.

"Call me anything you like, but for God's sake, just don't call me *'Finni-the-Pooh'!*"

Meet Trisha FitzGerald

Patricia FitzGerald was born and grew up in Ireland though she did spend a few brief years of her childhood life in Brazil.

After school, she studied Graphic Design and Visual Communications at the National College of Art and Design in Dublin, and worked for a short time as a freelance designer before moving to Germany. After her children were born, Patricia decided against further education in order to catch up with the now new fast-moving world of computer graphics, but instead, returned to a language school in Ireland to obtain qualifications in TEFL, Teaching English as a Foreign Language. Since then, as well as her job as an assistant in international business, she has been working freelance, translating and teaching commercial and general English.

Patricia was an EPPIE 2003 finalist with her first book "Making Tracks" (Wings ePress 2006), originally published under the title "Peggy Does a Runner". She has also written three other novels, "Casting Off" (Wings ePress 2005) and "There And Back", as well as a tongue-in-cheek article on epublishing for Scribesworld called "Frisson of Passion". Furthermore, Patricia is an active member of The Frankfurt Writers' Group.

Her daughters, Jenny and Nadia, are now in their twenties and she lives with her partner in a small Bavarian village. When not writing, she loves sailing, cycling and, of course, reading.

Other Works From The Pen Of

Trisha FitzGerald

Casting Off

Meg, in a moment of madness, throws caution to the wind and sets sail. Too late, she discovers she's cast off a lot more than merely a life of drudgery.

Making Tracks

Just graduated, Peggy Fitzpatrick and some friends flee Dublin city for a week of madness in the coastal village of Ballydereen. Four of them set off. Three come back.

Visit Our Website

For The Full Inventory
Of Quality Books:

Wings ePress, Inc
https://wingsepress.com/

Quality trade paperbacks and downloads
in multiple formats,
in genres ranging from light romantic comedy
to general fiction and horror.
Wings has something for every reader's taste.
Visit the website, then bookmark it.
We add new titles each month!

Wings ePress Inc.
3000 N. Rock Road
Newton, KS 67114